Unbiddable
Attraction

KATHIE DENOSKY
ROBYN GRADY
BARBARA DUNLOP

MILLS &
BOON

First Published in Great Britain 2016
By Mills & Boon, an imprint of HarperCollins*Publishers*
1 London Bridge Street, London, SE1 9GF

UNBIDDABLE ATTRACTION © 2017 Harlequin Books S. A.

Lured By The Rich Rancher, Taming The Takeover Tycoon and *Reunited With The Lassiter Bride* were first published in Great Britain by Harlequin (UK) Limited.

Lured By The Rich Rancher © 2014 Harlequin Books S. A.
Taming The Takeover Tycoon © 2014 Harlequin Books S. A.
Reunited With The Lassiter Bride © 2014 Harlequin Books S. A.

Special thanks and acknowledgement are given to Kathie DeNosky, Robyn Grady and Barbara Dunlop for their contribution to the *Dynasties: The Lassiters* series.

ISBN: 978-0-263-92946-1

05-0117

Our policy is to use papers that are natural, renewable and recyclable products and made from wood grown in sustainable forests.The logging and manufacturing processes conform to the legal environmental regulations of the country of origin.

Printed and bound in Spain
by CPI, Barcelona

LURED BY THE RICH RANCHER

BY
KATHIE DeNOSKY

Kathie DeNosky lives in her native southern Illinois on the land her family settled in 1839. She writes highly sensual stories with a generous amount of humor. Her books have appeared on the *USA TODAY* bestseller list and received numerous awards, including two National Readers' Choice Awards. Kathie enjoys going to rodeos, traveling to research settings for her books and listening to country music. Readers may contact her by e-mailing kathie@kathiedenosky.com. They can also visit her website, www.kathiedenosky.com, or find her on Facebook.

This book is dedicated to the authors of Dynasties: The Lassiters. It's been a pleasure working with you and I hope to do so again in the near future.

And a special dedication to my good friend and partner in crime, Kristi Gold, whose sense of humor is as wicked as my own. Love you bunches, girlfriend!

One

At the designated time on the Fourth of July, Chance Lassiter and his half sister, Hannah Armstrong, approached the doorway to the massive great room in the Big Blue ranch house. "This seems wrong. I just learned two months ago that I have a sister and now I'm giving you away," he complained.

"That's true," she said, smiling. "But since you and Logan are good friends, I think we'll probably be seeing each other quite often."

"You can count on it." He gazed fondly at his five-year-old niece waiting to throw flower petals as she preceded them down the aisle. "I told Cassie I would come over and take her into Cheyenne for ice cream at least once a week. And I'm not letting her down."

"You're going to spoil her," Hannah teased good-naturedly.

Grinning, he shrugged. "I'm her favorite uncle. It's expected."

"You're her only uncle," Hannah shot back, laughing. "You have to be her favorite."

When he first discovered that he had a half sister from the extramarital affair his late father had some thirty years ago, Chance had experienced a variety of emotions. At first, he'd resented the fact that the man he had grown up believing to be a pillar of morality had cheated on Chance's mother. Then learning that Marlene Lassiter had known her husband had a daughter and hadn't told him had compounded Chance's disillusionment. His mother had been aware of how much he missed having a sibling and he felt deprived of the relationship they might have had growing up. But in the two months since meeting Hannah and his adorable niece, he had done his best to make up for lost time.

Chance tucked Hannah's hand in the crook of his arm. "Besides the standing ice-cream date, you know that all you or Cassie have to do is pick up the phone and I'll be there for you."

"You and your mother have been so good to us." Tears welled in Hannah's emerald eyes—eyes the same brilliant green as his own. "I don't know how to begin to thank you both for your love and acceptance. It means the world to me."

He shook his head. "There's no need to thank us. That's the beauty of family. We accept and love you and Cassie unconditionally—no matter how long it took us to find you."

As they started down the aisle between the chairs that had been set up for the wedding, Chance focused on the red-haired little girl ahead of them. Cassie's curls bounced as she skipped along and her exuberance for throwing flower petals from the small white basket she carried was cute as hell. Of course, like any proud uncle, he thought everything the kid did was nothing short of amazing. But with an arm like that there wasn't a doubt in his mind that she could play for a major league baseball team if she set her mind to it.

Approaching the groom standing beside the minister in front of the fireplace, Chance waited for his cue before he placed his sister's hand in Logan Whittaker's. He kissed Hannah's cheek, then gave his friend a meaningful smile as he took his place beside him to serve as the best man. "Take care of her and Cassie," he said, careful to keep his tone low. "If you don't, you know what will happen."

Grinning, Logan nodded. "You'll kick my ass."

"In a heartbeat," Chance promised.

"You don't have anything to worry about," Logan said, lifting Hannah's hand to kiss the back of it as they turned to face the minister.

When the bespectacled man of the cloth started to speak, Chance looked out at the wedding guests. Except for Dylan and Jenna, the entire Lassiter clan had turned out in force. But his cousin and his new bride's absence was understandable. Their own wedding had only taken place a little over a week ago and they were still on their honeymoon in Paris.

As Chance continued to survey the guests, he noticed that his cousin Angelica had chosen to sit at the back of the room, well away from the rest of the family. She was still upset about the terms of her father's will and refused to accept that J. D. Lassiter had left control of Lassiter Media to her former fiancé, Evan McCain. Chance didn't have a clue what his uncle had been thinking, but he trusted the man's judgment and knew there had to have been a good reason for what he'd done. Chance just wished Angelica could see things that way.

He shifted his attention back to the ceremony when the minister got to the actual vows and Logan turned to him with his hand out. Chance took from his jacket pocket the wedding ring his friend had given to him earlier and handed it to his soon-to-be brother-in-law. As he watched Logan slide the diamond-encrusted band onto Hannah's ring finger, Chance couldn't help but smile. He had no intention of going down that road himself, but he didn't mind watching others get married when he knew they were meant for each other. And he had yet to meet two people better suited to share their lives as husband and wife than Hannah and Logan.

"By the power vested in me by the great state of Wyoming, I pronounce you husband and wife," the minister said happily. "You may kiss the bride."

Chance waited until Logan kissed Hannah and they turned to start back down the aisle with his

niece skipping along behind them before he offered
his arm to the matron of honor. As they followed
the happy couple toward the door, a blonde woman
seated next to his cousin Sage and his fiancée, Colleen, caught his eye.

With hair the color of pale gold silk and a complexion that appeared to have been kissed by the
sun, she was without question the most gorgeous female he'd ever had the privilege to lay eyes on. But
when her vibrant blue gaze met his and her coral
lips curved upward into a soft smile, he damn near
stopped dead in his tracks. It felt as if someone had
punched him square in the gut.

Chance had no idea who she was, but he had every
intention of remedying that little detail as soon as
possible.

Felicity Sinclair felt as if something shifted in the
universe when she looked up to find the best man
staring at her as he and the matron of honor followed
the newly married couple back down the aisle. He
was—in a word—perfect!

Dressed like the groom in a white Oxford cloth
shirt, black sport coat, dark blue jeans and a wide-
brimmed cowboy hat, the man was everything she
had been looking for and more. He was tall, broad-
shouldered and ruggedly handsome. But more than
that, he carried himself with an air of confidence
that instilled trust. She could only hope that he was
related to the Lassiters so that she could use him in
her PR campaign.

When he and the matron of honor continued on, Fee turned to the couple seated next to her. "Sage, would you happen to know the name of the best man?"

"That's my cousin Chance," Sage Lassiter said, smiling as they rose to their feet with the rest of the wedding guests. "He owns the majority of the Big Blue now."

Excited by the fact that the best man was indeed a member of the Lassiter family, Fee followed Sage and his fiancée, Colleen, out onto the flagstone terrace where the reception was to be held. She briefly wondered why she hadn't met him at the opening for the newest Lassiter Grill, but with her mind racing a mile a minute, she dismissed it. She was too focused on her ideas for the PR campaign. The Big Blue ranch would be the perfect backdrop for what she had in mind and there wasn't anything more down-to-earth and wholesome than a cowboy.

When her boss, Evan McCain, the new CEO of Lassiter Media, sent her to Cheyenne to take care of the publicity for the grand opening of the Lassiter Grill, she'd thought she would be back in Los Angeles within a couple of weeks. But she'd apparently done such a stellar job, her stay in Wyoming had been extended. Two days ago, she had received a phone call assigning her the task of putting together a public relations campaign to restore the Lassiter family image and Fee knew she had her work cut out for her. News of Angelica Lassiter's dissatisfaction with her late father's will and her recent association with notorious corporate raider Jack Reed had traveled like wildfire and tarnished the company's happy family image, and created no small amount of panic among some of the stockholders. But by the time she hung up the phone, Fee had already come up with several ideas that she was confident would turn things around and reinstate Lassiter Media as the solid enterprise it had always been. All she needed to pull it together was the right spokesperson in the right setting. And she'd just found both.

Of course, she would need to talk to Chance and get him to agree to appear in the television spots and print ads that she had planned. But she wasn't worried. She'd been told all of the Lassiters had a strong sense of family. Surely when she explained why she had been asked to extend her stay in Cheyenne and how important it was to restore the Lassiters' good name, Chance would be more than happy to help.

Finding a place at one of the round tables that had been set up on the beautifully terraced patio, Fee sat down and took her cell phone from her sequined clutch to enter some notes. There were so many good ideas coming to her that she didn't dare rely on her memory.

"Do you mind if I join you, dear?"

Fee looked up to find a pleasant-looking older woman with short brown hair standing next to her. "Please have a seat," she answered, smiling. "I'm Fee Sinclair."

"And I'm Marlene Lassiter," the woman introduced herself as she sat down in the chair beside Fee. "Are you a friend of the bride?"

Shaking her head, Fee smiled. "I'm a public relations executive from the Los Angeles office of Lassiter Media."

"I think I remember Dylan mentioning that someone from the L.A. office had been handling the publicity for the Lassiter Grill opening here in Cheyenne," Marlene said congenially. She paused for a moment, then lowering her voice added, "And when I talked to Sage yesterday, he said you were going to be working on something to smooth things over after Angelica's threats to contest J.D.'s will and her being seen with the likes of Jack Reed."

"Yes," Fee admitted, wondering how much the woman knew about the board of directors' concerns. Something told her Marlene Lassiter didn't miss much of what went on with the family. "I'll be putting together some television commercials and print ads to assure the public that Lassiter Media is still the solid, family-friendly company it's always been."

"Good," the woman said decisively. "We may have our little spats, but we love each other and we really are a pretty close family."

They both looked across the yard at the pretty dark-haired woman talking rather heatedly with Sage. It was apparent she wasn't the least bit happy.

"I know it's probably hard for a lot of people to believe right now, but Angelica really is a wonderful young woman and we all love her dearly," Marlene spoke up as they watched the woman walk away from her brother in an obvious huff. Turning to Fee, Marlene's hazel eyes were shadowed with sadness. "Angelica is still trying to come to terms with the death of her father, as well as being hurt and disillusioned by his will. That's a lot for anyone to have to deal with."

Compelled to comfort the older woman, Fee placed her hand on top of Marlene's where it rested on the table. "I'm sure it was a devastating blow to her. She worked so hard for the family business that many people just assumed she'd be running it someday."

"When J.D. started cutting back on his workload, Angelica knew he was grooming her to take over and we all believed she would be the one leading Lassiter Media into the future," Marlene agreed, nodding. "When he left her a paltry ten percent of the voting shares and named Evan McCain CEO, the girl was absolutely crushed."

Fee could tell that Marlene was deeply concerned for Angelica. "It's only been a few months since Mr. Lassiter's passing," she said gently. "Maybe in time Angelica will be able to deal with it all a little better."

"I hope so." Marlene shook her head. "There are times when even grown children have a hard time understanding the reasons their parents have for making the decisions they do. But we always try to do what's in our children's best interest."

It was apparent the woman's focus had shifted and she was referring to someone other than Angelica. Fee didn't have a clue who Marlene was talking about, but she got the distinct impression there might be more than one rift in the family.

"I don't have children, but I can imagine it's extremely difficult sometimes," she agreed. Deciding to lighten the mood, she pointed to the bride's table, where the wedding party would be seated. "I don't know who did the decorations for the reception, but everything is beautiful."

All of the tables were draped with pristine white linen tablecloths and had vases of red, white and blue roses for centerpieces. But the table where the newly married couple and their attendants would sit had been decorated with a garland made of baby's breath and clusters of red and blue rosebuds. It was in keeping with the holiday and utterly stunning.

"Thank you," Marlene said, smiling. "Hannah left the reception decorations up to me and I thought red, white and blue would be appropriate. After all, it is the Fourth of July." Marlene smiled. "We'll be having fireworks a bit later when it gets dark."

"Grandma Marlene, can I sit with you for dinner?" the adorable little red-haired flower girl asked, walking up between Fee and Marlene.

"Of course, Cassie," Marlene said, putting her arm around the child. "As long as your mother says it's okay."

"Momma said I could, but I had to ask you first," Cassie answered, nodding until her red curls bobbed up and down. She seemed to notice Fee for the first time. "I'm Cassie. I got a new daddy today."

"I saw that." Fee found the outgoing little girl completely charming. "That's very exciting, isn't it?"

Cassie smiled. "Yes, but Uncle Chance says that I'm still his best girl, even if Logan is my new daddy."

"I'm sure you are," Fee said, smiling back.

While the child walked around her grandmother's chair to sit on the other side of Marlene, Fee felt encouraged. She hadn't realized she had been talking to her new spokesman's mother and niece. Surely if Marlene knew about the public relations campaign and was all for it, her son would be, too. And with any luck, he would be more than willing to play a role in the publicity she had planned to help restore the Lassiters' reputation.

Seated next to his new brother-in-law at the head table, Chance was about as uncomfortable as an eligible bachelor at an old-maids convention. He didn't like being on display and that was exactly the way he felt. Every time he looked up from his plate, someone was either smiling at him, waving to him or just plain staring at him. It was enough to make the succulent prime rib on his plate taste about as appetizing as an old piece of boot leather.

Finally giving up, he sat back from the table and waited until he had to toast the bride and groom. Once he got that out of the way, as far as he was concerned, his duties as the best man would be over and he fully intended to relax and enjoy himself.

At least, Logan had decided they would wear sports coats and jeans instead of tuxedos or suits.

Hannah called Logan's choice of wedding clothes "casual chic." Chance just called it comfortable.

As he scanned the crowd, he looked for the little blonde that had caught his eye at the wedding. He hoped she hadn't skipped the reception. She was definitely someone he'd like to get to know.

He was almost positive she wasn't from the area. None of the women he knew looked or dressed like her. From her perfectly styled hair all the way down to her spike heels, she gave every indication of being a big-city girl, and he would bet every last penny he had that the red strapless dress she was wearing had a famous designer's name on the label. But it didn't matter that they came from two different worlds. He wasn't looking for anything permanent with anyone. All he wanted was for them to have a little summer fun while she was around.

When he finally spotted her, he barely suppressed a groan. She and his mother seemed to be deep in conversation and that couldn't be good. Since his mother had gotten a taste of what it was like to be a grandmother with Cassie, she had made several comments that she wouldn't mind him giving her another grandchild or two in the near future. Surely his mother wouldn't be talking him up as husband and father material.

He frowned. Of course, he couldn't be sure. She'd shocked the hell out of him a couple of months ago when she had admitted that she'd known all about the affair his late father had thirty years ago. Then his mother had surprised him further when she admitted that she was the one who paid child support to Hannah's mother all those years after his father's death. His mother's secrets had caused him no end of frustration and it had only been in the past few weeks they had started to repair the breach those issues had caused in their relationship. Surely she wouldn't run the risk of creating more problems between them.

Lost in thought, it took a moment for him to realize that Logan had said something to him. "What was that?"

"Time for your toast," Logan said, grinning. Lowering his voice, he added, "Unless you'd rather make us wait while you sit there and ogle the blonde seated next to Marlene."

"Did anyone ever tell you what a smartass you can be, Whittaker?" Chance grumbled as he took his champagne flute and rose to his feet.

He ignored his new brother-in-law's hearty laughter as he sincerely wished the couple a long and happy life together, then gifted them a thousand acres on the Big Blue ranch to build the new house he knew they had been planning. Now that the toast was out of the way and he had given them his gift, he was free to enjoy himself. And the first thing he intended to do was talk to the blonde.

Hell, he might even ask her to dance a slow one with him. Not that he was all that great at doing more than standing in one place and swaying in time to the music. He wasn't. But if the lady was willing to let him put his arms around her and sway with him, it would be worth the risk of looking like a fool.

Ten minutes later, after listening to several more toasts for the bride and groom, Chance breathed a sigh of relief as he headed over to the table where his mother, Cassie and the blonde sat. "I'm glad that's over," he said, smiling. "Now it's time for some fun."

"You did a fine job with the toast, son," his mother said, smiling back at him.

"Uncle Chance, would you dance with me?" Cassie asked as she jumped down from her chair and skipped over to him.

"You're my best girl. Who else would I dance with?" he teased, winking at the blonde as he picked Cassie up to sit on his forearm. "But we'll have to wait until the band starts. Will that be okay with you?"

Cassie nodded. "I hope they hurry. I'm going to pretend we're at the ball."

"Fee, this is my son, Chance," his mother introduced them. Her smile was just a little too smug as she rose to her feet. "While we wait for the dancing to begin, why don't you and I go inside the house to see if we can find your princess wand, Cassie?"

"Oh, yes, Grandma Marlene," Cassie agreed exuberantly. "I need my wand and my crown for the ball."

Chance set the little girl on her feet as the band started warming up. "I'll be waiting for you right here, princess." When his mother and niece started toward the house, he placed his hand on the back of one of the chairs at the table. "Mind if I join you, Fee?"

Her pretty smile caused an unexpected hitch in his breathing. "Not at all, Mr. Lassiter."

"Please, call me Chance." He smiled back as he lowered himself onto the chair his mother had vacated. "I don't think I've ever known anyone with the name Fee."

"It's actually short for Felicity." She brushed a wayward strand of her long blond hair from her smooth cheek as they watched Hannah and Logan dance for the first time as husband and wife. "My grandmother talked my mother into naming me that. It was her mother's name."

"Are you a friend of my sister?" he asked, wondering if she might be one of the teachers Hannah worked with in Denver.

"No, I'm a public relations executive with Lassiter Media," she answered as she picked up her cell phone from the table and tucked it into her purse. When she looked up, he didn't think he'd ever seen anyone with bluer eyes. "I work out of the Los Angeles office."

That explained why he'd never seen her before, as well as her polished career-girl look. But although she probably bought everything she wore from the shops on Rodeo Drive, Fee Sinclair had a softness about her that he found intriguing. Most of the career women he'd met were aloof and all business. But Fee looked approachable and as if she knew how to kick up her heels and have a good time when she decided to do so.

"I'll bet you worked on the publicity for the grand

opening of Lassiter Grill," he speculated, motioning for one of the waiters carrying a tray of filled champagne flutes. Asking the man to bring him a beer, Chance took one of the glasses of bubbling pink wine and handed it to Fee. "My cousin Dylan said he couldn't have been happier with the way you handled the opening."

"I didn't see you that evening," she commented.

He shook his head. "No, I had to be over in Laramie on business that day and didn't get back in time."

She seemed to eye him over the rim of her glass as she took a sip of the champagne. "I've also been put in charge of getting your family's image back on track what with all the controversy over J. D. Lassiter's will and Angelica's association with Jack Reed."

"So you'll be here for a few weeks?" he queried, hoping that was the case. "Will you be staying here at the ranch?"

"Lassiter Media has rented a house in Cheyenne, where they have employees from the L.A. office stay while they're in town on business," she said, shaking her head. "I'll be here at least until the end of the month."

Chance waited until the tuxedoed waiter brought him the beer he had requested and moved on before he commented. "I don't envy your job. Our reputation of being a solid family that got along well took a pretty big hit when Angelica pitched her little hissy fit right after my uncle's will was read. Do you know how you're going to go about straightening that out?"

"I have a few things in mind," she answered evasively.

Before he could ask what those ideas were, Cassie skipped up to them. "I'm ready to dance now, Uncle Chance. I have my wand and my crown."

"You sure do," he said, laughing as she tried to hang on to her pink plastic wand while she adjusted the tiara his mother had bought for her a few weeks ago. As if on cue, the band started playing a slower tune. Turning to Fee, he smiled. "I'm sorry, but I can't keep the princess waiting. I'll be right back."

Fortunately, all he had to do was stand in one place and hold Cassie's little hand as she pirouetted around him. The kid had definite ideas on the way a princess was supposed to dance and who was he to argue with her? He just hoped she didn't make herself too dizzy and end up falling flat on the floor.

When the dance was over and he and Cassie returned to the table, Chance held out his hand to Fee. "Would you like to dance, Ms. Sinclair?"

She glanced at her uncomfortable-looking high heels. "I...hadn't thought I would be dancing."

Laughing, he bent down to whisper close to her ear. "You witnessed the extent of my dancing skills with Cassie. I'm from the school of stand in one place and sway."

Her delightful laughter caused a warm feeling to spread throughout his chest. "I think that's about all I'll be able to do in these shoes anyway."

When she placed her soft hand in his and stood up to walk out onto the dance floor with him, it felt as if an electric current shot straight up his arm. He took a deep breath, wrapped his arms loosely around her and smiled down at her upturned face. At a little over six feet tall, he wasn't a giant by any means, but everything about her was petite and delicate. In fact, if she hadn't been wearing high heels, he could probably rest his chin on the top of her head.

"Chance, there's something I'd like to discuss with you," she said as they swayed back and forth.

"I'm all ears," he said, grinning.

"I'd like your help with my public relations campaign to improve the Lassiters' image," she answered.

He didn't have any idea what she thought he could do that would make a difference on that score, but he figured it wouldn't hurt to hear her out. Besides, he wanted to spend some time getting to know her better and although she might not be staying in Wyoming for an extended period of time, that didn't mean they couldn't have fun while she was here.

Before he could suggest that they meet for lunch the following day to talk over her ideas, she gave him a smile that sent another wave of heat flowing through him. He would agree to just about anything as long as she kept smiling at him that way.

"Sure. I'll do whatever I can to help you out," he said, drawing her a little closer. "What did you have in mind?"

"Oh, thank you so much," she said, surprising him with a big hug. "You're perfect for the job and I can't wait to get started."

He was pleased with himself for making her happy, even if he didn't know what she was talking about. "I don't know about being perfect for much of anything but taking care of a bunch of cattle, but I'll give it my best shot." As an afterthought, he asked, "What is it you want me to do?"

"You're going to be the family spokesman for the PR campaign that I'm planning," she said, beaming.

Because he was marveling at how beautiful she was, it took a moment for her words to register. He stopped swaying and stared down at her in disbelief. "You want me to do what?"

"I'm going to have you appear in all future advertising for Lassiter Media," she said, sounding extremely excited. "You'll be in the national television commercials, as well as…"

Fee kept on telling him all the things she had planned and how he figured into the picture. But Chance heard none of it and when the music ended, he automatically placed his hand at the small of her back and, in a daze, led her off the dance floor.

His revved up hormones had just caused him to agree to be the family spokesman without knowing what he was getting himself into. Un-freaking-believable.

Chance silently ran through every cuss word he'd ever heard, then started making up new ones. He might be a Lassiter, but he wasn't as refined as the rest of the family. Instead of riding a desk in some corporate office, he was on the back of a horse every day herding cattle under the wide Wyoming sky.

That's the way he liked it and the way he intended for things to stay. There was no way in hell he was going to be the family spokesman. And the sooner he could find a way to get that across to her, the better.

Two

The following day, Fee programed the GPS in her rented sports car to guide her to the restaurant where she would be meeting Chance for lunch. After their dance last night, he had insisted that they needed to talk more about his being the family spokesman and she had eagerly agreed. She was looking forward to getting her campaign started and his sister's wedding reception hadn't been the right time or place to discuss what she needed Chance to do.

When the GPS instructed her to turn north, Fee nervously looked around and realized she was heading in the same direction they'd driven the afternoon before on the way out of Cheyenne to the wedding. Sage and Colleen had invited her to accompany them to the Big Blue ranch for the wedding because she was alone in town and unfamiliar with the area. She'd been more than happy to accept the offer because her biggest concern when she'd learned that she would be spending more time in Wyoming was the fact that she was going to be completely out of her element. She had been born and raised in the San Fernando Valley and the closest she had ever been to a rural setting was her grandmother's pitiful attempt at a vegetable garden on the far side of her swimming pool in Sherman Oaks.

When the GPS indicated that her destination was only a few yards ahead, she breathed a sigh of relief that she wouldn't have to venture out of the city on her own. Turning into the gravel parking lot of a small bar and grill, she smiled when she parked next to a white pickup truck with Big Blue Ranch painted on the driver's door. Chance was leaning against the front fender with his arms folded across his wide chest and his booted feet crossed casually at the ankles.

Lord have mercy, the man looked good! If she'd thought he looked like a cowboy the night before in his white shirt, black sport jacket and black hat, it couldn't compare to the way he looked today. Wearing a blue chambray shirt, jeans and a wide-brimmed black cowboy hat, he was the perfect example of a man who made his living working the land. The type of man men could relate to and women would drool over.

"I hope I didn't keep you waiting long," she said

when he pushed away from the truck to come around the car and open her door.

"I've only been here a couple of minutes," he said, smiling as he offered his hand to help her out of the car.

Her breath caught. Chance Lassiter was extremely handsome at any time, but when he smiled he was downright devastating. She had noticed that about him the night before, but attributed her assessment to the excitement she'd felt at finding the perfect spokesman to represent his family. But now?

She frowned as she chided herself for her foolishness. Her only interest in the man or his looks was for the purpose of improving his family's image. Nothing more.

But when she placed her hand in his, a delightful tingling sensation zinged up her arm and Fee knew her reaction to his smile had nothing whatsoever to do with being anxious to start her ad campaign and everything to do with Chance's raw sexuality. He wasn't as refined as the men she knew in Los Angeles, but something told her that he was more of a man than any of them ever dreamed of being. She took a deep breath and ignored the realization. Her interest in him was strictly business and that's the way it was going to stay. Maybe if she reminded herself of that fact enough, she would remember it.

"I have some of the mock-ups of the print ads I'd like to run," she said, reaching for her electronic tablet in the backseat.

"Let's have lunch and talk before we get into any

of that," he said, guiding her toward the entrance to the restaurant.

"I suppose you're right," she agreed as they walked inside. "I'm just excited about starting this project."

His deep chuckle sent a warmth coursing throughout her body. "Your enthusiasm shows."

When they reached a booth at the back of the establishment, he asked, "Will this be all right? It's a little more private and we should be able to talk without interruption."

"It's fine," she answered, sliding onto the red vinyl seat. Looking around, Fee noticed that although the bar and grill was older and a little outdated, it was clean and very neat. "What's the special here?" she asked when Chance took his hat off and slid into the booth on the opposite side of the table.

"They have a hamburger that's better than any you've ever tasted," he said, grinning as he placed his hat on the bench seat beside him. "But I'm betting you would prefer the chef's salad like most women."

His smile and the sound of his deep baritone sent a shiver coursing through her. The man's voice alone would charm the birds out of the trees, but when he smiled, there wasn't a doubt in her mind that he could send the pulse racing on every female from one to one hundred.

Deciding to concentrate on the fact that he had correctly guessed her lunch choice, she frowned. For reasons she couldn't explain, she didn't like him thinking that she was predictable or anything like other women.

"What makes you think I'll be ordering the salad?" she asked.

"I just thought—"

"I can think for myself," she said, smiling to take the sting out of her words. "And for the record, yes, I do like salads. Just not all the time."

"My mistake," he said, smiling.

"Since it's your recommendation, I'll have the hamburger," she said decisively.

He raised one dark eyebrow. "Are you sure?" he asked, his smile widening. "I don't want you thinking I'm trying to influence your decision."

"Yes, I'm positive." She shrugged. "Unless you're afraid it won't live up to expectations."

He threw back his head and laughed. "You're really something, Felicity Sinclair. You would rather eat something you don't want than admit that I was right. Do you even eat meat?"

"Occasionally," she admitted. For the most part she lived on salads in L.A. But that was more a matter of convenience than anything else.

When the waitress came over to their booth, Chance gave the woman their order. "I can guarantee this will be the best hamburger you've ever had," he said confidently when the woman left to get their drinks.

Curiosity got the better of her. "What makes you say that?"

"They serve Big Blue beef here," he answered.

"It's the best in Wyoming, and several restaurants in Cheyenne buy from our distributor. In fact, my cousin Dylan and I made a deal when he decided to open a Lassiter Grill here to serve nothing but our beef in all of his restaurants."

"Really? It's that special?"

Chance nodded. "We raise free-range Black Angus cattle. No growth hormones, no supplements. Nothing but grass-fed, lean beef."

Fee didn't know a lot about the beef industry, except that free-range meat was supposed to be healthier for the consumer. But she did know something about Dylan Lassiter and the Lassiter Grill Group.

A premier chef, Dylan had started the chain with J.D.'s encouragement and had inherited full control of that part of the family business when J.D. died. Dylan was well-known for serving nothing but the finest steaks and prime rib in his restaurants, and Fee was certain that was why every one of them bore the coveted five-star rating from food critics and cuisine magazines. If he was confident enough to serve Big Blue beef exclusively in his restaurants, it had to be the best. And that gave her an idea.

"This is perfect," she said, her mind racing with the possibilities. "I'll have to give it a little more thought, but I'm sure we can use that for future Lassiter Grill advertisements, as well as the spots about the Lassiter family."

"Yeah, about that," Chance said slowly as he ran a hand through his short, light brown hair. "I don't think I'm right for what you have in mind for your ad campaign."

Her heart stalled. "Why do you say that?"

He shook his head. "I'm not a polished corporate type. I'm a rancher and more times than not I'm covered in dust or scraping something off my boots that most people consider extremely disgusting."

"That's why you're the perfect choice," she insisted.

"Because I've stepped in a pile of…barnyard atmosphere?" he asked, looking skeptical.

Laughing at his delicate phrasing, she shook her head. "No, not that." Now that she'd found her spokesman, she couldn't let him back out. She had to make Chance understand how important it was for him to represent the family and that no one else would do. "Not everyone can identify with a man in a suit. But you have that cowboy mystique that appeals to both men and women alike. You're someone who will resonate with all demographics and that's why they'll listen to the message we're trying to send."

"I know that's what you think and for all I know about this kind of thing, you might be right about me getting your message across to your target audience." He shook his head. "But I'm not real big on being put on display like some kind of trained monkey in a circus sideshow."

"It wouldn't be like that," she said earnestly. "All you'll have to do is pose for some still pictures for the print ads and film a few videos that can be used for television and the internet." She wasn't going to mention the few personal appearances that he might have to do from time to time or the billboard advertising that she had already reserved. Those were sure to be deal breakers, so she would have to spring those on him after she got a firm commitment.

When he sat back and folded his arms across his wide chest, she could tell he was about to dig in his heels and give her an outright refusal. "What can I do to get you to reconsider?" she asked out of desperation. "Surely we can work out something. You're the only man I want to do this."

A mischievous twinkle lit his brilliant green eyes. "The only man you want, huh?"

Her cheeks felt as if they were on fire. She was normally very clear and rarely said anything that could be misconstrued. "Y-you know what I meant."

He stared at her across the table for several long moments before a slow smile tugged at the corners of his mouth. "Come home with me."

"E-excuse me?" she stammered.

"I want you to come and stay at the Big Blue for a couple of weeks," he said, his tone sounding as if he was issuing a challenge. "You need to see how a working ranch is run and the things I have to do on a daily basis. Then we'll talk about how glamorous you think the cowboy way of life is and how convincing I would be as a spokesman."

"I didn't say it was glamorous," she protested.

"I think you referred to it as 'the cowboy mystique,'" he said, grinning. "Same thing."

"Is that the only way you'll agree to do my PR

campaign?" she asked, deciding that staying in the huge ranch house where the wedding had been held the night before wouldn't be an undue hardship.

The Lassiter home was beautiful and although a little rustic in decor, it was quite modern. If all she had to do to get him to agree to be part of the advertising was stay at the ranch for a week or so, she'd do it. She had a job promotion riding on the outcome of this project and she wasn't about to lose the opportunity.

"Nice try, sweetheart." His low chuckle seemed to vibrate straight through her. "I didn't say I would agree to anything if you came to the ranch. I said we'd talk."

Staring at him across the worn Formica table, Fee knew that she didn't have a lot of choices. She could either agree to go home with him and try to convince him to represent the Lassiters or start looking for another spokesman.

She took a deep breath. "All right, cowboy. I'll stay with you at the Big Blue. But only on one condition. You have to promise that you'll keep an open mind and give me a fair chance to change it."

"Only if you'll respect my decision and drop the matter if I choose not to do it," he said, extending his hand to shake on their deal.

"Then I would say we have an agreement," she said, extending her hand, as well.

The moment her palm touched his an exciting little shiver slid up her spine and Fee couldn't help but wonder what she had gotten herself into. Chance

Lassiter was not only the best choice for redeeming his family in the eyes of the public, he was the only man in a very long time to remind her of the amazing differences between a man and a woman.

Why that thought sent a feeling of anticipation coursing through her at the speed of light, she had no idea. She wasn't interested in being distracted by him or any other man. She had a job to do and a career to build and protect. As long as she kept things in perspective and focused on her goal of putting together a campaign that would redeem the Lassiters for any and all transgressions, she would be just fine.

The following morning, Fee had just put the finishing touches on preparing brunch when the doorbell rang, signaling her guest had arrived. "You have perfect timing," she said, opening the door to welcome Colleen Faulkner. "I just took the scones out of the oven."

"I'm glad you called and asked me over." Colleen smiled. "Sage is out of town for the day and I can definitely use a break from all of the wedding plans."

"Have you set a date yet?" Fee asked as she led the way down the hall to the kitchen.

"No." Seating herself at the table in the breakfast nook, Colleen paused a moment before she continued, "Sage is hoping if we wait a bit, things will settle down with Angelica."

Pouring them each a cup of coffee, Fee set the mugs on the polished surface and sat down on the opposite side of the small table. "When I saw her at the wedding the other night, I could tell she's still extremely frustrated with the situation. Has she given up the idea of contesting her father's will?" Fee asked gently.

She didn't want to pry, but it was no secret that Angelica Lassiter and the rest of the family were still at odds, nor was there any mystery why. The young woman wanted to break the will and regain control of Lassiter Media, while the rest of the family were reluctant to go against J.D.'s last wishes or bring into question the other terms of the will and what they had inherited.

"I don't think she's going to give up anytime soon," Colleen admitted, shaking her head. "Angelica is still questioning her father's motives and how much influence Evan McCain had in J.D.'s decision to take control of Lassiter Media away from her." Colleen gave Fee a pointed look. "But J.D. had his reasons and believe me, he knew what he was doing."

Fee had no doubt that Colleen knew why J. D. Lassiter had divided his estate the way he had—leaving his only daughter with practically no interest in Lassiter Media. Colleen had been his private nurse for some time before his death and she and J.D. had become good friends. He had apparently trusted Colleen implicitly, and with good reason. To Fee's knowledge, Colleen hadn't revealed what she knew about the matter to anyone.

"I just hope that I'm able to turn public opinion around on the matter," Fee said, dishing up the breakfast casserole and crisp bacon she had made for their brunch. "The Lassiters have for the most part been known as a fairly close, happy family and that image has taken its share of hits lately." She didn't want to mention that Sage had distanced himself from J.D. sometime before the older Lassiter died or that they had never really resolved the estrangement. It was none of her business, nor did it have anything to do with her ad campaign.

"The tabloids are having a field day with all this," Colleen agreed. They were silent for several long moments before she spoke again. "I'm a very private person and I'm not overly thrilled by the idea, but if you can use our wedding plans in some way to shift the focus away from whatever legal action Angelica is planning, I suppose it would be all right."

Taken by surprise at such a generous offer, Fee gave the pretty nurse a grateful smile. "Thank you, Colleen. But I know how intrusive that would be for you and Sage during a very special time in your lives."

"If it will help the Lassiters, I'll adjust," Colleen answered, looking sincere. "I love this family. They're very good people and they've welcomed me with open arms. I want to help them in any way I can."

Smiling, Fee nodded. "I can understand. But I think—at least I hope—I've found the perfect angle for my campaign and won't have to use your wedding."

"Really?" Colleen looked relieved. "May I ask what you're planning?"

As she explained some of her ideas for the videos and print ads featuring Chance as the family spokesman, Fee sighed. "But he's not overly happy about being in front of the camera. In fact, he's invited me to stay at the Big Blue for the next two weeks to prove to me that he's completely unsuitable."

Colleen grinned. "And I'm assuming you're going to use that time to convince him the exact opposite is true."

"Absolutely," Fee said, laughing. "He has no idea how persistent I can be when I know I'm right."

"Well, I wish you the best of luck with that," Colleen said, reaching for a scone. "I've heard Sage mention how stubborn Chance could be when they were kids."

Fee grinned. "Then I'd say he's met his match because once I've made up my mind I don't give up."

"The next couple of weeks should be very interesting on the Big Blue ranch," Colleen said, laughing. "What I wouldn't give to be a fly on the wall when the two of you butt heads."

"I'm not only hoping to have his agreement within a week, I'd like to get a photographer to start taking still shots for the first print ads," Fee confided in her new friend. "Most of those will start running by the end of the month."

"It sounds like you have things under control." Colleen took a sip of her coffee. "I'll keep my fingers crossed that you get Chance to go along with all of it."

"Thanks," Fee said, nibbling on her scone.

She didn't tell Colleen, but she had to get him on board. Her entire campaign was based on him and his down-to-earth cowboy persona. The Lassiter family had been ranching in Wyoming for years before Lassiter Media became the communications giant it was today. Besides the down-to-earth appeal of a cowboy, it just made sense to capitalize on the family's Western roots. She wasn't going to let a little thing like Chance's reluctance to be in front of the camera deter her from what she knew would be an outstanding promotion.

On Monday afternoon when Chance parked his truck in front of the house Lassiter Media had rented for visiting executives, he felt a little guilty about the deal he had made with Fee. He had promised that he would consider her arguments for his being part of her PR campaign and he did intend to think about it.

It wasn't that he didn't want to help the family; he just couldn't see why one of his cousins wasn't more suitable for the job of spokesman or for that matter, even his mother. She was the family matriarch and had been since his aunt Ellie had died over twenty-eight years ago. They all knew more about Lassiter Media than he did. He was a rancher and had been all of his life. That's the way he liked it and wanted it to stay. Besides, he'd never been the type who felt the need to draw a lot of attention to himself. He had always been comfortable with who he was and hadn't seen any reason to seek out the approval of people whose opinions of him didn't matter.

All he wanted was to get to know Fee better and that was the main reason he'd suggested that she stay with him on the ranch. They could have some fun together and at the same time, he could prove to her that he wasn't the man she needed for her ad campaign. He knew she wasn't going to give up easily and would probably still insist that he was the best choice. But he seriously doubted she was going to make a lot of headway with her efforts.

Getting out of the truck, he walked up to the front door and raised his hand to ring the bell just as Fee opened it. "Are you ready to go?" he asked as his gaze wandered from her head to her toes.

Dressed in khaki slacks and a mint-green blouse, she'd styled her long blond hair in loose curls, making her look more as if she was ready for a day of shopping in some chic, high-end boutique than going to stay at a working cattle ranch. He hadn't thought it was possible for the woman to be any prettier than she had been two days ago when they'd had lunch, but she'd proved him wrong.

"I think I'm about as ready as I'll ever be," she said, pulling a bright pink suitcase behind her as she stepped out onto the porch.

His eyebrows rose when he glanced down at the luggage. It was big enough to fit a body and if the bulging sides were any indication, there just might be one in there already. It was completely stuffed and he couldn't imagine what all she had in it.

"Think you have enough clothes to last you for two weeks?" he asked, laughing.

"I wasn't sure what I would need," she answered, shrugging one slender shoulder. "Other than attending the wedding the other night, I've never been on a ranch before."

"My place does have the convenience of a washer and dryer," he quipped.

"I thought it would," she said, giving him one of those long-suffering looks women give men they think are a little simpleminded. "That's why I packed light."

When he picked up the suitcase, he frowned. The damn thing weighed at least as much as a tightly packed bale of hay. If this was her idea of "packing light," he couldn't imagine how many pieces of luggage she'd brought with her for her stay in Cheyenne.

Placing his other hand at the small of her back, he noticed she was wearing a pair of strappy sandals as he guided her out to his truck. "I'm betting you don't have a pair of boots packed in here," he said, opening the rear door on the passenger side of the club cab to stow the suitcase.

"No. I didn't expect to be needing them," she answered. She paused a moment before she asked, "What would I need them for?"

He laughed. "Oh, just a couple of things like walking and riding."

"I…I'm going to be riding?" she asked, sounding a little unsure. "A…horse?"

"Yup." He closed the rear door, then turned to help her into the front passenger seat. "Unless you want me to saddle up a steer so you can give that a try."

She vigorously shook her head. "No."

"You do know how to ride, don't you?"

There was doubt in her pretty blue eyes when she looked at him and he knew the answer before she opened her mouth. "The closest I've ever been to a horse is seeing them in parades."

"Don't worry. It's pretty easy. I'll teach you," he said, giving her what he hoped was an encouraging smile as he placed his hands around her waist.

"W-what are you doing?" she asked, placing her hands on his chest. The feel of her warm palms seemed to burn right through the fabric and had him wondering how they would feel on his bare chest.

"You're short and…the truck is pretty tall," he said, trying to ignore the hitch he'd suddenly developed in his breathing. "I thought I'd help you out."

"I assure you, I could climb into the truck," she said.

"I'm sure you could," he said, smiling. "But you want to shoot me a break here? I'm trying to be a gentleman."

Staring down at her, it was all he could do to keep from covering her lips with his and kissing her until the entire neighborhood was thoroughly scandalized. His heart stuttered when he realized she looked as if she wanted him to do just that.

He wasn't sure how long they continued to gaze at each other, but when he finally had the presence of mind to lift her onto the seat, he quickly closed the truck door and walked around to climb in behind the steering wheel. What the hell was wrong with him? he wondered as he started the engine and steered away from the curb. He'd never before been so completely mesmerized by a woman that he forgot what he was doing. Why was Fee different? What was it about her that made him act like an inexperienced teenager on his first date?

"I still don't understand…why you insisted on coming to get me," she said, sounding delightfully breathless. "I could have driven…to the ranch."

"You could have tried," he said, focusing on her statement instead of her perfect coral lips. "But that low-slung little sports car wouldn't have made it without drowning out when you forded the creek. That's why I suggested you leave it here. If you need to go somewhere, I'll be more than happy to take you."

"When we drove to the ranch for the wedding, I don't remember anywhere along the way that could happen," she said as if she didn't believe him. "The roads were all asphalt and so was the lane leading up to the ranch house." She frowned. "I don't even remember a bridge."

"There isn't one," he answered. "Most of the year it's just a little slow-moving stream about three or four inches deep and about two feet wide," he explained. "But July is the wettest month we have here in Wyoming. It rains almost every day and the stream doubles in size and depth. That little car sits so low it would stall out in a heartbeat."

"Why don't you build a bridge?" she demanded. "It seems to me it would be more convenient than running the risk of a vehicle stalling out."

He nodded. "Eventually I'll have the road to my place asphalted and a culvert or bridge put in. But I only inherited the ranch a few months ago and I've had other things on my mind like cutting and baling hay, mending fences and moving cattle from one pasture to another."

"Hold it just a minute. Your place?" She frowned. "You don't live on the Big Blue ranch?"

"I've never lived anywhere else," he admitted. "I just don't live in the main house."

"There's another house on the ranch?" she asked, her tone doubtful.

"Actually there are several," he said, nodding. "There's the main house, the Lassiter homestead where I live, as well as a foreman's cottage and a couple of smaller houses for married hired hands."

"The only buildings I saw close to the ranch house were a couple of barns, a guest cottage and a stable," she said, sounding skeptical.

"You can't see the other places from the main house," he answered. "Those are about five miles down the road where I live."

"So I won't be staying with Marlene?" she inquired, as if she might be rethinking her decision to stay with him.

"Nope. The actual ranch headquarters is where we'll be staying," he said, wondering if Fee was apprehensive about being alone with him. She needn't be. He might want to get to know her on a very personal level, but he wasn't a man who forced his attentions on a woman if she didn't want them.

Frowning, she nibbled on her lower lip as if deep in thought. "I was led to believe that the main house was the ranch headquarters."

Chance almost groaned aloud. Nothing would please him more than to cover her mouth with his and do a little nibbling of his own. Fortunately, he didn't have time to dwell on it. They had arrived at the stop he'd decided to make when he learned she didn't have a pair of boots.

Steering his truck into the parking lot at the Wild Horse Western Wear store on the northern outskirts of Cheyenne, he parked and turned to face her. "My uncle built the main house when he and my late aunt adopted Sage and Dylan. That's where we have our family gatherings, entertain guests, and Lassiter Media holds corporate receptions. The actual ranch headquarters has always been at the home my grandfather and grandmother built when they first came to Wyoming. I renovated it about seven years back when my uncle turned the running of the ranch over to me. I've lived there ever since."

She looked confused. "Why not have the headquarters at the main house? Doesn't that make more sense?"

Laughing, he shook his head. "Headquarters is

where we sort cattle for taking them to market and quarantine and treat sick livestock. A herd of cattle can be noisy and churn up a lot of dust when it's dry. That's not something you want guests to have to contend with when you're throwing a party or trying to make a deal with business associates."

"I suppose that makes sense," she finally said, as if she was giving it some serious thought.

"Now that we have that settled, let's go get you fitted for a pair of boots," he suggested, getting out of the truck and walking around to help her down from the passenger seat. "How many pairs of jeans did you bring?"

"Two," she said as they walked into the store. "Why?"

"I'm betting your jeans have some designer dude's name on the hip pocket and cost a small fortune," he explained as he walked her over to the women's section.

"As a matter of fact, I did get them from a boutique on Rodeo Drive," she said, frowning. "Does that make them unsuitable?"

"That depends," he answered truthfully. "If you don't mind running the risk of getting them torn or stained up, they'll be just fine. But if they're very expensive, I doubt you'll want to do that. Besides, they probably aren't boot cut, are they?"

"No. They're skinny jeans."

He swallowed hard as he imagined what she would look like in the form-fitting pants. "We'll pick up a few pairs of jeans and a hat."

"I don't wear hats," she said, her long blond hair swaying as she shook her head.

Without thinking, Chance reached up to run his index finger along her smooth cheek. "I'd hate to see your pretty skin damaged by the sun. You'll need a hat to protect against sun and windburn."

As she stared up at him, her pink tongue darted out to moisten her lips and it was all he could do to keep from taking her into his arms to find out if they tasted as sweet as they looked. Deciding there would be plenty of time in the next two weeks to find out, he forced himself to move. He suddenly couldn't wait to get to the ranch.

"Let's get you squared away with jeans and boots," he advised. "Then we'll worry about that hat."

Three

Fee glanced down at her new jeans, boots and hot-pink T-shirt with *I love Wyoming* screen-printed on the front as Chance drove away from the store. When had she lost control of the situation? When they walked into the store, she hadn't intended to get anything but a pair of boots and maybe a couple pairs of jeans.

She had to admit that Chance had been right about her needing the boots. Her sandals definitely weren't the right choice of footwear if she was going to be around large animals. Even his suggestion about getting new jeans had made sense. She'd paid far too much for the stylish denim she'd purchased in one of the boutiques on Rodeo Drive to ruin them.

But when he had suggested that she might want

to start wearing the boots right away to get them broken in, that's when her command of the situation went downhill in a hurry. She'd had to put on a pair of the new jeans because the legs of her khaki slacks hadn't fit over the tops of the boots. Then she'd taken one look at her raw silk blouse with the new jeans and boots and decided to get something more casual, motivating her to get the T-shirt. She glanced at the hat sitting beside her on the truck seat. She'd even given in to getting the hat because his argument about protecting her skin had made sense.

Looking over at Chance, she had to admit that a shopping trip had never been as exhilarating as it had been with him. When she stepped out of the dressing room to check in the full-length mirror how her new jeans and T-shirt fit, she'd seen an appreciation in his brilliant green eyes that thrilled her all the way to her toes. It certainly beat the practiced comments of a boutique employee just wanting to make a sale.

She sighed heavily. Now that they were actually on the road leading to the ranch, she couldn't help but wonder what she'd gotten herself into. On some level, she had been excited about the new experience of being on a working ranch. It was something she'd never done before and although she felt as if she would be going into the great unknown, she had thought she was ready for the challenge. But if the past hour and a half was any indication of how far out of her element she was, she couldn't imagine what the next two weeks held for her.

Preoccupied with her new clothes and how ill-prepared she had been for her stay at the ranch, it came as no small surprise when Chance drove past the lane leading up to the main house on the Big Blue ranch. They had traveled the thirty or so miles without her even realizing it.

Now as she watched the lane disappear behind them in the truck's side mirror, Fee felt the butterflies begin to gather in her stomach. It was as if they were leaving civilization behind and embarking on a journey into the untamed wilderness.

She was a born and bred city dweller and the closest she had ever been to any kind of predatory wildlife was in the confines of a zoo. There was a certain comfort in knowing that there were iron bars and thick plates of glass between her and the creatures that would like nothing more than to make a meal out of her. But out in the wilds of Wyoming those safety measures were nonexistent and she knew as surely as she knew her own name there were very large, very hairy animals with long claws and big teeth hiding behind every bush and tree, just waiting for the opportunity to pounce on her.

"Do you have a lot of trouble with predators?" she asked when the asphalt road turned into a narrow gravel lane.

Chance shrugged. "Once in a while we have a mountain lion or bobcat wander down from the higher elevations, but most of the time the only wildlife we see are antelope and deer."

"Doesn't Wyoming have bears and wolves?" she asked, remembering something she'd read about their being a problem when she'd gone online the night before to research ranching in Wyoming.

"Yeah, but they're like the big cats. They usually stay up in the mountains where their food sources are," he said slowly. "Why?"

"I just wondered," she said, looking out the passenger window.

She didn't like being afraid. It took control away from her and made her feel inadequate. Fee couldn't think of anything that she hated more than not being in charge of herself. But that was exactly the way she was feeling at the moment. But as long as the really big, extremely scary wildlife stayed in the mountains where they belonged, she'd be just fine.

As she stared at the vast landscape, hundreds of black dots came into view. As they got closer, she realized the dots were cattle. "Are all those yours?"

"Yup. That's some of them."

"How big is this ranch?" she asked, knowing they had been on the property for several miles.

"We have thirty thousand acres," Chance answered proudly. "My grandparents settled here when they first got married. Then when Uncle J.D. inherited it, he kept buying up land until it grew to the size it is now." He laughed. "And believe it or not, I'm going to be checking into leasing another ten or twenty thousand acres from the Bureau of Land Management next year."

"Isn't the ranch big enough for you?" she asked before she could stop herself. It seemed to her that much land should be more than enough for anyone.

"Not really." He smiled as he went on to explain. "The Big Blue has around six thousand head of cattle at any given time. Since our cattle are grass-fed year-round we have to be careful to manage the pastures to keep from overgrazing, as well as make sure we have enough graze to mow for hay in the summer to put up for the winter months. That's why we keep a constant check on grazing conditions and move the herds frequently. Having the extra land would give us some breathing room with that, as well as expanding the herd."

His knowledge about the needs of the cattle he raised impressed her and Fee made a mental note of the information. Since he supplied beef for the Lassiter Grill Group, it was definitely something she could envision using if she was assigned future promotions for the restaurant chain.

When Chance stopped the truck on top of a ridge, Fee's breath caught at the sight of the valley below. It looked like a scene out of a Western movie. "This is where you live?"

Smiling proudly, he nodded. "This is the Lassiter homestead. The house wasn't always this big, though. When I did the renovations before I moved in, I added several rooms and the wraparound porch on to the original log cabin."

"It's really beautiful," Fee said, meaning it. She pointed to two small houses on the far side of the valley. "Are those the cottages you mentioned for the married hired hands?"

"Slim and Lena Garrison live in one and Hal and

June Wilson live in the other," Chance answered. "Slim is the ranch foreman and Hal is the head wrangler." He pointed toward a good-size log structure not far from the three barns behind the house. "That's the bunkhouse, where the single guys stay."

"This would be the perfect place to film some of the videos I'm planning," Fee said, thinking aloud. She noticed that Chance didn't comment as he restarted the truck and drove down into the valley. "You do realize that I'm not going to give up until you agree to be the Lassiter spokesman, don't you?"

"It never crossed my mind that you would," he said, grinning as he parked the truck in front of the house. He got out to come around and open her door. "You're here to try to talk me into taking on the job and I'm going to try to convince you that you'd be better off finding someone else."

Anything she was about to say lodged in her throat when he lifted her from the truck and set her on her feet. She placed her hands on his biceps to steady herself and the latent strength she felt beneath his chambray shirt caused her pulse to race and an interesting little flutter in a part of her that had no business fluttering.

"Why do you keep...doing that?" she asked.

"What?"

"You keep lifting me in and out of the truck," she said, even though she enjoyed the feel of his solid strength beneath her palms. "I'm perfectly capable of doing that for myself."

"Two reasons, sweetheart." He leaned close to

whisper, "I'm trying to be helpful. But more than that, I like touching you."

Her breath caught and when her gaze locked with his, she wasn't sure if she would ever breathe again. He was going to kiss her. And heaven help her, she was going to let him.

But instead of lowering his head to capture her lips with his, Chance took a deep breath a moment before he stepped back and turned to get her luggage from the backseat. She did her best to cover her disappointment by looking beyond the house toward the fenced-in areas around the barn.

"What are all these pens used for?" she asked.

"We use the bigger ones for sorting the herds during roundup," he answered as he closed the truck door. "The smaller ones are for sick or injured animals that need to be treated or quarantined. The round one we use for training the working stock or breaking them to ride."

"You have all that going on at one time?" she asked, starting toward the porch steps.

"Sometimes it can be pretty busy around here," he said, laughing as he opened the front door for her.

When Fee entered and looked around the foyer, she immediately fell in love with Chance's home. The log walls had aged over the years to a beautiful warm honey color and were adorned with pieces of colorful Native American artwork along with cowboy-related items like a pair of well-worn spurs hanging next to a branding iron. Although the Big Blue's main ranch house, where she had attended the wedding, was quite beautiful, it had a more modern feel about it. Chance's home, on the other hand, had that warm, rustic appeal that could only be achieved with the passage of time.

"This is really beautiful," she said, gazing up at the chandelier made of deer antlers. "Did you decorate it?"

"Yeah, I just look like the type of guy who knows all about that stuff, don't I?" Laughing, he shook his head. "After I finished adding on to the cabin and modernizing things like the kitchen and bathrooms, I turned the house over to my mom for the decorating. She has a real knack for that kind of thing."

"Marlene did a wonderful job," Fee said, smiling. "She should have been a professional interior decorator."

"She was too busy chasing a houseful of kids." Before she could ask what he meant, he nodded toward the stairs. "Would you like to see your room?"

"Absolutely," she said as they started upstairs. She couldn't believe how eager she sounded about the bedroom, considering the moment they had just shared out by the truck. To cover the awkwardness, she added, "I can't wait to see what your mother did with the bedrooms."

When they reached the second floor, Chance directed her toward a room at the far end of the hall and opened the door. "If you don't like this one, there are four more you can choose from."

"I love it," Fee said, walking into the cheery room.

The log walls were the same honey color as the ones downstairs, but the room had a more feminine feel to it with the yellow calico curtains and bright patchwork quilt on the log bed. An antique mirror hung on the wall above a cedar-log dresser with a white milk glass pitcher and bowl on top. But her favorite feature of the room had to be the padded window seat beneath the double windows. She could imagine spending rainy afternoons curled up with a good book and a cup of hot peach tea on that bench.

"Your private bathroom is just through there," he said, pointing toward a closed door as he set her luggage on the hardwood plank floor.

"Thank you, Chance." She continued to look around. "This is just fine."

"I'll be downstairs in the kitchen if you need anything. When you get your things unpacked, come on down and we'll see what there is for supper." He stepped closer and lightly touched her cheek with the back of his knuckles. "And just so you know, I am going to do what both of us want."

"W-what's that?" she asked, wondering why the sound of his voice made her feel warm all over.

Her heart skipped a beat when his gaze locked with hers. But when he lightly traced her lower lip with the pad of his thumb, a shiver of anticipation slid up her spine and goose bumps shimmered over her skin.

"I'm going to kiss you, Fee," he said, his tone low and intimate. "And soon." Without another word, he turned and walked out into the hall, closing the door behind him.

Staring after him, she would have liked to deny that he was right about what she wanted. But she couldn't. She had thought he was going to kiss her when he came to get her at the rental house this afternoon and then again when they arrived at the ranch. Both times she'd been disappointed when he hadn't.

With her knees wobbling, she crossed the room to sit on the side of the bed. What on earth had gotten into her? She had a job to do and a promotion to earn. She didn't need the added distraction of a man in her life—even if it was only briefly.

But as she sat there wondering why he was more tempting than any other man she'd ever met, Fee knew without a shadow of doubt that the chemistry between herself and Chance was going to be extremely hard to resist. Every time he got within ten feet of her, she felt as if the air had been charged by an electric current, and when he touched her, all she could think about was how his lips would feel on hers when he kissed her. She could tell from the looks he gave her and his constant desire to touch her that he was feeling it, as well.

But she had her priorities straight. She was focused on her goal of becoming Lassiter Media's first vice president in charge of public relations under the age of thirty. She wasn't going to risk her career for any man and especially not for a summer fling—even if the sexy-as-sin cowboy had a charming smile and a voice that could melt the polar ice caps.

* * *

"Did you get the little lady squared away?" Gus Swenson asked when Chance entered the kitchen.

Too old to continue doing ranch work and too ornery to go anywhere else, Gus had become the cook and housekeeper after the renovations to the homestead had been completed. If it had been left up to him, Chance would have just had Gus move into the homestead and that would have been that. After all, Gus had been his dad's lifelong best friend—he was practically family. But Gus's pride had been at stake and that's why Chance had disguised his offer in the form of a job. The old man had grumbled about being reduced to doing "women's work," but Chance knew Gus was grateful for the opportunity to live out the rest of his days on the ranch he had worked for the past fifty years.

"Yup. She's in the room across the hall from mine," Chance answered, walking over to hang his hat on a peg beside the back door.

Reaching into the refrigerator, he got himself a beer and popped off the metal cap. He needed something to take the edge off the tension building inside him.

In hindsight, it might not have been the smartest decision he'd ever made to put Fee in the room across from the master suite. If touching her smooth cheek was all it took to make him feel as restless as a bull moose in mating season, how the hell was he going to get any sleep? He tipped the bottle up and drank half the contents. Just the thought of her lying in bed within feet of where he would be, wearing something soft and transparent, her silky blond hair spread across the pillow, had him ready to jump out of his own skin.

"You still got the notion you're gonna talk her outta makin' you a movie star?" Gus asked, drawing him out of his unsettling insight.

"I told you she wants me to be the spokesman for her PR campaign," Chance said, finishing off the beer. "That's a far cry from being in a movie."

"You're gonna be in front of a camera, ain't ya?" Gus asked. Before Chance could answer, the old man went on. "I've got a month's pay that says you'll end up doin' it."

Chance laughed as he tossed the empty bottle in the recycling container under the sink. "That's one bet you'll lose."

The old man grunted. "We'll see, hotshot. You ain't never asked a woman to come stay here before and that's a surefire sign that she's already got you roped. It's just a matter of time before she's got you fallin' all over yourself to do whatever she wants."

Deciding there might be a ring of truth to Gus's observations and not at all comfortable with it, Chance changed the subject. "Did Slim check on the north pasture's grazing conditions today?"

He didn't have to ask if Gus had seen the ranch foreman. The old guy made a trip out to the barn every afternoon when the men came back to the ranch for the day, to shoot the breeze and feel as if he was still a working cowboy.

Gus shook his head. "Slim said they couldn't get to it today. He had to send a couple of the boys over to the west pasture to fix a pretty good stretch of fence that last storm tore up and the rest of 'em were movin' the herd over by the cutbank so they can start mowin' for hay next week."

"I'll take care of it tomorrow," Chance said. He had intended to show Fee around the ranch anyway; he could include the northern section of pasture as part of the tour.

"Something smells absolutely wonderful," she said, walking into the kitchen.

"Thank you, ma'am." Bent over to take a pan of biscuits out of the oven, Gus added, "I don't fix anything real fancy, but I can guarantee it'll taste good and there's plenty of it."

"Fee Sinclair, this is Gus Swenson, the orneriest cowboy this side of the Continental Divide," Chance said, making the introductions.

When Gus straightened and finally turned to face her, Chance watched a slow grin appear on the old man's wrinkled face. "Real nice to meet you, gal." He stood there grinning like a damned fool for several moments before a scowl replaced his easy expression. "Where's your manners, boy? Don't just stand there blinkin' your eyes like a bastard calf in a hailstorm. Offer this little lady a seat while I finish up supper."

"Thank you, but I'd be more than happy to help you finish dinner," Fee offered, smiling.

"I got it all under control, gal," Gus said, reaching into the cabinet to get some plates.

"Could I at least set the table for you?" she asked, walking over to the butcher block island, where Gus had set the plates. "I really do want to help."

Gus looked like a teenage boy with his first crush when he nodded and handed her the dinnerware. "I appreciate it, ma'am."

"Please call me Fee," she said, smiling as she took the plates from the old man.

When she turned toward the table, Gus grinned like a possum and gave Chance a thumbs-up behind her back. "Why don't you make yourself useful, boy? Get some glasses and pour up somethin' for all of us to drink."

As Chance poured three glasses of iced tea and carried them to the table, he couldn't get over the change in Gus. Normally as grouchy as a grizzly bear with a sore paw, the crusty old cowboy was downright pleasant to Fee—at least as close to it as Gus ever got. If he didn't know better, Chance would swear that Gus was smitten.

Twenty minutes later after eating a heaping plate of beef stew, homemade biscuits and a slice of hot apple pie, Chance sat back from the table. "Gus, you outdid yourself. I think that was one of the best meals you've ever made."

"Everything was delicious," Fee agreed, reaching over to cover the old man's hand with hers. "Thank you, Gus."

The gesture caused Gus's cheeks to turn red above

his grizzled beard. "You're more than welcome, gal. Can I get you anything else? Maybe another piece of pie? We got plenty."

Smiling, Fee shook her head. "I couldn't eat another thing. I'm positively stuffed."

Chance rose to take his and Fee's plates to the sink. If anyone was falling all over themselves to do whatever Fee wanted, it was Gus. The old guy was practically begging her to let him do something—anything—for her.

"Would you like to go for a walk after I help Gus clear up the kitchen?" Chance asked, wanting to spend a little time alone with her.

"That would be nice," she said, getting up from the table. "But I want to help with the cleanup first."

"You kids go on and take your walk," Gus said as he got to his feet. "There ain't nothin' much to do but put the leftovers in the refrigerator and load the dishwasher."

"Are you sure, Mr. Swenson?" Fee asked, her voice uncertain.

"The name's Gus, little lady," the old geezer said, grinning from ear to ear. "And I don't mind one bit."

Chance turned to stare at Gus to see if the old man had sprouted another head and a new personality to go with it. He'd never in his entire thirty-two years heard Gus sound so amiable. What was wrong with him?

"Are you feeling all right?" Chance asked, frowning.

"I'm just fine," Gus answered, his smile warning

Chance to drop the matter. "Now, you kids go ahead and take that walk. I'm gonna be turnin' in pretty soon. I'll see you both at breakfast in the mornin'."

Chance shook his head as he reached for his hat hanging on the peg and opened the door. He suddenly knew exactly what was wrong with Gus. Damned if the old fart wasn't trying to play matchmaker.

As they left the house, Fee looked confused. "It's not that late. Is Gus really going to bed this early?"

Chance shook his head. "No, but he's got a set of priorities and in the summer it's baseball. The Rockies are playing the Cardinals on one of the satellite TV channels tonight and he wouldn't miss that for anything. He's going to hole up in his room watching the game."

They fell silent for a moment as they started across the yard toward the barn. "Do you mind if I ask you something, Chance?"

"Not at all. What do you want to know?" he asked, barely resisting the urge to put his arm around her.

To keep from acting on the impulse, he stuffed his hands into the front pockets of his jeans. She had only been on the ranch a couple of hours and he didn't want her to feel as if he was rushing things.

"Earlier this afternoon, you said your mother didn't have time to become an interior decorator because she was too busy chasing after a houseful of children." She paused as if she wasn't sure how to word her question. "I was under the impression that the only sibling you had was your sister."

He nodded. "She is. But up until a couple of months ago, I thought I was an only child."

Fee's confusion was written all over her pretty face. "Am I missing something?"

"Hannah is the product of an affair my dad had when he was out on the rodeo circuit," Chance admitted, still feeling a bit resentful. Although he loved and accepted his half sister, he still struggled with the fact that his father had cheated on his mother. "My mom, dad and uncle J.D. knew about her, but the rest of the family didn't find out until a couple of months ago."

"Okay," Fee said slowly. "But if all your mother had was you, who were the other kids she was running after?"

"Working for Lassiter Media, you've probably heard that Uncle J.D.'s wife died within a few days of having Angelica." When Fee nodded, he continued, "Uncle J.D. had his hands full trying to raise three little kids on his own. Mom helped out as much as she could, but she had me and Dad to take care of and was only able to do so much. Then after my dad got killed four years later, my uncle suggested that Mom and I move into the main house with him and his kids. By that time he had opened the Lassiter Media office in L.A. and traveled back and forth a lot. He needed someone he trusted to take care of his kids and my mom was the obvious choice. She knew and loved the kids and they all considered her a second mother anyway."

"That makes sense," she agreed. "Was your parents' home nearby?"

"We lived here at the homestead." He couldn't help but feel a strong sense of pride that he was the third generation to own this section of the ranch. "My dad was more of a cowboy than Uncle J.D. ever thought about being and when he wasn't riding the rough stock in a rodeo somewhere, Dad was working here at the ranch. After my uncle built the main house, Uncle J.D. gave this part of the Big Blue to us."

"No wonder the family is extremely close," Fee said thoughtfully. "Sage, Dylan and Angelica are more like your siblings than they are cousins."

As they walked into the barn, Chance gave in to temptation and casually draped his arm across her slender shoulders. She gave him a sideways glance, but he took it as a good sign that she didn't protest.

"The only time the four of us weren't together was at night when we went to bed," he explained. "Uncle J.D. gave my mom and me one wing of the house so that we would have our privacy, while he and his kids took the other wing."

"You must have had a wonderful childhood with other children to play with," Fee said, sounding wistful.

"I can't complain," he admitted. "What about your family? Do you have a brother or sister?"

She shook her head. "I was an only child."

When she failed to elaborate, Chance decided to let the matter drop. It was clear she didn't want to talk about it and he'd never been one to pry. If Fee wanted to tell him about her family, he would be more than happy to listen. If she didn't, then that was her call.

Walking down the long aisle between the horse stalls, Chance pointed to a paint mare that had curiously poked her head over the bottom half of the stall door. "That's the horse you'll learn to ride tomorrow."

Fee looked uncertain. "It looks so big. Do you have one in a smaller size?"

"You make it sound like you're trying on a pair of shoes," he said, laughing. "Rosy is about as small as we have around here."

"I'm not so comfortable with large animals," she said, shaking her head. "When I was little girl, my grandmother's next door neighbor had an overly friendly Great Dane that knocked me down every time I was around him. I know he wasn't trying to hurt me, but I ended up with stitches in my knee from his friendly gestures." She eyed the mare suspiciously. "She's bigger than he was."

He guided Fee over to the stall. "I promise Rosy is the gentlest horse we have on the ranch and loves people." Reaching out, he scratched the mare's forehead. "She'll be the perfect starter horse for you and she won't knock you down."

"Rosy likes that?" Fee asked.

He nodded. "You want to try it?" When she shook her head, he took her hand in his. "Just rub Rosy's forehead like this," he said, showing her how. "While you two get acquainted, I'll go get a treat for you to feed her."

"I don't think that's a good idea, Chance." He heard the hesitancy in her voice as he walked across the aisle into the feed room. "She looks like she might have pretty big teeth. Does she bite?"

He shook his head as he walked back to the stall with a cube of sugar. "Rosy might nip you unintentionally, but she's never been one to bite." He placed the cube on Fee's palm. "Just keep your hand flat and Rosy will take care of the rest."

When Fee tentatively put her hand out, the mare scooped up the sugar cube with her lips. "Oh my goodness!" Fee's expression was filled with awe when she turned to look at him. "Her mouth is so soft. It feels just like velvet."

Seeing the wonder in her eyes and her delighted smile, Chance didn't think twice about closing the gap between them to take Fee in his arms. "Do you remember what I told you this afternoon?"

The glee in her vibrant blue eyes changed to the awareness he'd seen in them earlier in the day. "Y-yes."

"Good." He started to lower his head and was encouraged when she brought her arms up to encircle his neck. "I'm going to give you that kiss now that we've both been wanting."

When he covered her mouth with his, Chance didn't think he had ever tasted anything sweeter. He took his time to slowly, thoroughly explore her soft lips. They were perfect and clung to his as if she was eager for him to take the kiss to the next level. When she sighed and melted into him, he didn't think twice about tightening his arms around her and deepening the caress.

The moment his tongue touched hers, Chance felt a wave of heat shoot from the top of his head all the way to the soles of his feet. But when she slid her hands beneath the collar of his shirt to caress the nape of his neck, it felt as if his heart turned a somersault inside his chest. The magnetic pull between them was more explosive than anything he could have imagined and he knew as surely as he knew his own name it was inevitable—they would be making love. The thought caused the region south of his belt buckle to tighten so fast it left him feeling lightheaded.

Easing away from the kiss before things got out of hand, he gazed down at the dazed expression on her pretty face. She was as turned on as he was and, unless he missed his guess, a little confused by how quickly the passion had flared between them.

"I think we'd better call it a night," he said, continuing to hold her.

"I-it would…probably be a good…idea," she said, sounding as breathless as he felt.

"Mornings around here start earlier than you're probably used to," he advised, forcing himself to take a step back.

When he put his arm around her and started walking toward the open doors of the barn, she asked, "How early are we talking about?"

He grinned. "Well before daylight."

"Is it that imperative to get up so early?" she asked, frowning.

"The livestock get breakfast before we do," he explained, holding her to his side. "Besides, in the summer we get as much done as we can before the hottest part of the day. The earlier we get up and get started, the better chance we have of doing that."

"I suppose that makes sense," she said as they climbed the porch steps and went into the house. "Why don't you wake me up when you get back to the house after you feed the livestock?"

"Hey, you're the one who's here to observe what a real cowboy is all about," he reminded, laughing. "That includes the morning chores as well as what I do the rest of the day."

"No, I'm here to talk you into being the spokesman for your family's PR campaign," she shot back. "It was your idea that I needed to see what you do."

Walking her into the foyer of the homestead and up the stairs, they fell silent and Chance cursed himself as nine kinds of a fool the closer they got to their bedrooms. After he had put her in the room across the hall from his, he'd realized that it probably hadn't been one of his brightest ideas. But now that he knew the sweetness of her lips and how responsive she was to his kiss, there wasn't a doubt in his mind that it was the dumbest decision he'd made in his entire adult life. But at the time, he'd thought she might like the room with the window seat. It was the only one of the six bedrooms that was the least bit feminine.

When they stopped at the door to her room, he barely resisted the temptation of taking her back into his arms. "Sleep well, Fee."

"You, too, Chance," she said, giving him a smile that sent his blood pressure skyrocketing.

He waited until she went into her room, then quickly entering his, he closed the door and headed straight for the shower. Between the kiss they'd shared in the barn and the knowledge that at that very moment she was probably removing every stitch of clothes she had on, he was hotter than a two-dollar pistol in a skid-row pawn shop on Saturday night.

He'd have liked nothing more than to hold Fee to him and kiss her senseless. But that hadn't been an option. If he had so much as touched her, he knew he wouldn't have wanted to let her go. And that had never happened to him before.

It wasn't as if he hadn't experienced a strong attraction for a woman in the past. But nothing in his adult life had been as passionate as fast as what he had felt with Fee when he kissed her. He hadn't counted on that when he asked her to stay with him. Hell, the possibility hadn't even been on his radar.

Quickly stripping out of his clothes, he turned on the water and stepped beneath the icy spray. Maybe if he traumatized his body with a cold shower, he'd not only be able to get some sleep, maybe some of his sanity would return.

As he stood there shivering uncontrollably, he shook his head. Yeah, and if he believed that, there was someone, somewhere waiting to sell him the Grand Canyon or Mount Rushmore.

Four

Fee yawned as she sat on a bale of hay in the barn and watched Chance saddle Rosy and another horse he'd called Dakota. She couldn't believe that after he'd knocked on her door an hour and a half before the sun came up, he'd gone on to feed all of the animals housed in the barns and holding pens and met with his ranch foreman to go over the chores for the day—all before breakfast.

Hiding another yawn with her hand, she decided she might not be as tired if she'd gotten more rest the night before. But sleep had eluded her and she knew exactly what had caused her insomnia. Not only had Chance's kiss been way more than she'd expected, it had caused her to question her sanity.

Several different times yesterday, she had practi-

cally asked the man to kiss her and when he finally
had, she'd acted completely shameless and all but
melted into a puddle at his big booted feet. Thank
goodness he'd kept it fairly brief and ended the kiss
before she'd made a bigger fool of herself than she
already had.

Then there was the matter of the promise she'd
made to herself years ago. She'd seemed to forget
all about her vow to never put her career in jeopardy
because of a man.

"You're not your mother," she whispered to herself.

Her mother had been a prime example of how that
kind of diversion could destroy a career, and Fee was
determined not to let that happen to her. Rita Sinclair
had abandoned her position as a successful financial advisor when she foolishly fell head over heels
in love with a dreamer—a man who chased his lofty
ideas from one place to another without ever considering the sacrifices his aspirations had cost her.
Maybe he'd asked her to marry him because she had
become pregnant with Fee or maybe he'd thought it
was what he wanted at the time. Either way, he had
eventually decided that his wife and infant daughter were holding him back and he'd moved on without them.

But instead of picking up the pieces of her life
and resuming her career, Fee's mother had settled
for working one dead-end job after another that left
her with little time for her daughter. Her mother had
died ten years ago, still waiting for the dreamer to

return to take her with him on his next irresponsible adventure. Fee suspected that her mother had died of a broken heart because he never did.

When she'd been old enough to understand the life her mother had given up for her father, Fee had made a conscious decision to avoid making the same mistakes.

Although he wasn't her boss, Chance's family owned the company she worked for and that was even worse. She could very easily end up getting herself fired.

She tried to think if she'd heard anything about Lassiter Media's policy on fraternization. Would that even apply in this situation? Chance wasn't an employee of the company, nor was he an owner. But he was closely related to those who were and she'd been sent to smooth over a scandal, not create another one.

"I don't know what you're thinking, but if that frown on your face is any indication, it can't be good," Chance said, breaking into her disturbing thoughts.

"I was thinking about the PR campaign," she answered, staring down at the toes of her new boots. "I should be working on ideas for the videos and print ads."

Technically it wasn't really a lie. She had been thinking about the reasons she'd been sent to Wyoming and how losing her focus when it came to him could very easily cost her a perfectly good job.

Squatting down in front of her, Chance used his index finger to lift her chin until their gazes met.

"What do you say we forget about fixing the Lassiter reputation today and just have a little fun?"

The moment he touched her, Fee could barely remember her own name, let alone the fact that she had a job she might lose if she wasn't careful. "You think I'm going to have fun riding a horse?" she asked, unable to keep the skepticism from her voice.

"I promise you will," he said, taking her hands in his. Straightening to his full height, he pulled her to her feet, then picked up her hat where she had placed it on the bale of hay when she sat down. Positioning it on her head, he pointed to Rosy. "Now, are you ready to mount up and get started?"

"Not really," she said, wondering if workers' compensation would cover her falling off a horse since she was only learning to ride in an effort to get him to agree to be the Lassiter spokesman. Eying the mare, Fee shook her head. "Is it just me or did she get a lot bigger overnight?"

"It's just you," he said, laughing as he led her over to the mare's side. He explained how to put her foot in the stirrup and take hold of the saddle to pull herself up onto the back of the horse. "Don't worry about Rosy. She's been trained to stand perfectly still until you're seated and give her the signal you're ready for her to move."

"It's the after I'm seated part that I'm worried about," Fee muttered as she took a deep breath and barely managed to raise her foot high enough to place it in the stirrup. Grabbing the saddle as Chance had instructed, she tried to mount the horse but found the task impossible. "How is stepping into the stirrup any help when your knee is even with your chin?" she asked, feeling relief flow through her. If she couldn't mount the horse, she couldn't ride it. "I guess I won't be able to go riding. At least not until you get a shorter horse."

"It takes a little practice," he answered, grinning. "Besides, the horse isn't as tall as you are short."

She shook her head. "There's nothing wrong with being short."

"I didn't say there was," he said, stepping behind her.

Fee's heart felt as if it stopped, then took off at a gallop when, without warning, he placed one hand at her waist and the other on the seat of her new jeans. Before she could process what was taking place, Chance boosted her up into the saddle. Her cheeks heated and she wasn't sure if it was from embarrassment or the awareness coursing through her.

But when she realized she was actually sitting atop Rosy, Fee forgot all about sorting out her reaction to Chance. Wrapping both hands around the saddle horn, she held on for dear life. "This is even higher than I thought it would be. I really do think a shorter horse would work out a lot better."

"Try to relax and sit naturally," he coaxed. He reached up to gently pry her hands from the saddle. "You don't want to be as stiff as a ramrod."

When the mare shifted her weight from one foot to the other, Fee scrunched her eyes shut and waited for the worst. "I thought you said she would stand still."

"Fee, look at me," he commanded. When she opened first one eye and then the other, the promise in his brilliant green eyes stole her breath. "Do you trust me?"

"Yes." She wasn't sure why, given that she hadn't known him all that long, but she did trust him.

"I give you my word that I won't let anything happen to you," he assured her. "You're completely safe, sweetheart."

Her heart stalled and she suddenly found it hard to draw a breath. The sound of his deep voice when he used the endearment caused heat to fill her. Why did she suddenly wish he was talking about something besides riding a horse?

Unable to get her vocal cords to work, she simply nodded.

"Good." He checked to make sure the stirrups were adjusted to the right length. "Now I want you to slightly tilt your heels down just below horizontal."

"Why?" she asked even as she followed his instructions.

"Shifting your weight to your heels instead of the balls of your feet helps you relax your legs and sit more securely," he explained. "And it's more natural and comfortable for both you and Rosy." He took hold of the mare's reins, then reached for his horse's reins, as well. "Now are you ready to go for your first ride?"

"Would it make a difference if I said no?" she asked, already knowing the answer.

Grinning, he shook his head. "Nope."

"I didn't think so." Fee caught her breath when the mare slowly started walking beside Chance as he led both horses out of the barn. But instead of the bumpy ride she expected, it was more of a smooth rocking motion. "This isn't as rough as I thought it would be."

"It isn't when you relax and move with the horse, instead of against it," he said, leading them over to the round pen he had mentioned was used for training. Once he had his horse tied to the outside of the fence, he opened the gate and led the mare inside. "Hold the reins loosely," he said, handing Fee the leather straps. He walked around the pen beside Rosy until they had made a complete circle. "Now, I'm going to stand right here while you and Rosy go around."

A mixture of adrenaline and fear rose inside of Fee like a Pacific tsunami. "What am I supposed to do?"

"Just sit there and let Rosy do the rest," he said calmly. "I promise you'll be fine."

As the horse carried her around the enclosure, Fee noticed that the mare kept turning her head to look back at her. "Yes, Rosy, I'm scared witless. Please prove Chance right and don't do anything I'll regret."

To her surprise the mare snorted and bobbed her head up and down as if she understood what Fee had requested as she continued to slowly walk around the inside of the fence.

By the time Rosy had made her way back around to the gate for the second time, Fee began to feel a little more confident. "This isn't as difficult as I thought it would be."

"It's not," Chance said when the mare stopped in front of him. "Are you ready to take a tour of the ranch now?" he asked, patting the mare's sleek neck.

"I…guess so," Fee answered, not at all sure she was ready to ride outside of the enclosure. But Rosy seemed to be willing and Fee felt some of her usual self-confidence begin to return.

"Don't worry," Chance said, as if reading her mind. He opened the gate to lead the mare out. "Rosy is kid broke and you're doing great for your first time on a horse."

Fee frowned. "What does kid broke mean?"

"Her temperament and training make her safe enough to let a little kid ride her with minimal risk of anything happening," he said, mounting his horse. "And I'll be right beside you."

As they rode across the pasture and headed toward a hillside in the distance, she reflected on how far out of her element she was. Up until today, her idea of adventure had been a shopping trip to one of the malls in the San Fernando Valley the day after Thanksgiving.

But she had to admit that riding a horse wasn't as bad as she thought it would be. In fact, the more she thought about it, the more she realized she was actually enjoying the experience. And if that wasn't un-usual enough, they were traveling across a deserted expanse of land where wild animals roamed free and she wasn't all that afraid of being something's next meal. Unbelievable!

Fee glanced over at the man riding beside her. What was it about Chance that could get her to do things that were totally out of character for her and without much protest on her part?

Staring out across the land, she knew exactly why she was willing to step out of her comfort zone and try new things. She trusted Chance—trusted that he wouldn't ask anything of her that she couldn't do and wouldn't allow anything to harm her.

The realization caused her heart to skip a beat. She didn't trust easily and especially when it came to men. The fact that she had already placed her faith in Chance was more than a little disturbing. Why was he different?

It could have something to do with the fact that so far, he was exactly what he said he was—a hard-working rancher who was more interested in draw-ing attention to the quality of the beef he raised than being in the limelight himself. Or maybe it was the fact that he was vastly different from any of the men she knew in L.A. Although great guys, most of them would rather sit behind a desk in a climate-controlled office than be outside getting their hands dirty.

She wasn't sure why she trusted Chance, but one thing was certain: she was going to have to be on her guard at all times. Otherwise, she just might find herself falling for him and end up out of a job.

As they rode up the trail leading to the north pasture, Chance was proud of the way Fee had taken to horseback riding. At first, she had been extremely apprehensive about getting on a horse, but she'd at least had the guts to try. That was something he admired.

In fact, there were a lot of things about her that he appreciated. She was not only courageous, she was dedicated. He didn't know any other woman who would go to the lengths she had in her effort to do her job and do it right. Fee was willing to do whatever it took to get him to agree to be the spokesman in her ad campaign, even if that meant getting up at a time most city dwellers thought was the middle of the night and riding a horse for the first time. And from what Sage had told him, she was sensitive to others. Apparently, Colleen had tentatively offered to let Fee use their upcoming wedding as part of the PR campaign to improve the Lassiters' image, but she hadn't wanted to exploit their big day and had politely declined.

"Rosy and I seem to be getting along pretty well," Fee said, bringing him back to the present.

"So you're having a good time?" he asked, noticing how silky her hair looked as a light breeze played with the blond strands of her ponytail.

"Yes," she said, giving him a smile. "I didn't think

I would, but I really am. Of course, I might not feel the same way if I was riding a different horse."

"I was pretty sure you and Rosy were…a good match," he said, distracted by the faint sound of a cow bawling in the distance. Staring in the direction the sound came from, he spotted a large black cow lying on her side about two hundred yards away. It was clear the animal was in distress. "Damn!"

"What happened?" Fee asked, looking alarmed.

"I'm going to have to ride on ahead," he said quickly. "You'll be fine. I'll be within sight and Rosy will bring you right to me."

Before Fee had the chance to question him further or protest that he was leaving her behind, he kicked Dakota into a gallop and raced toward the cow. The bay gelding covered the distance quickly and when he reached the cow, Chance could tell that not only was she in labor, she was having trouble delivering the calf.

Dismounting, he immediately started rolling up the long sleeves on his chambray shirt. He could tell from her shallow breathing that the animal had been at this awhile and was extremely weak. He was going to have to see what the problem was, then try to do what he could to help. Otherwise there was a very real possibility he would lose both the heifer and her calf.

"What's wrong with it?" Fee asked when she and Rosy finally reached the spot where the cow lay.

"I'm pretty sure the calf is hung up," he said, taking off his wristwatch and slipping it into the front pocket of his jeans. He reached into the saddlebags tied behind Dakota's saddle and removed a packet of disinfectant wipes.

Fee looked genuinely concerned. "Oh, the poor thing. Is there anything you can do to help her? Should you call the veterinarian?"

"The vet will take too long to get here." Walking over to the mare, he lifted Fee down from the saddle and set her on her feet. "I'm going to need you to hold the heifer's tail while I check to see what the problem is," he said, taking several of the wet cloths from the packet to wipe down his hands and arms. "Do you think you can do that, Fee?"

He could tell she wasn't at all sure about getting that close to the animal, but she took a deep breath and nodded. "I'll do my best."

"Good." He couldn't stop himself from giving her a quick kiss. Then catching the cow's wildly switching tail, he handed it to Fee. "Hold on tight while I see if the calf's breech or it's just too big."

While Fee held the tail out of the way, Chance knelt down at the back of the animal. He wished that he had some of the shoulder-length gloves from one of the calving sheds back at ranch headquarters, but since that wasn't an option, he gritted his teeth and proceeded to do what he could to help the heifer. Reaching inside, he felt the calf, and sure enough, one of the legs was folded at the knee. Pushing the calf back, he carefully straightened its front leg, then gently but firmly pulled it back into the birth position.

"Will she be able to have the calf now?" Fee asked, her tone anxious as she let go of the tail and put distance between herself and the cow.

"I hope so," he said, rising to his feet. Using more of the wipes, he cleaned his arm as he waited to see if the heifer was going to be able to calve. "I'll have to check my records when I get back to the house, but I'm pretty sure this is her first calf."

When the cow made an odd noise, Fee looked worried. "Is she all right?"

"She's pretty tired, but we should know within a few minutes if she'll be able to do this on her own," he said, focusing on the cow to see if there were any more signs of distress. When he saw none, he walked over to Fee.

"And if she can't?" Fee asked.

"Then I become a bovine obstetrician and help her out," he answered, shrugging. "It wouldn't be the first time and it won't be the last."

"This is definitely one of those jobs you mentioned that most people would consider disgusting."

"Yup." He noticed the heifer was starting to work with her contractions and that was a good sign she at least wasn't too exhausted to try.

"Maybe a lot of people find something like this distasteful, but I think it's rather heroic," Fee said, thoughtfully. "You care enough about the animals on this ranch to make sure they're well taken care of and if that means getting your hands dirty to save one of them or to help relieve their suffering, then that's what you do."

He nodded. "I'm responsible for them and that includes keeping them healthy."

Chance had never really thought about his job the way Fee had just pointed out. Sure, he liked animals—liked working with them and being around them. He wouldn't be much of a rancher if he didn't. But he had never really thought about what he did as heroic. To him, taking good care of his livestock was not just part of the job description, it was the right thing to do.

"Oh my goodness," Fee said suddenly when the calf began to emerge from the cow. Her expression was filled with awe. "This is amazing."

Confident that the animal was going to be able to have the calf without further intervention on his part, he used his cell phone to call ranch headquarters. He needed to get one of his men to come out and watch over the heifer until she and the calf could be moved to one of the holding pens close to the barn.

When the calf slid out onto the ground, Chance walked over to make sure it was breathing and checked it over while the heifer rested. "It's a girl," he said, grinning as he walked back to Fee.

"Is the momma cow going to be all right?" Fee asked.

He nodded as he draped his arm across her shoulders. "I think she'll be just fine. But Slim is sending one of the boys out here to see that she gets back to the ranch, where we can watch her and she can rest up a little. Then she and her baby will rejoin the herd in a few days."

Fee frowned. "Why was she out here by herself to begin with?"

"Livestock have a tendency to want to go off by themselves when they're in labor," Chance explained.

"For privacy." She nodded. "I can understand that."

He watched the cow get up and nudge her baby with her nose, urging it to stand, as well. "She had probably done that yesterday when the men moved the herd and they just missed seeing her. Normally, our cattle calve in the spring, but she apparently got bred later than usual, throwing her having her calf to now."

"But they will be back at the ranch house and I'll be able to see the calf again?" she asked, looking hopeful as, after several attempts, the calf gained her footing and managed to stand.

"Sure, you'll be able to see her." He grinned. "But I somehow got the impression you didn't like big animals all that much and might even be a little afraid of them."

"This one is different," she insisted, her voice softening when the calf wobbled over to her mother and started to nurse. "It's a baby and not all that big yet. Besides, the fence will be between me and her momma."

Seeing the cowboy he'd called for riding toward them, Chance led Fee over to Rosy. "Our replacement is almost here. Are you ready to mount up and finish checking on the grazing conditions before we head back to the house?"

"I suppose," she said, lifting her foot to put it into the stirrup. "This would be a whole lot easier if Rosy was shorter."

As he stepped up behind her, Chance took a deep breath and got ready to give her a boost up into the saddle. Touching her cute little backside when she'd mounted the mare the first time had damn near caused him to have a coronary. He could only guess what his reaction would be this time.

The minute his palm touched the seat of her blue jeans, a jolt of electric current shot up his arm, down through his chest and straight to the region south of his belt buckle. His reaction was not only predictable, it was instantaneous.

Feeling as if his own jeans had suddenly gotten a couple of sizes smaller in the stride, he waited to make sure Fee was settled on Rosy before he caught Dakota's reins in one hand and gingerly swung up onto the gelding's saddle. He immediately shifted to keep from emasculating himself. Fee hadn't been on the ranch a full twenty-four hours and he was already in need of a second cold shower.

As they started toward the north pasture, Chance decided it was either going to be the most exciting two weeks of his life or the most grueling. And he had every intention of seeing that it was going to be the former, not the latter.

While Chance called his mother to make arrangements to take Cassie for ice cream the next day, Fee helped clean the kitchen after dinner. "Gus, it was the most amazing thing I've ever seen. He knew exactly what to do and everything turned out fine for the momma cow, as well as for her baby."

She still couldn't get over the efficiency and expertise Chance had demonstrated with the pregnant cow. What he'd had to do to help the animal was messy and disgusting, but he hadn't hesitated for a single second. He had immediately sprung into action and taken care of her and her calf to make sure they both survived.

It was hard to believe how many facets there were to Chance's job. He not only had to keep extensive records on all of the livestock, he had to be a land manager, an experienced horseman and an impromptu large-animal veterinarian. And she had a feeling that was just the tip of the iceberg.

"Don't go tellin' him I said so 'cause I don't want him gettin' bigheaded about it," Gus said, grinning. "But that boy's got better cow sense than even his daddy had. And that's sayin' somethin'. When Charlie Lassiter was alive there was none better at ranchin' than he was. He knew what a steer was gonna do before it did."

Fee remembered Chance telling her that his father had run the ranch when he wasn't out on the rodeo circuit. "How did Chance's father die? Was he killed at a rodeo?"

"It was one of them freak accidents that never shoulda happened." Gus shook his head sadly as he handed her a pot he had just finished washing. "Charlie was a saddle bronc and bareback rider when he was out on the rodeo circuit, and a damned good one. He always finished in the money and other than a busted arm one time, never got hurt real bad. But about three years after he stopped rodeoin' and went to ranchin' full time, he got throwed from a horse he was breakin'. He landed wrong and it snapped his neck. Charlie was dead as soon as he hit the ground."

"That's so sad," she said, drying the pot with a soft cotton dish towel before hanging it on the pot rack above the kitchen island.

"The real bad thing was Chance saw it all," Gus said, his tone turning husky.

"Oh, how awful!" Fee gasped.

Gus nodded. "After Charlie started bein' at home all the time, that little kid was his daddy's shadow and followed him everywhere. It weren't no surprise to any of us that Chance was sittin' on the top fence rail watchin' Charlie that day."

Fee's heart broke for Chance and it took a moment for her to be able to speak around the lump clogging her throat. "How old…was Chance?"

"That was twenty-four years ago," Gus answered. He cleared his throat as if he was having just as hard a time speaking as she was. "That would have made Chance about eight."

She couldn't stop tears from filling her eyes when she thought about Chance as a little boy watching the father he idolized die. Although she'd never really known her father and hadn't been all that close to her mother, she couldn't imagine watching someone she loved so much die in such a tragic way. That had to have been devastating for him.

"Well, that's taken care of," Chance said, walking into the room. He had called his mother to let her know what time they would be stopping by the main house tomorrow to take his niece to get ice cream. Marlene was keeping Cassie while Hannah and Logan were on their honeymoon, and she could probably use a break. "Mom said she would have Cassie ready tomorrow afternoon for us to come by and get her."

Without thinking, Fee walked over and wrapped her arms around his waist to give him a hug. She knew he would probably think she'd lost her mind, but she didn't care. The more she found out about Chance Lassiter the more she realized what a remarkable man he was. He'd suffered through a traumatic loss as a child, but that hadn't deterred him from following in his father's footsteps to become a rancher. And from what she'd seen at the wedding a few nights ago, he had gone out of his way to become close to the half sister and niece that he hadn't even known existed until just recently.

"Don't get me wrong, sweetheart," he said, chuckling as his arms closed around her. "I'm not complaining in the least, but what's this for?"

Knowing that if she tried to explain her actions, she'd make a fool of herself, she shrugged and took a step back. "I'm still amazed that you knew what to do today to save the momma cow and her baby."

He smiled. "How would you like to take a walk out to the holding pen to check on them?"

"I'd like that," she said, meaning it. "Gus and I just finished up the dishes."

Gus nodded. "I'll see you at breakfast. I've a baseball game comin' on the sports channel in a few minutes."

As Gus went to his room to watch the game, she and Chance left the house and walked across the yard toward the barn. She glanced up at him when he reached out and took her hand in his. It was a small gesture, but the fact that it felt so good to have him touch her, even in such a small way, was a little unsettling. Was she already in way over her head?

"Looks like we may have to cut our walk short," Chance said, pointing to a bank of clouds in the distance. "We might get a little rain."

"From the dark color, I'd say it's going to be a downpour," Fee commented as they reached the pen where the cow and calf were being held.

"Even if it is a downpour, it probably won't last long," he answered. "We get a lot of pop-up thundershowers this time of year. They move through, dump a little water on us and move on."

Noticing a covered area at one end of the enclosure, she nodded. "I'm glad to see there's shelter for them if it does start raining."

"Cattle don't usually mind being out in the rain during the summer months," he said, smiling. "It's one of the ways they cool off."

"What's another?" she asked, watching the little black calf venture away from her mother.

"If there's a pond or a river, they like to wade out and just stand there." He grinned. "Sort of like the bovine version of skinny-dipping."

"I can't say I blame them," she said, laughing. "I would think it gets rather hot with all that hair." When the calf got close to the fence, Fee couldn't help but feel a sense of awe. "She's so pretty. What are you going to name her?"

He chuckled. "We normally don't name cattle."

"I guess that would be kind of difficult when you have so many," she said, thinking it was a shame for something so cute not to have a name.

He nodded. "If they're going to be kept for breeding purposes, we tag their ears with a number. That's the way we identify them and keep track of their health and how well they do during calving season."

"I don't care," Fee said, looking into the baby's big brown eyes. "She's too cute to just be a number. I'm going to call her Belle."

"So before we take her and her mother to rejoin the herd, I should have her name put on her ear tag instead of a number?" he asked, grinning as he reached out and caught her to him.

She placed her hands on his chest and started to tell him that was exactly what she thought he should do, but she stopped short when several fat raindrops landed on her face. "We'll be soaked to the bone by the time we get back to the house," she said when it started raining harder.

Chance grabbed hold of her hand and pulled her along in the direction of the barn. "We can wait it out in there."

Sprinting the short distance, a loud clap of thunder echoed overhead as they ran inside. "That rain moved in fast," she said, laughing.

"Unless it's a big storm front, it should move through just as fast." He stared at her for several seconds before he took her by the hand and led her midway down the long center aisle to a narrow set of stairs on the far side of the feed room. "There's something I want to show you."

When he stepped back for her to precede him up the steps, she frowned. "What is it?"

"Trust me, you'll like it," he said, smiling mysteriously.

"I'm sure that's what a spider says to a fly just before it lures him into its web," she said, looking up the stairs to the floor above. She didn't know what he had up his sleeve, but she did trust him and smiling over her shoulder at him, climbed the stairs to the hayloft. When they stood facing each other at the top of the stairs, she asked, "Now, what is it you wanted to show me?"

He walked her over to the open doors at the end of the loft. "We'll have to wait until it stops raining and the sun comes back out," he said, taking her into his arms.

A shiver coursed through her and not entirely from her rain-dampened clothes. The look in Chance's eyes stole her breath and sent waves of goose bumps shimmering over her skin.

"Chance, I don't think this is a good idea," she warned. "I'm not interested in an involvement."

He shook his head. "I'm not, either. All I want is for both of us to enjoy your visit to the ranch."

"I need to talk to you about the PR campaign," she said, reminding him that she wasn't giving up on him being the family spokesman.

He nodded. "I promise we'll get to that soon. But right now, I'm going to kiss you again, Fee," he said, lowering his head. "And this time it's going to be a long, slow kiss that will leave both of us gasping for breath."

Fee's heart pounded hard in her chest when his mouth covered hers and a delicious heat began to spread throughout her body as she raised her arms to encircle his neck. True to his word, Chance took his time, teasing with tiny nibbling kisses that heightened her anticipation, and when he finally traced her lips with his tongue to deepen the caress, Fee felt as if she would go into total meltdown.

As he explored her slowly, thoroughly, he slid his hand from her back up along her ribs to the underside of her breast. Cupping her, he lightly teased the hardened tip with the pad of his thumb and even through the layers of her clothing the sensation was electrifying. A lazy tightening began to form a coil in the pit of her stomach and she instinctively leaned into his big, hard body.

The feel of his rigid arousal nestled against her

soft lower belly, the tightening of his strong arms around her and the feel of his heart pounding out a steady rhythm against her breast sent a need like nothing she had ever known flowing from the top of her head all the way to the soles of her feet.

Her knees wobbled, then failed her completely as he continued to stroke her with a tenderness that brought tears to her eyes. She had been kissed before, but nothing like this. It felt as if she had been waiting on this man and this moment her entire life.

The thought frightened her as little else could. Pushing against his chest, she took a step back to stare up at him. "I'm not good at playing games, Chance."

"I'm not asking you to play games, Fee." He shook his head. "We can have fun while you're here, and when you go back to L.A., you'll have the memory of the good time we had. As long as we keep that in mind, we should be just fine."

She stared at him for several long seconds as she waged a battle within herself. He wasn't asking for anything more from her than the here and now. But there was one problem with his reasoning. She wasn't entirely certain she could trust her heart to listen. Lowering his head, he kissed her again.

"I do believe, Fee Sinclair, that you have the sweetest lips of any woman I've ever known," he whispered close to her ear.

Another tremor of desire slid through her a moment before he pulled back and pointed toward the open doors of the loft. "This is what I wanted you to see."

Looking in the direction he indicated, Fee caught her breath. A brilliantly colored full rainbow arched across the bluest sky she had ever seen.

"It's gorgeous," she murmured.

"Did you know that in some cultures the rainbow symbolizes a new beginning or a new phase in a person's life?" he asked, kissing her forehead as he held her to him and they watched the vibrant prism fade away.

She swallowed hard as she turned her attention to the man holding her close. What was it about being wrapped in Chance's arms that made her feel as if she was entering a new phase in her life—one that she hadn't seen coming and was powerless to stop? And one that made her extremely uneasy.

Five

Standing at the ice-cream counter in Buckaroo Billy's General Store on the outskirts of Cheyenne, Chance glanced through the window at Fee and his niece seated under a big yellow umbrella at one of the picnic tables outside. Cassie was talking a mile a minute and it seemed that Fee was somehow keeping up. That in itself was pretty darned amazing. The kid usually had him confused as hell by the speed she changed subjects. He loved her dearly, but sometimes Cassie had the attention span of a flea and hopped from one topic to another faster than a drop of water on a hot griddle.

Paying for their ice cream, he juggled the three cones and a handful of paper napkins as he shouldered open the door. "A scoop of chocolate fudge brownie for you, princess," he said, handing Cassie the frozen treat. Turning to Fee, he grinned. "And mint chocolate chip for you."

"Uncle Chance!" Cassie exclaimed, pointing to his vanilla ice cream. "You were supposed to try something new this time."

"Where's your sense of adventure, Mr. Lassiter?" Fee asked, laughing.

"I like vanilla," he said, shrugging as he dropped the napkins onto the table and sat down. He should have known Cassie would remember he was supposed to try a new flavor. The kid had a mind like a steel trap. Grinning, he added, "But next week, I promise I'll leave what I get up to you two. How does that sound?"

Cassie's red curls bobbed when she nodded her approval. "I like that. I'll ask Momma what you should have when she gets home." True to form, she looked at Fee and took the conversation in another direction. "My mommy and daddy are on their moneyhoon. That's why I'm staying with Grandma Marlene."

"You mean honeymoon?" Chance asked, winking at Fee. He could tell she was trying hard not to laugh at Cassie's mix-up, the same as he was.

"Yeah. They went on a boat." Cassie shook her head. "But I don't know where."

"After much debate, Hannah and Logan went on a Caribbean cruise," Chance explained to Fee.

She smiled at his niece. "That sounds like a nice honeymoon."

"They're going to bring me back a present," Cassie added as she licked some of the chocolate dripping onto her fingers. When she started to touch her tongue to the ice cream in her usual exuberant fashion, the scoop dislodged from the cone and landed on the top of her tennis shoe. Tears immediately filled her big green eyes and her little chin began to wobble. "I'm sorry. It…fell…Uncle Chance."

"Don't cry, princess," he said gently as he reached over and gave her a hug. "It's all right. I'll get you another one."

While Fee used the napkins to clean off Cassie's shoe, he went back into the store to replace her ice-cream cone. By the time he returned a couple of minutes later, Cassie was all smiles and chattering like a magpie once again.

His mind wandered as his niece and Fee discussed the newest version of a popular fashion doll—and he couldn't help but notice every time Fee licked her ice cream.

"Chance, did you hear me?" Fee asked, sounding concerned.

"Oh, sorry." He grinned. "I was still thinking about doll accessories."

She gave him one of those looks that women were so fond of when they thought a man was full of bull roar. "I said I'm going to take Cassie to the ladies' room to wash her hands."

He nodded. "Good idea."

As he watched Fee and his niece walk into the store, he shook his head at his own foolishness and rose to his feet to walk over to his truck to wait for them to return. If he and Fee didn't make love soon, he was going to be a raving lunatic.

But as he stood there thinking about the danger to his mental health, he realized that making love with Fee wasn't all he wanted. The thought caused his heart to pound hard against his ribs. He wasn't thinking about an actual relationship, was he?

He shook his head to dispel the ridiculous thought. Aside from the fact that neither of them was looking for anything beyond some no-strings fun, he was hesitant to start anything long-term with any woman. His father had been the most honorable man he had ever known and from what he remembered and everything everyone said, Charles Lassiter had loved his wife with all his heart. If his father couldn't remain faithful, what made Chance think that he could do any better?

"Uncle Chance, Fee said we could play fashion show with my dolls the next time she's at Grandma Marlene's house," Cassie said, tugging on his shirtsleeve. "When will that be?"

He'd been so preoccupied with his unsettling thoughts that he hadn't even noticed Fee and Cassie had returned. "I'll talk to Grandma Marlene and see what we can work out," he said, smiling as he picked Cassie up to sit on his forearm. "How does that sound, princess?"

Yawning, Cassie nodded. "Good."

"I think someone is getting sleepy," Fee said when

Chance opened the rear passenger door and buckled Cassie into her safety seat.

"She'll be asleep before we get out of the parking lot," he said, closing the door and turning to help Fee into the truck.

When he got in behind the steering wheel and started the engine, Fee smiled. "After she goes to sleep, we'll have some time to talk."

"About the campaign?" he guessed, steering the truck out onto the road.

"I'd like to hear what your main objections are to being the spokesman," she said, settling back in the bucket seat.

"Being the center of attention isn't something I'm comfortable with and never have been," he said honestly.

"But it would only be some still photos and a few videos," she insisted. "We could even cut out the few personal appearances unless you decided you wanted to do them."

"Yeah, those are out of the question," he said firmly. As far as he was concerned those appearances she mentioned had been off the table from the get-go. "Like I told you the other day at lunch, I don't intend to be a monkey in a sideshow. What you see with me is what you get, sweetheart. I wouldn't know how to be an actor if I tried."

"What if we filmed the video spots on the ranch?" she asked, sounding as if she was thinking out loud. "I could have a cameraman take some footage of you riding up on your horse and then all you would have to do is read from a cue card." She paused for a moment. "We could probably even lift still shots from that."

He could tell she wasn't going to give up. "I'm by no means making any promises," he said, wondering what he could say that would discourage her. "But I'll have to think a little more about it."

"Okay," she said slowly. He could tell she wasn't happy that she hadn't wrangled an agreement from him.

Reaching over, he covered her hand with his. "I'm not saying no, Fee. I'm just saying I need more time to think it over."

When she looked at him, her expression hopeful, he almost caved in and told her he would be her spokesman. Fortunately, she didn't give him the opportunity.

"That's fair," she said, suddenly grinning. "But just keep in mind, I'm not giving up."

"It never occurred to me that you would," he said, laughing.

Fee sat in the middle of the bed with her laptop and an array of papers spread out around her on the colorful quilt. She was supposed to be working on the Lassiter PR campaign. But in the past hour, she had found herself daydreaming about a tall, handsome, green-eyed cowboy more than she had been thinking about ways to restore the public's faith in his family.

Watching him interact with his niece that afternoon had been almost as eye-opening as witnessing his skill at helping a cow give birth to her calf. Both times she had seen him interact with his niece, he had listened patiently when the child spoke and always made Cassie feel as if everything she said was of the utmost importance to him. Someday Chance was going to be a wonderful father and Fee couldn't help but feel a twinge of envy for the woman who would bear his child.

Her heart skipped a beat and she shook her head to dispel the unwarranted thought. What was wrong with her? Why was she even thinking about Chance having a child with some unknown woman?

It shouldn't matter to her. By the end of her month's stay, she would be back in Los Angeles scheduling commercial spots for the family campaign and working toward her goal of becoming Lassiter Media's first female public relations vice president under the age of thirty. And unlike being in Wyoming, she would enjoy the convenience of not having to drive forty miles just to reach a town where she could shop or dine out.

But as she sat there thinking about her life back in L.A., she couldn't seem to remember what the appeal of living there had been. Her condo building was filled with people she didn't know and didn't care to know. And for reasons she couldn't put her finger on, the job promotion didn't seem nearly as enticing as it had a week ago.

As she sat there trying to figure out why she was feeling less than enthusiastic about her life in California, there was a knock on her closed door. Gathering the papers around her to put back in the file folder, she turned off her laptop and walked over to find Chance standing on the other side of the door.

"It's a clear night and the moon is almost full," Chance said, leaning one shoulder against the door frame. "How would you like to go for a ride?"

"On a horse? Surely you can't be serious." She laughed as she shook her head. "I'm not that experienced at riding during the day. What makes you think I would be any better at night? Besides, don't wild animals prowl around more in the dark? There's probably something out there with sharp teeth and long claws just waiting for me to come riding along."

"Slow down, sweetheart. You're sounding a lot like Cassie," he said, laughing. "We won't be going far and other than a raccoon or a coyote, I doubt that we'll see any wildlife. Besides, you won't be riding Rosy. You'll be on the back of Dakota with me."

She gave him a doubtful look. "And you think that's an even better idea than me riding Rosy?"

He grinned as he rocked back on his heels. "Yup."

"I'll bet you even have a cozy little saddle made for two stashed in the tack room," she quipped.

"You're so cute." Laughing, he straightened to his full height and took her by the hand to lead her downstairs. "No, they don't make saddles for two people. We're going to ride bareback."

"Oh, yeah, that's even safer than me riding Rosy at night," she muttered as they left the house and started toward the barn.

"It is if you're a skilled horseman and you know your horse."

"Just remember, I'm counting on you to be right about that," she said, unable to believe she was going along with his scheme.

When they reached the barn, he led Dakota out of his stall and put a bridle on the gelding. Then turning, he loosely put his arms around her. "Thanks for going with me and Cassie today," he said, kissing her temple. "I know she enjoyed talking to you about her dolls."

"She's a delightful little girl. Very bright and outgoing," Fee said. "I had a wonderful time talking to her." Grinning, she added, "But I'm really surprised that you didn't join in the conversation when we were discussing the latest doll accessories."

"I'll be the first to admit I don't know diddly-squat about dolls." He chuckled. "But if you want to talk toy trucks or action figures, I'm you're guy."

"I'll take your word for that, too," she said, staring up into his eyes. "But all joking aside, I really did have fun chatting with your niece."

"What about me?" he whispered, leaning forward. "Did you have a good time talking with me?"

A quivering excitement ran through her body at the feel of his warm breath feathering over her ear and she had to brace her hands on his biceps to keep her balance. The feel of rock-hard muscle beneath his chambray shirt caused heat to flow through her veins.

"Yes, I always enjoy talking to you," she answered truthfully.

"I like spending my time with you, too." Lowering his head, he gave her a kiss so tender her knees threatened to buckle before he stepped back, took hold of the reins and a handful of Dakota's mane, then swung up onto the horse. "Turn your back to me, Fee."

When she did as he instructed, he reached down and effortlessly lifted her to sit in front of him on the gelding. Straddling the horse, she was glad Chance was holding on to her. "Whoa! This is a lot higher than sitting on Rosy."

Chance's deep chuckle vibrated against her back as he tightened his arm around her midsection and nudged the gelding into a slow walk. "I promise you're safe, sweetheart. I won't let you fall."

She knew he was talking about a fall from the horse, but what was going to keep her from falling for the man holding her so securely against him?

Fee quickly relegated the thought to the back of her mind as Dakota carried them from the barn out into the night and she gazed up at the sky. Billions of stars created a twinkling canopy above and the moon cast an ethereal glow over the rugged landscape.

"This is gorgeous, Chance." She shook her head. "I've never seen so many stars in the night sky before."

"That's because of smog and too many lights in the city to see them all," he answered, his voice low and intimate. He tightened his arms around her. "Are you chilly?"

She could lie and tell him that she was, but she suspected that he already knew her tiny shiver was caused by their close proximity. "Not really," she admitted, leaning her head back against his shoulder. "It's just that something this vast and beautiful is humbling."

They rode along in silence for some time before she felt the evidence of his reaction to being this close to her against her backside. So overwhelmed by the splendor of the night, she hadn't paid attention to the fact that her bottom was nestled tightly between his thighs. But it wasn't his arousal that surprised her as much as her reaction to it. Knowing that he desired her caused an answering warmth to spread throughout her body and an empty ache to settle in the most feminine part of her.

"Chance?"

"Don't freak out," he whispered, stopping Dakota. "I'm not going to deny that I want you. You're a desirable woman and I'm like any other man—I have needs. But nothing is going to happen unless it's what you want, too, sweetheart."

Before she could find her voice, Chance released his hold on her and slid off the horse to his feet. He immediately reached up to help her down, then wrapping his arms around her, gave her a kiss that caused her toes to curl inside her boots before he set her away from him.

Disappointed that the kiss had been so brief, she

tried to distract herself by looking around. Something shiny caught her attention and taking a few steps closer, she realized it was the moon reflecting off of a small pool of water. Surrounded on three sides by cottonwood trees, she could see wisps of mist rising from its surface and the faint sound of running water.

"Is that a natural spring?" she asked.

"It's actually considered a thermal spring even though the temperature never gets over about seventy-five degrees," Chance said, walking over to stand beside her. "I used to go swimming in it when I was a kid."

"It's that deep?" she asked, intrigued. Even with just the light from the moon, she could see a shadowy image of the bottom of the pool.

"It's only about four feet deep over by the outlet where it runs down to the river." He laughed. "But to a ten-year-old kid that's deep enough to get in and splash around."

Fee smiled as she thought of Chance playing in the water as a child. "I'm sure you had a lot of fun. I used to love going to the beach when I was young, and my grandmother's house had a swimming pool."

"We always had a pool up at the main house," he said, nodding. "But it's not as much fun as this. Have you ever been skinny-dipping?" he asked.

"No." She laughed. "Besides not really having the nerve to do it, I would have hated causing Mr. Harris next door to have a coronary, or scandalizing his wife to the point where she refused to go to the senior center with my grandmother to play bingo."

He gave her a wicked grin and reached down to pull off his boots and socks. "I will if you will."

"Skinny-dip? Here? Now?" She shook her head. "Have you lost your mind? Aren't you worried someone will see you?"

He tugged his shirt from his jeans and with one smooth motion released all of the snap closures. "Sweetheart, it's just you, me and Dakota out here. And since he's a gelding, all he's interested in is grass."

She glanced over at the horse. "What if he runs away and leaves us stranded out here?"

"He's trained to ground tie." He reached to unbuckle his belt and release the button at the top of his jeans. "As long as the ends of the reins are dragging the ground, he'll stay close." His grin widened. "Are you going to join me?"

"I don't think so." She wasn't a prude, but she wasn't sure she was ready to abandon years of her grandmother's lectures on modesty, either.

"Now who isn't being adventurous?" he teased.

"Trying a different flavor of ice cream is completely different than taking off all of your..." Her voice trailed off when Chance shrugged out of his shirt.

The man had the physique of a male model and she had firsthand knowledge of how hard and strong all those muscles were. She thought about how every time he helped her into his truck or lifted her onto one of the horses, he picked her up as if she weighed nothing.

Unable to look away when he unzipped his fly and shoved his jeans down his long muscular legs, Fee felt a lazy heat begin to flow through her veins. "I can't believe you're really going to do this."

"Yup, I'm really going to do this," he repeated as he stepped out of his jeans and tossed them on top of his shirt. When she continued to stare at him, he grinned as he hooked his thumbs into the waistband of his boxer briefs. "I'm not the least bit shy and don't mind you watching one little bit, but unless you want to see me in my birthday suit, you might want to close your eyes now."

"Oh!" She spun around. "Let me know when you're in the water."

"All clear," he announced. When she turned back, Chance was standing up in the pool. The water barely covered his navel. "You really should join me. The water is the perfect temperature."

"I can't," she said, shaking her head as she avoided looking below his bare chest. "It isn't deep enough."

"You know you want to," he said, grinning.

She didn't believe for a minute that he would keep his eyes averted as she was doing, but he was right about one thing. She was tempted to throw caution to the wind and go skinny-dipping for the first time in her life.

"I don't have a towel to dry off with." Her statement sounded lame even to her.

"We can dry off with my shirt," he offered.

"And you promise not to look?" she asked, knowing that his answer and what he would actually do were probably two different things.

"Scout's honor I won't look while you undress and get into the water," he said, raising his hand in a three-finger oath.

"Then close your eyes," she said decisively as she reached to pull the tail of her T-shirt from her jeans.

When he did, she quickly removed her boots and socks, then stripped out of her clothing before she had a chance to change her mind. Stepping into the water, she immediately covered her breasts with her arms and bent her knees until the water came up to her neck.

"I can't believe I'm actually doing this," she said between nervous giggles.

"Look at it this way," he said, opening his eyes. His low, intimate tone and the look on his handsome face as he moved through the water toward her made Fee feel as if he had cast a spell over her. "It's something you can check off your bucket list."

"I don't have a list," she said slowly.

"I'll help you make one." His gaze held hers as he reached beneath the water and lifted her to her feet. Taking her into his arms, he smiled. "Then I'll help you check off all of the new things you're doing."

Her arms automatically rose to encircle his neck and the moment her wet breasts pressed against his wide, bare chest a jolt of excitement rocked her. "You said you wouldn't look."

"I haven't…yet." His slow smile caused a nervous

energy in the deepest part of her. "But I never said I wouldn't touch you."

As he lowered his head, Fee welcomed the feel of his firm mouth covering hers. Chance's kisses were drugging and quickly becoming an addiction that she wasn't certain she could ever overcome.

The thought should have sent her running as fast as she could to the Cheyenne airport and the earliest flight back to L.A. But as his lips moved over hers with such tenderness, she forgot all the reasons she shouldn't become involved with him or any other man. All she could think about was the way he made her feel.

When he coaxed her to open for him, she couldn't have denied him if her life depended on it. At the first touch of his tongue to hers, it felt as if an electric current danced over every one of her nerve endings and a tiny moan escaped her parted lips. She wanted him, wanted to feel his arms around her and the strength of his lovemaking in every fiber of her being.

The feel of his hard arousal against her lower belly was proof he wanted her just as badly. The realization created a restlessness within her and she was so lost in the myriad sensations Chance had created, it took her a moment to realize he was ending the kiss.

"As bad as I hate to say this, I think we'd better head back to the house." His voice sounded a lot like a rusty hinge. "I have a good idea where this is headed and I don't have protection for us."

Covering her breasts with her arms, she nodded

reluctantly. There was no way she could deny that the passion between them was heading in that direction. Thank goodness he had the presence of mind to call a halt to it.

"Turn around."

He laughed. "Really? Our nude bodies were just pressed together from head to toe and you're worried about me seeing you?"

Her cheeks heated. "Feeling is one thing, seeing is entirely different."

"If you say so," he said, doing as she requested.

Hurriedly getting out of the water, Fee turned her back to him, used his shirt to quickly dry herself and then pulled on her panties and jeans. But when she searched for her bra, she couldn't seem to find it anywhere.

"Looking for this?" Chance asked.

Glancing over her shoulder, he was standing right behind her with her bra hanging from his index finger like a limp flag. "I thought you were supposed to stay in the water with your back turned until I got dressed," she scolded, taking her lacy brassiere from him to put the garment on.

"I stayed in the water right up until you started searching for your bra." She heard him pulling on his clothes. "After you dried off, you dropped my shirt on it when you reached for your panties."

"You watched me get dressed? You swore you wouldn't peek."

"Yeah, about that." He turned her to face him and the slow smile curving his mouth caused her to catch her breath. "I was never a Scout so that oath earlier didn't really count. But just for the record, I told you before I kissed you that I hadn't looked *yet*. I didn't say I wasn't going to." He gave her a quick kiss, then bent to pull on his socks and boots.

While he walked over to where Dakota stood munching on a patch of grass, Fee picked up his damp shirt and waited for him to help her onto the gelding's back. She should probably call her boss at Lassiter Media and arrange for someone else to take over the PR campaign, then head back to L.A. to get her priorities straight before she committed career suicide. But she rejected that idea immediately. No matter how difficult the assignment, she had never bowed out of a project and she wasn't going to back down now.

She was just going to have to be stronger and resist the temptation of Chance Lassiter. But heaven help her, she had a feeling it was going to be the hardest thing she'd ever have to do.

Chance lay in bed and damned his sense of responsibility for at least the hundredth time since he and Fee had returned to the house. He hadn't taken her on the moonlight ride with the intention of seducing her. On the contrary, it had simply been something he thought she might enjoy and he'd been right. She'd loved seeing all the billions of stars twinkling in the night sky.

At least, that's the way things had started out. What he hadn't allowed himself to consider was the effect her body would have on his when they rode double. Her delightful little bottom rubbing against the most vulnerable part of him had quickly proven to be the greatest test of his fortitude he'd ever faced. Then, if he hadn't been insane enough, she'd noticed the spring and he'd had the brilliant idea of going skinny-dipping.

"Yeah, like that didn't have disaster written all over it," he muttered as he stared up at the ceiling.

If he'd just stayed on his side of the pool and hadn't touched her or kissed her, he wouldn't be lying there feeling as if he was ready to climb the walls. But the allure of her being so close had been more than he could fight and once he'd touched her, he couldn't have stopped himself from kissing her any more than he could get Gus to give up baseball.

But what had really sent him into orbit had been her response. The minute their lips met, Fee had melted against him and his body had hardened so fast it had left him feeling as if he might pass out. The feel of her breasts against his chest and his arousal pressing into her soft lower belly had damn near driven him over the edge and he'd come dangerously close to forgetting about their protection.

Fortunately, he'd had enough strength left to be responsible. But that hadn't been easy.

He punched his pillow and turned to his side. No two ways around it, he should have known better. But he'd been fool enough to think that he could control the situation and ended up being the victim of his own damned arrogance.

He'd known full well the moment he'd laid eyes on her at Hannah and Logan's wedding, a spark ignited within him and with each day since the fire had increased to the point it was about to burn him up from the inside out. He wanted her, wanted to sink himself so deeply within her velvet depths that neither of them could remember where he ended and she began. And unless he was reading her wrong, it was what she wanted, too. So why was he in bed on one side of the hall and she in bed on the other now?

With a guttural curse that his mother would have had a fit over, Chance threw back the sheet and sat up on the side of the bed. Two hours of tossing and turning had gotten him nowhere. Maybe a drink would help him calm down enough to get a few hours of sleep.

Pulling on a pair of jeans, he didn't bother with a shirt as he left the master suite and stared at the closed door across the hall. He'd like nothing better than to go into that room, pick Fee up and carry her back to his bed. Instead, he forced himself to turn and walk barefoot down the hall to the stairs.

When he reached the kitchen, he went straight to the refrigerator for a beer, and then walked out onto the back porch. Hopefully, the beer and the cool night air would work their magic and help him relax.

Chance took a long draw from the bottle in his hand and stared out into the night as he tried to forget about the desirable woman upstairs. He needed to make a trip into town tomorrow for some supplies, as well as to stop by Lassiter Media's Cheyenne office to pick up his tickets for Frontier Days at the end of the month. Because Lassiter donated the use of some of their audio and video equipment for the annual event, the rodeo organizers always gave the company complimentary tickets. He attended the finals of the event every year and he thought Fee might enjoy going with him, even if she was back at the rental house by then.

Lightning streaked across the western sky, followed by the distant sound of thunder. It appeared the weather was as unsettled as he was, he thought as he downed the rest of his beer and headed back inside.

As he climbed the stairs a flash of lightning briefly illuminated his way and by the time he started down the upstairs hall, a trailing clap of thunder loud enough to wake the dead rattled the windows and reverberated throughout the house. He had just reached the master suite when the door to Fee's room flew open. When she came rushing out, she ran headlong into him.

"Whoa there, sweetheart." He placed his hands on her shoulders to keep her from falling backward. "What's wrong?"

"What was that noise?" she asked breathlessly.

"It's getting ready to storm," he said, trying his best not to notice how her sweet scent seemed to swirl around him and the fact that she had on a silky red nightgown that barely covered her panties.

"It sounded like an explosion," she said, seeming as if she might be a little disoriented.

"It's just a little thunder." He should probably be

ashamed of himself, but he had never been more thankful for a thunderstorm in his life. "You have storms in L.A., don't you?"

Nodding, she jumped when another clap of thunder resounded around them. "Not that many. And I never liked them when we did."

Chance put his arms around her and tried to remind himself that he was offering her comfort. "I guess I'm more used to them because at this time of year we have one almost every day."

"Really? That many?" She was beginning to sound more awake.

He nodded. "Occasionally we'll have severe storms, but most of the them are a lot like Gus— more noise than anything else."

"I think I'm glad I live in L.A. The city noise masks some of the thunder," she said, snuggling against his bare chest. "I'd be a nervous wreck if I lived here."

Chance felt a little let down. He wanted her to love the Big Blue ranch as much as he did even if she was only in Wyoming for a short time. But it wasn't as if he had been hoping she would relocate to the area. All he wanted was a summer fling.

Right now, he didn't have the presence of mind to give his unwarranted disappointment a lot of thought. Fee was clinging to him as if he was her lifeline and her scantily clad body pressed to his wasn't helping his earlier restlessness one damn bit. In fact, it was playing hell with his good intentions, causing his body to react in a way that she probably wouldn't appreciate, considering the situation.

"I'm going to drive into Cheyenne tomorrow to pick up some supplies and rodeo tickets," he said in an effort to distract both of them. "I thought we could have lunch at Lassiter Grill. Dylan and Jenna are back from their honeymoon and I figured you might like to see them."

"I'd like that very much." Her long blond hair brushed against his chest when she nodded. "Jenna and I became pretty good friends when I worked on the ads for the grand opening," she added, oblivious to his turmoil. "I also helped her out when one of the reporters became obsessed with her at the opening of Lassiter Grill and started asking questions about her and her father."

Sage had told him about Jenna's father being a con artist and that the man had made it look as if she'd been in on one of his schemes. He'd also mentioned the incident with the reporter at the restaurant's opening and how effectively Fee had handled the situation.

"Then that's what we'll do," he said, finding it harder with each passing second to ignore the heat building in his groin.

Another crash of thunder caused Fee to burrow even closer and Chance gave up trying to be noble. He had reached his limit and he was man enough to admit it.

"Fee?"

When she raised her head, he lowered his and

gave in to temptation, consequences be damned. It wasn't as if he'd been able to sleep anyway. He was going to give her a kiss that was guaranteed to keep them both up for the rest of the night.

Six

When Chance brought his mouth down on hers, Fee forgot all about her vow to be strong and try to resist him. The truth was, she wanted his kiss, wanted to once again experience the way only he could make her feel.

As his lips moved over hers, a calming warmth began to spread throughout her body, and she knew without question that as long as she was in his arms she would always be safe. But she didn't have time to think about what her insight might mean before he coaxed her with his tongue.

When his arms tightened around her and he deepened the kiss, she felt as if her bones had turned to rubber. The taste of need on his firm male lips, the feel of his solid bare chest pressed against her breasts and the hard ridge of his arousal cushioned by her stomach sent ribbons of desire threading their way through her.

He brought his hand around from her back up along her ribs. When he cupped her breast, then worried the taut peak with his thumb, her silk nightie chafing the sensitive nub felt absolutely wonderful and she closed her eyes to savor the sensation.

"I know all you want from me right now is reassurance," he said, nibbling kisses from her lips down the column of her neck to her collarbone. "But I've wanted you from the moment I first saw you at my sister's wedding." He left a trail of kisses from her chest to the V neckline of her short nightgown before pulling away. "If that's not what you want, too, then now would be the time for you to go back into your room and close the door."

Opening her eyes, she saw the passion reflected in his and it thrilled her. Fee knew what she should do. She should return to her room, pack her things and have him take her back to the corporate rental house in Cheyenne the first thing tomorrow morning. But that wasn't what she was going to do. It could very well prove to be the biggest mistake she'd ever made, but she wasn't going to think about her job or the danger of doing something foolish that could cause her to lose it.

"Chance, I don't want to go back to my room," she said, realizing she really didn't have a choice in the matter. They had been heading toward this moment since she looked up and watched him escort the matron of honor back up the aisle at his sister's wedding.

He closed his eyes and took a long, deep breath before he opened them again and gazed down at her. "I'm not looking for anything long-term, Fee."

"Neither am I," she said truthfully.

She ignored the little twinge of sadness that accompanied her agreement. She wasn't interested in anything beyond her time in Wyoming. At the end of her stay, she would go back to her life in California and he would stay here on the Big Blue ranch. Other than a trip back to film the video for the Lassiter PR campaign, they wouldn't be seeing each other again. That's the way it was supposed to be—the way it had to be.

"Let's go into my room, sweetheart," he said, taking her by the hand to lead her across the hall to the master suite.

The lightning flashed and thunder continued to rumble loudly outside, but Fee barely noticed as Chance closed the door behind them and led her over to the side of his king-size bed. When he turned on the bedside lamp, she looked around. The furniture was made of rustic logs, and with the exception of a silver picture frame sitting on the dresser, the room was decorated in the same Western theme as the rest of the house. The photo inside was of a young boy and a man who looked a lot like Chance. Before she could ask if it was a picture of him and his father, Chance caught her to him for a kiss that sent waves of heat coursing through her and made her forget everything but the man holding her.

"Do you have any idea how many times I've thought about doing this over the past week?" he asked as he ran his index finger along the thin strap of her nightie. "Every time I've looked at you, it's all I can think about."

"I hadn't…really given it…a lot of thought." Did he expect her to form a coherent answer when the intimate tone of his voice and his passionate words were sending shivers of anticipation through every part of her?

Needing to touch him, she placed her palms on his chest. "I have, however, thought a lot about you and how much I've wanted to do this." She ran her fingertips over the thick pads of his pectoral muscles and a heady sense of feminine power came over her when she felt a shudder run through him. "Your body is perfect. I thought so when we were at the spring." She touched one flat male nipple. "I wanted to touch you then, but—"

"By the time the night is over, I intend for both of us to know each other's body as well as we know our own," he said, sliding his hands down her sides to the lace hem of her nightgown.

His sensuous smile caused an interesting little tingle deep inside her as he lifted the garment up and over her head, and then tossed it aside. He caught her hands in his, took a step back and held her arms wide. His eyes seemed to caress her, the need she detected in their green depths stealing her breath.

"You're absolutely beautiful, Fee."

"So are you, Chance."

He gave her a smile that curled her toes, then brought her hands back up to his broad chest. "Ladies first."

She realized that he wanted her to feel comfortable with him and was willing to allow her to explore him before he touched her. His concession caused emotion to clog her throat. She'd never known any man as thoughtful and unselfish as Chance Lassiter.

Enjoying the feel of his warm bare flesh beneath her palms, she ran her hands down his chest to the ripples of muscle below. When she reached his navel, she quickly glanced up. His eyes were closed and his head was slightly tilted back as if he struggled for control.

"Does that feel good?" she asked, kissing his smooth skin as she trailed her finger down the thin line of dark hair from his navel to where it disappeared into the waistband of his jeans.

"Sweetheart, if it felt any better, I'm not sure I could handle it," he said, sounding as if he'd run a marathon. When she opened the snap, he stopped her and took a step back. "I don't want you to get the wrong idea. I'd love nothing more than to have you take my jeans off me, but this time it's something I have to take care of myself."

Slightly confused, she watched him ease the zipper down and when his fly gaped open, she realized the reason for his concern. "If I had tried… Oh, my… That could have been disastrous."

Grinning, he nodded as he shoved his jeans down

his long, heavily muscled legs and kicked them over to join her nightgown where it lay on the floor. "When I got up to go get a drink, I just grabbed a pair of jeans. I didn't bother putting on underwear."

Fee had purposely kept her eyes above his waist in the pool, but as she gazed at him now, she realized how truly magnificent his body was. Chance's shoulders were impossibly wide, his chest and abdomen sculpted with muscles made hard from years of ranch work. As her gaze drifted lower, she caught her breath. She'd felt his arousal when they'd gone skinny-dipping, but the strength of his desire for her was almost overwhelming.

"Don't ever doubt that I want you, Fee," he said, taking her into his arms. He lowered his head to softly kiss her lips, then nibbled his way down to the slope of her breast. "You're the most desirable woman I've ever met."

Her pulse raced as he slowly kissed his way to the hardened peak. But the moment he took the tip into his mouth, it felt as if her heart stopped and time stood still. Never in her entire twenty-nine years had she experienced anything as exquisite or electrifying as the feel of Chance's soft kiss on her rapidly heating body. When he turned his attention to her other breast, her head fell back and she found it hard to draw in enough air.

"Does that feel good?" he asked.

Unable to speak, she merely nodded.

Taking a step back, he held her gaze with his as he hooked his thumbs in the waistband of her bi-

kini panties and slowly pulled them down her legs.
When they fell to her ankles and she stepped out of
them, he smiled and wrapped his arms around her.
The feel of her softer skin pressed to his hard flesh
caused her to sag against him.

He swung her up into his arms to carefully place
her on the bed and she didn't think she'd ever felt
more cherished. She watched him reach into the bedside table to remove a foil packet, then tucking it
under his pillow, Chance stretched out on the bed
beside her. He'd no sooner taken her back into his
arms when lightning flashed outside and a loud clap
of thunder caused the windows to rattle.

When the lamp flickered several times, he gathered her to him. "It looks like we might lose power."

The feel of all of him against her caused a shiver
of excitement to course through her. "I'd forgotten
it was even storming."

"And I intend to make sure you forget about it
again," he said, covering her mouth with his.

He kissed her tenderly and ran his hand along her
side to her hip. The light abrasion of his calloused
palm as he leisurely caressed her was breathtaking,
but when he moved his hand to touch her intimately,
Fee wasn't certain she would ever breathe again.

As he stroked her with a feathery touch, the ache
of unfulfilled desire coiled inside her. She needed
him more than she'd ever needed anything in her life,
but she wanted to touch him—to learn about him the
same as he was learning about her.

When she moved her hands from his chest and

found him, he went completely still a moment before he groaned. "You're going to ruin…all my… good intentions, Fee."

"What would those be?" she asked as she measured his length and girth with her palms.

"I'd like to make this first time last…a little longer than what it's going to…if you keep doing that," he said, taking her hands to place them back on his chest. He took several deep breaths, then reached beneath his pillow. "I want you so much, I'd rather not finish the race before you get to the starting gate, sweetheart."

When he arranged their protection, he took her back into his arms and kissed her as he nudged her knees apart. Then capturing her gaze with his, he gave her a smile that sent heat coursing through her veins. "Show me where you want me, Fee."

Without a moment's hesitation, she guided him to her and he joined their bodies in one smooth thrust. He went perfectly still for a moment and she knew he was not only giving her time to adjust to being filled completely by him, he was also struggling to gain control.

"You're so beautiful and perfect," he finally said as he slowly began to rock against her.

"So are you," she managed as her body began to move in unison with his.

Fee felt as if she had been custom-made just for him and as Chance increased the rhythm of his thrusts, she became lost in the delicious sensations of their lovemaking. Heat filled her as she started climbing toward the fulfillment they both sought.

Unable to prolong the inevitable, she reluctantly gave herself up to the tension building within her. As waves of pleasure coursed through every cell in her being, she clung to him to keep from being lost. A moment later, she felt his body stiffen and knew he'd found his own satisfaction.

Wrapping her arms around his shoulders when he collapsed on top of her, Fee held him tight. She had never felt closer to anyone in her entire life than she did to Chance at that moment and she didn't want the connection to end.

The thought that she might be falling for him crossed her mind and caused her a moment's panic, but she gave herself a mental shake. It was true that she cared for him more than she could remember caring for any man, but that didn't mean she was falling in love with him. Chance was intelligent, caring and the most selfless man she'd ever met, and any woman would be lucky to win his heart. But she wasn't that woman.

The next morning as Chance got dressed, he smiled at the woman curled up in his bed. Fee was sound asleep and he wasn't going to wake her. They had spent most of the night making love and she had to be every bit as tired as he was. But he had chores to do and a ranch to run. Otherwise, he'd crawl back in bed, make love to her again and then hold her while they both slept.

As he stepped out into the hall, he regretfully closed the door behind him. He had never met any woman who felt as good or as natural in his arms as Fee did. She was amazing in just about every way he could think of, and even though she was a good nine or ten inches shorter than his six-foot-one-inch frame, when they made love they fit together perfectly.

Yawning as he entered the kitchen, he smiled when he thought about why he was so tired. "Gus, Fee and I are going into Cheyenne later this morning," he said, walking straight to the coffeemaker to pour himself a cup of the strong brew. "Is there anything you need me to pick up while I'm there?"

"Can't think of a thing," Gus said, opening the oven. "Where's Fee?"

"The storm kept her awake most of the night," Chance answered, going over to sit down at the table. "I thought I'd let her sleep in this morning."

When Gus turned, he stared at Chance for several long seconds before he slammed the pan of biscuits he had just removed from the oven onto the butcher-block island. "What the hell are you thinkin', boy?"

"What do you mean?" He was used to Gus and his off-the-wall questions and normally managed to figure out what the old man was talking about. But Chance had no idea what he'd done to piss the old boy off this early in the morning.

"I wasn't born yesterday," Gus said, shaking his head. "That storm moved on just past midnight and if you hadn't been awake with her, how would you know she didn't sleep?"

With his coffee cup halfway to his mouth, Chance stopped to glare at his old friend, then slowly set it down on the table. "Watch it, Gus. You're about to head into territory that isn't any of your concern."

"That little gal up in your bed ain't the kind of woman you bed, unless you're willin' to change her name," Gus said, ignoring Chance's warning.

"When did you become an expert on the subject of women?" Chance asked, doing his best to hold his anger in check out of respect for Gus's age and the fact that he was more like family than an employee.

"I never said I was an expert." Gus walked over to shake his finger at Chance. "But there's women you have a good time with and the kind you court for a while and marry." He pointed his index finger up at the ceiling. "That little gal upstairs is the courtin' kind."

"She's not interested in getting serious any more than I am," Chance said defensively.

"That may be what she's sayin'," Gus insisted. "And she probably even believes it. But I've heard how she goes on about you and the look in her eyes when you walk in a room." He grunted. "Your momma wore the same look every time she looked at your daddy."

"Yeah and we both know how that turned out," Chance muttered.

"Boy, don't go judgin' a man till you walk a mile

in his boots," Gus advised. "Your daddy loved your momma more than life itself."

"Is that why I've got a half sister from the affair he had with Hannah's mother?" Chance shot back before he could stop himself. He loved that he finally had a sibling, but the truth of the matter was, Charles Lassiter had cheated on his wife and that was something Chance wasn't sure he could ever come to terms with.

"Your daddy made a mistake and till the day he died, he did everything he could to make it up to your momma." Gus shook his head. "She forgave him, but I don't think he ever did forgive himself."

"Well, that's something I'll never have to deal with," Chance said, shrugging. "You can't cheat on your wife if you never get married."

Gus stared at him for a moment before he sighed heavily. "I never took you for a coward, boy."

Before Chance could tell Gus to mind his own damn business, he heard Fee coming down the stairs. "We'll finish this later."

"There ain't nothin' to finish," Gus said stubbornly. "I've said all I'm gonna say about it."

"Chance, why didn't you wake me?" Fee asked, entering the kitchen. "I wanted to help you feed Belle and her mother this morning."

"I thought I'd let you sleep in." Rising to his feet, Chance walked over and got a cup from the cupboard to pour her some coffee instead of taking her into his arms and kissing her the way he wanted to. "I know the storm kept you up last night and thought you could use the sleep." When Gus coughed, he glared at the old fart a moment before he walked over to set her coffee on the table. "I'll go out to the barn and give Slim the list of things I want him and the boys to get done today. Then after breakfast we'll feed the cow and calf before we take off to go into Cheyenne."

Her smile sent his hormones racing. "Great! I'll help Gus finish breakfast while you go talk to your foreman."

As Chance walked out of the house and across the yard, he thought about what Gus had said and how irritated he'd been with the old guy. Gus had been best friends with Charles Lassiter for years and it was only natural that he would defend him. And Chance had to admit that being out on the rodeo circuit had probably been lonely for his father without his family with him. But as far as Chance was concerned there was no excuse for infidelity. When a man committed himself to a woman, he didn't go looking for relief in another woman's arms.

That's why Chance had made the decision to remain single. Finding out a couple of months ago that a man like his father hadn't been able to resist temptation was enough to make Chance question a lot of things about himself. With the exception of his college girlfriend, he'd never been in a relationship for any real length of time. He'd always thought that was because he hadn't met the right woman. But could it be a clue he was incapable of committing himself to one woman? He wasn't sure and until he knew the answer to that question, his best bet would be to avoid getting too deeply involved with anyone. He certainly didn't want to run the risk of causing any woman the emotional pain that he was certain his mother had gone through.

He shook his head as he walked into the barn. He didn't know why he was giving anything Gus said a second thought. Gus had never been married and to Chance's knowledge the old guy hadn't had a date in more than twenty-five years. That wasn't exactly a glowing recommendation for Gus's advice on matters of the heart.

Besides, there were too many differences between Chance and Fee for anything to work out between them. She was a city girl who loved spending a day at the spa or in a boutique on Rodeo Drive, while he would rather go skinny-dipping or attend a rodeo. And then there was the matter of their jobs. She had a nice clean office in a climate-controlled skyscraper in downtown L.A. and his job required being out in all kinds of weather, doing things that most people considered dirty and thoroughly disgusting.

He took a deep breath and faced the facts. When Fee had to go back to L.A., he would tell her to get in touch with him whenever she was in town, kiss her goodbye and let her go. That was just the way it would have to be. But what he couldn't figure out was why the thought of her leaving made him feel completely empty inside.

"Chance is amazing with animals," Fee said to Jenna Montgomery-Lassiter after they enjoyed lunch at her new husband's restaurant. Chance and Dylan had gone into the office to discuss an increase in the amount of beef the Big Blue supplied to the Lassiter Grill chain, giving the women time for a little girl talk.

"Colleen and I have come to the conclusion that all of the Lassiter men are pretty amazing," Jenna agreed, grinning. "They aren't necessarily easy to love, but they are more than worth the effort."

"I'm sure they are," Fee said, smiling. "But I'm not in love with Chance."

Jenna gazed at her for several long moments. "Are you sure about that?"

Fee nodded. "We're just friends. I'm trying to talk him into helping me with the PR campaign to improve the Lassiter public image." Laughing, she added, "And he's trying to talk me out of it."

She felt a little guilty about not applying more pressure in her arguments to get him to agree to be the spokesman. But she sensed that the "hard sell" approach wouldn't work with him. If anything, it would make him that much more determined not to take on the job. And then there was the distraction he posed. Much of her time had been taken up with thinking about how soft his kisses were and how his touch made her feel as if she was the most cherished woman in the world.

"I'm sure Chance has been *very* persuasive," Jenna commented, her smile indicating that she knew something Fee didn't.

"What do you mean?" Fee couldn't imagine what her friend was alluding to.

Without answering, Jenna reached into her purse, handed Fee a small mirror, then tapped the side of her own neck with her index finger.

Looking into the mirror, Fee gasped and immediately pulled her long hair forward to hide the tiny blemish on the side of her neck. "I... Well, that is... We..." She clamped her mouth shut. There wasn't anything she could say. The little love bite on the side of her neck said it all.

To ease her embarrassment, Jenna smiled as she reached over to place a comforting hand on Fee's forearm. "It's barely noticeable and I probably would have missed it completely if I hadn't had one myself when we were on our honeymoon in Paris."

Her cheeks feeling as if they were on fire, Fee shook her head. "I haven't had one of those since I was a sophomore in college."

"The Lassiter men are very passionate," Jenna said, her tone reflecting her understanding. "It's one of the reasons we love them so much."

"I told you, Chance and I aren't in love," Fee insisted.

"I know," Jenna interrupted. "But I've seen the way you look at each other." She smiled. "If you two aren't there yet, it's just a matter of time."

Fee wasn't going to insult Jenna's intelligence by trying to deny that she was having to fight to keep herself from falling head over heels for Chance. "We're so different. I'm completely out of my element on the ranch, the same as he would be in a city the size of L.A."

"Differences are what makes things interesting," Jenna replied. "Heaven only knows, Dylan and I had our share. But if you really care deeply for someone, you work through the issues." She paused a moment. "I was certain that the implications of my father's illegal activities were going to tear Dylan and I apart. But we worked through that and our relationship is stronger than ever. If we can get past something like that, a little thing like distance between you and Chance should be a piece of cake to work out." She smiled. "You could always move here."

Fee stared down at her hands folded on top of the table for several seconds before she met Jenna's questioning gaze. "It's not just the distance of where we live that we'd have to work around," she said slowly. "I have a career that I won't give up." She sighed. "I won't bore you with the details, but my mother gave up a very promising career as a financial adviser because she fell in love with my father. After he left us, she'd been out of her field for so long, she decided it would be impossible to catch up." She shook her head. "I don't intend to give history the opportunity to repeat itself."

"I can understand wanting to maintain your independence," Jenna said, nodding. "But I don't think Chance would ever ask you to give up your career. He just doesn't impress me as being that type of man."

They both fell silent before Fee decided it was

time to lighten the mood. "Enough about that. Tell me about your honeymoon. I've never been to Paris. I've heard it's beautiful."

"It is," Jenna said, her eyes lighting up with enthusiasm. "Dylan spent a lot of time there when he was traveling through Europe and couldn't wait to show me all the little-known places he had discovered."

While her friend talked about the sites her husband had shown her in Paris, as well as the delectable French cuisine, Fee's thoughts strayed to Jenna's observations. If others could see how she felt about Chance, she probably was beginning to fall for him. He was a wonderful man and no matter how much she might deny it, she cared more deeply for him with each passing day and especially after making love last night.

But she couldn't allow herself to fall *in love* with Chance. Besides the fact that he had made it clear he wasn't looking for a relationship, she had far too much to lose. Not even taking into account the loss of her career, Fee could very easily end up facing a lifetime of heartache for a love that he could never return.

"Chance tells me you want him to be the family spokesman for the campaign," Dylan said, when he and Chance walked back to the table.

Fee nodded. "I believe he could be very convincing in getting the message across to the stockholders, as well as the public, that Lassiter Media is as solid as ever."

Dylan grinned as he and Chance took their seats. "I agree."

"Only because you're afraid she'll ask you to do it *if* I decide against it," Chance shot back.

"Well, there is that," Dylan said, laughing.

As she watched the two cousins' good-natured banter, Fee smiled. Of the three Lassiter men, she knew she had made the right choice. Chance wasn't as closed off as Sage and although Dylan was more open and outgoing than his brother, he had an air of sophistication about him that she didn't think would appeal to all demographics.

But she felt heartened by the exchange between Chance and Dylan. Chance hadn't said he wouldn't do the campaign; he had emphasized the word *if.* That had to mean he was considering the idea. Now all she had to do was get a firm commitment from Chance to be the family spokesman and she could start scheduling the video shoot.

A sadness began to fill her as she thought about what that meant. Once she had his agreement and the footage was filmed, she would go back to L.A. and he would stay on at the Big Blue. They might see each other occasionally at a Lassiter function, but eventually they would lose touch completely. Her chest tightened at the thought. No matter how many times she told herself that was the way it had to be, she knew it wasn't going to make their parting any easier. And she knew as surely as she knew her own name that she would be leaving her heart behind when she had to go.

Seven

Two days after their lunch with Dylan and Jenna, Chance watched Fee and his niece sitting cross-legged on the floor in the great room of the main ranch house having a good old time with Cassie's dolls. Fee was encouraging when the little girl wanted to try something different, listened attentively to everything Cassie said and wasn't the least bit put off by the child's constant questions.

No doubt about it, Fee was going to be a wonderful mother someday. The sudden thought that he wouldn't be the man giving her babies caused a knot to twist in his gut. Where had that come from? And why?

When he got up from the couch, Fee gave him a questioning look. "I think I'll go see if Mom needs help with dinner," he explained, thinking quickly. There was no way in hell he could tell her the real reason he was leaving the room.

"I should check to see if Marlene needs me to set the table," she said, starting to rise to her feet.

"No, you go ahead and have fun with your beauty pageant or fashion show or whatever it is you and Cassie are doing there," he said, forcing a laugh. "Mom loves to cook and probably already has everything under control. But I thought I'd offer just in case."

She smiled and the knot in his gut tightened painfully. "If I'm needed to do something, don't hesitate to come and tell me."

"I won't," he said, practically jogging from the room. The truth was, he needed to put some distance between them in order to come to terms with the fact that at some point in time another man was going to be holding her, loving her and raising a family with her. Up until two months ago when he learned about his father's failings, Chance had thought he'd have a shot at a family like that someday. Now he wasn't so sure that would ever happen.

Slowing his pace when he reached the hall, he walked into the kitchen, where his mother was getting ready to take a pot roast from the oven. If there was one thing Marlene Lassiter loved to do, it was cook, and even though the Lassiters could easily afford a world-class chef, she had always insisted on making the family meals herself. The only time he had ever known her to turn over the chore to some-

one else was when the ranch hosted a party or reception that required the hiring of a caterer.

"When are Hannah and Logan supposed to be
back from the Caribbean?" he asked, walking over
to take the pair of oven mitts from her. Opening the
oven, he lifted the roast out and sat it on the counter
for her. "I thought they were only going on a seven-
day cruise."

"They got back from the cruise last night, but they
are going to spend a few days in New Orleans seeing the sights before they fly back to Cheyenne," his
mother said, smiling. He could tell that he and Fee
had pleased her by accepting her dinner invitation
when they'd brought Cassie back from her weekly
trip for ice cream.

That only added a good dose of guilt to the feelings already twisting his gut. As he leaned against
the counter and watched her arrange the roast on a
platter with the potatoes and carrots around it, he
decided there was no time like the present to get
things out in the open and put them to rest once and
for all. "Mom, I've been curious about something."

"What's that, dear?" she asked, turning to tear up
lettuce for a salad.

"Why didn't you tell me about Hannah years ago
instead of waiting until she showed up a couple of
months back?" he asked point-blank.

He heard her soft gasp a moment before she
stopped making the salad to turn and face him. "I
know you feel cheated about not knowing you had
a sister all these years, but it's the way it had to be,

son. Hannah's mother didn't want her to know or have anything to do with the Lassiters. Whether I agreed with her decision or not, I respected those wishes because Hannah was her child, not mine."

"I know that's what you told me when we first met Hannah," Chance said slowly. "But why didn't she want Hannah to know about us?"

Marlene stared at him for a moment before she spoke. "I don't suppose it will hurt to tell you now." She sighed. "Ruth Lovell was a very bitter woman. She wanted your father to leave me and marry her. When he told her that wasn't going to happen, she refused to let Hannah have anything to do with any of us." She shook her head. "The ones who suffered the most from her decision were your father and Hannah. He didn't get to see his daughter more than a few times and she was too young to even know who he was."

"Did Dad ever try to get custody?" If he had been in his father's shoes, which he wouldn't have been in the first place, he'd have moved heaven and earth to be with his child.

Marlene nodded. "Your father consulted several lawyers, but back then a married man trying to gain custody of a child from an affair didn't have nearly the rights he has today."

Chance hesitated a moment, but since his mother brought up the subject of his father's affair, he was going to ask the question that had been bothering him since he learned about Hannah. "Why did you stay with him after he cheated on you with another woman? Weren't you angry and hurt by what he'd done?"

A faraway look entered his mother's eyes as if she might be looking back in time at the choices she'd made. "When Charles told me about his affair with Ruth Lovell, I was crushed," she admitted. "He was the love of my life and he'd betrayed me." She looked directly at Chance. "And don't think for a minute it was easy for me to stay with him or eventually forgive and start trusting him again. It wasn't. I struggled with that for quite some time before I accepted that your father had made a mistake he couldn't change, but one that he regretted with all of his heart."

"What finally convinced you to give him another chance?" he asked, still not fully comprehending her motivation to stay with a man who cheated on her.

"I finally realized that he was just as crushed by what he'd done as I was," she said, turning back to finish making the salad. "I only saw your father cry two times in his life—the day you were born and the day he told me about the affair."

"But how could he have done that to begin with?" Chance asked, unable to understand how a man could do something like that to the woman he loved.

"Back then, riders didn't fly home after a rodeo," Marlene said, setting the salad on the table. "They had to drive from one to another and that required them to be away from home for weeks at a time if they wanted to make any money at it. Your father got lonely and Ruth was there when I wasn't." She shrugged. "And I suspect alcohol was involved because after that I never saw your father take another drink."

"That's still no excuse for sleeping with another woman," Chance insisted.

"He was a man, Chance." She smiled sadly. "And men make mistakes. Some of the mistakes they make can be easily fixed, while others can't." Laying her hand on his arm, she looked him square in the eyes. "I know how much you worshipped your father and how disappointed in him you were when you learned that he wasn't perfect. But remember this, son. He had already ended the affair and I would have never known what he'd done if he hadn't told me right after it happened."

"Why did he tell you?" Chance frowned. "He could have kept his mouth shut and you wouldn't have had to suffer through all the emotional upset."

Marlene nodded. "That's true. But your father was an honorable man and if he hadn't told me and begged my forgiveness for what he'd done, it would have eaten him alive." She opened the cabinet, then handed him some plates to set the table. "I want you to think about the kind of courage it took for him to make his confession. He stood a very real chance of losing everything he loved. But he couldn't live with that kind of secret between us." She reached up to cup his cheek with her hand. "Don't let his one error in judgment distort your memories of him. He was every bit the good, upstanding man you've always thought him to be."

Chance realized that his mother was talking about more than just his father. In her way, she was telling him not to let his father's one failure affect the choices he made.

As he set the table, then went to tell Fee and Cassie that dinner was ready, he thought about what his mother had said. It was true his father had made a grievous mistake. But the man had been compelled to be truthful and make amends, even though it could have cost him his marriage. That did take a hell of a lot of courage. But it had also been the right thing to do.

Standing at the doorway of the great room, Chance watched Fee and his niece still playing with the dolls. Had he been too harsh in judging his father for simply being human? Had he used Charles Lassiter's transgression as an excuse to avoid falling in love?

When Fee looked up and smiled at him, his heart stalled. He could see his future in her eyes and he had a feeling that if he didn't find the answers to his questions, and damned quick, he could very well end up regretting it for the rest of his life.

When they returned to ranch headquarters after having dinner with Marlene and Cassie, Fee knew she should spend the rest of the evening going over her notes and at least make another attempt to get Chance's agreement to be the family spokesman. It had been days since she'd thought about improving the Lassiter family image, the job promotion she wanted or her life back in L.A.

Why didn't that bother her more? Just a couple of weeks ago, all she could think about was becoming the vice president in charge of public relations. Now, it didn't seem to matter as much as it once had.

"Thanks for being so patient with Cassie," Chance said as they entered the house. "I can't believe all the questions a five-year-old can come up with."

"I didn't mind at all. I enjoyed being with her." Smiling, Fee forgot all about her concerns regarding her lack of interest in the job promotion as she thought about his niece and the fun she'd had playing fashion show with the child. "Cassie's a bright, inquisitive little girl with a very active imagination."

He laughed as they walked down the dark hall toward the stairs. "That's a nice way of saying she's a handful."

"I could say the same thing about her uncle," Fee teased as they went upstairs.

When they reached his room, Chance led her inside, closed the door behind them and immediately took her into his arms. His wicked grin promised a night filled with passionate lovemaking, and the thought of what she knew they would be sharing caused her pulse to beat double time.

"I'll show you just how much of a handful I can be," he whispered. His warm breath feathering over her ear caused excitement and anticipation to course through her.

Lowering his head, he kissed her, and his desperation was thrilling. He wanted her as badly as she wanted him. His need fueled the answering desire deep inside her and stars danced behind her closed eyelids from its intensity.

"I thought I would go out of my mind this evening, watching you and not being able to touch you," he said as he nipped and kissed his way from her lips to the hollow below her ear. "All I could think about was getting you home."

"What did you intend to do when we got here?" she asked, feeling as if there wasn't nearly enough oxygen in the room.

"This for starters," he answered, tugging her mint-green tank top from the waistband of her jeans. Pulling it over her head, he tossed it aside, unhooked her bra and whisked it away. When he cupped her breasts with his hands, he kissed one taut nipple. "And this," he added, paying the same attention to the other tight peak.

Fee impatiently grasped the lapels of his chambray shirt, releasing all of the snaps with one quick jerk. Shoving the fabric from his shoulders, she placed her palms on his warm bare flesh.

"I love your body," she said, mapping the ridges and valleys of his chest and abdomen with her fingertips. "It's absolutely beautiful."

His hands stilled for a moment as he took a deep breath. "Guys have too many angles and hard edges to be beautiful," he said, his voice deep with passion. "But a woman's body is softer and has gentle curves that drive a man crazy with wanting," he added, gliding his hands down her sides to her hips. "That's true beauty, sweetheart."

As he unfastened her jeans, his heated gaze held hers and the promise in his dark green eyes stole her breath. He didn't need just any woman. He needed her. The knowledge sent a wave of heat washing over her and unable to remain passive, she unbuckled his belt and released the button at the top of his jeans.

Neither spoke as they stripped each other of their clothing. Words were unnecessary. They both wanted the same thing—to lose themselves in the pleasure of being joined together as one.

"I need you," Chance said as he kicked the rest of their clothing into a heap on the floor.

"I need you, too," she said, her body aching to be filled by him.

Without another word, Chance lifted her to him and Fee automatically wrapped her legs around his waist. Bracing the back of his shoulders against the wall, he lowered her onto him in one breathtaking movement. Fee's head fell back as she absorbed his body into hers, the feeling so exquisite it left her feeling faint.

He immediately began a rhythmic pace that sent a flash fire of heat flowing through her veins. All too quickly Fee felt herself climbing toward the culmination of their desire and she struggled to prolong the sensations, even as she raced to end them.

Her body suddenly broke free from the tension holding them captive and she gave herself up to the pleasure surging through every cell in her body. She heard Chance groan her name as he thrust deeply into her one last time, then holding her tightly against him, shuddered from the force of his own release.

As they slowly drifted back to reality, Chance suddenly went completely still for a moment before he cursed and set her on her feet. "I'm so sorry, Fee," he said, closing his eyes and shaking his head as if he'd done something he regretted.

"What are you sorry about?" she asked, becoming alarmed by his obvious distress.

When he opened his eyes and looked directly at her, she could see guilt in their emerald depths. "I was so hot and needed you so much, I forgot to use a condom."

Fee's heart came up in her throat and her knees threatened to give out as she made her way over to the side of the bed to sit down. She'd never had to face the possibility of becoming pregnant before. "I can't believe this."

Reaching for the folded comforter at the end of the bed, she wrapped it around herself as she tried to think. The possibility that she would become pregnant from this one time without protection had to be small. She remembered reading somewhere that there was only a 20 to 30 percent chance of success each month when a couple was trying to become pregnant. Surely that percentage went down significantly when a couple only had unprotected sex once. Of course, all of that meant absolutely nothing to the women who became pregnant after just one time in defiance of the statistics.

"Fee, look at me." Chance had put on his boxer briefs and was kneeling in front of her. Taking her hands in his, he shook his head. "I'm sorry, sweetheart. It's my fault and I take full responsibility."

Staring at him, it was her turn to shake her head. "I can't let you take all the blame. I didn't remember, either."

He looked as if he might be calculating the odds. "I doubt that you'll become pregnant from this one time." He took a deep breath and gently squeezed her hands in a comforting gesture. "But if you do, I swear I'll be at your side every step of the way."

"I'm sure the probability is small," she said, distracted.

What was wrong with her? Shouldn't she have a stronger reaction to the circumstances? Or was she simply in a state of shock?

Before she could sort out her feelings, Chance lifted her to the middle of the mattress, removed his boxer briefs, then stretched out beside her. Covering them both with the comforter, he pulled her into his arms and cradled her to his chest.

Kissing the top of her head, he ran his hands along her back in a soothing manner. "Fee, could I ask you something?"

Still trying to sort out her reaction to the turn of events, she simply nodded.

"I know our deal was for you to stay two weeks," he said slowly. "But I'd like for you to stay here with me until you go back to L.A. Maybe by that time we'll know for sure if you're pregnant."

"Okay," she said slowly.

She really didn't want to go back to the rental house Lassiter Media had provided for her. For one thing, she would miss Chance terribly. And for another, being alone while she waited to see if their carelessness had produced an unexpected pregnancy wasn't something she wanted to do.

"There's something else I'd like to know," he said, clearing his throat.

"What's that?" she asked.

"Would it be so bad if you did have my baby?" he asked quietly.

Leaning her head back, she searched his handsome features as she tried to formulate an answer. How could she explain what she didn't understand? Part of the reason she was struggling with the situation was the fact that she wasn't nearly as upset at the thought of being pregnant as she would have been just a couple of weeks ago.

"I'd rather not be pregnant," she finally said, trying to be as honest as possible. "But if I am, the answer is no. I wouldn't mind at all for you to be the baby's father."

Sitting on a bale of hay outside the feed room in the barn, Chance propped his forearms on his knees and stared down at the toes of his boots. He should be shot, propped up and shot again. Not even when he was a teenager with more hormones than good sense had he forgotten to use protection. It was something his uncle J.D. had stressed from the time he'd had "the talk" with Chance and his two cousins when they entered puberty until they all went off to college.

What had been different about last night? Why had he lost control with Fee when he'd never done that with any other woman?

If anything, he should have been more careful with her than he'd ever been. He'd fought against it—had even tried to deny it was happening—but she meant more to him than life itself.

His heart stalled and he felt as if he'd taken a sucker punch to the gut. It was the last thing he'd thought would happen, but he'd fallen in love with her.

As he tried to catch his breath, he realized he'd been a damned fool. Although Chance had no intention of telling Gus, the old cuss had been right. Fee wasn't a woman a man had a little fun with and then moved on from. She was the type of woman a man wanted in his life, his bed and his heart. Forever.

So what was he going to do about it? What could he do about it?

He knew she had feelings for him. Otherwise, she wouldn't have slept with him, nor would she have agreed to extend her stay with him. But she had made it clear she wasn't looking to get involved in anything long-term. Of course, if it turned out she was pregnant, he couldn't think of anything more long-term than raising a kid together. But that didn't mean she would marry him, nor would he expect her to. As far as he was concerned, marriage should be based on love, not because a baby was on the way.

"Whoa!" he said aloud. Was he really thinking about marriage?

As he turned the notion over in his mind, he wasn't certain that was something he wanted to do. He still hadn't completely forgiven his father's infidelity, even though his mother obviously had. If a man like Charles Lassiter could stray, what guarantees did Chance have that he wouldn't?

When he looked up to see Fee walking down the barn aisle toward him, Chance knew he had his answer. He would rather die than do anything to hurt her. If temptation presented itself, he had no doubt that he could walk away from it without so much as a backward glance.

But he wasn't going to spring the idea on her just yet. He needed to think things through and do a little planning.

"Did you finish helping Gus get everything cleared up from supper?" he asked, unable to stop grinning.

"He's already retired to his room for the Rockies game," she said, nodding. She tilted her head to one side. "You look happy. What happened?"

When she reached him, he patted his thigh. "Have a seat, sweetheart. I have something I want to ask you."

She gave him a suspicious glance, then sat down on his leg and put her arms across his shoulders. "What?"

"I intended to ask you the other day when I picked up the tickets, but forgot about it once we had lunch with Dylan and Jenna at Lassiter Grill." He gave her a quick kiss. "Would you like to go to the finals rodeo events at Cheyenne Frontier Days with me?"

"That sounds like a lot of fun," she said, smiling. "I've never been to a rodeo before."

Her delighted expression caused a warmth to spread from his chest throughout his body. She looked happy and he knew there wasn't anything he wouldn't do to please her.

Taking a deep breath, he placed his index finger under her chin to tilt it up until their gazes met. "We both know I'm not overly comfortable being in the public eye," he said, choosing his words carefully. "It's just not my thing. I'm happy staying right here on the ranch, doing what I do best—taking care of livestock and arguing with Gus. But I've been think-ing if you really want me to be the Lassiter family spokesman, I'll do it as long as we limit it to just a few pictures and a video or two."

Her excitement was palpable. "Really? You're going to do my campaign?"

"Yeah, I'll do it," he said, loving the way she threw her arms around his neck. When she gave him a kiss that left them both gasping for breath, he decided right then and there, he'd climb a barbed wire fence buck naked if that's what she wanted.

"Let's go back to the house," she said, standing up to take him by the hand.

"Why?" He hooked his thumb toward the horse stalls. "I thought you might like to go for a ride."

She gave him that look again—the one all women used when they thought men were being overly obtuse. "You're about to get lucky and you're going to stand here and tell me you want to go for a horseback ride?"

"No, ma'am."

"I didn't think so," she said, laughing as he hustled her toward the house.

Eight

A week after Chance told her he would be her spokesman in the ad campaign, Fee should have been elated. She had scheduled the first video shoot for the following week, had the first of the on-air spots reserved for the commercials and was well on her way to becoming the vice president of public relations at Lassiter Media. So why wasn't she thrilled?

She knew exactly why. Her time in Wyoming was drawing to a close and when the videographer left to go back to L.A. to edit the footage, she would be returning with him. A lump clogged her throat and for the first time in her life, Fee understood a little more about the choices her mother had made all those years ago. It was going to be the hardest thing she'd ever had to do to walk away from this man.

Blinking back tears, she decided not to think about it now. She would face that day at the end of next week. For now she was with him and she wasn't going to waste a single minute of what little time they had left together.

Seated in the huge covered grandstand with him, she turned her attention to the men on horseback as they roped calves. As soon as the animal had been stopped at the end of the rope, the cowboy would jump from his horse, tie three of the calf's legs together with lightning-fast speed, then wait to see if it stayed bound for a specified length of time. It was interesting to see how fast the cowboys accomplished the task and the level of skill they all possessed. She admired them all for their ability, but quickly decided if she had to do the task it might never get done.

Glancing over at Chance, she smiled. He had been wonderful telling her about the rich history of Frontier Days, explaining the way cowboys were awarded prize money and points toward qualifying for the National Finals Rodeo at the end of the year and patiently answering her questions about the different events. Fee found all of it fascinating and enjoyed every minute of what she'd seen thus far.

"What's next?" she asked, looking forward to more excitement.

"Saddle bronc riding," he answered, nodding toward horses that were being loaded into the bucking chutes. "This is one of the events my dad competed in."

"From what Gus told me, your father was very

successful at this and another event," she said while they waited for the action to begin.

Chance nodded. "He competed in the bareback riding as well as the saddle bronc riding." He smiled proudly. "Dad was world champion in both events several times before he retired."

"How old was he when he decided to quit?" she asked.

"He was thirty-six," Chance answered, staring at the media pit across the arena in front of the other grandstand.

She looked to see what he was so interested in all of a sudden. "Is something wrong?"

"No, I was just checking to see who was operating the cameras this year," he said, shrugging. "Lassiter Media donates the use of some of their audio and video equipment every year and I was just checking to see if any of the Lassiter technicians I'm acquainted with are helping out."

"I didn't realize those big screens belonged to Lassiter," she said, noticing for the first time the huge screens mounted on top of long trailers pulled by semis.

He nodded as he checked his watch. "We've donated the use of equipment for the rodeo as long as I can remember."

"I'll have to keep that in mind," she said thoughtfully. Even though she doubted she would need the information for publicity, it was nice to have it just in case.

When Chance checked his watch again, she frowned. "Do you have somewhere you need to be?"

"Not really." He grinned. "I was just thinking it's about time to get something else to eat."

"Where on earth do you put all that food?" she asked. They had stopped by the chuck wagon cook-off when they first arrived at the rodeo grounds and enjoyed heaping plates full of some of the delicious fare once fed to the men on cattle drives in the old West. "I'm positively stuffed."

"I've used a lot of extra calories the past few weeks," he said, his grin suggestive. "Especially at night."

"Forget I mentioned it," she said, laughing.

When one of the chutes opened and a cowboy on a horse burst into the arena, Fee turned her attention to the action in front of her. At times, all four of the horse's hooves were off the ground as the animal appeared to do aerial acrobatics in its effort to dislodge the rider. Well before the eight-second buzzer went off, the unfortunate cowboy landed on the ground in an undignified heap while the horse continued to buck its way around the arena.

"He doesn't get any points for that, right?" she turned to Chance and asked.

"Nope. He won't get a score, money or points," he answered, checking his watch before he rose to his feet. "While you watch the rest of the saddle bronc riding, I think I'm going to see about getting some food on a stick and maybe a basket of nachos. Do you want me to bring you a corn dog or something else?"

"No, thank you. But before you go, maybe you could explain something to me."

He nodded. "Sure, what do you want to know?"

"Why do men and children like their food on a stick?" she asked.

Laughing, he leaned down to kiss her cheek. "Sweetheart, fair food always comes on a stick and just tastes better that way. Same goes for food at a rodeo."

"I'll take your word for it," she said, unable to believe how many different foods had been put on sticks, dipped in batter and deep-fried at today's event. At one concession stand she'd even seen a sign for fried ice cream—on a stick, of course.

"Will you be all right?" he asked. "I'll only be a couple of minutes."

Smiling, she nodded. "I'll be right here when you get back."

As she turned her attention to the action in front of her, she marveled at the fact that most of the cowboys were able to stay in the saddle for even eight seconds. If she tried to ride a horse like that, she'd be lying on the ground after the first jump.

When the announcer informed the crowd that the saddle bronc event was over and the bareback riding was about to begin, she sat back in her seat to wait for Chance. What could be keeping him so long? Surely he wasn't visiting every concession stand in his quest for food on a stick.

"Dear, I'm sorry to bother you, but would you

mind letting me out?" an elderly woman asked, pointing to the aisle a few seats away.

"Not at all," Fee said, smiling. She stood up to allow the woman to pass in front of her.

"Thank you, dear." The older woman sighed. "My grandson decided he needs another soft drink."

Fee started to tell the woman it was no trouble at all when she heard her name over the public address system. She hadn't been paying attention as she spoke with the woman but now, when she looked up, she was riveted. There was Chance on the huge video screen across the arena, and he was asking, "…Will you marry me?"

She hadn't heard the beginning of his message, but she didn't need to. Chance was asking her to marry him? Why would he do that? And why did he have to do it in such a public way?

He'd made it perfectly clear weeks ago that he didn't want a permanent relationship. She knew he was fond of her and that he desired her, but he hadn't once told her that he loved her.

It suddenly dawned on her that the man who said he wasn't looking for anything permanent had only made the gesture because he thought she might be pregnant. She couldn't think of anything more humiliating than to be blindsided with a marriage proposal in a huge crowd when all Chance was trying to do was assuage his conscience.

The camera scanned the crowd, then zeroed in on her, and she gasped when she saw herself on the giant screens on either side of the grandstand. Her larger-than-life image wore the legendary deer-in-the-headlights expression and when the crowd started chanting "say yes," panic set in. She had to get out of there. She needed time to think and a rodeo arena filled with thousands of strangers wasn't the place to do it.

She felt as if she couldn't breathe as she quickly descended the steps of the grandstand. She'd fallen in love with Chance in spite of all her best efforts not to and if he loved her, his grand gesture would have been sweet and she would have seriously considered agreeing to be his wife. But she refused to marry a man who didn't return her love and only offered because there might be an unexpected pregnancy.

Fee wasn't her mother. She wasn't about to enter into a marriage because a man felt obligated to offer or because he was trying to rectify a mistake. She wanted him to love her as much as she loved him.

Digging through her purse, she managed to retrieve her cell phone. Her hands shook so badly she almost dropped it as she called and arranged for a cab to meet her on the street outside the rodeo grounds. As she made her way to the exit, she decided not to go back to the house Lassiter Media had rented. It was the first place Chance would look for her and at the moment, he was the last person she wanted to see.

No, she was going to the airport to buy a ticket on the first available commuter plane to Denver. From there she could take a flight back to L.A. It was where she could think and where she had the best chance of forgetting the cowboy who had broken her heart.

When Chance saw the look on Fee's face and watched her take off as if the hounds of hell were chasing her, his heart sank. She wasn't just getting away from the cameras. She was making a run for it. He didn't know exactly where she would go, but he knew as surely as he knew his own name that he wouldn't find her anywhere on the rodeo grounds.

Checking with the security office to make sure he was right about her leaving, one of the older guards recognized him as a Lassiter and, taking pity on Chance, showed him the surveillance tape of Fee hurrying through the east exit. Thanking the man, Chance went straight to his truck and climbed in. He felt like a damned fool. He'd gone against every one of his reservations about being the center of attention, told her he loved her and asked her to marry him in front of thousands of people, and she had thrown his proposal back in his face.

He'd told her how uncomfortable he was in front of a camera. Didn't she realize what his gesture meant—that he loved her and was sincere when he asked her to marry him?

He drove straight to the rental house. He knew better than to think Fee would go back to the ranch. The Big Blue was the last place she'd go because she knew he would be there.

The fact that she obviously didn't want to be

around him made Chance feel as if someone had reached in and ripped his heart from his chest. But as he navigated downtown Cheyenne and finally turned onto the street where the rental was located, he shook his head. What had he expected? Beyond great sex, they had very little in common. She was a city girl who had made it crystal clear she was more interested in climbing the corporate ladder than having a man in her life. And he was a country boy who would rather spend his nights gazing at billions of stars in the western sky than watch the moon rise over a skyscraper in L.A.

Parking his truck, he got out and walked up to knock on the door. The rental car was still in the driveway, but when Fee didn't answer, he walked back to the truck and sat there for several long minutes. She was either inside and just not answering the door or she was elsewhere. His money was on the latter.

As he started the truck and drove away, he decided that either way it didn't matter. She'd let him know in no uncertain terms what was important to her. And he wasn't it.

"Momma, Uncle Chance said Fee flew the car a few days ago," Cassie said, skipping ahead of Chance as they entered Hannah and Logan's house after their weekly trip for ice cream.

When his sister and brother-in-law walked into the foyer, Hannah gave Chance a questioning look. "Coop," he corrected. "Fee flew the coop."

"Yeah, that." Cassie frowned. "I was going to tell her today that I decided to call her Aunt Fee."

"Maybe you can tell her another time, sweetie," Hannah said, her gaze never leaving Chance's. "Logan?"

With his usual perceptiveness, Logan Whittaker nodded. "Cassie, why don't you and I go watch that new video cartoon Grandma Marlene got for you?" Logan suggested. "I think your mom wants to talk to your uncle Chance." He nodded at Chance as he led Cassie toward the media room. "My wife is amazing. If anyone can help you see the error of your ways, she can."

Chance frowned. "The error of *my* ways?"

Logan shrugged. "Take my word for it, ninety-nine percent of the time it's a man's fault."

"Let's go into the kitchen and I'll make us a cup of coffee," Hannah said, leading the way down the hall. "You look terrible. You haven't been sleeping well, have you?"

"Not really." When they entered the room, Chance sat down at the table in the breakfast nook while his sister started the coffeemaker. "There's really nothing to figure out, Hannah. I'm here and Fee isn't. End of story."

He appreciated his sister's concern, but he'd lain awake in his big empty bed for the past three nights, wondering how he could have been so wrong about Fee. He'd been sure she had started to care for him the way he cared for her. Obviously, he'd been wrong. Otherwise she wouldn't have left him standing at the rodeo looking like the biggest fool on the whole damned planet.

"Why don't you tell me what happened and let me decide if there's a way you might be able to turn this around?" She sat his coffee in front of him, then took a seat on the opposite side of the table. "Marlene said Gus told her you went to Frontier Days with Fee and came home without her."

Chance groaned. He should have known Gus would send out an alert to all interested parties. "Do you three have some kind of hotline to keep tabs on me now?"

"No, but that's a thought," Hannah shot back. "Now are you going to tell me what happened or am I going to have to get Logan in here to put his cross-examination skills to good use."

"You had to go and marry a lawyer, didn't you?" Chance said, stalling.

He had always been of the opinion that the more you picked at a wound the longer it took to heal. But as much as he wanted the aching in his chest where his heart used to be to end, he suspected the pain of Fee's rejection would be with him for the rest of his life.

"Yes, but don't hold Logan being a lawyer against him," Hannah said, grinning. "I had my doubts at first, but all in all he's turned out to be a pretty good guy. Now, tell me what happened."

Knowing his sister wasn't going to give up until she got to the bottom of what took place between him and Fee, Chance shrugged. "I asked Fee to marry me and she took off."

Hannah shook her head. "I know that. If Marlene hadn't told me, I would have read about it in the newspaper." She gave him a sympathetic smile. "It's not every day a Lassiter proposes and gets turned down in front of a crowd of people."

"Yeah, it wasn't pretty," he said, still disgusted with himself.

"So start over. You've left out some important details. What happened between our wedding reception and you asking Fee to marry you?"

When he told her about the deal he had come up with for Fee to stay with him on the Big Blue, he had to admit it didn't sound all that good. "Looking back, it wasn't one of my better ideas."

"You think?" Hannah asked sarcastically. "If you weren't my brother I'd swear you were a snake in blue jeans and boots. It sounds like you were planning her seduction more than you were trying to talk her out of making you the Lassiter family spokesman."

"I realize that now." He ran his hand over his face as he tried to wipe away some of the regret. "But at the time, all I wanted was to keep things light. I wasn't looking for anything permanent and she made it clear she wasn't, either. I figured we could have a little harmless fun together and when the time came, I'd go my way and she'd go hers."

Hannah shook her head. "It backfired on you, didn't it? You fell in love."

Chance nodded and took a sip of the coffee Hannah had placed in front of him. He really didn't want it, but he didn't want to hurt her feelings. He'd caused enough of those lately. He didn't want to add more. For the past couple of months, his mother had been upset because he made it clear he resented her not telling him about Hannah years ago, Cassie was upset that Fee had left and he'd obviously upset Fee when he asked her to marry him. Hell, he was beginning to think he couldn't win with females.

"So you fell in love, but Fee didn't?" Hannah prodded when he remained silent.

"To tell you the truth, I'm not sure," he admitted. "I thought she felt the same as I do. At least, she acted like she cared for me. But that obviously isn't the case."

"Trying to get something out of you is like trying to pull teeth." His sister sighed. "What gave you the idea she loves you? And did you actually tell her you love her?"

"I didn't tell her until just before I proposed," he answered, staring at his coffee cup.

"Well, what did she say?" He could tell Hannah was getting frustrated, but he didn't particularly care to share the most embarrassing moment of his entire life.

"I don't know what she said because we weren't together," he admitted.

"Okay, you're going to have to tell me how that works," Hannah said, looking confused a moment before her eyes narrowed. "Don't tell me you called her or sent her a text."

"No. I'm not that boneheaded." As he explained about telling Fee he loved her and proposing on the big screen at Frontier Days, he realized he should have told her sooner and in a more private way. "That might not have been the right timing." He'd figured that out on the lonely drive back to the Big Blue that same day.

"Oh, my God, Chance," Hannah gasped. "You seriously didn't do that, did you? I assumed you had told her you love her previously. I wasn't aware that was the first time."

Nodding, he finished off his coffee. "Once again, not one of my better ideas."

"Having a man tell her for the first time that he loves her is a very tender moment for a woman," Hannah said slowly, as if choosing her words carefully. "She doesn't necessarily want an audience of thousands to intrude on that. Especially when they're chanting *say yes* to a marriage proposal she didn't expect."

"Yeah, I got that when she took off," he said, nodding. He shook his head as he decided that he might as well tell Hannah the entire story. "There's something else."

His sister nodded. "I thought there might be. What else happened?"

"Nothing. At least not yet." He took a deep breath. "It's probably remote, but there is the possibility that Fee might be pregnant."

"That's the real problem right there," Hannah said, her tone adamant. "I don't think it's that Fee doesn't love you, Chance."

"Yeah, what's not to love?" he asked sarcastically. "I'm the guy who can't even propose to a woman without screwing it up."

"Don't be so hard on yourself," she said, placing her hand on his. "It really was a sweet gesture and if circumstances were different, everything might have worked out the way you intended. But I wouldn't be the least bit surprised if Fee thinks you proposed only because of the possible pregnancy."

The thought had crossed his mind, but that wasn't the case at all. Unfortunately, Fee didn't know that. "To tell you the truth, that had nothing to do with my decision to propose."

He had realized he loved her the night they had dinner at his mother's. But Fee didn't know that and if there was even the slightest possibility he could convince her, they might still have a chance.

When he remained silent, Hannah's eyes sparkled with excitement. "You're going to Los Angeles, aren't you?"

"I'm thinking about it," he said, feeling more hopeful than he had in the past three days.

Hannah got up and rounded the table to give him a hug. "I realize we haven't known about each other for more than a couple of months, but you're my brother and I want you to be happy. Take that leap of faith, Chance. You'll never know if you don't."

"Thanks for the advice, Hannah." He hugged her

back. "At first I had a real hard time with the fact that our dad had an affair with your mother. But if he hadn't, I wouldn't have you and Cassie in my life. And that's something I wouldn't trade for anything."

"I know what you mean," she said, nodding. "It took me a while to forgive my mother for not letting me know that I had a family who wanted me in their life. But letting go of the past has a way of making way for the future." Hannah gave him a pointed look. "And speaking of the future, you have something you need to do."

"Yeah, I guess I do," he said slowly.

Hannah took the cordless phone from its charger on the wall and handed it to him. "Now, call the Lassiter hangar and make arrangements for the corporate jet to take you to Los Angeles. You have some serious groveling to do." Laughing, she added, "And if you can refrain from making any more grand declarations in front of thousands of people, you might get another chance with Fee."

Chance shook his head. "You just had to bring that up, didn't you?"

"Of course." She smiled. "I've heard sisters are supposed to do that."

"Do what?" he asked, frowning.

She laughed as he dialed the phone. "Remind their brothers when they've been real boneheads."

Nine

"Hi, Becca," Fee said as she closed the door behind her friend. "Thanks for coming over."

"What's up, Fee?" Her friend looked concerned. "You sounded stressed when you called. Is everything all right?"

Fee shook her head. "Not really."

"Since you asked me to come over instead of meeting you somewhere for lunch, I assume you need a shoulder," Becca said, sitting in the chair flanking Fee's couch.

The director of the Lassiter Charitable Foundation, Becca Stevens had asked for Fee's help with publicity on several different occasions for the charity events put on by the Lassiters. Over the years, they had become good friends and frequently shared the highs and lows of their careers—and of their personal lives from time to time.

"Actually, I was going to tell you that there's a very good possibility I'll be leaving Lassiter Media within the next few weeks," Fee said, curling up in one corner of the couch.

"Why?" Clearly shocked, Becca sat forward in the chair. "I thought you love your job."

"I do," Fee admitted. "But after my trip to Wyoming, I think it's time for me to move on."

"What happened in Wyoming?" Becca's eyes narrowed suddenly. "You met a man, didn't you?"

"Yes." Fee shrugged one shoulder. "But I broke the rules."

Her friend looked confused. "What rules are you talking about?"

"Mine," Fee answered. "I got close to someone… and…it's just time for a change." She didn't want to go into details because it was simply too painful to explain.

Sitting back in her chair, Becca shook her head. "But you're in line for vice president of public relations—a position that I know you wanted."

"With my work experience, I don't think I'll have a problem finding another position elsewhere," Fee said, knowing she didn't sound at all enthusiastic about it. She loved working for Lassiter Media and would have continued to work there indefinitely if she hadn't met a ruggedly handsome cowboy who stole her heart.

"Before we talk about where you'll look for an-

other job, tell me about the man you got close to,"
Becca said gently. When Fee didn't say anything,
Becca's eyes grew wide and Fee knew her friend
had figured it out. "You got involved with one of
the Lassiters."

Tears filled her eyes as Fee nodded. "He's J.D.'s
nephew."

"So he doesn't work for Lassiter Media?" Becca
asked. When Fee shook her head, she continued,
"Then I don't see the problem." She frowned. "Actually, even if he did work for Lassiter there shouldn't
be an issue. As far as I know there isn't any kind of
company policy on dating another employee."

"It's...complicated," Fee said, sniffing back her
tears.

Becca seemed to consider her answer. "I take it
that things didn't work out between you?"

"No." Fee closed her eyes for a moment in an effort to regain her composure. "I know it wouldn't
happen often, but I don't want to risk running into
him at one of the corporate functions or one of your
fund-raisers. And I've handed over the Lassiter family PR campaign to someone else for the same reason."

"I can understand that." Becca smiled sadly. "But
I'm really going to miss working with you on the
publicity for the foundation."

Fee dabbed at her eyes with a tissue. It was completely out of character for her, but for the past few
days, everything made her cry.

"Enough about me and my problems," she said,

trying to lighten the mood. "Tell me what's been going on with you for the past month."

"Aside from the fact that donations for the foundation are way down and it's Jack Reed's fault, not a lot," Becca answered.

"He's a corporate raider," Fee commented. "Don't tell me he's started setting his sights on raiding charity foundations now."

"Not exactly," Becca said, her pretty face reflecting her anger. "He's been buying up blocks of Lassiter Media shares in an attempt at a hostile takeover. In light of the way he chops up companies and sells them off piece by piece, our contributors have backed off and haven't been nearly as generous with their donations. Some of the recipients of our funding are shying away from the association with Lassiter Media, too, especially with what's going on with Angelica. She seems to be in cahoots with Jack and that makes everyone nervous. I'm just glad her father isn't alive to see the way she's acting. I don't think he would be overly pleased."

"That's terrible," Fee said, upset by the news. "The Lassiter Charitable Foundation does so much good for so many people. How bad is it?"

"If something doesn't change—and soon—I'm going to have to start making cuts." Becca shook her head. "But I'm not going down without a fight. I'm going to pay Mr. Reed a visit and try to make him see reason."

"I hope you're successful," Fee said, meaning it.

"I've heard he's quite ruthless and doesn't care about anything that doesn't serve his own interests."

Becca took a deep breath. "He hasn't met me. I can be just as cutthroat as the next person when it's something I've worked hard to build and truly believe in."

"Something tells me Mr. Jack Reed has met his match," Fee said, managing a smile.

When Becca checked her watch, she rose to her feet. "I hate to run, but I need to get some things together for that meeting."

Fee rose to give her a hug. "Thanks for stopping by. Good luck and please let me know how it goes. I know if anyone can make Jack Reed see reason, you'll be the one to do it."

"And good luck to you, Fee," Becca said, hugging her back. "I wish you would change your mind, even if you aren't going to do the campaign or get the vice president job. I'm going to miss you terribly."

"We'll still be able to get together for lunch or dinner," Fee offered. "I'll let you know when I get another job."

Opening the door to see her friend out, Fee's breath lodged in her throat and she felt the blood drain from her face. Chance was coming up the walk. Dressed in a white Western-cut shirt, jeans, boots and his ever-present wide-brimmed black hat, he looked more handsome than any man had a right to look.

"Who is that?" Becca asked, sounding impressed.

When Fee remained silent, understanding dawned

on Becca's face. "That's him, isn't it?" She glanced from Fee to Chance and back again. "No wonder you broke your rule. He's gorgeous." Giving Fee another quick hug, Becca whispered, "Good luck working this out with him, too."

Watching Chance tip his hat as Becca passed him on the sidewalk, Fee felt tears threaten. How could she simultaneously be so happy to see him and feel as if her heart was breaking all over again?

"Hi, Fee," he said when he reached her door.

"What are you doing here, Chance?" she managed, thankful that her voice didn't sound as shaky as she felt.

"We need to talk."

"I don't think that would be a good idea," she said, her heart pounding hard against her ribs. Why couldn't he leave her alone to salvage what was left of her heart?

"I do," he said calmly. "Now are you going to ask me in or are we going to discuss this right here on your doorstep?"

Before she had a chance to answer, he placed his hands on her shoulders, guided her back into her condo and shut the door behind them. Her skin tingled from the warmth of his hands even through her clothing and she walked over to put the coffee table between them. If she didn't, she couldn't be sure she wouldn't turn to him and make a complete fool of herself by throwing herself into his arms.

"Why are you here?" she asked again.

"I'm here for your answer," he said simply.

"I thought you would figure out what my answer was when I left Cheyenne," she said, feeling tears fill her eyes.

"Oh, I figured it out right about the time I watched you run down the steps of the grandstand. It was kind of hard to miss on a JumboTron. But I want you to tell me face-to-face," he insisted, taking a step toward her. "You're going to have to look me in the eyes and tell me that you don't love me and don't want to be my wife."

She held out her hand to stop him. "Chance, please don't do this. Please don't…make me…say it."

He held up a DVD case she hadn't noticed before. "Maybe we should go back and replay my proposal so you can see the look in my eyes when you ran away. Then you can give me your answer."

"Why are you doing this?" she asked brokenly. "You don't love *me*. You only asked me to marry you because you think I might be pregnant."

"That's where you're wrong, sweetheart. I told you I love you before I asked you to marry me."

Her knees felt as if they had turned to rubber and she lowered herself onto the couch before they gave way. "No, you didn't. I would have remembered it if you had."

"I wondered if you might have missed that. That's why I brought this along—to prove it." He went to her television and put the disk in the DVD player, switching both machines on.

An image of Chance standing next to one of the rodeo announcers appeared on the screen. The man was saying that someone had a very special message for one of the ladies in the crowd. She watched Chance take a deep breath before he smiled and looked directly into the camera. "I love you, Felicity Sinclair. Will you marry me?"

Fee gasped as she remembered how she'd been distracted by the elderly woman trying to get past her in the grandstand. "I didn't hear you say you love me." She stared down at her tightly clasped hands in her lap. "All I heard was your proposal."

"Believe me, sweetheart, there's no way in hell I would have been on camera with all those people watching if I didn't love you," he stated.

As she thought about the sincerity in his eyes, as well as the number of times he'd told her he wasn't comfortable being the center of attention, she realized what he said must be true. He did love her. "I'm sorry, Chance," she said, wiping a tear from her cheek. "I panicked."

Chance walked over, squatted down in front of her and lifted her chin with his finger until their gazes met. "Just for the record, I'll admit that I'm a pretty traditional kind of guy. But I don't happen to believe that a man and woman should get married just because a baby is on the way."

"You don't?" she asked, loving the feel of his touch, even if it was just his finger on her chin.

He shook his head. "I believe two people should be in love and want to spend the rest of their lives together before they take that step."

"You want to spend the rest of your life with me?"

she asked, feeling hope begin to rise within her, even though the thought of marriage scared her as little else could.

"I do," he said firmly. "I never expected to find a woman I couldn't live without. A woman who invaded my dreams and made me burn for her by simply walking into the room. Then I saw you at Hannah and Logan's wedding and all that changed. I want to spend the rest of my life with you, Fee. I want to make love to you every night and wake up each morning with you in my arms. Is that what you want, too?"

She caught her lower lip between her teeth to keep it from trembling. "I'm…afraid, Chance."

Moving to sit beside her on the couch, he pulled her onto his lap and cradled her to him. "What are you afraid of, Fee?"

The gentle tone of his deep voice and the tender way he held her to him were so tempting. Did she dare trust that his love for her was as strong as hers was for him? Did she have the courage to reach for what she never thought she would ever have?

"I need to tell you why I'm so career driven and why the thought of being in love scares me to death," she said, wanting him to understand part of the reason she'd panicked.

"You can tell me anything," he said, kissing her temple. "There's nothing you can say that will ever stop me from loving you."

"When my mother met my father, she was a successful financial adviser in a prestigious firm in downtown L.A.," she explained. "She immediately fell in love with him and in no time was pregnant with me."

"They got married?" Chance guessed.

"Yes, but I have a feeling it would have never happened if my mother hadn't been pregnant." Fee shook her head. "From what my grandmother told me, my father wasn't the kind of man who stayed in one place for long and he eventually got tired of having a wife and baby in tow. When he decided to leave, he didn't even say goodbye. He just walked out and left us in a second-rate motel somewhere in eastern Arizona with no money and no way to get back to California."

"How did you get back home?" he asked, tightening his arms around her in a comforting gesture.

"Nana sent my mother enough money to pay for a train ticket and the outstanding motel bill." Sighing, she finished, "My mother never got over him, nor did she ever resume her career."

"I'm sorry, sweetheart," he said, gently stroking her hair. "Did he divorce her?"

"A few years after we went back to L.A., she received a set of divorce papers in the mail with instructions to sign them and return them to an attorney in Las Vegas." Fee shrugged. "She voluntarily gave up everything for him and would have followed him to the ends of the earth if that was where he wanted to go. And he couldn't even be bothered to come back and tell her it was over." She shook her head. "Even though they divorced, she held out hope that he would come back one day. She died ten years ago, still waiting for that to happen."

"And you've been afraid all these years that if you fell in love you would turn out like her?" Chance guessed, his voice filled with understanding.

"I know it sounds foolish, but I didn't want to be dependent on a man for my happiness, nor was I willing to give up my only means of support," she answered, nodding. "I didn't want to be like my mother."

"That's something you never have to worry about, Fee," Chance said, capturing her gaze with his. "I would never ask you to give up anything for me or change anything about yourself. I love you for who you are—the intelligent, independent, beautiful woman that took my breath away the moment I laid eyes on her."

Staring into his brilliant green eyes, she knew that she never really had a choice in the matter. She loved this man with all of her heart and soul and had from the moment their eyes met at his sister's wedding.

"I love you, Chance Lassiter," she whispered. Tears flowed down her cheeks as she released the last traces of her fear and embraced the only man she would ever love.

"I love you, too, Fee," he said, crushing her to him. "But I still need an answer, sweetheart."

A joy she'd never known before filled her entire being. "If you'll ask the question again, I'll be more than happy to give you an answer."

Setting her on the couch, he got down on one knee

in front of her. His smile was filled with more love than she ever dreamed of. "Felicity Sinclair, will you do me the honor of becoming my wife?"

Another wave of tears spilled down her cheeks as she nodded and threw her arms around his shoulders. "Yes, yes, yes."

He took her into his arms then and gave her a kiss that left them both gasping for air. "About your career," he said, holding her close. "Do you want me to move to L.A. or would you like to live on the Big Blue ranch and telecommute?"

"Chance, I would never ask you to leave the Big Blue," she said, shaking her head. "That ranch is your life."

He shook his head. "Nope. You are." Touching her cheek, he added, "I love the Big Blue ranch, but I love you more. If living in L.A. is what you want, I'll adjust. My home is wherever you are, Fee."

"I don't want you to give up being a cowboy— my cowboy," she said, kissing him. "I'll move to the ranch and telecommute if that can be arranged." She paused. "If I even have a job with Lassiter."

"Why do you think you wouldn't?" he asked, frowning.

"I handed the Lassiter campaign over to one of my colleagues and told Evan McCain that I might be looking for employment elsewhere," she said hesitantly. "I even mailed the keys to the rental house and the car to the Lassiter Media office in Cheyenne, instead of returning them myself."

"That's not going to happen. You're not going to

lose your job," he said, shaking his head. "I won't be the spokesman unless you're in charge of the campaign."

"But it's all set up with another PR executive," she argued. "They probably won't let me take it back."

"Don't be so sure. I think we can make that happen, as well as setting it up for you to telecommute," he said, laughing. "You're forgetting that your future husband has a little bit of pull with your bosses."

"I suppose you do, don't you, Mr. Lassiter?" she said, laughing with him. "It will make it easier to do the family-image campaign if I'm on the job site." She paused. "You are still going to be my spokesman, aren't you?"

"I'm anything you want me to be, Fee," he promised. "Name it and I'll do it, sweetheart." His expression turned serious. "Now that we have that settled, I have one more question for you."

"What's that?" she asked.

"Don't take this wrong... It really doesn't matter, but I was just wondering... Do you know if you're pregnant?" he asked cautiously.

"I'm not sure," she said honestly. "I haven't taken a pregnancy test."

He nodded. "If you're not pregnant now, you will be eventually."

"You think so?" she asked, grinning.

"Sure thing, sweetheart. The man you're going to marry has been in a perpetual state of arousal since he met you." Chance gave her a sensual grin that sent heat flowing through her veins. "Just say the word and I'll be more than happy to give you all the babies you want."

"Did you hear what I said?" she asked, unable to stop smiling.

Clearly confused, he frowned. "You said you're not sure—that you hadn't taken a test."

Nodding, she kissed him soundly. "The key words in that are *not sure,* cowboy."

As understanding dawned, his grin got wider. "Do you know something I don't?"

"I'm almost a week late," she said, nodding. "Since I'm as regular as clockwork, I would say there's the possibility that the first of all those babies you promised me is on the way."

He wrapped her in a bear hug. "I guess we beat the odds, sweetheart."

"It appears that the remote possibility wasn't so remote after all," she said, hugging him back.

"God, I love you," he said, kissing her cheeks, her forehead and the tip of her nose.

"And I love you, cowboy. With all my heart."

* * * * *

TAMING THE
TAKEOVER TYCOON

BY
ROBYN GRADY

Robyn Grady was first contracted by Mills & Boon in 2006. Her books feature regularly on bestsellers lists and at award ceremonies, including the National Readers' Choice Awards, the Booksellers' Best Awards, CataRomance Reviewers' Choice Awards and Australia's prestigious Romantic Book of the Year.

Robyn lives on Australia's gorgeous Sunshine Coast, where she met and married her real-life hero. When she's not tapping out her next story, she enjoys the challenges of raising three very different daughters, going to the theater, reading on the beach and dreaming about bumping into Stephen King during a month-long Mediterranean cruise.

Robyn knows that writing romance is the best job on the planet and she loves to hear from her readers! You can keep up with news on her latest releases at www.robyngrady.com.

For Penny and Gracie,
Two very cool ladies.
xoxo

One

The Robin Hoods of this world were Becca's heroes. As she watched Jack Reed strike a noble pose then draw back and release an arrow that hit dead center of his target, the irony wasn't lost on her.

Jack Reed was no Robin Hood. He was anathema to everything she stood for. To every living, breathing thing she believed in. Beyond all else, people ought to give back— even sacrifice—to support others who need help. Some mistook that level of compassion for weakness, but Becca was far from easy prey.

Looking *GQ*-hot in jeans and a white button-down, cuffs folded back on strong forearms, Reed lowered the bow and focused on his guest. The slant of his mouth was so subtle and self-assured, Becca's palm itched to slap the smirk off his face. She might have done it, too, if she thought it'd shake him up some. But it was said displays of true emotion only amused him.

Jack Reed owned a property in his hometown of Chey-

enne, Wyoming, as well as two residences here in L.A.:
an ultramodern penthouse apartment in a downtown high-
rise building that he'd purchased as well as this spectacular
Beverly Hills estate. With a quiver slung across his broad
back, he sauntered over the manicured lawn to meet her.
Although he was expecting her visit, Becca doubted he
would welcome what she had to say.

She introduced herself. "Becca Stevens, director of the
Lassiter Charity Foundation." She nodded at the target. "A
perfect bull's-eye. Well done."

"I took up archery in college," he said in a voice so deep
and darkly honeyed, the tone was almost hypnotic. "I try
to squeeze some practice in every week."

"Difficult with your schedule, I imagine." All that dismantling of companies and banking the proceeds had to
take up oodles of time. "I appreciate you seeing me."

His smile, designed to disarm, got bigger. "Any friend
of J.D.'s is a friend of mine."

"If J. D. Lassiter were alive, he might not count *you* as
a friend at the moment."

The smile widened more. "Straight for the jugular, Ms.
Stevens?"

Given Jack Reed was a highly successful corporate
raider, he ought to be used to the approach. "I thought
you'd appreciate it."

"I only want to help Angelica Lassiter reclaim what she
rightly deserves."

Becca let out a humorless laugh and then sighed. "Ah,
sorry. Just the idea of someone like you being in any way
self-sacrificing…"

His gaze sharpened. "Angelica was J.D.'s only child."

"You're forgetting Sage and Dylan."

"They are Ellie Lassiter's orphaned nephews, adopted
after J.D. and Ellie had been told by doctors—"

"I know the background, Jack."

"Then you'll also know that Angelica, J.D.'s own flesh and blood, was his favorite—that he'd entrusted her with the running of Lassiter Media those crucial months before his death. It makes no sense that his will should insult her with a paltry ten percent while controlling voting interest of J.D.'s multibillion-dollar company goes to Angelica's ex-fiancé—" Jack paused for effect "—even if J.D. had handpicked Evan McCain for his daughter."

"J.D. might have liked Evan for a son-in-law. No one would argue he has remarkable business sense." Becca joined Jack as he headed off toward his target. "But Angelica trusted Evan. They fell in love."

"Betrayed by the man she was ready to marry. Tragic, wouldn't you say?"

Oh, please. "Evan had nothing to do with J.D.'s will."

"Maybe. Maybe not. But nothing stops him from re-instating to Angelica what should be hers now. He could do the decent thing by the woman he professes to love." Jack's lips twitched. "I don't know how he sleeps at night."

An image flashed into Becca's mind—Jack Reed lying butt naked on a rumpled sheet, fingers thatched behind his head, an unmistakable thirst reflecting in the depths of his glittering onyx eyes. Nerve endings ignited and flashed over her skin. The tingle raced through to her core, all the way down to her toes.

Reed was an attractive man; she would go so far as to say he was exceptional. If half of what the tabloids published was true, hoards of women had surrendered to the drugging heat she felt radiating off him now. The effect was gripping—beguiling—and, in Becca's case, about as welcome as boiling water on a third-degree burn.

As they continued to walk, she tried to stay focused.

"I'm here to implore you, in J.D.'s memory, to show some human decency. Walk away from this. After her father's death, Angelica's in no shape to link arms with the likes of you."

"Don't underestimate Angelica." His classically chiseled profile hardened as his chin lifted a notch. "She's stronger than you think."

"Right now, she's desperate."

He laughed, a somehow soothing and yet cynical sound. "You don't beat around the bush, do you, Becca?"

No time. "You own an interest in Lassiter Media and rumors are rife. People are bracing for a hostile takeover bid. The charity's donations are down. Regular beneficiaries are actually looking at other options. Want to guess why?"

"I'm sure you'll tell me."

Damn right she would. "The name Jack Reed means trouble—the kind of trouble clear-minded people run a mile to avoid."

He blinked slowly and grinned as if the description was something to savor. "As long as Angelica wants my help, I'll give it."

"You sought her out," she reminded him, "not the other way around."

"Your point?"

Her heart was pounding in her ears. No one wanted to make an enemy of this man, but Becca had a principle to defend. A fight to win. Hell, she'd faced worse situations than this and survived.

"I know what you're up to," she said as they neared the target, "even if Angelica can't or won't face the truth. After you've used her to gain majority control over Lassiter Media interests, you'll aim the next arrow at her back. You'll sell off Lassiter assets like you have with every other company you've acquired."

"Got it. I wear the black hat."

"Simple, isn't it?"

"If only."

Lord above, how she wanted to shake this man. "Seriously, how much money does one person need? Is this worth betraying your friend's memory? J.D.'s family?"

"This is not about money."

"With you, it's always about money."

His jaw flexed as he stopped in front of the target and freed the arrow.

"I understand your desire to help, but Angelica and I have this covered. And make no mistake." His uncompromising gaze pierced hers. "We intend to win."

Becca's focus shifted from the steely message in his eyes to the arrow's bright red feathers, the shaft's long straight line and finally the weapon's potentially lethal head. Then she thought of this man's lack of empathy— his obsession with self-enrichment. How could this superb body harbor such a depraved soul? How could Jack Reed live with himself?

Becca took the arrow from his hand, broke the shaft over a knee and, shaking inside, strode away.

Jack watched Becca Stevens's spectacular behind as she marched off in a fiery temper and had to smile.

When Becca had contacted his office hoping to meet, instinct had said to shake her off. If ever Jack set his sights on a target, he committed to that goal two hundred percent. No one and nothing would sway him. In certain circles, the term pathological was used to describe his drive.

No offense taken.

The same circles might suggest that his reasons for meeting Becca today had been selfish. That it was probable to very likely he would take advantage of his position in this Lassiter standoff for personal gain. And where Becca was concerned, Jack did mean personal.

As she disappeared over the rise, he smiled again.

What a woman.

His cell phone rang. Jack checked out the caller I.D. and, toeing Ms. Stevens's broken arrow aside, connected. "Logan. What've you got?"

"Just making sure we're still on track."

Coming from humble beginnings, Logan Whittaker had worked hard to build a successful career. As a partner at Drake, Alcott and Whittaker Attorneys based in downtown Cheyenne, Wyoming, Logan had looked after J. D. Lassiter's affairs, including the execution of J.D.'s last will and testament. The document had cast some challenges Logan's way. Some unanticipated rewards, as well. Through work associated with settling the will's terms, he had found his future wife.

"I've spoken with Angelica Lassiter again this morning," Jack said. "She's still going forward."

"You're sure about that? I've told Angelica more than once the will is airtight. J.D. was in his right mind when he drafted the terms. With majority voting interest, Evan McCain will remain chairman and CEO of Lassiter Media no matter how many punches she wants to throw. I thought she was finally coming around, listening to reason."

Jack headed back toward the shooting line. "Sure, she has reservations. Her father was a huge influence on her life. Even with him gone, it goes against the grain to disappoint him and battle that will. But her heart and soul are in that company, Logan. She has J.D.'s stubborn streak as well as his keen bent for business."

"How hard will you push her?"

"This isn't my first rodeo." When the attorney audibly exhaled, Jack wasn't fazed. "You're acting under strict instruction here."

"I'm aware of my obligations, damn it. This still leaves a god-awful taste in my mouth."

That all came with the territory…with being obligated, no matter what.

"No one said you had to like it," Jack said.

Logan huffed. "You're one hard-nosed son of a bitch, you know that?"

"That from a corporate lawyer." *Funny.*

As Jack reached back to draw an arrow from his quiver, Logan asked, "How did your meeting with Becca Stevens play out?"

Logan was aware of Becca's phone call and today's arrangements.

"She might run Lassiter Charity Foundation," Jack said, "but Becca is no Mother Teresa. She put on her boxing gloves and told me to back the hell away."

"Did you toss her off your property?"

Remembering the fire blazing in those beautiful green eyes, Jack held the phone between his ear and shoulder as he slotted the arrow's notch against his bow's string. "I would've asked her to stay for lunch if I thought she wouldn't try to run a butter knife through my heart."

"Will she be a problem?"

"Lord, I hope so."

Logan groaned. "For God's sakes, Jack. Tell me you plan to keep your pants on here."

"After the way you mixed Lassiter business up with pleasure, you're in no position to lecture."

When J.D. had bequeathed five million big ones to a mystery woman who didn't want to be found, Logan had not only tracked her down, damned if he hadn't taken her to bed, and more than once. Talk about calling the kettle black.

"I won't deny certain lines got blurred," Logan admitted. "But I fell in love with Hannah Armstrong and married her. I'll hand my resignation in to the bar the day anything approaching marriage enters your head."

Jack laughed. What an idea.

After the men disconnected, Jack resumed his stand behind the shooting line. He drew back the arrow and, enjoying the tension of the bowstring as he took aim, thought of Becca Stevens—the undisguised malice in her eyes, the sweeping conviction of her words. Then he imagined how darn good she would feel folded in his arms...how sweet her smooth, scented skin would taste beneath his lips. In his mind, Jack heard her whimper his name and then cry out as he sank into her again and again.

Jack released his shot and then shaded his brow to measure the result. When was the last time he'd missed a target's center gold ring? This arrow had sailed clean over the top.

Felicity Sinclair's blue eyes sparkled as she shifted her chair closer to the café table and lowered her voice. "Becca, I have something I need to ask."

"About Lassiter Media?"

As Lassiter Media's recently promoted vice president of public relations, Fee was always brimming with ideas. Since Becca's appointment with the Lassiter Charity Foundation two years ago, the women had worked closely. More than that—they'd become good friends, the kind who shared everything, during good times as well as bad.

Winding golden-blond hair behind a dainty ear, Fee explained, "My question has to do with Chance Lassiter."

"That would be your *fiancé* Chance Lassiter," Becca teased.

As Fee reached over to grip her friend's hand, the magnificent diamond on her third finger threw back light slanting in through the window.

"You were there when I needed to vent about that mess last month," she said. "I have to say, it feels a little strange calling Cheyenne home. I love L.A...."

"Well, you're here now. You'll simply have to visit often." Becca squeezed her hand. "Promise?"

"And you promise to drop in on us at the Big Blue."

"I'll bring my Stetson."

Chance Lassiter was J.D.'s nephew, the son of the billionaire's deceased younger brother, Charles. Chance had managed his uncle's world-famous cattle ranch—the Big Blue—and while he'd been rocked by J.D.'s unexpected death, he'd gladly accepted, via his uncle's will, controlling interest in the ranch he loved more than anything...although now, of course, his vivacious wife-to-be had taken pride of place in the charming cowboy's heart.

Fee sat back. "I can hardly wait for the wedding. Which brings me back to that question. Becca, would you be a bridesmaid?"

Emotion prickled behind Becca's eyes. Fee would make a *stunning* bride and, given her talent for organizing grand occasions, the ceremony was bound to be nothing short of amazing. Becca was even a little envious.

Marriage and starting a family were nowhere near a priority, but one day Becca hoped to find Mr. Right—a kindred spirit who got off on giving back and paying forward. This minute, however, all her energies were centered on helping the foundation survive the storm J.D.'s unexpected death and will had left behind.

Of course, there was *always* room for the wonderful women in her life and their very special requests.

Becca hugged her friend. "Fee, I would be honored to be a bridesmaid at your wedding."

The women discussed styles for dresses as well as flowers for bouquets before the conversation turned to a far less pleasant topic.

As coffees arrived, Fee asked, "Have you spoken with Jack Reed yet?"

Suddenly feeling queasy, Becca nodded. Fee knew that she had hoped to get in Jack's ear.

"The backyard of his Beverly Hills mansion houses an Olympic-standard archery field."

Fee's lip curled. "Your regular Robin Hood."

"The joke of the decade, right?" Becca pulled her decaf closer. "I let him know how his association with Angelica is weighing on Lassiter Media, not least of all the foundation. A lot of the funding comes from Lassiter accounts, but other benefactors are shutting doors in our face. While the notorious Jack Reed has a chance of pulling off a takeover bid and then tearing everything apart, we might as well have leprosy."

Fee flinched. "Jack does have a reputation."

Huge understatement. "He's the most ruthless corporate raider this country has given breath to. I hate to think of how quickly he'd chop up the company and sell off the pieces if he had a chance. He doesn't give a flying fig where or how the foundation ends up." Becca held her stomach when it churned again. "He's a scourge on mankind."

"You have to admit though…" Fee lifted her cup to her lips. "He is charismatic."

"If you can call a snake charismatic."

"And incredibly good-looking."

Becca huffed—and then gave it up. "Sure. The guy is hot, in a Jay Gatsby kind of way."

"Gatsby was gorgeous."

"Gatsby was a crook."

"Sweetie, let's face it. Jack Reed is *smoking*."

Becca's stomach pitched again. "I was taught that power should be used for good. If you have brains and position, for God's sake, help those less fortunate—even a *little* bit."

"Good luck convincing Jack Reed of that."

"Greed." Becca shuddered. "It's a disease." When the waitress delivered their coffees, she pointed to an item on the menu. "Can I have a caramel fudge brownie, please?"

As the waitress made a note and walked away, Fee studied her friend curiously. "Since when do you have a sweet tooth?"

"In school I was always the chubby kid who tried to get out of gym. If ever I felt anxious—upset—I'd reach for cake or candy."

Then she'd joined the Peace Corps and all that had changed. Her life had taken its sharpest turn yet.

Fee set her cup down. "Well, you're the poster girl for svelte now."

"That craving for sweet stuff doesn't win too often anymore. Don't worry," Becca said as the waitress delivered the brownie. "I'll fit into my bridesmaid's dress."

"I wouldn't care if you were a size two or a twenty." Fee had an awesome athletic build but she didn't judge any book by its cover. "I just hate to see you this rattled."

Becca bit into the brownie. As chocolate crumbs fell apart on her tongue, she almost sighed. She tried not to indulge; so many in this world did without. But, dear God, this was good.

"I believe in the foundation," she said, sucking caramel off a thumb. "I believe in the work it does. Do you know how much we've helped with homeless services, with youth camps, with disaster relief?"

When she slid over the plate to share, Fee broke off a corner of the brownie.

"Your team does an incredible job," Fee said and popped it in her mouth.

"And everyone on my staff wants to keep doing our job—raising funds, making a difference—one person and family at a time."

Fee's mouth twisted. "Unfortunately, it's not your company."

At the moment Lassiter Media was at the center of a tug-of-war primarily between Evan and Angelica, two people who ought to be working, and living, together, not pulling each other apart.

"J.D. couldn't have wanted this dissention within the family when he drew up his will."

"Given their connection," Fee added, "how hard she worked in the company the months before her father's death, I don't get how he left Angelica so little. It doesn't make sense."

Becca broke off more brownie and mulled as she chewed. "John Douglas Lassiter was a smart man," she reflected. "A good man with a big heart. The foundation was way more than a tax dodge to J.D. I *have* to believe he had a good reason for the way his will was arranged."

"He must have known Angelica would fight."

"Even her brothers are against her now." At first, Angelica's siblings had supported her attempts to find ways to challenge the will. No longer. "No one is left on her side."

"No one except Jack the Slasher Reed."

"For everyone's sakes, I hope she gives it up soon, before any more damage is done." To the family as well as the company, including the foundation.

"With Jack Reed egging her on, don't hold your breath."

An image formed in Becca's mind…Jack Reed with a quiver slung over his back. He looked so arrogant. So flat-out sexy and self-serving. Becca growled. "It all comes back to Jack."

"You're not finished with him, are you?"

"I can't give up." Becca pushed the plate aside. "I'm not made that way."

Fee sighed. "Problem is Jack Reed's not made that way, either."

Two

Jack waited until the end of the week and then buckled.

Dusting off a tux, he organized a ticket for the Lassiter Charity Foundation gala ball. By the time he'd finished at the office and then showered and drove over, he was unfashionably late. The keynote speaker had long since finished entertaining and educating the glittering crowd. Desserts had been served and suitable music wafted around the ballroom, coaxing couples onto a dance floor that sprawled beneath prisms of light cast by a spectacular Swarovski chandelier.

As he headed toward the VIP tables, Becca Stevens noticed him. Mild surprise registered on her face before she turned in her chair to gauge his approach. Loose, salon-tousled curls mantled her shoulders. Her ears and throat were free of jewels. Sitting proud and erect in a white strapless gown that accentuated her curves and teased the imagination, she gave an impression that lay somewhere between temptress and saint. When Jack stopped before her, she looked up at all six-plus feet of him and arched a brow.

"Did you notice?" she asked.

"That you look exquisite tonight?"

Her narrowing gaze sent a warning. *Don't flirt.*

"When you walked into the room," she explained, "people stopped talking. I think a lot stopped breathing. They don't expect to see you at a charity night. Although in this case they might—given it's a Lassiter Media event."

"Because I'm the big bad wolf here to gobble up everything I can sink my fangs into and then spit out the bones."

She shrugged a bare shoulder. "Not to put too fine of a point on it."

"Would it surprise you to know that I give to charity?"

"The Jack Reed Foundation for Chronic Self-Indulgence?"

He rubbed a corner of his grin. "You're cute, you know that?"

"Wait till I get started."

The only other couple left at the table was engrossed in a private conversation. If the room had indeed been distracted by his appearance, the socialites and Fortune 500 reps were back to mingling as far as Jack could tell.

He took the vacant seat next to Becca's. "When I donate, I do it anonymously."

Becca brought a glass of water to her lips. "How convenient."

"It's your job to blow this foundation's bugle. How much you give away, how much you help the disadvantaged. Publicity equals exposure, equals a greater chance of raising even more funds and getting the money to those who need it."

As the music swelled and lights dimmed more, he leaned closer and caught the scent of her perfume—a hin

of red apple, feminine. Way too sexy for her own good—
at least where he was concerned.

"But tell me," he went on, "if you had as much personal
wealth as I do, would you need to go around bleating to
everyone how generous you were?"

"I will never have that much personal wealth. Don't
want it. Don't need it. I'm nothing like you. Not in any
way, shape or form." When his gaze dropped to skim her
lips, she frowned slightly before pushing to her feet. "Don't
even think about going there."

No denying he was attracted to Becca Stevens. He had
wanted to tip closer, sample those lips, invite her to help
fuel the spark. If he wasn't mistaken—and Jack was rarely
wrong—there was a part of Becca that wanted that, too.

"Am I that obvious?" he asked, getting to his feet.

"You're ridiculously easy to read."

"In certain things."

"I'll give you a list. Tell me what I'm missing."

As waiters served coffee, Jack crossed his arms. "Go
ahead."

"You have an insatiable thirst for money. Correction.
For *power*. You like expensive toys. Jets and yachts and
prestige cars. You enjoy beautiful women hanging off your
arm, the more the merrier. Above all else, you love calling the shots. Being the king of your cancerous castle."

Jack frowned.

Ouch.

"I like being the boss," he said. "So do all CEOs. So
did J.D."

"You're missing my point. And, sorry, but you're not
in J.D.'s league."

"He might argue with you on that."

Her look was almost pitying. "Modesty is so not your
strong suit."

"Perhaps you'd care to find out what is."

"You know, for a smart guy, you just don't get it."

When she breezed out of the room, Jack followed her onto the terrace. He found her standing by a railing, facing a twinkling downtown view. A breeze caught a layer of her gown's skirt; gossamer-thin fabric billowed out, ruffling behind her like filmy wings.

As he headed over, she tossed him an annoyed glance before gripping the railing like she wanted to wring someone's neck. "You can't take a hint, can you?"

"Let's not play that kind of game," he drawled. "You wanted me to follow. You're just not sure how to handle things now that I have."

She faced him. "I'm passionate about my work at the foundation. More passionate than I've felt about anything before in my life, and that's saying something."

"It's how a person uses her passion that counts."

"How about for good rather than evil?"

Most people thought of Jack Reed that way. Evil incarnate. Difference was that Becca wasn't afraid to tell him point-blank.

Hell, she was right. Everyone was. If he could get his paws on Lassiter Media, if he could truly sink his teeth into a vein, he wouldn't let go until he'd drained it all. That was his profession. What he did best.

But with Becca Stevens looking at him as if malevolence might be contagious, for just a second Jack almost hoped he wouldn't get the chance. A part of him actually wanted to let this colossal Lassiter Media opportunity slide off into the water.

Of course, that wasn't possible. Wasn't—*sane*. Neither was continuing to annoy poor Ms. Stevens. It wasn't her fault she was caught up in this fight, any more than Jack could help the part he had to play.

"It's time my black cape and I flapped away before the

first hint of dawn turns us into dust." He affected a bow. "Good night, Becca."

She caught up with him at the entrance back into the ballroom, slotting herself between his chest and the door. Jack didn't know whether to smile and relax or frisk her for a wooden stake.

"What if I show you how serious I am?" she said. "I'll prove to you how much good this foundation does. Have you ever visited homeless shelters, soup kitchens? If you see firsthand, you'd have to understand. You can't be *that* big of a monster...can you?"

"You mean it's possible I might have human emotions after all?"

When she allowed a small smile, Jack grinned, too. "Give me a month," she said, "and I'll change your mind."

"Change my mind about what?"

"About dismantling Lassiter Media's assets."

Interesting. "You think Angelica and I can win?"

Becca lifted her chin. "Four weeks."

"One day."

"One week."

"On one condition."

"Name it."

What the hell. "I'd rather show you."

He slid a hand around her waist and drew her in as his mouth dropped over hers.

She went stiff against him. Hands balled into fists against his chest. He waited for her to tear away and call him every name under the sun. Short of her scratching his eyes out, Jack figured it was worth it.

Instead, her fists melted and palms slowly spread before her fingers knotted, winding into his jacket lapels. Then, making a strangled sound in her throat, she pressed in plumb against him. Jack relaxed into it, too.

As his palm on her back tugged her closer, his other

hand slipped beneath the curls at the warm base of her neck. Gradually her lips parted under his. Kneading her nape, he tilted his head at more of an angle at the same time the tip of his tongue slid by her teeth.

She stiffened again and this time broke away. Short of breath, eyes wild, she wiped her mouth on her arm. Then she called him a name Jack had been called more than once but never by a lady.

"What was *that* supposed to be?"

Jack ran a hand back through his hair. "You tell me."

She siphoned down air, half composed herself. "Fine," she said. "I will. That was a mistake. A big fat *never again*."

"Unless you decide you want to."

She stabbed a finger at his nose. "You repulse me."

"Do you want to hear my condition or not?"

Puzzled, she blinked twice. "Condition?"

"To give you one week to change my mind."

Her throat bobbed as she swallowed and pushed curls back from her brow. "Oh. Right."

"My condition is that we are civil toward each other."

She muttered, "Figures that would be your idea of civil."

It wasn't the time to mention that she had kissed him right back.

"Do we have an agreement?" Jack hesitated and then ribbed her anyway. "Or are you afraid you might find my dark charm irresistible?"

Her slim nostrils flared. "I'd sooner sell my soul to the devil."

"Be careful what you wish for." Jack pulled open the door and noise from the ballroom seeped out. "I'll collect you from your office Monday, ten a.m. sharp."

"I'll arrange my own transport. I'll meet you—"

"Uh-uh. I make the rules. The challenge for you now is to change the game."

"Using any means available?"

Jack smiled into her spirited green gaze. "What an appealing thought."

Three

Early Monday, as Jack finished up his first call of the working week, the vice president of Reed Incorporated crossed over to his desk. A financial dynamo with a killer background in trading, Sylvia Morse set her hands on her hips.

"What exactly are you doing?"

Sylvia had been standing inside his office door for the past few minutes, so, trick question?

"What do you mean what am I doing?" Jack asked.

"I want the lowdown. No B.S. Not to me. You just got off the phone from Angelica Lassiter—*again*. You've moved mountains to acquire every Lassiter Media share you can lay your hands on. You'd do anything to get a hold of hers."

Sylvia's brunette razor-cut looked somehow spikier today, and her normally light gray gaze was definitely darker. He almost asked whether her caffeine addiction had escalated to substances that caused memory loss or confusion, but then Jack remembered her brother was in rehab again and went with the direct approach instead.

He set down his pen. "What the hell is up with you this morning?"

"You're in bed with Angelica Lassiter," Sylvia went on, "to help her regain control of J.D.'s company."

"Metaphorically speaking, absolutely."

"And?"

"Sylvia, you've been my right hand here for five years. Nothing's changed."

"So, you intend to buy up, buy in and then put into play the most efficient, financially rewarding way to sell off the various pieces of Lassiter Media. Except that isn't Angelica Lassiter's plan."

Jack slumped. *Et tu, Sylvia?* "I thought our moral compasses were in sync."

"This is different."

"It's never different." He picked up the pen, put his head down. "Trust me."

"God knows I want to, but something's missing. Unless you're more ruthless than even I thought, and I know you pretty well."

"Better than anyone."

"I'm on your side, Jackie-boy. Always. But, while you'd never admit it publicly, even you must have limits. J. D. Lassiter was a friend. You'd call in on each other's homes in Cheyenne. I thought that kind of relationship would put a spin on things."

"You thought wrong."

"So, feelings never get in the way of business."

Jack got to his feet. "Feelings don't get in the way of anything. Period."

He moved to a nearby credenza. Last week, he'd been sorting through a spread of figures on a boat company he was keen to acquire. Easy money—or it would be in a few months after he'd taken over and maximized the various resources.

"I value your work," Jack told Sylvia, thumbing through the top pages of Baldwin Boats' annual financials. "I value *you*. But if ever you decide you want to, you know—move on—I'd only ever wish you well."

"Where in blazes would you ever find another me?"

Jack returned her mocking grin. "Wouldn't be easy." Then it clicked. "Oh, okay. Sure. I get what this is about."

Her face opened up. "You do?"

"You've been working day and night on the Lassiter deal. Crazy hours. Follows you want a bigger cut when the demolition ball starts swinging."

The intensity in her gaze deepened again before her expression eased and a crooked smile appeared. "Guess you are as big a hard-ass as they say." She crossed over, scanned a spreadsheet. "Baldwin Boats."

Pushing the prickly issue of Lassiter Media aside, Jack nodded. "I'm ready to move on it."

"I spoke with David Baldwin late Friday. He wants you to meet with him. He asked if you'd like a tour of the factory."

Jack had already seen the factory. Damn it, he knew all he needed to know.

He hung his head and winced. "I hate this part."

"You mean the part where a struggling businessman who's put his entire life into a company thinks there might be a chance of talking you into injecting some much-needed capital and becoming partners?"

"Yeah, Sylvia. That part. I've told him we'll put together a good offer. The best he'll get before his company is forced into bankruptcy. I'm not interested in having a beer with the boys out back."

David Baldwin had recently made an appointment to discuss his situation. His company, while not huge, had ongoing contracts and sizeable assets. Baldwin Boats was also in financial strife with no easy way out. Same story. Bad economy, rising costs and taxes. Jack had said he thought they could do business. *His* kind of business, not Baldwin's. On that, he'd been clear.

Baldwin made beautiful boats but Jack wasn't in the manufacturing trade. To his way of thinking, Baldwin could either come out of this with something via Reed Incorporated's offer, or he could walk away with nothing due to bankruptcy. Despite popular opinion, Jack wasn't completely heartless, even where Lassiter Media was concerned. He hoped David Baldwin grabbed the buoy he had tossed rather than clinging to blind hope and going under.

"Just let him know," Jack said, "that we'll have a firm offer to him by end of the month."

When Sylvia turned to leave, he called after her.

"Just a heads-up. Becca Stevens paid me a visit."

"The director of Lassiter Media's Charity Foundation, right?"

"She threw out a challenge. If I gave her some time, she would change my mind about going after the company."

"You're joking."

"She wants to show me where the money goes."

"And you said go jump."

"I gave her a week."

Sylvia's jaw dropped. It took her time to recover. "You schedule your days down to the minute."

"If I play my cards right, I might be able to glean some valuable inside information."

Sylvia was shaking her head. "I've run checks on everyone of any note at the company. Becca Stevens is former foster care and post-grad Peace Corps. She might look delectable on the outside but that woman is no cream puff. If you're planning to ensnare Becca with your charms, tread carefully. She's smart and she's tough and she'll do anything to win."

Jack ran a finger and thumb down his tie. "We should get on like two peas in a pod." Catching the time on his watch, he moved to grab his jacket. "I'm meeting with Joe Rivers to discuss the logistics on that opportunity in China, and then I'm off to meet Ms. Stevens."

"Off to *seduce* Ms. Stevens, you mean." Sylvia angled her head. "Unless she's a step ahead of you."

"How so?" He shrugged into his jacket.

"Maybe she plans to do the seducing."

"To work her way into my heart and save her foundation?"

"I'm not kidding. My information says she's extremely resourceful."

He winked and swung open the door for them both. "Lord, I hope so."

As Jack Reed's luxury black sedan swerved off Sunset and into the Lassiter Media Building's forecourt, Becca strode over and swung open the passenger-side door. She settled into the soft leather seat while, hands locked on the wheel, Jack assessed her quizzically.

At the gala ball, he'd caught her off guard. In a designer tuxedo he'd been born to wear, every aspect of his star quality had been amplified tenfold. The white slash of his smile had almost knocked Becca off her chair. By the time he'd stopped at the table, her heart was thudding in her throat, in her ears. She thought she'd hid his effect on her pretty well.

Until that kiss.

Their head-spinning, utterly unforgivable kiss.

Today Becca was prepared. Alert and armed and ready for anything.

"Nice ride," she said, buckling up. "Smells new." And

while she would never admit it out loud, Jack smelled good, too. Fresh and woodsy and one hundred percent male.

"I know when we agreed to do this I said *my rules,* but I didn't expect you to wait outside for me. I'd have come up to collect you."

"Time is money."

"Well, that's…considerate of you."

"I was talking about the foundation's time and money."

The uncertain look on his face cleared and his dark eyes gleamed as he grinned. "Of course you were."

When he flicked a questioning glance at her legs, Becca secretly quivered. The look wasn't meant to be intimate, but her body didn't seem to know the difference. Warmth washed through her veins, the same shot of heat that had made rubber bands of her ligaments when Jack had kissed her that night.

Becca's hands bunched in her lap.

Don't think about that now.

"Do you wear jeans to the office often?" he asked, steering onto the road.

"Depends what I have planned for the day."

She sounded cool and collected despite her nails digging into her palms. His nearest arm and thigh were too close. Even in the air-conditioning, his body heat was tangible, enough to make her upper lip and hairline sweat.

"Where are we headed?" he asked, changing up gears.

"A high school." Nodding at the stoplights, Becca set her mind to the task. "Next right here."

"A school, huh? Someone need a new gym?"

She studied his profile, the hawkish nose, that confident air. "You really have no idea, do you?"

"I thought that's what this week was about. Giving me a clue."

She planned to do a truckload more than that.

"How well do you remember your teenage years?"

she asked. "You'd have done well in sport. Football's my guess." He only smiled. "You got good grades, too, right? I bet you didn't have to try."

"Chemistry was tricky."

"But you knew what you liked. What resonated. And your parents could afford an Ivy League school."

"I worked hard when I got there."

"What kind of car did you drive?"

He named a luxury German make.

"Fresh off the assembly line?" she asked.

His laugh was warm and deep. "You think you can guilt me out, Becca?"

"I hope I can open your eyes."

He looked across at her again and this time when he took in her jeans, Becca sensed he was labeling her, slotting her into another compartment in his head. The very idea set her teeth on edge.

"You didn't come from money," he said.

He didn't need to know the whole story—or not at this early stage in the game.

"My parents own a bakery."

He threw her a surprised look and held it before concentrating again on the traffic.

"I'm one of four," she went on. "We kids were taught that we needed to take responsibility for others in society who were less fortunate. Giving back and being community-minded are the secret not only to a happy life but also a happier world. During my senior year, I volunteered at hospitals and nursing homes...."

Attention on the road, his gaze had gone glassy. Becca cleared her throat.

"Am I boring you, Jack?"

"You could never bore me." He rubbed his freshly shaven jaw, which still had the shadow of persistent stubble. "It's just that I've traveled a few miles since school."

She appealed to Jack Reed's ego. "I can't imagine how much you've learned since then. How much you could pass on."

"Is that what we're doing? You want me to give a talk to schoolkids about aiming for the stars?"

"A fair percentage of the kids we'll see today have battled depression and suicidal thoughts and some have even attempted to end their own lives."

From the way a pulse had suddenly begun to pop in his cheek, finally she had his attention.

She indicated a driveway. "In there."

The public secondary high school had around three thousand students, grades nine through twelve. Its multistory red-brick buildings, landscaped with soaring palm trees, had been used as filming locations for several movies and TV shows. After parking the car, they headed for an area by the front chain-link fence where a mass of students had gathered. The kids were cheering as a stream of riders on bicycles flew past in a blur of Lycra color and spinning wheels. A couple of students waved a big sign: *Ride for U.S.*

"Do you ride a bike, Jack?" Becca asked over the hoots and applause from the excited mob jostling around them.

"Not one with pedals. Not for a while."

"These people are riding from coast to coast to bring awareness and help to teenagers who can't see a light at the end of their tunnel. Whose parents might be alcoholics, prostitutes, drug addicts or dealers. A lot of those kids bring themselves up. They might be taught to fetch drugs or another bottle of booze from the cabinet."

As the last of the bikes shot past, Jack gazed on, looking strangely indifferent. Detached.

She tried again. "The Lassiter Foundation donates to this cause every year, and we help decide where and how funds raised ought to be spent."

He took out a pair of shades from his inside breast pocket and perched them on his nose. "A big job."

"Not compared to the effort this bunch puts in."

Some students were fooling around with a football. When a toss went off track, Jack reached and effortlessly caught the ball before hurling it back to the boys. Then, impassive again, he straightened his shades.

"You don't have any children?" she asked.

"I'm not married."

"The two don't necessarily go hand in hand."

"No children."

"That you know of."

He exhaled. "Right."

The crowd started to head back into the building. "How freaky would it be to find out that you'd fathered a child say twenty years ago when you were cruising around in that gleaming new Beamer, acing your assignments, planning out your future with waves of twenty-four-carat-gold glitter."

"I might have a reputation, but I've always been responsible where sex is concerned."

"Right there we have a difference in understanding. How can a big-time player be responsible where sex in concerned?"

His smile was thin. "Takes practice."

"We're getting off topic. Point is that from day one you led a privileged life. Most kids aren't that lucky. Most children could use a hand on their way to reaching adulthood."

Inside the gymnasium, she and Jack sat to one side at the back in the bleachers while the leader of Ride for U.S. addressed the students. Tom Layton was a professional counselor Becca knew through various channels. He had incredible insight into the minds of young adults, a gift he used to full advantage. As he spoke to the audience,

Tom and Becca made eye contact. Tom winked to say hi but didn't miss a beat.

"Good, isn't he?" she whispered across to Jack. "Everything seems so *life or death* to teens. Tom gets that. A child needs all his strength going forward because the real test is later in life when he has to follow his own star, when he needs to develop a thick skin toward those who might want to trash his dream, for whatever reason."

Minus the sunglasses now, Jack trained his hooded gaze on her. "Would it surprise you to learn that you and I aren't so different, Becca?"

"It would surprise the living hell out of me."

His eyebrows drew together and damned if she didn't sense something real shift in Jack Reed. Not compassion or empathy exactly. That would have been too much to ask. It was more of a fleeting *connection* that fell through her fingertips, like loose grains of sand, before she could truly grasp it.

While Tom listed signs that everyone should watch for when identifying a peer who needed help, Becca scanned the audience. The geeks up front were all ears, some even taking notes. The lot in the middle alternated between sneaking looks at smartphones and zoning out, daydreaming about extracurricular activities. The mob in the back—the ones who really needed to listen—were restless. It was difficult to see a bright future when home life sucked everything into a vortex of gray. She and Tom wanted to help change that.

Thirty minutes later, as the principal thanked his guests and a round of applause went up, Jack immediately stood to stretch his spine. Becca looked up the entire length of him. God, he was tall.

"Still awake?" she asked, standing, too.

"Sure." He stretched again. "Coffee would be good though."

As they headed down the bleacher aisle, she helped bring the bigger picture into focus.

"The foundation works with school counselors across the country to get help to students who are under imminent threat. Who need our help now. This minute. We put on camps where they can talk about their problems in a safe and encouraging environment. Where they can share everything with others they identify with. It's important these kids know they're not alone."

At the bottom on the bleachers, Jack held up a hand. "Excuse me a moment? I need to make a call."

Okay. She'd drowned him with information, trying to make every second count. Now she needed to ease her foot off the pedal. Mix it up a bit.

"No problem," she said. "Go ahead. I'll wait here."

Jack drew out his cell and thumbed in a number as he strolled across the floor. By the time he'd disconnected, he'd wound back and was approaching a group who included Tom Layton. When the two men shook hands and spoke, Becca debated whether or not to join them. But they only talked for a moment before Tom sent a friendly wave her way and let Jack go. As Jack drew closer, she couldn't hide her smile.

"That was nice," she said.

"Sure. Nice guy." Jack rested his hand on her arm and eyed the exit. "Let's go."

Logic told Becca to remove herself from his touch. This wasn't a date.

Then again, giving her a guiding hand wasn't exactly an inappropriate gesture, either. If she wanted the chance to push her case going forward, she had to choose her battles. Jack had accepted her challenge, but he could walk away at any time.

And, secretly…

A part of her liked the contact. Crazy, dangerous, stupid. Still, there it was.

As he led her toward the gym doors, Becca made a suggestion.

"We could go back to the office for that coffee. My barista skills are renowned in that building."

"You're not afraid of being hit by a grenade," he said, "or ambushed by gunfire? That's why you waited outside this morning, isn't it? You wanted to keep this arrangement and the questions as quiet as possible."

Her step almost faltered. "I told you why I met you downstairs."

"You're not worried some people might think you're getting too friendly with the foe?"

"If I was worried about my reputation, I wouldn't invite you back, now, would I?" Sliding her arm away from his, she turned his assumption on its head. "Maybe it's you who's afraid to front up at Lassiter Media."

His slanted grin oozed sex appeal. "Yeah," he said. "That must be it."

As they entered the parking lot, Becca took stock. She'd decided to ease back on the info dump, and she'd got rattled at the idea of her loyalties ever being questioned, but she still needed to keep the dialogue open and evolving. She had to keep Jack close. *So, big breath and moving on.*

"Now that's settled," she said, walking alongside of him, "are we on for coffee?"

"If Danishes are involved."

"You're a fan?"

"Can you spell cheese, blueberry, apple toffee?"

Suddenly Becca could taste all her favorites. "How about cinnamon or custard?"

"Now you're talking."

"With my family owning a bakery, there was lots of cake growing up. *Too* much."

He gave her an odd look and then smiled. "You can never have too much cake."

Becca could have argued. She also wanted to know what that strange look was about. Instead she smiled as he opened the car door for her. If she let him in a little more, maybe he would open up to her, too. And then surely light and a sprinkling of goodness would fall among the shadows. Even where blackhearted Jack Reed was concerned.

Jack parked in a space outside of the Lassiter Media Building. After switching off the ignition, he lifted his chin to loosen his tie. He was serious about needing a coffee—extra strong. At each turn this morning, he'd been taken off guard.

Firstly, he was sure Sylvia had said that Becca had been a foster kid. Was she lying about the bakery? Something hinky was going on there.

Second, he, too, was a benefactor of Ride for U.S. When Tom Layton had spotted him and Becca in the bleachers together, Jack had seen speculation flare in the younger man's eyes. It wasn't a reach to think Tom had wondered whether he and Becca had partnered up in some charity-minded capacity. So, before Tom had the chance to wander over and all kinds of questions were asked, Jack had made an excuse and had "bumped" into him. Then, on the quiet, he'd let Tom know nothing had changed. *No one* needed to know who Reed Incorporated gave to, when, how or particularly why—unless it was the taxman.

If Becca wanted to stand behind general consensus and believe his character was a step away from sludge, Jack was used to being pegged as a villain. Hell, wearing that label where Becca was concerned was probably best. When the Lassiter deal went his way and the ax began to fall all around her, she might be hurt but at least she wouldn't be surprised.

On the upside, he had heard everything she'd said about problems facing young adults. Depression, self-harm, suicide…he wished he could wave a wand and all the damage—past, present and future—would be fixed.

Becca got out of the car before Jack had a chance to swing around and open her door.

"Will we personally choose our Danishes?" she asked over the roof of the car. "Or should we have them delivered?"

On the way back from the school, she'd mentioned a good bakery near the office.

"We'll go have a look," he said.

"Cheese, blueberry and apple toffee, right?"

Slipping on sunglasses, he met her at the trunk. "And cinnamon and custard."

She laughed, an effervescent, sexy sound that suited her far better than a scowl. "Just how much can you eat? Or am I buying for the whole office?"

"I'm buying," he said. "Might as well throw in a couple of chocolate chip muffins while we're at it."

"Now that's getting dangerous." They headed off toward the mall via the building's entrance. "And it's *my* treat. No argument. You're my guest." She playfully eyed him up and down. "A guest with a very big appetite."

"And growing by the minute."

Her smile changed in a knowing, measured way at the same time her gaze flicked to his mouth. Every one of Jack's extremities began to tingle.

Maybe she's the one doing the seducing.

Earlier, he had scoffed at Sylvia's suggestion, but the idea of Becca Stevens as calculating seductress out to save the world wasn't so far-fetched. Would she think that flirting, or even sleeping with him, might gain her information…curry favor…change his mind? After the kiss they had shared, he knew her hormones wouldn't object even if her conscience did.

Out of the corner of his eye, Jack saw a woman emerge from the building's main entrance. The slender build, dark brown hair and matching eyes were unmistakable. Angelica Lassiter was so absorbed in her thoughts, she almost ran into them without noticing. Recognizing Jack first, she sagged and let out a ragged sigh.

"Thank God. How did you know I'd be here?" she asked. Then she saw Becca.

Angelica was strong-willed, like her dad. But right now, with those dark-brown eyes wide and questioning, she looked as if she was teetering on an edge.

Jack spoke to Becca first. "Can we do this later?"

She said, "Of course," before offering Angelica an awkward goodbye. As Becca moved inside the building, Jack looped his arm through Angelica's.

"C'mon. Let's walk."

Four

"What are you doing with Becca Stevens?" Angelica asked as Jack ushered her away from the Lassiter Media Building and down the busy boulevard sidewalk.

"Becca's worried about the foundation's future," he said.

Angelica nodded deeply. "She does a brilliant job there. Her heart is totally in the right place. But, Jack, don't think for a minute she's on our side. She doesn't like you. Given our association, I'm sure she doesn't like me much at the moment, either."

Angelica could easily have grown up a spoiled pain. She'd come along later in Ellie Lassiter's life, after J.D. and his wife had been warned against ever trying to conceive. Ellie had died just days after giving birth to a healthy baby girl. Elevated blood pressure had brought on a stroke.

Years earlier, Ellie and J.D. had adopted her orphaned nephews, Sage and Dylan. After Ellie's death, J.D. and the boys had showered all their love and attention on Angelica, who had developed into a remarkably caring, career-minded woman.

It was no secret that J.D. had been grooming his daughter to take over Lassiter Media. When J.D. had died suddenly from a massive coronary, everyone was shocked to hear his final wishes at the will's reading. But, one by one, all had accepted the inexplicable terms. All except Angelica and, of course, Jack.

"Yep, Becca supports Evan."

"And if you want her to switch camps," Angelica went on, "you're wasting your time. When that woman makes up her mind about something, there's no changing it. And frankly, Jack, I don't see any point in trying."

"You've got it mixed up. Becca came to me. She wants me to see where the foundation's money goes. All the good it does."

He thought better of admitting he was hoping to pick up some Lassiter intel along the way. He wouldn't add to the tally of his baser tactics where Angelica's opinion of him was concerned.

She was mulling over his words. "Becca wants to inspire you enough that you'll back off from any takeover bid, and all the bad publicity and doubt plaguing the foundation will disappear along with you."

She stopped and sat heavily down on a vacant bench at a bus stop.

"I *hate* that the company is suffering," she said. "I hate that my family can barely look at me anymore." She exhaled a shaky breath as he sat alongside of her. "It's getting to me, Jack. Grinding me down until my head feels like it might explode."

"Trust me," he said. "We're in a good place with this."

"I rang Dylan this morning, a sisterly call to see how he and Jenna are doing."

Dylan had got involved with Jenna Montgomery, a flo-

rist in Cheyenne. Jack had heard that the couple had weathered some severe relationship storms before recently tying
the knot.

"Of course, the conversation swung onto the will,"
Angelica went on. "I got so stirred up, I could have hit
something. Out of everyone, I never thought Dylan would
turn against me. We were so close when we were young.
I thought we still were."

After high school, Dylan had set sail to see the world.
Odd jobs in restaurants had grown into head chef opportunities in premiere establishments. Five years ago, J.D.
asked him to head the Lassiter Grill Group with restaurants in L.A., Vegas, Chicago and now their hometown,
Cheyenne. He'd inherited complete control of the restaurant business when J.D. died.

"Dylan told me again," Angelica said, "that I needed to
accept Dad's wishes. That I should bury the hatchet and
get on with my life." Staring into the noisy downtown traffic, she bit her lip and shook her head. "I needed to talk
to Evan. Thrash it out. Know what he said? Evan said I
should settle down. Sitting in *my* chair, in *my* office. Can
you believe it?"

As a tear rolled down her cheek, Jack fished out a
pressed handkerchief from his inside breast pocket.

Gritting her teeth, Angelica dabbed her face. "I can't
get my mind around the fact that Evan somehow conspired
with my father to do this. Or maybe Evan somehow conspired against us both."

Jack wanted to put his arm around her. Squeeze her
hand. But Angelica didn't need sympathy. She needed
firm direction. He sat forward, elbows on thighs, fingers
thatched between knees.

"Evan's right," he said.

As the 302 bus growled by, she shot Jack a glance. "Excuse me?"

"You do need to settle down. Then you need to refocus and never let that target out of your sights. You can't afford to let emotion get in the way."

"Just sometimes, Jack…sometimes I wonder whether we're doing the right thing. Whether it's worth it."

"You wonder whether you ought to give up your inheritance because Sage and Dylan don't approve?" Pulling out all the stops, Jack turned toward her. "Sage was never close to J.D. He's a billionaire in his own right, for God's sakes, and yet he got twenty-five percent of Lassiter Media in the will. And Dylan? Why, he's happy as a pig in mud since he's snagged controlling interest of the Lassiter Grill Group. Then there's you. J.D.'s only child through blood. His little princess. Tell me how the hell it works when you get a lousy ten percent and the man you trusted enough to want to marry walks away with controlling voting interest of *your* father's company." Jack sneered. "I don't give a rat's furry behind whether or not Sage or Dylan or anyone else approves of your attempt to get what's rightfully yours."

Angelica's shoulders squared slightly and she blinked several times as if her eyes might be stinging.

"I miss Dad so much," she said. "I wish I could talk to him now. Let him make sense of it all. I'm torn between wanting to fold and being outraged that he could embarrass and hurt me like this. I worked my rear end off for that company. It was all I thought, ate. *Slept*." She swallowed back emotion and brushed away another tear. "I'm just so tired of it all."

Jack almost groaned aloud. He'd valued J.D.'s friendship, but if he'd been alive and standing in front of him now, Jack would have plowed him in the jaw, what Jack stood to make out of this deal be damned.

Angelica dabbed her cheek again. "I'm a wimp."

"Hey, would I team up with a wimp?"

When he bumped her shoulder, she almost grinned.

"Sylvia and I are working nonstop," he said, "finding ways to boost our position in the company's shares. It won't be long now. We're almost there. Okay?"

A genuine smile flickered at the corners of her mouth before her gaze narrowed, searching his.

"In the past, you've only ever wanted to tear down and sell off companies you'd acquired. Why is Lassiter Media any different?"

"You really need to ask?"

"Everyone's asking."

"J.D. was a close friend. I've known you since you were a skinny kid with braids. I'm doing precisely, to a *T*, what your father would want me to do."

"Except it goes against his final wishes."

"That can't have been his intent. Search your heart and tell me you don't agree."

Her gaze narrowed again.

"You would never betray me, would you, Jack?"

As a shiver ran up his spine, Jack looked her dead in the eye. "No, Angelica," he said. "I would never betray you."

Jack followed Angelica back to the Lassiter family mansion, which sat on two acres of Beverly Hills north of Sunset. J.D. had bought the Spanish Colonial revival twenty years ago when he'd created the L.A. office. Built in the 1930s, the mansion retained its original wrought-iron detail, leaded glass and homemade Spanish tiles. In recent years, however, Angelica had contributed much in the way of decorating its 11,000 feet of luxury living space. It had been more her home than J.D.'s.

When Jack and Angelica began to go over some figures and she asked him to stay for lunch, of course, he accepted. He even helped her prepare enough egg salad sandwiches to feed ten. Then they sat and ate in the lanai, taking in the sparkling pool and the flawless blue sky of late summer. By the time they had talked through everything and Angelica felt positive again about going forward, the sun was arcing toward the west.

As she accompanied Jack through the living room with its soaring ceiling to the front entrance, for the hundredth time he considered the part he was playing in this unfolding drama. Complex and uncomfortable, even for him. Still, as he had said to Angelica earlier, they need only keep their eyes on the target.

"I shouldn't have kept you this long." Angelica looked weary, resting her cheek against the opened door edge as Jack stepped onto the extravagant porch.

"I'm here anytime you need me."

"Becca Stevens must be wondering where you got to."

"She probably welcomed the break."

"I doubt that."

When Angelica sent him a fond smile, Jack held her shoulder. "You'll be okay."

"You were always a good friend to my father…to me. I don't know what I'd do without you."

"You'll never have to worry about that."

There was a spring in Jack's step as he crossed to his car. He had helped Angelica—or *not* helped, depending on which team a person rooted for. On top of that, even after having his fill of egg salad, Jack was still fanging for those Danishes.

Steering out onto the main road, he put through a call to the Lassiter Foundation and gave his name. He was transferred to Becca's assistant.

"Sorry, Mr. Reed. Ms. Stevens left for the day."

Jack checked the dash clock. A little after four. "She's gone home?" he asked.

"I couldn't say."

He reverse head-butted the seat. *Damn.*

"Do you have her private number?"

"Sorry, sir. I can't give that out."

Jack knew he could get it easily enough. Not the point. Nothing was more important to Becca than saving her foundation, which translated into putting all her efforts into trying to talk him around. Surely her nose wasn't put out because Angelica had needed him earlier.

So, what had come up that was so urgent? Was Becca playing hard to get? He wasn't that desperate for Danish.

When his cell rang a minute later, he connected without checking the ID.

It wasn't Becca.

"Hey, Jack. David Baldwin here."

Jack flinched but put a smile in his voice. "Hey. How's it going, David?"

"Call me Dave. Have you got a few minutes? I'd like to show you something."

"Sylvia already mentioned another factory tour."

"She let me know. You've seen enough there."

"And you'll have an offer by end of the month." Silence echoed down the line. "Dave, you there?"

"I wanted to speak with you about a personal matter."

Damn it. He should've checked that caller ID. "I'm not sure I can help with any personal issues."

"Actually it's about me helping you."

"I'm tied up at the moment, but sit tight and we'll get that offer—"

"This is about family, Jack. It's about…a journey."

Jack had heard it all before in a hundred different ways from just as many different people. The times they had spoken, David Baldwin had come across as a good guy who'd worked hard and considered his employees to be just that…family. Now, he wanted Jack to get involved, drag his financial butt out of the fire and save his business. Save the day.

And, hey, there was something about David Baldwin that gave Jack pause. Something in the deep brown of his eyes that made him care. But this association could end only one way and that was not with the two of them sharing Christmas dinners.

"I'll be in touch soon," Jack said. "Another call's coming through. Take care."

He disconnected. A single beat later, pain ripped through his chest—a stab followed by one almighty twist. Stopping at lights, he winced, massaging the spot.

Not heartburn or, God forbid, a heart attack. Just this Lassiter issue getting to him. The Baldwin business, too. If David wanted to save his family, best of luck. Jack couldn't help.

And, while she might never accept it—while she would want to see his head on a spike when this was done—Jack couldn't help Becca Stevens, either.

The next morning, Jack's cell phone woke him.

Rubbing his eyes, Jack grabbed it, checked the caller ID—lesson learned—and connected.

"Jack?" Becca sounded puzzled. "Did I wake you?"

He sat up, ran a hand through his hair. The bedside clock read eight-oh-five. *Holy crap.* He always had trouble getting to sleep, but what the hell time had he finally nodded off last night?

"I thought I'd call early," she went on. "I have a plan."

Jack smothered a yawn. "I like plans."

"Can I come over and tell you about it?"

"I thought you might have been, well…"

"Pissed at you after ditching me yesterday? I understand your situation with Angelica. She feels backed into a corner."

"The only way out is to fight."

"Or to accept. Even forgive."

He swung his feet over and onto the floor. "Ultimately, that's up to her."

"It'd help if you stopped pushing her."

Jack grinned. "I thought you said you understood."

He heard her sigh. At least she didn't argue.

"What time can I come over?" she asked.

She certainly was eager. "Why not the office?"

"It'd save time."

He couldn't argue with that. "I'll just jump in the shower."

It was on the tip of his tongue to suggest that he'd wait for her. *Bad Jack.*

"See you in thirty then," she said.

Naked, he crossed to the bathroom. "I'll be here." *With bells on.*

Jack answered his booming doorbell wearing tatty jeans that hung low on his hips. He hadn't bothered to put on a shirt. When he lifted an arm to lean against the jamb and his epic six-pack firmed up even more, Becca could have drooled.

Look into his eyes. Not the big, bronzed chest or that strip of skin south of his navel, damn it. Look at his eyes.

"Morning," he said. "You're late."

A lousy ten minutes. And she wouldn't give him the satisfaction of asking where the rest of his clothes were, either. Even his feet were bare; who knew toes could be sexy?

The other time she had visited, an older man with an impeccable air had seen her through to the back lawn. "I thought the butler would answer the door," she said.

"Merv's not a butler." His arm slid down as he stepped back to allow her inside. "He looks after things for me on the home front. It's his day off."

"Did you grow up having a person like Merv around

to mix your chocolate milk?" she asked, stepping into the double-story, marble-decked foyer that smelled of money.

"I did."

"Must be nice."

He laughed. "Still trying to guilt me out?"

"Just saying…"

"Merv does a great job. In return he is paid extremely well."

She pinned up a smile. "Then everyone's happy."

Jack must have been six-two or -three. In peep-toe flats that matched her simple white summer dress, Becca felt way less than her average height. When his scent filled her lungs, she fought the absurd urge to wither against him…even drag her lips all over those pecs. His chest was that good.

Before he shut the door, he did a double-take at her ride parked in the forecourt. "Tell me that's not a company car."

"My '63 Fiat Bambino is what's known as a true classic."

He squinted, looking harder—admiring the distinctive light mint-green shade, perhaps. "Are those dinky wheels even roadworthy?"

"I'm pretty sure it'll get us where we need to go."

He gave her a doubtful look. "*Pretty* sure."

"Are you ready?"

He shut the door and set his hands on the band of his jeans. She fought the urge to fan herself. She'd seen that body before, on a billboard advertising men's underwear.

"Ready to go where?" he asked.

"First of all," she pointed out, "you'll need clothes." *Or I'll go insane.* "Three to four changes."

"Sounds interesting."

"Oh, it will be."

With anticipation gleaming in his eyes, he nudged his

chin toward the stairs. "Come up while I pack. I might need further instruction."

As he headed off, Becca hesitated. But it wasn't as if he planned to throw her down on his bed and manacle her wrists to the posts. He wasn't that depraved. At least, she didn't think he was.

Steeling herself, she jogged up the stairs behind him.

"You didn't say where you're taking me," he said over one beautiful broad shoulder.

"On an adventure." *A journey.*

"Should I let anyone know?"

"Anyone, as in Angelica Lassiter?"

"She needs my support, now more than ever."

Becca's stomach pitched and she groaned. "God, I feel for her. I really do."

"But not enough to side with her."

"You know the answer to that."

At the top of the stairs, he turned left down a wide corridor. Examining the mouthwatering way his muscled back tapered to the incredible seat of those jeans, she kept close.

"Here's an idea," he said. "While you're trying to convince me to step back from a takeover, I could try to convince you to come join the dark side."

Join Jack Reed? *Ha!*

"I'm not the least drawn to the dark side."

He waited for her to catch up before continuing. "Not even a little bit?"

"Not even the teensiest baby thimbleful."

"Nothing in this world is simply black or white, you know."

She refrained from rolling her eyes. "Just pack, Jack."

They crossed a double threshold into a massive private suite. In this separate sitting room, blue brocade couches offered luxurious seating. Shelves filled with tomes lined an entire wall. An uneven pile of books lay stacked on an otherwise tidy desk. The room smelled of sandalwood. Masculine, soothing and unsurprisingly arousing.

Jack moved into an adjoining suite—the master bedroom. Becca took a calming breath and stayed precisely where she was.

"Will I need a dinner suit?" he called out while she ran a fingertip over book spines. Business, philosophy, a number of classics. One entitled *The Witchery of Archery*.

"No suit," she called back. "It'll be easy living all the way."

She moved to check out what was hung inside a large glass casing on a neighboring wall. "This bow looks like it belongs in a museum," she said loud enough for him to hear.

His deep disconnected voice filtered out from the bedroom. "It's thousands of years old, found preserved in ice in Norwegian mountains. The bow is made of elm. The arrow tip's slate. I won't say what I had to do to get hold of it."

She felt her eyes bulge. *Wow.* "This really does belong in a museum."

"I've had offers."

She took in the authentic Persian rug a few feet away. "Don't need the money, right?"

"It's not about money."

"It never is," she muttered, "when you eat caviar five days a week."

He went on, "It's about pride. It's about passion. A person should never give those away."

Passion… Becca peered out the window over his home archery field.

"So, have you ever split an arrow down the middle?" she asked, strolling over toward the view. "You know, like in the movies."

"That's a one-in-ten-thousand shot."

"So, that would be no?" she teased.

"I'm pretty good with apples though."

"On heads?"

"Just call me William Tell."

"I was thinking more Robin Hood, in reverse. Robbing from the poor to give to the rich."

"What about the theory that Robin Hood was nothing more than an outlaw?"

"In that case, I have the bases covered."

He emerged from the bedroom looking edible in a black polo shirt and tailored dark pants. Overnighter in hand, a wry smile on his face, he sauntered over.

"So now I'm a thief?"

"There is that theory," she said, "yeah."

As he lowered the case to the floor, his face came closer until the tip of his nose very nearly met hers. A tingling wave washed through her before settling in her chest.

"You're not worried that while we're away I might steal another kiss?" he asked close enough for his breath to brush her mouth.

Her suddenly sensitive nipples pushed against the lace cups of her bra. But now that she knew what to expect— knew just how to play this—it was within her power to resist.

She crossed her arms. "Like I said. Zip chance of defecting to the dark side."

While they were away, Becca planned to remind herself of that every minute of every day.

Five

Becca steered her Bambino north up Highway 1, tawny-colored hills on one side, awesome ocean bluffs and beaches on the other. With the windows rolled down, breathing in sweet oleander-scented air, she suggested that they play "Did you know?"

"Did you know," she began, "that there are no deaf birds or fish?"

Jack's dark hair ruffled around the sunglasses parked on his head. "I did *not* know that," he said, sounding suitably impressed.

"Did you know that one in every three hundred and fifty babies born have permanent hearing problems? Until twenty years ago, most children born with hearing problems weren't detected until they were two to three years of age. Now ninety-five percent of newborns are screened."

"That's good to hear." His grin was kick-ass sexy. "No pun intended."

After steering through a stomach-dropping curve, she

flicked over another look. Elbow hitched on the window ledge, foot tapping to 104 on the radio dial, Jack looked relaxed. Becca was stoked that he'd gone for this road trip idea even if it was simply because he needed the break from his desk. Of course, she knew Jack hadn't got to the top of his game by slacking off. No doubt he hoped this trip would be in some way beneficial, either by garnering information from her that might help advance his and Angelica's takeover plans, or by believing that he might actually pull off taking her to bed.

If she'd shared this smoldering chemistry with any other man, Becca might well have acquiesced. All kinds of sparks zapped around the room whenever she and Jack were together. But this week was not about romance. Definitely not about sex. It was about persuading a ruthless rich man not to add Lassiter Media to his wall of trophies. Becca wanted to reach Jack Reed's more human and merciful side. She wanted to help him accept that true pride came with peace of mind and compassion, not suffocating wealth and majority indifference.

Jack needed to find himself, and she was going to help shine the light. She'd started by planting him in the audience at a high school, making him a part of the swirl and the thrust. This morning she would introduce him to another foundation-funded scheme, as well as a person who had returned from the brink of despair to get her life back.

Later, Becca aimed to completely remove Jack from his cutthroat corporate element. She wanted to strip his defenses bare, make him forget who he was while nurturing his higher self. She had to believe there was some part of Jack Reed who would connect with the joys and importance of simple things, and also recognize that others less fortunate needed help to achieve even that connection.

She was excited about the little friend she had lined up for that part of their journey. Becca's friend, the owner of a gorgeous little dog, had come up with the idea. Chichi's antics could soften the hardest of hearts.

"Auditory areas of the brain," Becca went on now, "are most active not only when a child listens but also when he reads. Isn't that amazing?"

"How's your foundation involved?"

"It isn't *my* foundation. Not really."

"But the dream is to head your own charity someday?"

"If I did, it'd help all kinds of causes, like Lassiter's foundation does. I couldn't choose just one."

"If you had to?"

Concentrating on the snaking road, Becca ran through worthy causes in her mind.

"I'd want to give hope to homeless kids," she finally said. "I spent time in foster care." She pulled up in her seat and then took another sweeping turn. "I lucked out with my last family."

"The one with the bakery."

Ah... The smell of freshly baked bread and cinnamon-apple fritters in the morning. By then, she had felt transported to heaven.

"It was the first time and place I remember ever feeling truly safe. And loved." Such a beautiful, warm, *vital* feeling. "I was eleven, the age when a kid starts to mature, to change...when we question everything three times over and still have more to ask. But my parents seemed to have all the answers."

"How'd they manage that?"

"With patience and kindness. Plenty of communication. Talking. But mainly listening."

"Which brings us back to *did you know*."

She smiled. *Right*. "Did you know that the foundation is helping fund clinical trials of auditory brainstem implants in children?"

"You're really into kids."

"We all started out as one."

When he didn't reply, she glanced across again. He was studying the ocean. A pulse popped steadily above his jaw. Had she made him truly think or was she simply boring his pants off? Not that she needed that image in her head. It was tough enough battling the epic visual of his bare chest and arms when he'd opened his front door earlier that day. The memory alone made her breath come short.

"I got one for you," he said suddenly.

"One what?"

"A did you know."

Cool. "Shoot."

"Did you know, once a long time ago, I almost got married?"

Becca's grip on the wheel slipped and the Bambino swerved before she corrected and got back onto their side of the road. She pushed out a shaky breath.

"Jesus, Jack, don't throw those curveballs while I'm driving."

Jack Reed's reputation as a corporate raider was trumped only by his name as a player. He was always on the hunt for something or someone to jump into bed with, before moving on to some other project.

Seriously. *Marriage?*

"So…what happened?" She smirked. "Did she break your heart?"

"In a sense. She died."

Gravel sprayed as the car veered onto the shoulder. Was this a bad joke? Given the tight line of his mouth, she guessed not.

"Jack…" *God.* "I'm sorry."

"Like I said. It was a long time ago. A *lifetime* ago." His gaze sharpened on hers as his eyebrows knitted together. "You okay?"

"I just…wasn't expecting that."

Not for one minute.

He studied her white-knuckled grip on the steering wheel. "Want me to drive?"

"That could work." He might even enjoy it. "Except… this clutch slips a bit. The steering wheel wobbles a lot of the time. She's a temperamental beast."

"But full of heart."

Exactly. "I think she's worth the trouble."

When she looked across, Jack's thoughtful gaze probed hers. "I was thinking the same thing."

Becca parked the *antique-mobile* out front of a redbrick single-story building. With its barred, round-arch windows, it was a cross between last-century public housing and urban old-English church.

During the rest of the drive, they'd spoken more about charities, including the fact that J.D. had left a good deal of cash to the Lassiter Charity Foundation. That segued into a discussion that touched upon the recent grand opening of the Lassiter Grill in Cheyenne. Jack had attended the opening with Angelica, which hadn't gone down so well with the Lassiter "in" crowd. He mentioned that he hadn't been invited to Dylan's wedding to Jenna Montgomery; it had been very much a family-only affair.

Becca had then trilled about Felicity Sinclair's upcoming nuptials to Chance Lassiter. Jack couldn't see himself being invited to that shindig, either.

Now, as he and Becca walked up the rickety cement-block path, Jack pushed that other business aside to focus on a neat rainbow painted over the building's entrance.

He scratched his chin. "Are we here to listen to a sermon?"

Becca reached back to release her ponytail and shake it out. "We're here to test your powers of observation."

Like observing how her hair unraveled around her

shoulders like spools of gold silk? The way her every gesture and expression carried the conviction of what she believed in? Above all else, Becca believed in herself—what she was about and why.

She resembled Jack in that regard.

Not that he needed to explain himself to anyone—not for any reason. Although, when they'd played that game earlier in the car, he had given in to the impulse to throw a private snippet out there: if Krystal hadn't died, they would have been married. Things would have been different.

Jack rarely thought about that period of his life. It stirred up unpleasant feelings, doubts, memories—well, obviously.

"How would you rate yourself?" Becca asked. "On observation."

"I see what I need to see."

"What you *want* to see."

His gaze skimmed her lips. "That, too."

He swung open the front glass door and they crossed to a counter. A vase of marigolds sat at one end, a framed headshot announcing "Employee of the Month—Brightside House" on the other. Becca addressed the receptionist.

"Hi, Torielle. Mind if I take a guest through?"

The woman had a magic smile, the type that made a person want to beam back. "You know you're welcome here anytime, Becca. Anytime at all."

"Torielle Williams, this is Jack Reed."

Torielle's dark-chocolate gaze flickered—perhaps she recognized the name and its recent connection to the Lassiter scandal in the media. But her smile didn't waver.

"Pleased to meet you, Mr. Reed. Let me know if there's anything you need."

As they headed down a corridor, Jack felt Becca's energy swell and glow. She was a natural leader, a person who got the job done. Knowing she was out for his scalp would have upset a lesser opponent. Instead Jack found himself absorbing her spirit. What might they accomplish if Becca and he sat on the same team?

"This facility helps long-term unemployed women not only find work but also regain their self-esteem," she said. "No matter the color, creed, age or background, we do whatever needs to be done to get them back into contributing, earning and growing as individuals."

They stopped at a window that opened onto another room. Inside, a group was immersed in doing nails and makeup. Numerous rails of women's clothing were lined neatly off to one side.

"Every obstacle is tackled," Becca said, "from grooming and carriage to interview skills and continuing education."

Jack stole a look at Becca's hands resting on the window ledge. Her nails were cut short, no polish. Her makeup was minimal, too, if she wore any at all. Her kind of bone structure and flawless skin didn't need any help. Good diet, plenty of uninterrupted sleep. Jack imaged her opening her eyes each morning and bouncing out of bed. He usually hit the snooze button at least twice. Insomnia was a bitch.

Farther on, they stopped at another window and saw a well-dressed woman addressing a room full of women who were taking notes. Then the next room was a gym. Exercise classes were in full swing—spin bikes, Pilates, ball games.

"Everyone's enjoying themselves," he said.

"Exercise releases endorphins. Feeling good is addictive, Jack." Her shoulder nudged his arm. "You got to keep it pumping."

Jack grinned. "You like to push yourself."

"That's the way to success."

"As long as you don't burn out."

"No chance of that when you're doing what you love."

"And you love what you're doing."

"Every minute."

"Even troubleshooting problems like me?"

They faced each other and she tilted her head, as if she were trying to see him more clearly—see the good.

"You, Jack, are a challenge."

"But redeemable?"

"Everyone's redeemable." Her fingers tapped his shirt-front. "Even you."

Next was a stop at a newer facility separate from the main building. Groups of young children were painting, playing dress-up, making mud pies. Minders were engrossed in helping, sharing, laughing.

"A child-care facility?" he asked.

"And after-school facilities with a bus service to deliver and collect the kids. There's a nursery for the newborns, too."

As they walked along a fence lined with fragrant yellow flowers, Becca explained.

"In the States, more women than men are poor, and the poverty gap is wider here than anywhere in the Western world. When parents separate or divorce it's more likely that mothers will take on the financial responsibilities of raising the kids. Childcare costs can be crippling, never mind medical expenses. While we get a woman prepared to interview for jobs, we make certain any children are properly supervised and cared for."

A little girl with pink track shoes and big brown eyes saw Becca and waved her paintbrush hello over her head. Becca waved back and blew her a kiss before leading Jack back into the main building.

"Who was that?" he asked.

"Wait a minute and I'll let you guess."

They entered a room. Women sitting at half a dozen computer workstations glanced up and greeted them both.

Becca sat at a vacant desk and logged in while Jack stood behind her, attention on the computer screen. She opened up a file labeled "Before." There were countless entries each catalogued by a headshot.

"These are just some of the women who the facility has helped," she said, enlarging a "Before" image. Not only did the woman look disheveled, her resigned expression said she'd accepted that disappointment was her lot in life.

"She never finished high school," Becca said, studying the screen. "For years she suffered in a domestic violence situation. Her husband put her in hospital more than once but she never pressed charges because she feared the next beating would be worse. Her teeth were broken. Can you imagine the agony of feeling discriminated against because of your smile? She was living in a shelter with her children when she came to us."

"Did she get a job?"

From her seat, Becca grinned up at him. "You don't recognize her?"

"No." Then he blinked, focused harder. "Wait…" Something in those eyes… "Torielle?"

"Just two years ago."

Of course. "The receptionist with the dynamite smile."

"We have several professionals, including dentists, who donate their time. Now Torielle helps out here part-time and is working toward completing a college degree."

"And the girl waving her paintbrush, saying hello…?"

"Chelsea, Torielle's four-year-old daughter. She has two older brothers in grade school, twins. The boys both want to become jet pilots. They're smart enough, too. Chelsea wants to be a ballerina—every little girl's dream, and why not?"

"A happy ending," Jack said as Becca clicked to Torielle's "After" picture. The difference, the pride—real pride—shone from the inside out.

"We want to set these facilities up all over the country," Becca said.

"But they need ongoing support."

"The way we see it, we give a little now and society gets a whole lot back later."

Becca pushed to her feet and smiled into his eyes, a beautiful smile Jack had seen before but not as clearly as he did this minute. Becca was one of those uniquely special individuals who bobbed up every now and then. Unselfish, exuberant. She was physically attractive but it was her attitude that made everything about her shine...even when she was chewing someone out.

"Are you ready for a change of pace?" she asked.

His gaze swept over her silken waves of hair. "What do you have in mind?"

"Something different." She winked. "Something fun."

Six

"My God. What the hell *is* that?"

Frowning at Jack's remark, Becca crossed over to the small, seemingly unsupervised dog. "You're lucky he's not sensitive," she said.

They had driven from Brightside House a short distance to a small, quiet parking lot located this side of a beach. When they'd gotten out of the car, this little guy had been waiting alone as planned. Chichi would play a role in Becca's weeklong challenge. Her overriding strategy was to reach Jack's more human, less sophisticated side. He couldn't help but lower his defenses with this cute dog around.

For the next two days of her remaining six, she would hide Jack away from all the temptations and reminders that drove his *conquer and take all* mentality. He needed to get back to basics, and appreciate that everyone deserved a chance to achieve at least that, too.

Now, studying the dog, Jack visibly shuddered. "Sorry, but that's got to be the ugliest mutt I've ever seen."

"Haven't you heard?" Crouching, Becca stroked the wispy tuft of hair on the dog's head. "Beauty is skin deep."

"Except when ninety-five percent of the skin is bald and dappled—" he shuddered again "—and please, not scaly, too."

"He's a Chinese-crested Chihuahua mix."

"If you say so." He flipped a finger at its head. "Do you think its tongue always lolls out the side of its mouth like that?"

She dropped a kiss between the puppy's ears. "Cute, huh?"

"God as my witness, I've never seen anything like it."

"Chichi will be joining us on our road trip."

Jack's head went back. "You know this dog?" As if to answer for her, Chichi sneezed and Jack shrank back. "Whatever it's got, let's hope it's not contagious. Does he smell?"

"Not as well as a bloodhound."

"That's not what I meant."

As she ran a palm down Chichi's hairless back, his pink tongue lolled out more. "Did you have a dog growing up?"

"Would it be too unkind to suggest those bobble eyes look possessed?"

"Jack?" *Focus.* "Growing up?"

"Yeah. We had a King Charles."

"To go with the thoroughbreds, right?"

Chichi's skinny tail with its pompom tip whipped the sandy ground; he got the joke.

Becca pushed to her feet. "He wants you to pick him up."

Jack crossed his arms and puffed out his chest. "You pick him up."

"That's pathetic."

Jack hashed it out some more and finally exhaled. He edged forward, gingerly hunkered down and scooped the dog up. Chichi's eyes grew heavy, contented, looking up into his. "Are you running some kind of weird dog make-over campaign?"

"We all need to be loved."

Jack shot her a look. "You're not trying to get me to adopt this thing, are you? Because my lifestyle isn't con-ducive, to say the least."

"He's on loan from a friend." The longtime owner of the café right next to this parking lot.

As Chichi's head and tongue craned up, Jack recoiled. "And the friend wants it back?"

"Oh, c'mon. You're not that harsh."

He arched a brow. "I have it on good authority that I am."

From many, including Becca. And yet Jack must have owned a soul at some point. He'd wanted to marry that woman, hadn't he? Ipso facto, he'd been in love, a self-sacrificing condition from all accounts. Of course, he could've simply been trying to screw with her brain. She wouldn't put it past him. And yet somehow, deep down, Becca knew he'd told the truth, at least about that.

Still gazing up at Jack, Chichi put his miniature paw on his chest. What a picture.

"He's really taken to you," she said.

The dog yipped and one side of Jack's mouth twitched— almost a grin. "He sounds like a mouse."

Moving closer, Becca ran a palm over Chichi's head. When the dog laid his ear against Jack's chest, her fingers skimmed that solid warmth, too, and for one drugging moment she imagined herself curled up in those capable arms, snuggling in against that sensational rock of a chest.

"He loves the sand and water," she said.

"That's my cue to take him for a walk while music plays over a slow-motion montage."

"I'm not aiming that high." Yet. She did, however, want to bring out Jack's softer, more compassionate side.

When Jack set him on the ground, Chichi trotted off down the wooden-slat path to the beach. Then he stopped and looked back, as if making sure he was being followed.

Shielding his gaze from the sun, Jack surveyed the quiet area. "We'll need a leash."

"It's a leash-free beach."

"So a bigger dog can just romp up and have him for lunch?"

"Hasn't happened yet."

"A hawk might swoop and carry him off. I'm *serious*."

Becca was laughing. Was Jack embarrassed or just being difficult? Either way, she was going to win. She skirted around the rear to give him a good push. But when she set her palms on his back, ready to shove, heat swirled up her arms, zapping her blood all the way to her core. At the same time, Jack spun around and, playing, caught her hands.

She should have stepped back then and put some physical distance between them. But his expression changed so quickly from games to that intense, dark gaze searching hers…when a thick vein in his throat began to throb, she couldn't help it. Becca felt mesmerized by the beat.

Chichi's yip broke the trance. The sound of waves washing onto shore faded back up. Again, she felt wind pulling through her hair. Light-headed, she edged back at the same time Jack reached to bring her closer. He missed catching her by a whisker.

Gathering herself, Becca nodded toward Chichi. "Go on," she said in an unintentionally husky voice. "He's waiting."

"What about you?"

"I have someone to see." Her friend, Chichi's owner.

He took two purposeful steps, closing the gap between them again. Had he suddenly grown six inches? Becca felt dwarfed...very nearly consumed.

"Becca, you said this was fun time."

Her heart was pounding so hard, she had to swallow against the knot lodged in her throat before tacking up a smile.

"So..." She shrugged. *"Have fun."*

But Jack didn't move. If he reached for her hand now, Becca wasn't sure which way it might go. How easy would it be to pretend they were a regular couple out for the day with their dog on the beach. But this wasn't about her. Definitely wasn't about them *as a couple.*

The intensity in Jack's expression finally eased. When he bent to slip off his shoes, Becca released that breath. As he trotted off down onto the beach, Chichi scampered back up, trying to scoot between his legs on each step. When Jack almost stumbled, Becca laughed. Glancing back, he laughed, too—a hearty, deeply stirring sound that in some ways touched Becca's heart.

She had to believe...

There must be hope for us all.

Amidst a clump of dried seaweed, Jack found a stick to toss while Becca disappeared in through the front door of a café located next to the parking lot. When what's-his-face let out a bark, Jack refocused and hurled the stick toward the water. He watched the dog scamper off, kicking up sand as he went. It was a perfect Californian day, Jack was a fan of the beach and, okay, this dog was half-cute in a sincerely *off* kind of way. But Jack's mind was stuck on Becca. First, he understood the visit to Brightside House. Becca had wanted to bring him up close and personal with the good work her foundation was doing, the real life peo-

ple the funds helped. The way she had highlighted Torielle's dramatic change in circumstances had been a nice
touch. It was obviously a worthwhile and solid program.

But what was she thinking lumping him with a dog?
Was this introduction somehow linked to opening his eyes
in connection to a pet adoption agency, perhaps? Whatever Becca was hatching here had to do with advancing
her cause of coaxing him away from a takeover bid.

She would be pleased to hear that this morning had
made him think.

More importantly, Becca made him *feel*. Whenever they
touched, even a brush, Jack felt it to the marrow of his
bones—they had sexual compatibility through the roof.
And a minute ago, he'd put a finger on at least one reason
for that. Becca wasn't *playing* hard to get. She *was* hard
to get. It wasn't happening, not in this lifetime, even while
they both felt temptation gnawing and growing between
them. With Becca, ethics came first, last and everywhere
in between.

If they should happen to come to some understanding
regarding the rescue of her beloved foundation, she would
worry that a rogue like him could always go back on his
word. She might suggest a contract with special clauses,
Jack supposed…in which case, perhaps he could slip in a
couple of special private conditions of his own.

Nah. That was low, even for him.

Jack was between throws and watching Becca from a
distance as she spoke with a woman on the veranda of the
café when his cell phone rang. After checking the caller
ID, he pressed the phone to his ear.

"Angelica just called," Logan said. "She wanted my
opinion again."

"And you said?"

Logan recited his standard response. "She needs to accept the terms of the will."

"But she resisted."

"She still can't believe J.D. would do this to her. She's convinced there's some kind of conspiracy going on."

Jack transferred the cell to his other hand and tossed the stick again. "Poor kid."

"Angelica's hardly a child."

"There's a part of me that still sees her that way."

Jack had felt for Angelica having grown up without her mother, although from all reports her aunt had done a great job as a substitute. J.D.'s longtime widowed sister-in-law, Marlene, still resided in a private wing of the homestead belonging to the Big Blue.

Of course, her son, Chance, had inherited a whopping sixty percent of the ranch. Real generous of J.D. It must have made Angelica wonder if what appeared to be favoritism was gender-related. It made Jack wonder, too. If J.D. had sired a son rather than a daughter, would he have structured his will differently, leaving out the complications that Angelica was experiencing now?

Jack hadn't thought about being a father himself, not since he'd been in love with Krystal back in college. He'd been a different person then. His own most recent will left everything to Sylvia and some friends as well as to charity.

Ha. Wouldn't that make Becca's day.

Chichi was dancing on his hind legs, tongue flapping, wanting to play *fetch* some more.

"I'm away from the office the rest of the week," Jack told Logan, throwing the slimy stick yet again. Logan didn't need to know why he was away. The attorney was tetchy enough about this final stretch as it was.

"But you'll keep your cell on," Logan said.

"Angelica knows I'm available to talk day or night."

"And if she wants to speak face-to-face?"

"I'm there. No question."

A pause. "Maybe it would be better if you *weren't* available for a while."

"Can't do that, Logan. We agreed to play by the rules."

"Yeah." He exhaled. "I know."

When Jack caught sight of Becca leaving the café and heading down toward the entrance to the beach, he signed off.

Becca joined him on the sand a couple of minutes later.

"You were on the phone," she said. "Business?"

"Always."

"Nothing too urgent?"

"It's in hand." He glanced at the café. "I was hoping you might bring back supplies."

"What about you, Chichi?" Becca asked, bending and patting her thighs. "Hungry, little fella?"

The dog sneezed and barked and then picked up the stick and dropped it at Jack's feet again.

"His batteries don't wind down," he told Becca. "I've tossed that stick a hundred times."

"A hundred?"

"Definitely fifty."

"So, you've got those endorphins pumping?"

As a sea breeze picked up, pulling her summer dress back against the curves and valleys of her body, Jack nodded. "You could say I'm pumped, yeah."

She waved for them both to follow. As Jack jogged after her, he glanced over a shoulder. Chichi was sitting, stuck beside that stupid stick. Jack whistled through his fingers.

"Yo. Get a move on, slowpoke."

Chichi scampered up and damned if he didn't leap into Jack's arms like a circus act. Jack pulled his head away from that feral tongue and then caught up with Becca.

"So, tell me about the foundation's link to animal shelters." If that's what this was about.

"No links to shelters. I simply thought that while we

were here you two could meet," she said innocently as she collected Jack's loafers because his hands were full. "Pets are good for humans."

"So are other humans."

"Yep. Having friends is important."

"What would you say to you and me becoming friends?"

She gave a small smile. "Oh, Jack, you know that's not possible."

"But it *would* be possible if I backed away from Lassiter Media?"

A glimmer of hope lit her eyes. "That sure would be a start."

As they walked up to the café, Jack ran over that last bit of conversation in his mind. If he were to spend time with Becca outside of this current context, he would have preferred to tick the "sex between consulting adults" box. And yet he had asked about them becoming *friends? And* he'd meant it. Clearly he had left off the "with benefits" part.

Jack was reading the name on the café's facade, *Hailey's Favorite Haunt,* when a van rolled up alongside the Bambino; the insignia of a top-rating tabloid entertainment news show was stenciled on the side. Jack's antennae twitched. Over the years, he'd tackled his fair share of reporters—truckloads since word of his possible takeover bid for Lassiter Media had leaked. But that crew wasn't here to hassle him. Normally he planned every minute of his day, from first call in the morning to final perusal of documents at night. However, Becca had drawn up this itinerary. No one knew he was here, not even Sylvia. The crew had probably pulled up to grab a coffee for the road.

Then a man jumped out the side door of the vehicle with a camera perched on his shoulder, and Jack paused. Next, a well-dressed woman with a mic climbed out the front passenger side, immediately focused on him and smiled like he was expecting her. Jack set his jaw.

Was this ambush somehow a part of Becca's weeklong deal? If so, he was not amused.

Seven

On their way up to the café, Becca heard someone call out Jack's name. She stopped to track down the source. A tall, slender woman in a bright tangerine skirt-suit and a man with a news camera balanced on one shoulder were ambling across the parking lot, headed their way.

An ice-cold feeling cut through her middle. No one other than her friend had known to expect her at this time. So what was a tabloid TV crew doing here? And what kind of spin would they put on her presence here with Jack?

Holding Chichi close, Jack asked, "Know anything about this?"

She shook her head.

"Lord knows how they'll twist this."

Jack growled. "God, I hate the media."

Becca's hackles went up. "You did happen to notice the name of the company you want to take over, didn't you? Lassiter *Media*. Not that you intend to keep it long." Keep it *whole*.

He repositioned Chichi against his chest. "We can be chewing each other out when that reporter reaches us or we can feed her crumbs and hopefully they'll slouch off."

The reporter and her cameraman were seconds away. Becca exhaled. "Any idea what crumbs?"

A wicked grin eased across his face. "I have a couple in mind."

"Mr. Reed, isn't it?" the reporter asked when she reached them. "Jack Reed. And you're Becca Stevens, head of the Lassiter Charity Foundation. Do you have a moment to answer a few questions?"

Jack replied for them both. "No trouble at all."

"Mr. Reed, you're aware of the publicity and unrest surrounding speculation that you and Angelica Lassiter may succeed in a takeover bid of Lassiter Media after she was shut out of running the company. Would you care to comment on this secluded get-together between yourself and a respected member of Evan McCain's umbrella management team?"

"Ms. Stevens and I have business to discuss regarding the foundation," Jack replied.

The reporter cocked her head and then made a point of eying Jack's loafers, which Becca still held.

"A leisurely day at the beach seems an odd way to discuss business," she said. "Could this be viewed more as a date? And if so, Ms. Stevens, how will you explain this kind of rendezvous to your Lassiter colleagues who are pretty down on Mr. Reed at the moment?"

Becca's blood pressure spiked. This might not look kosher at first glance, but her colleagues would never believe that she'd turned Benedict Arnold. They knew where her heart lay and it was not with Jack Reed.

"As Mr. Reed explained," she replied with barely a tremor in her voice, "today is strictly business."

The reporter's sky-blue eyes narrowed to slits. "So the

rumors regarding a romantic liaison between the two of you are unfounded?"

That hit her in the chest. *"What the—?"*

"My sole purpose today," Jack replied, "is to build on my already solid support of the Lassiter Charity Foundation. Now, we're late for an appointment. I'll thank you both to leave us to our privacy."

Becca rubbed a throbbing temple. She'd never suffered from migraines but she was sure she was getting one now.

How would Evan McCain react if or when this hit the airwaves? She had wanted to keep quiet about her long shot plan to crack Jack's enigmatic side and in some way at least sway his thinking. Now she would need to contact Sarah, her assistant, as well as Evan, to reassure them that she hadn't shifted camps, and never would.

Or maybe it would be wiser to simply call this all off now.

After Jack set Chichi down, Becca led him around the café's wide veranda to an ocean-facing table set with a reserved sign.

"You realize the dog has followed us," Jack said quietly, casting glances at the other guests sprinkled inside the café as well as out here in the fresh air.

"No problem," Becca said. "Trust me."

They were taking their seats when Becca's friend appeared in her trademark denim skirt and vest. They'd had a conversation earlier at this very table when she'd left Jack on the beach.

"Jack Reed," Becca said, "meet Hailey Lang."

"Pleased to meet you," Hailey said with the hint of a Texas twang. Her family had moved over from Houston twenty years ago when Hailey was eight. "I saw you tripped up by some pesky reporter."

"They appeared out of nowhere," Becca said, and then

noticed how Hailey averted her gaze before she spoke again, upbeat this time.

"How you doing there, Chichi?"

Now Jack looked between the dog and Hailey. "You know each other, too?"

"He's my baby," Hailey said while Chichi sat patiently by her feet, his tail fanning the wood planking. "He's a bit of a celeb around these parts."

Jack leaned back in his chair. "He does kind of grow on you."

"So, Chichi's going on a trip with you guys. One of his favorite things is riding shotgun."

"He's partial to sticks, too. Which reminds me…" Jack got to his feet. "If you'll excuse me, I need to wash up before lunch."

As Jack moved off, Hailey crouched down beside Becca's chair. "Becca, honey, I think I might need to apologize."

"For reserving us the best table in the house?"

"The reporter who gave you grief just now…" She leaned closer. "Thing is I have a regular who comes in most days around brunch time for our Delite Mushroom Omelet. Anita's daughter works for the same cable show. Anita talks about her all the time, how she's a hound, always after a big scoop. I think Anita overheard part of our conversation earlier about what you're doing here with Jack Reed. I think she tipped her daughter off."

Becca thought back. "You mean the redhead with a French twist, who was sitting a couple of tables over?" Becca had felt that woman's eyes on them a few times earlier.

"Anita McGraw has a keen ear for gossip. And if there's none around, she'll make dirt up." Hailey sighed. "Is it going to cause much trouble, hon?"

Nothing could be done about it now. And Becca didn't

want Hailey to feel responsible or to worry. "It'll be fine," she assured her friend as Jack returned to the table.

She would make those phone calls to Sarah and Evan's office. She'd decide then on whether or not to cancel this challenge.

Looking halfway relieved, Hailey pushed to her feet.

"Do I need a menu?" Jack asked, pulling his chair in. "I'm open to suggestions."

Hailey piped up. "Chef's salad and specialty pizza. That's with prosciutto, caramelized pear and goat cheese."

"I'm in," Becca said.

"Times two. So, how did you two become friends?" Jack asked, shaking out a napkin to place on his lap.

"Coming up two years ago, Becca broke down just over there, this side of the median strip." Hailey nodded toward a section of road. "Chichi let me know someone needed help. He zipped right up to me, turning circles like his tail was on fire."

"Water pump," Becca explained. "It'd been coughing all the way up the coast. The hood was spewing steam."

"I have a cousin just round the corner—the best mechanic in town," Hailey went on. "His specialty is old cars."

"*Classic* cars," Becca corrected. "He wanted to buy it, remember?"

"I sure do," Hailey said. "You wouldn't take the money even when he doubled the going rate. I don't *ever* see you giving up those wheels."

"There's no accounting for taste," Becca agreed. "Hailey ended up giving me a bed for the night while the repairs were done. Chichi slept at my feet."

Hailey sighed at Chichi, who was still gazing adoringly up at her. "That dog there is a fine judge of character."

Jack grinned. "And yet he likes me?"

"We were watching you two on the beach." Hailey winked at Jack. "He likes you a *whole* lot."

Becca had a moment of what psychologists term cognitive dissonance. She knew Chichi was a good gauge of character. She also knew he liked Jack. And yet Jack was not of good character. It made her brain hurt.

Hailey headed off. "I'll get this order under way and finish packing that ice chest for you all."

"Ice chest?" Jack asked, pouring water for them both from a carafe. "Are we going on a picnic?"

"Not a picnic, as such," Becca said and he grinned.

"Another one of your secret destinations?"

"With no chance of reporters this time." She lifted her glass. "One hundred percent guaranteed."

But first, she'd check with the boss.

Three hours later, watching out for media tails the whole way, Becca pulled the Bambino up in the middle of freaking nowhere—or, rather, somewhere east of Fresno.

Chichi was asleep on Jack's chest. The drool went from his neck to—he didn't want to think about it. With the dog's head and that tongue hanging out the window more than half the time, the car's side panel must be Slime City by now.

Jack surveyed the area. Dense woods. Lonely cabin. Cooler shadows creeping in.

"What is this?" he asked. "Boot camp?"

Becca jerked on the parking brake. "Actually...yeah."

While Becca got out of the car, Jack wondered how he could extricate himself without disturbing the dog. Which was crazy...except, with one leg kicking and eyelids twitching, the mutt looked like he was having a nice dream. When Becca opened the passenger side door, Chichi stirred, stretched and expelled a big smelly yawn. Then he jumped onto a carpet of pine needles and trotted off into the woods.

Becca was at the trunk. Jack eased out from the car and stretched out his own kinks, frowning as he watched the dog's cotton-top tail disappear among the trees.

"Aren't you worried about him?"

"Chichi's been here before," she said, handing over Jack's bag. "He knows his way around."

"Does he know his way around a mountain lion?"

"Don't forget the black bears and rattlesnakes."

She was screwing with him, but a chill rippled up Jack's spine just the same.

Heading for the door, she added, "He'll come the minute you call."

"If you're not worried, I'm not worried."

Jack grabbed the ice chest from the backseat and shut the door with a hip. "What did Hailey pack in here? Cement blocks?"

"Bread, fruit, cheese, refreshments—"

"Beer?"

"And wine."

They were most definitely set then. For what exactly, he had no idea.

"I got the high school visit and Brightside House. Forgive me if I sound slow, but what am I doing way the heck out here with a dog?"

"For two days and nights, I've kidnapped you," she said, heading for the front door. "Transported you away from your obsession with killer deals and accruing power so that you can get in touch with reality and learn some lessons on how to unleash your truer, less egocentric self."

"After which I will accept a higher calling and disavow my evil ways."

"*Ahh*…doesn't that sound heavenly?"

"It sounds like you're dreaming."

"Some of the world's biggest dreams have come true because someone believed and made others believe, too."

When a couple of huge examples came to mind, he couldn't argue the point. "And the mutt?"

"I knew he'd make you smile in a different way than you're used to."

"So, I'll change my mind about Lassiter Media because I played with a dog? Because I smiled differently?" *Come on.*

"Actions trigger emotions that link with the process of decision-making. I'm hoping that sometime this week, you'll not only smile differently, but start to *think* and choose differently, too."

Okay, fine. "Does Evan know about this cozy getaway?"

"He does now. I phoned him before we left the café. I didn't want him finding out from…other sources."

Like that tabloid show. "And he was okay with it?"

"He said he trusts my judgment and admires my determination."

"In that case, you get an A for creativity. Except you're forgetting one thing. Even when I want to, I never let emotions dictate my decisions."

Her expression didn't waver. "Then we'll simply call this a break from civilization."

Sure. Although he could do without the overgrown rat, he wouldn't object to hanging out here alone with this beautiful woman. Maybe he could put a spin on things and have *Becca* thinking differently by the time they left. And he wasn't talking business.

Inside, the place was quiet and dark enough at four in the afternoon to need to turn on the light. But Becca continued on from the front door without flicking a switch. Jack gave his eyes time to adjust. The room was sparsely furnished, no window dressings. Some walls were plastered. Others displayed exposed logs. It smelled like raccoons might have lodged in the cupboards over winter.

"Who owns this place? The foundation?"

He found Becca in a room that housed a double-bed covered with a patchwork quilt and matching pillows. A painting, featuring wilted poppies, hung above the headboard. Becca was setting her bag near a lopsided free-standing wardrobe.

"The cabin belongs to my parents," she said.

"When was it last used?" Jack sniffed the musty air. "1965?"

"Are you uncomfortable?" She faced him, hands on hips. "Out of your silver-spoon element?"

"Wasn't that the idea?"

With a wistful smile, she peered out the window at the trees. "We used to vacation here for a week every year. No television or hairdryers or—"

"Electricity?"

A camping lantern sat perched on top of a set of drawers. She flicked a switch and white light filled much of the space. "Ta-dah!"

Loving her bright smile, he moved closer. "Very rustic." He stopped before her, close enough to absorb the contentment and pride shining in her eyes. "Is there a second bedroom?"

"There is—complete with two sets of bunk beds, meant for kids, not a man of your sizable build."

His heart gave a running jump. "So, one bed?"

"And a cot." She nodded toward a corner. A saggy camper bed was tucked away among the shadows.

Oh. "Right." He scratched a temple. "That might work." *Not.*

"Guess we don't need to draw straws. I get the cot."

Jack growled as she moved across to inspect it. "Becca, I'm not letting you spend the night on that."

"Lots of people sleep on benches, in doorways, alleys, under bridges, in subways and behind Dumpsters—"

"Okay, okay." He'd heard enough. Guess her first point in bringing him here had been made. "I'll take the cot."

"You'll break it."

"If I do, I'll reimburse you." And see a chiropractor, end of discussion. "But it's a long way from lights-out. What do you have planned until then? Ghost stories around a campfire?"

Jack had a couple up his sleeve. She might even need two strong arms to help with the fright factor.

"A campfire?" she asked. "You mean outside with the bears and rattlesnakes?"

Jack paused. *Good point.*

"First we make the beds," she said. "Then a nice relaxing bath to wash off the travelers' dust."

An image of the two of them together caressing in a deep, sudsy hot tub faded up in his mind. Pure fantasy. Still, he didn't want to put a damper on her idea.

He rocked back on his heels. "Sounds good."

"Great. We'll need maybe ten buckets' full."

"Full of what?"

"Water. We don't exactly have a bath or a shower. We do, however, have a washtub."

Jack waited for the punch line.

His grin dropped.

She was serious.

"Aren't you going to let me know how many people go without adequate plumbing?"

"Don't need to. You worked it out yourself."

He grinned. *Lesson two: check.*

Becca moved to the drawers and found some sheets while he took his place on the other side of the bed. She fluffed out the lower sheet and proceeded to pull the elasticized end under the top corner of the mattress. He did the same on his side of the bed and then tackled the lower corner.

It was a cinch.

As she fluffed out the top sheet, she asked, "Ever made a bed before?"

He scoffed. "I'm sure I have."

"You'd have a housekeeper now, of course."

"Weekdays."

"How long has she worked for you? It's a woman, yes?"

"Mary's worked for me maybe four years."

"Long-time employee?"

"You could say that."

"So, Mary who?"

"Why do you want to know my housekeeper's last name?" What did that have to do with her plan to turn him around on the takeover question?

"I'm curious is all."

As they both stretched the sheet across the middle of the mattress, Jack searched his memory and came up a blank. "It'd be in my phone."

She moved to the end of the bed. "Uh-huh."

From across the mattress, Jack narrowed his eyes at her. "You know all your employees' names off the top of your head?"

"It's fine, Jack. Honest."

"Now you're patronizing me?"

"Is this you being defensive?"

"I'm more than happy with who I am."

She slipped her side of the sheet under the mattress. "Well, that's the main thing, isn't it."

"Why do I feel as if you just insulted me?" he asked, scooping under his end.

"You're smart enough to work it out."

"Just say I'm not."

She joined him on his side of the bed. "You live such a

privileged life, you take for granted clean sheets, and those who change them for you. Lots of children have to do their own laundry. Lots of people would do anything for any kind of bed to sleep on. Want to hear more."

He rubbed the back of his neck. "Not right now."

"Want to learn how to do a hospital corner then?"

Jack moved back to give her room. She bent to collect the dangling edge of the sheet and hold it out from the bed. Then she scooped the linen under the mattress and all the way up. At least he thought that's what she'd done. Call him a man, but even after the speech, Jack was more interested in the view of her legs and those buns.

Straightening, she turned to him. "Think you can do that?"

He feigned an uncertain look. "I might need help."

She moved back to her side, and nodded at the to-be-hospital-tucked bottom corner. "Go ahead. Have a go."

He crossed over and picked up the sheet at the wrong point.

"That's a little too far along," she said. "Let the sheet drop and naturally fold and try again."

He did as she instructed and then grabbed the sheet in a different spot.

"Here," she said patiently. "Like this."

She nudged in front of him and bent over again. Jack didn't see what happened next. He faintly heard some instructions. "…fold the lowest bit…smooth it under…" On autopilot, he moved in. His hand covered hers and they both tucked the sheet in.

"Like that?" he asked, close to her ear.

She didn't stiffen or jump away, so he closed his eyes and absorbed the moment. When she finally began to straighten, they disengaged and then simply stood there in the light and shadow, his hand holding hers as time ticked on and anticipation soared. When he coiled his arm around the front of her waist, he felt her intake of air. Pressing in behind her more, he imagined her biting her lip as she fought the urge to let nature take its course.

He brushed his lips over her temple, her cheek, all the while soaking up her scent. When he nuzzled her earlobe, he felt her quiver against him…heard her quiet, needful sigh. As he dragged his mouth down the side of her throat, bit by bit she tilted her head.

He nipped down the slope where neck met shoulder while his fingers left hers to skim the front of her dress. Through the cotton, he felt the start of her panties and, lower, the subtle rise of her mound. When she groaned— a low, wanting sound—half his blood supply rushed to a predetermined point.

"Jack…?" she murmured.

He hummed against her skin. *"Hmmm?"*

"The bed."

"What about the bed?"

"We were making it."

He dragged his grin back up to her ear. "I like making it with you."

When his fingers delved between her thighs, she made a husky noise in her throat that lit a fire in the pit of his belly. As his free hand slid up her side and under her breast, her head rocked back against his chest and her hand gripped his. Her voice was smoky now.

"This isn't what we're here for."

They were here to cut him off from reality and clobber him over the head with how little others had, how in need many of the less fortunate were.

"Okay." He nipped the side of her throat a little harder. "I'll stop."

When he didn't remove the hand between her legs, her grip over his tightened, not to drag him away but to hold his hand in place. His other palm dragged up over her breast and oh-so-lightly squeezed. She melted a moment before she pulled both his hands away and spun around. When she opened her mouth to speak, he got in first and lowered his head over hers.

Eight

Eight

When Jack pulled her close and his mouth captured hers, any objection Becca might have had dissolved like a tea-spoon of sugar in hot water. As the kiss deepened, she reached to wind her arms around his neck. A moment more and she arched all the way in.

She would have denied it earlier, even to herself. The admission would have been incongruous, shameful. Inexcusable. She hadn't brought Jack here for this...and yet, secretly, Becca Stevens—the woman—had waited for this moment.

Now she couldn't think past the sensations sizzling through her system. Her breasts felt tender crushed against his chest. Suddenly her insides were filled with an emotion that felt like a swell of liquid fire.

Cupping her jaw, Jack held her mouth to his as he dropped back onto the bed, bringing Becca down along with him. Lips still locked, she tangled one leg around his and knotted her fingers in his clean dark hair while both his palms traced down her sides then slid over the rise of her behind.

Becca arched up and then ground down against him. Through their clothes she felt him already hard and ready. Reaching back, she clapped a hand over his where he was kneading the flesh above one thigh.

When he delved under her dress and down the back of her panties, a giant flash went off through her body. This all felt so new and necessary. So incredibly wrong and wonderfully right. She needed to get naked with Jack. She would *die* if she couldn't feel his hot skin on hers. She could barely breathe, the physical longing was so strong. So beautiful and bad and brilliantly intense.

As that first kiss broke down into hungry snatches, she wiggled to help him ditch her underwear. When he grabbed the hem of her dress and started to tug it over her head, she sat up and lifted her arms in the air. Straddled over his hips, her head back and eyes closed, she leaned in as he scooped her breasts out of their lace cups. His palms were big and hot and, dear heaven, just rough enough.

He was alternating between rolling and lightly plucking her nipples when she reached behind to unsnap her bra.

Her mistake was glancing down, seeing herself pretty much naked, thighs spread over a fully clothed man who, less than a week ago, she wouldn't have spat on let alone enjoyed mindless sex with.

Jack Reed. Number-one enemy...

What the hell am I thinking?

"I can't do this," Becca said, sweeping up the dress to cover what she could.

"Don't worry." He craned up to nuzzle her throat. "I'll guide you through."

"I mean this is a mistake."

His lips grazed her chin. "No mistake."

A hand curled around the side of her neck. Next she

knew, she was flipped onto her back and Jack was crouching, towering over her, unbuttoning his shirt, shrugging it off. His chest was so broad and bronzed, her fingertips tingled to sample every delicious mound and rung. When he maneuvered out of his pants and boxer shorts, she felt blood rush to her cheeks. This was moving much too fast.

He set a hand down next to her head. As one hot knee prized itself between hers, panic set in and both her hands shot out. She pushed against his pecs as he lowered himself onto her. A questioning look took hold in his eyes before he pulled slowly back and then frowned.

"You want to stop," he said—not a question, although the set of his mouth said it pained him to have to say it.

"One minute we were making the bed," she stammered. "The next…"

"You were kissing me."

"You kissed me!"

His grin flashed white. "You kissed me back."

She had. And, damn it, she wanted to kiss him again. Hard and deep and dirty. But this was wrong on so many levels, it made her head spin. And even if it were right…

Becca snatched a look down the length of his body and focused on that serious erection. As her heart pounded, she swallowed and then moistened her lips.

"Jack, we don't have protection."

"I have condoms."

"You do?" Wait. He *knew* this would happen?

"Better to be prepared than sorry," he pointed out.

Well, sure…except…it just reminded her how prepared Jack had been on so many other occasions. With so many other women.

She shook her head. *No.* "I can't do this."

"Do what?"

"This." She held her cheeks. "*Sex.* With you."

He hesitated and then, exhaling long and hard, he

brought her hand to his lips and tenderly kissed the palm. "I can't say I'm not bitterly disappointed," he murmured and then proceeded to kiss each fingertip.

Damn, he felt good, looked amazing, smelled divine. But even without the Lassiter complication, this was not a wise choice. Jack was a self-professed player. Sex was nothing more to him than sport. It meant as much as hitting a bull's-eye with an arrow.

While they'd been at the café, Becca had got away to make that phone call to Evan McCain. Then she'd explained the situation to her assistant. If the interview aired, she wanted everyone to know it was a beat up. But what would the world think if *this* ever got out?

She wiggled out from beneath him and set both feet on the floor. Avoiding his gaze, she put on her bra and shimmied back into her dress. It seemed that her panties, however, had disappeared. When she stood, she felt giddy... spacey...as if those last few moments had happened to somebody else on a distant planet.

Behind her, the bed squeaked; Jack had found his feet, too.

"I saw a lake when we drove in," he said as Becca listened to him shake out and then shrug back into his clothes. "I need to cool down and a washtub of water ain't gonna cut it."

He skirted around the bed, stood before her and then lifted her chin. His dark gaze was disappointed but also understanding.

"Why don't you come keep me company?"

Her stomach gave a kick and she found an excuse. "I should unpack...fix up this bed."

"Becca, I should warn you, if you say bed again in the next thirty seconds, I won't be held responsible for my actions."

Inside she shouted, *BED, BED, BED!*

Then she crossed her arms to stop herself from bringing him close.

"You go cool off," she said. "I'll be fine here."

He crossed to the bedroom door. "I'll find the mutt while I'm gone."

When she didn't reply, he kept going, through the main room and out the front door. Becca found her underwear, shoved her panties on and then sat on the side of the bed like a lump.

At the end of three solid minutes, her body was *still* vibrating—humming and smoldering with unruly heat. The unspent energy was driving her nuts! None of that was about to subside unless, or until, she did something about it.

She thought of the lake's cool mirrored surface, of swimming until she was too tired to move or so much as think about humping Jack Reed half the night. She made fists of her hands, tried to think rational thoughts. In the end, she grabbed two towels from the closet, her bikini from her bag and ran after Jack to catch up.

Becca got to the lake in time to see Jack cannonball off the pier and into the water. His clothes were hung on a branch near the bush she decided to hide behind. Waiting at the end of that pier, Chichi yipped, skidded forward and then jumped in, too.

That dog loved the water. Jack appeared to be a strong swimmer, too. He power-stroked a good length before flip-turning to head off in a different direction. He swam up to Chichi, who alternated between madly lapping at the water and barking excitedly. Treading water, Jack laughed, a sound that echoed across the lake, through the treetops and then down to wrap around Becca.

The water sure looked good. So did those dynamite arms and shoulders, that brilliant smile and slick dark brown hair. So good, in fact, Becca was forced to admit a truth.

Even if Jack Reed *was* a villain and these feelings were wrong and the world might shun her if anyone ever found out—there was no way around it. She liked Jack. She liked his smile and his wit. God help her, she liked his kiss.

Behind the bush, she changed into the bikini. When he started off again, swimming freestyle in the opposite direction, she darted down the pier, all the way to the end and, without stopping, dived into the deep.

Spearing through the cold water gave her a jolt, but, man, was it refreshing! Becca held her breath as long as she could. When she surfaced, Jack was right there, waiting not an arm's length away.

She yelped.

Chichi barked.

And Jack…well, he just grinned.

"How the hell did you do that?" she asked. He'd been at least ten yards away. Then it clicked. "You *knew* I followed you," she said, working hard to tread water.

"Bears make less noise."

"Why didn't you wait for me?"

"This was more fun."

Seriously? "Scaring me half out of my wits like that?"

"You weren't scared." As he waded closer, cool ripples lapped at her neck and chin. "You wanted to surprise me. I just turned it around."

He looked so relaxed and one step ahead of the game, she couldn't give it up that easily.

"I got to thinking that a swim would save filling up the washtub." When his smile spread, Becca tried to frown. "What's so funny?"

"You are." Although he'd be tall enough to stand at this depth, he began to paddle around her, his long, strong arms swerving inches beneath the surface. "Fess up. You wanted to come play."

He'd waded closer...near enough for Becca to reach out and touch.

"Maybe," she agreed. "This part of our week together is supposed to be about acknowledging your less complicated side. About seeing the bigger value in simple pleasures and understanding you can help bring them to others."

His smile changed again around the corners of his mouth. It was even sexier, more knowing. Mischievous and so hot.

But then he shook his head.

"What?" she asked, barely keeping her chin above the surface. Treading water, her limbs were feeling the burn now.

"I'm not doing it this time."

"Doing what?"

"You want me to sweep you over. You want me to kiss you. Only when we get started, you'll remember your higher purpose and make up some lame excuse why we ought to stop."

She objected to the one thing she could. "My excuses aren't lame."

He kept circling her, looking at her with that exasperating smile. He filled his mouth with water and squirted a fountain off to one side.

"Why don't you come over here?" he finally said.

Becca tried to stare him down but, in the end, she bit her lip and admitted, "This isn't very mature, is it?"

"Can we agree that we should be grown-up about the fact that we're attracted to each other?"

As he slid closer, she imagined his tongue rather than the water swirling over her belly, between her legs.

She nodded. *Damn it. Yes.*

"You know the consequences?" he asked.

She nodded again.

"And you still want this?"

Big breath. "Uh-huh."

Hot, strong fingers curled around her shoulders. Then their mouths joined and she was swept into the sublime haven of his arms.

He held her against his chest as their kiss played out—savoring, teasing, probing, until nothing else existed except the two of them and these sizzling, secret feelings.

When he broke the kiss, his lips stayed close. "Still okay?"

She rubbed her dreamy smile over his. "Okay isn't the word."

He tasted her lips again. "Wrap your legs around me."

She looped her arms around his neck and circled his hips with her legs, digging her heels in behind his thighs. He cupped her bottom and pulled her through the water, closer to him. As the length of his erection met the strip between her thighs, a jet of warm sparks flew through her veins. Her breath caught at the same time her head rocked back.

His hands slid under her behind. Then she felt his touch inside her bikini's crotch. His teeth dragged one half of her bikini top aside until the nipple was exposed and moist warmth covered that tip bobbing just above water level. While he drew that nipple back onto his tongue, his fingers slipped slowly up and down, over and between her folds. When his head pulled back a little and the edge of his teeth grazed her nipple, one finger slipped all the way inside of her.

She gasped, shuddered from top to toe, and then held his head in place against her breast.

The tip of his tongue rimmed the areola as he expertly massaged her down below. Every time his finger slid up, the tip grazed her G-spot, while one of his other fingers slipped up the outside, nudging the swollen bead hiding at the top of her folds. His pace was slow and steady, the perfect speed and pressure. Before long, she joined in with the rhythm, her hips rocking with his mesmerizing caress.

With each passing second, the sensations increased. As tingling heat ripped through her bloodstream, she needed to feel his mouth on hers again. She had to have him kissing her in a penetrating, all-or-nothing kind of way. Only the things his lips and teeth and tongue were doing added to the climb—a slope so steep, she had to gasp, the air was so thin.

When her orgasm broke, Becca curled into herself before she ground down against him and then released a cry that must have carried halfway to Montana. As she continued to shudder and groan, Jack watched a flow of raw emotions redefine her beautiful face. Holding her, loving her... This water might be chilly but he was rock-hard.

When he felt her floating down, he brought both his arms up around her waist to hold her against his chest. As her hot cheek nestled against the slope of his neck, he swirled her slowly through the water. Her ragged breathing gradually eased. Every now and then, her legs would twitch and then tighten around him again. He pressed a kiss to her crown, closed his eyes and wished every day could be as good as this.

After a few moments, she gave a big sigh, slid a palm over his shoulder and gradually lifted her face to his. Her smile was faraway. Satisfied. The loveliest smile he'd ever seen.

"You look like you could do with a nap," he joked.

"Are you kidding?" she asked groggily. "I may never let you sleep again."

Was she saying she wanted to do this every night? Jack could certainly arrange that. For a time, at least. Once they got back to the city, no doubt she would want to return to their former relationship…the one where she pretended to hate him.

She stretched her arms high over her head and then withered back against him, her lips landing on the pulse he felt beating at the side of his neck. The tip of her tongue tickled the spot.

"Hmm, you taste good," she murmured against his skin. "I want to taste every inch of you."

"Well, we're going to have to get out of the water for that."

She smiled up into his eyes. "Why?"

"A…we'll get all pruny. B…it's getting cold. C…something's nibbling at my toes and I don't need the distraction. D…"

"We don't have any protection," she finished.

Her dreamy gaze was growing clearer.

"We might have to shift camp, but look on the bright side," he said. "No one has to sleep on the cot."

Her legs tightened around him again. "I'll race you to shore."

"Okay, but I really don't think—"

Jack grunted as she used her feet against his abdomen to push off.

He let her have a head start and then sprang into action.

A moment later, when the water got too shallow for freestyle, he jumped up and stomped and splashed onto shore. Laughing and splashing too, she beat him by a nose. The prize was Jack crash-tackling her onto a patch of soft, long grass, working it so she landed on top of him, not vice versa. Then he rolled so she was pinned beneath him, his giggling prisoner.

In fact, Becca was laughing so much, she started to cough. He eased her up to a sitting position and patted her back. He didn't miss the fact that her body was even more sensational without all that water getting in the way. Personal preference, of course…and Becca Stevens was his.

"I brought towels," she said, spluttering again and then visibly shivering. Goosebumps erupted all down her arms.

Jack pushed to his feet and crossed over to sweep up the towels she'd left at the foot of the bush he had seen her hide behind earlier. When he turned to join her again, something struck him as strange. As…missing. Becca was sitting straighter, alert. With a curious gaze, she scanned the water.

Jack's throat thickened.

Where the hell was the dog?

Nine

"Can you see him anywhere?" Becca asked.

When Jack handed over a towel but didn't reply, she called Chichi's name nice and loud. Only eerie silence, sprinkled with cicada clicks, came back. She called again, and as the seconds ticked by, a feeling of dread filled her.

"He must be around somewhere," Jack said, lashing a towel around his hips before helping Becca to her feet as she wrapped her towel under her arms.

"I haven't seen him since I dived in," she said, scanning the woods for any sign.

Holding the towel around her chest, she crossed to the water's edge and called again. A sick feeling built high in her stomach and rose in her throat. When Jack, being supportive, gripped her shoulder, emotion prickled behind her nose.

Keep it together. Don't panic. Not yet.

Becca had lived alongside people, including babies and young children, who'd been forced to survive without adequate or clean water, with barely enough to eat, and little or no prospect of bettering their lives in a way most folks here took for granted. During her Peace Corps days, she'd kept strong, kept going. Rarely had she shed a tear, not because she hadn't felt anguish and despair, but because time spent crying was less time being productive. Being a positive role model.

And yet here she was, tears in her eyes, because she'd lost sight of a little dog.

But there was more to it than that. She'd been so self-absorbed in satisfying those urges, she hadn't given another thought to Hailey's dog. To her friend's four-legged baby. How would she explain that?

"Has he been here before?" Jack asked.

"Not to the lake, but he loves splashing around in the surf and diving into Hailey's pool at home. He likes the water."

"Yeah. I got that. He's probably dog-paddling up a storm right now, swimming across from the other side."

Becca crossed her arms, hugging herself, as she scanned the area again. Everything was so still. She called out his name, and then called it again, more loudly. As loudly as she could.

Jack gently turned her to face him. Holding her gaze with his, he gave a brave smile. "I'll find him, okay? You have my word."

His promise was supposed to make her feel better. But what was Jack's word really worth? He wasn't renowned for jumping on a steed and galloping to anyone's rescue. Angelica might disagree, but she was clinging to any port in the storm her father's death and will had brewed up.

"If we can't find him—" she said.

"We'll find him."

"But if we can't…how will I ever tell Hailey? She loves that dog like a child."

Jack skirted around in front of Becca and herded her back toward the trees, away from the lake. "You sit. I'll search. Deal?"

She didn't argue, but she had no intention of sitting back and doing nothing.

They quickly changed back into their clothes and Jack set off to circumnavigate the lake. Every now and then he brought cupped hands to his mouth and called out Chichi's name. As Becca headed off the other way, she sent up a prayer.

When she told Hailey this story, she needed it to have a happy ending.

It didn't look good.

Jack was halfway around the lake, calling out the pooch's name, searching the scrub nearest the water's edge. Not a peep. He'd assumed that Chichi had been paddling by himself in the lake before this.

Now he felt worse than any names reporters or broken businessmen had ever called him. Why hadn't he even given the little guy, who'd been paddling furiously, a second thought? Obviously because he had other things on his mind.

It was getting dark and he'd scoured most of the perimeter of the lake when he decided to head back. Becca had set off in the opposite direction. Looking back now and then, he'd seen her either wandering into or coming out of the woods, searching among the trees and shrubs. They'd both been calling for over an hour.

When they met back at the pier, Jack wrapped Becca in his arms. After a moment, she hugged him back. He grazed his lips through her hair. "We'd better go while there's still some light."

She nodded against his chest and then they walked hand in hand back down the trail. It might as well have been a funeral march. He couldn't help this situation, but he could at least try to keep Becca's mind on other things.

"We never had a cabin in the woods growing up," he said, giving her hand a squeeze.

"Don't suppose you need one when you own a five-star chalet in the snow."

She wasn't serious but there wasn't a hint of a tease in her voice, either. He tried again.

"What were the other kids in your family like?"

"I was the youngest, then Emily, Abigail and Faith."

"Still keep in touch?"

"Emily's in the U.K. now. She married a doctor."

"Good for her."

"Abigail is an elementary school teacher and Faith is travelling the world. She's in Burma at the moment, I think."

"Did you share any time with them here at the lake house?"

"Not recently. I've had Hailey up a couple of times."

She lowered her head and he tried to pick up their pace, to distract her from thinking about the dog and because night was falling fast. They needed to get back to the cabin.

"Anyone else?" he asked.

"A couple of friends from the office."

"Any male friends?"

She gave him a look. "You really want to know?"

He shrugged. *Your call.*

She didn't exactly grin. "Although it's rather personal… no. I've never brought any male friends to the cabin."

"You don't want to get personal?"

"I don't have anything to hide. What you see is what you get."

"What I see is a beautiful, feisty, determined woman who always puts others before herself."

Instead of a smile, the compliment brought on a frown. "Don't overdo it."

He blew out a breath. Guess it was going to be a long, cold night. So he might as well say what he felt.

"Has anyone ever told you that you have trouble accepting compliments?"

"I don't need compliments."

"Because you're tough."

"Because I already feel fine with who I am."

"Whereas I need lots of work."

She only looked the other way. Her hand felt limp in his. He had the sense she might be more comfortable severing the link. On one level, that annoyed him. Not an hour ago, she'd come apart in his arms as if it was her last feel-good moment before the world ended. He'd thought they'd been pretty tight then.

On the other hand, he understood…she felt gutted. He felt like crap, too.

By the time they made it back to the cabin, Becca wished she'd never heard the name Jack Reed. But not for the reasons he might have thought. She didn't blame Jack one bit for Chichi's disappearance. That dog had been her responsibility and she'd screwed up.

During the search, she'd not only thought ahead to Hailey's tears when she discovered the news, but also sifted through every grain of logic that said it was a good idea to kidnap Jack for a few days. She'd believed that coming here—experiencing this with her—would touch and bring out his more humble, benevolent side.

But Jack had been in the game a long time. Did she have any hope of swaying his plans to take over Lassiter Media and do what instinct told him to do: make a huge profit off selling the company piecemeal? No one could convince Angelica of Jack's deeper motives, just as no one could have told Becca she should have kept from sticking her nose in.

But not everything could be fixed, including, it would seem, her physical attraction toward Jack. Today she'd let her emotions rule her head in a spectacular way. On one level she didn't regret the time they'd spent in the lake together. She had never imagined that such intensity of sensation could truly exist. The height of her climax had turned her inside out.

On another far more practical level, while she had not set out to use the possibility of sex as a motivator, the fact remained that Jack had agreed to this challenge not because he thought for a moment she might be able to change his mind in a week about taking over Lassiter Media, but because a woman had confronted and intrigued him. Getting closer to her had been a challenge in itself. She'd pretty much handed herself to him on a platter. She was no different, in that regard, from any other woman he'd successfully seduced.

So why did she feel as if what had happened between them in the lake had been special? Why did she feel as if it truly mattered to him? Maybe because it had mattered to her. She felt a connection with Jack that made her want to leave their other, more complicated worlds behind.

When they got to the cabin, the door was ajar. In her stupid hurry to catch up with Jack, she'd bolted without shutting the damn thing. Now she walked in first.

"Want me to light a fire?" he asked, following her inside.

"It's not cold enough."

"Might get cold later."

He was trying to be supportive. He truly felt bad about how this afternoon had ended. He'd done his best to try to find poor Chichi.

Turning to him, she found a smile. "Thanks for trying to find him. I appreciate it."

In the shadows, she couldn't make out his face other than by the moonlight slanting in through the doorway.

"Becca...I'm sorry. I don't know what else to say."

"You don't need to say anything. Just sit with me awhile. Who knows? He might still come back." Chichi might not have drowned or been bitten by a snake or—

Becca caught a tear as it ran down her cheek. She apologized. "I'm not usually such a baby."

"You're not being a baby. You have feelings. Everyone has feelings."

"Even you."

"Yeah." She imagined she saw his smile. "Even me."

She reached up on tiptoe, rested a palm on his shirt and dotted a kiss on his cheek. "I'll get the lantern."

"You sit down," he said. "I don't need you tripping over something and breaking your leg."

"But I know this place—"

"And I'm telling you...*asking* you...please. Let me."

She surrendered and felt her way around to sit on the couch in front of the unlit fireplace. A moment later, a bright light from the main bedroom illuminated a wedge of the wooden floor in front of her. Telling herself that they would find Chichi tomorrow, and all would be well, she waited for Jack to return. Instead he called out.

"Becca, can you come here?"

She pushed to her feet and followed the light. Jack stood next to the set of drawers. He held the lantern high so most of the room was lit. Looking at the partly made bed, he grinned as he said, "Look who the cat dragged in."

Near the headboard, Becca saw two glowing eyes pop up. She blinked. And then she covered her mouth to smother the yelp—of delight, not fright.

Jack chuckled. "Seems Chichi decided to beat us home."

She rushed over, folded the cool little dog in her lap and smothered him in kisses. Wagging his tail, he lapped it all up.

"I know what this means," Jack said, moving closer.

Becca was still cuddling Chichi close. "What's that?"

"There won't be just the two of us sharing that bed tonight."

As low as she had felt a moment ago, now she felt as if she could fly. She didn't want to think about any regrets she might have in the morning. As Chichi jumped off the bed and leapt onto the camper cot, she only wanted to celebrate.

Ten

Becca reached up and pulled him down. As her mouth latched onto his, they fell back onto the bed.

Sometime later, when she let him come up for air, Jack arched a brow.

"Does this mean we have to get naked?"

They were lying facing each other. Now she sat up, grabbed the hem of his shirt and pulled it up. Then she dropped warm, hungry kisses all over his chest while her fingers kneaded his sides.

Her mouth slid lower and lower. The tip of her tongue was circling his navel when she unzipped his fly. Jack pushed up on his elbows. If she was about to do what he thought she would do, he was all for it. He helped her pull off his pants and boxer briefs. Then she snatched the dress off over her head. The bra landed on the coat stand in the corner. He wasn't sure where the panties went.

He was sitting at the foot of the bed while she stood before him. Ready to go, he fell back and then shot up again.

"Condoms," he said, ready to spring over to his bag for supplies.

But Becca was slotting herself between his parted thighs. Her breasts were at eye level. What was a man to do?

He dropped slow, moist kisses around one nipple while plucking and lightly pinching the other. Her fingers drove through his hair, over the back of his scalp then across to each shoulder as she arched into him and made noises in her throat that only excited him more.

His other hand fanned down the curve of her ribs, waist, hip. When his fingers slid between her legs and found her wet, he remembered why he'd sat up in the first place.

While he sucked and plucked and gently rubbed, he spoke around that nipple. "Rubbers…"

She pulled his head away, snatched a penetrating kiss that blew his mind and then lowered onto her knees on the floor. A second before her lips met the tip of his erection, he heard her murmur, "Not yet."

As her head lowered more, a series of bone-melting sensations rippled over his skin. At first she simply held him in her mouth. Then her tongue got into the act, swirling around the ridge, rolling one way then the other, tickling the tip. When she began to hum, the vibration at the base of her throat drifted along her tongue and teeth.

He clutched the sheet and clenched his jaw.

He wasn't normally this excited this soon. It had to be all the buildup—in the lake, coming home—and because she knew just what to do and how to do it, as if they had been together like this before. Of course, before this week, she would have jumped off a cliff rather than…well, do what she was doing now.

He shifted enough to scoop her around the waist and lift her up and onto the bed. As she lay there looking at him with hungry eyes, he cautioned her with a finger.

"Stay right there. Don't move."

With a cheeky grin, she crossed her heart.

He found his bag, ripped the condom box open and, crossing back, rolled the rubber on. Becca's arms were tucked under the pillow behind her head. Her hair had dried. In the lantern light, the mussed waves glistened around her face. Then she drew up one knee, angled her hips in a provocative pose, and he crawled up the mattress until he was kissing her again. He couldn't bring her close enough as they rolled together on the sheets.

His breathing was heavy by the time he urged her over onto her back and positioned himself between her thighs. As he entered her slowly, he watched her eyes widen, her back arch and lips part. Then she smiled. He wanted to say how beautiful she was, not just her face or her body, but the way she made him feel—truly alive for the first time in years.

When her legs wrapped around his thighs and her pelvis slanted up, he closed his eyes and gave himself over to sensation.

He'd wanted this, their first time together, to last all night. She fit him so well—everywhere. The physical friction building between them was the sweetest he'd ever known. And as heat began to blaze and then to rage, Jack found himself picturing them here together like this for more than two nights.

For longer than either one could ever allow.

Becca's entire body was left buzzing—floating. All the rumors were true. Jack Reed was not only smoking hot in bed, in her opinion, he was legendary.

They were lying on their backs side by side, both gazing blindly at the ceiling. Basking in the afterglow, they were still panting and smiling. Becca's skin was cooling. The payoff had been so unbelievably good, she only wanted to do it again.

"I wonder if that dog planned this," he said.

"What do you mean?"

"If Chichi hadn't wandered off," he explained, "we wouldn't be here doing this."

"If we hadn't lost him in the first place," she pointed out, "we would have done this beside the lake."

"And right now mosquitoes would be feasting on our backsides." He kissed her nose. "Our little friend did us a favor."

"After half scaring me death."

"He didn't know."

She laughed. "Jack Reed, crusader for misunderstood mutts."

"Make that misunderstood *ugly* mutts."

"Not kind, and yet I can see it on a T-shirt. On the letterhead of a charity. Maybe you should get one of your own."

"A dog?"

"And a charity."

He shifted up on an elbow and cupped his jaw in his palm. "Maybe I should."

His smile was so close, and with his heavy hand resting on the dip of her waist… Becca felt so lucky. And somehow also sad. If she didn't know Jack's background, if he wasn't so forthright in embracing his less-flattering side, she might be fooled into believing they were made for each other.

In reality, of course, two people couldn't be less suited to each other. This physical chemistry might be explosive, but what a person believed in was a thousand times more important than how skilled and connected they were in the bedroom. She stood for sacrifice and the betterment of society. Jack stood for self-gain, for power at the expense of anything and anyone who stood in his way.

"Does the lake have fish?" he asked, toying with a wave of her hair.

"My dad used to fish here all the time."

"Any poles around?"

"In the shed." She drew a wiggling line down the middle of his steamy chest. "You like fishing?"

"My father took me fly-fishing a couple of times."

"Fond memories?"

"Sure. We didn't get to spend that much time together."

"Why's that?"

"He ran his own company. That means putting in the extra hours when employees get to go home to their families."

"If it was his company, he could have made a choice to go home rather than stay."

"Not that simple. Before I came along, my father was bankrupt. They lost their house and more than a few fair-weather friends. At the same time my mother landed in the hospital with pneumonia. She almost died. On one of those fishing trips, Dad told me that when he thought she might not pull through, he'd made a vow. If only she lived, if they could spend a long and happy life together, he would take care of her the way she deserved."

"He blamed himself for her illness?"

"He felt responsible for his family. She recovered and their luck seemed to change. He started up another company, finance lending this time, and it took off. But he always had one eye on the past, the other on the future. He never allowed himself to drop the ball. His priority was making sure we were cared for."

"Even if he couldn't share what was most precious of all."

"His time? I knew he loved us both. But there were sacrifices. You can't have everything."

"Do you see much of them now?"

"They passed away ten years ago within months of each other."

"That must have been hard."

"We've all got to go sometime. Better to go in your seventies than…" His jaw tensed and he looked away.

Was he remembering the woman he had loved in college? Did he wonder what they might have shared and conquered together if she had lived? Becca wasn't sure he would have taken his father's route and dedicated his life to a company in order to ensure security for his family. She would rather believe that he'd have taken his own son fly-fishing often—spent quality time with those he loved.

Jack sat up. "Hey, you want a beer? A glass of wine?"

"Beer," she said, reaching over the side of the bed to find her dress.

"Stay put. I'll find the bathroom, clean up and bring back supplies. Can I take the light?"

"Be my guest."

While he was gone and she was left in the shadows, Becca shimmied under the top sheet and waited. She heard Chichi's collar rattle from the cot in the corner as he scratched himself. She'd had plans to set Jack to work while they were here. Chopping wood, fixing loose shingles, sanding back walls, cooking simple meals. Nothing so out of the ordinary for normal folk. Her goal had been to highlight the difference between the big-time "haves" and people who had to struggle. There were plenty of them out there.

There wasn't much work going on at the moment.

Soon, he was back carrying the ice chest in one hand, flashlight in the other. Becca took the light and he jumped in under the sheet and then set the chest down between them. As he cracked open one beer and handed it over, she picked up the thread of their conversation.

"Sounds as if you had good parents."

"I was lucky," he admitted, cracking open one for himself. They saluted each other and pulled down a mouthful. Becca didn't drink beer often, but in this setting, on this night, it felt right.

"I've never found out who my birth mother was," she said, resting the beer on her lap. "I didn't want to complicate anyone's life by dropping back in."

"Isn't it usually the other way around? A biological parent not wanting to make waves in the adult child's life?"

"I figure it might not be easy, but there are ways to track down a baby who's been gobbled up in the system. If she didn't want to know, it's better left alone."

"You never wanted to know the reasons?"

"Not anymore. Can't change yesterdays. And I didn't have such a hard time, even those first eleven years."

"Were you with lots of families?"

"Two others. I was provided for. Nobody abused me. But…" She brought the beer to her lips, swallowed another mouthful and confessed what she hadn't told anyone before. "I knew something was missing. Something key. Sometimes I felt…*invisible*." Sometimes she felt that way still. But not with Jack. Even right from the start. "It's hard to describe."

"Did you feel that way a lot?"

"Whenever I did, I read. Sometimes the same book over and over."

"What was your favorite?"

"When I was very young, *Cinderella*."

"A classic. Like the Bambino."

She smiled. "I fell in love with the idea of a fairy godmother. When all the lights went out at night, I'd sit up in bed and gaze out the window for what seemed like hours. I thought if only I wished hard enough, all my dreams would come true."

"What dreams?"

"I was an overweight, painfully shy girl. I wouldn't say boo to save myself. But in my dreams I was a princess, like Cinders. I simply needed my godmother to wave her wand and work her magic."

He was grinning. "Well, of course."

"If ever I saw a mouse," she went on, "I would close my eyes and wish for it to change into a beautiful white steed. I'd daydream that my dress was a gorgeous billowing gown made of white satin. Naturally a prince would happen along, fall on one knee and beg me to marry him."

Jack's eyes were smiling. "Naturally."

"The ring he'd ask me to wear was either a big diamond circled by priceless rubies, or a pearl surrounded by a sparkling sea of sapphires. Something right out of yesteryear."

"And then?"

Becca put her beer down. "Then I grew up, got a degree, joined the Peace Corps."

His expression changed. "Tell me about that."

"I served as a volunteer in the Dominican Republic for two years."

"That would be right after college?"

"Uh-huh. I helped to teach the youth how to make good choices. We talked to women about reproduction health and nutrition. There's so much poverty and unemployment. It's hard to imagine my life back there now. Those two years shaped me more than anything before or since. I know the true value of a safe, soft place to land."

"I had dreams of saving the world, too, once."

"*No*. Really?"

"I'd finished my engineering business degree. I was going to fly to Africa to help build housing."

Was he serious? "Jack, have you ever told anyone else that?"

"What? And destroy my image?"

She grinned. "So, you were going by yourself?"

"With my girlfriend. My fiancée. We were going to leave everything behind. Start fresh."

Lying on her side, Becca laid her cheek on her outstretched arm and searched his eyes.

"What was she like?"

He seemed to think back. "Krystal was soft. Delicate. She was studying criminal law. Her father was a defense attorney, and then became a judge later in his career. I never thought she was cut out for it. She didn't fit with the idea of courtroom drama and getting murderers off on a technicality. She was gentle. Easily hurt. Entirely giving."

Becca's heart was beating faster.

"You wanted to protect her."

Like Jack's father had wanted to protect his mom.

"I imagined us married with a couple of boys," he said. "I'd come home from work every day and she'd have a delicious dinner waiting. Later, while she took some downtime, I'd play with the kids."

Becca smiled softly. "I can imagine you doing that." She really could. "Can I ask...how did she die?"

His jaw tightened. "Her father was one mean son of a gun. Krystal was never good enough for the judge. She was an only child, so it was up to her to follow in her dad's giant footsteps. Carry on the legacy. She began to flunk classes. She wasn't looking after herself. When she came down with mono, it laid her up for weeks. Then we spent Thanksgiving at her parents'. Big mistake. Her father went from cool, to frosty, to flat-out belligerent. At the table, he started attacking her, telling her that she had to try harder. If that was her best, it wasn't near good enough."

Becca felt ill. "Poor girl."

"I gave him a piece of my mind. Then I was in *everyone's* bad books."

It was true. A person could say what they like about

their own family, but God help anyone else who tried to bring them down.

"Krystal was depressed for weeks after that. Then, a few days before Christmas, the dark cloud seemed to lift. She was smiling again. She said that she'd come to accept that she couldn't get away from disappointing her father, but that was okay."

Becca knew what was coming.

A muscle in his jaw flexed before Jack ended, "She didn't see that Christmas morning. I found her in the bathroom."

"Oh, Jack ..."

"Her father blamed me. Hell, *I* blamed me."

Was this the reason he'd looked so distant when they'd visited that school—the day she'd lectured him about vulnerable young adults? He had already learned that lesson on his own.

"You shouldn't blame yourself," she said, holding his hand. "She needed professional help."

"Instead her boyfriend added to the pressure." He exhaled. "So, you see, sometimes it's not so good to be handed your future, whether you think you want it or not. Big shoes are hard to fill."

Was that his way of justifying his position with Angelica? If they should succeed in overthrowing Evan McCain, was that perspective meant to stave off guilt over persuading Angelica to later sell off the pieces?

He studied her face for a long moment before casting a look at the ice chest. Shifting his hand from under hers, he flipped open the lid again and put a casual note in his voice.

"So, what else have we got? Eggs, bacon, tomatoes? You have gas in the kitchen?"

"Yeah. I do."

Becca was still processing everything he'd divulged.

How many more layers were there to this man? What other wounds was he covering up? Her first eleven years of her life hadn't been a picnic, but she hadn't had anyone close to her die. Jack had lost the woman he had loved as well as both his parents. Some people grieved by putting up a wall. Shutting off certain parts of themselves. Was that Jack?

"What say I whip you up an omelet?" he said.

She tried to be light. "You cook?"

"Not well."

"Can you chop wood?"

"If required."

It wasn't cool enough for a fire. Becca peered inside the ice chest. "There's crackers and strawberries and three kinds of cheese. And look at this…" She drew out a package. "Belgian chocolate."

"Even better than Danishes."

She broke off two pieces and slotted one bit in his mouth, the other in her own.

"I should mention that I have a chocolate addiction," she said around her mouthful.

"Chocolate's good for you."

He popped another square into her mouth and she smiled as she took in every line of his face.

"If you're a chocoholic," he said, "you need to try this."

He broke off another piece of chocolate and set a strawberry on top. "Open up," he said, and she did.

As she chewed and sighed, he made his own chocolate-strawberry stack.

"Oh, God." She sighed. "This is so good."

His lips came close to taste hers. "I totally agree."

Eleven

After their picnic and talk in bed, Becca fell asleep in Jack's arms.

He lay there for he didn't know how long, thinking back on how he'd opened up about that piece of his past. The words had come remarkably easy. The emotion hadn't been as painful as he'd remembered. Time healed all wounds? Maybe that was true. It was the scars he couldn't seem to kick.

Jack closed his eyes for a moment. When he opened them again, morning light was streaking in through the window, warming the room with a gauzy golden glow. Smiling, Jack stretched. *Man,* he felt good. And the reason was lying right here alongside of him.

He reached out to bring Becca close—and came up empty. The only sign of her was the impression left on the sheet.

Jack sat up.

The cot was empty, too. Other than birds chirping and

squawking outside, all was quiet. The screened window was open, letting in pine-scented fresh air. No smog. No traffic. No meetings.

No phone calls?

Was there even reception out here?

Jack swung out of bed, grabbed some jeans and pulled them on. Then he found his phone. Some texts and three voicemails. One from Logan, one from Angelica and one from David Baldwin.

Wearing cutoffs and a T-shirt that read "Choose Happiness," Becca entered the room. Her flawless face broke into a big smile. "You're up!"

Something pleasant tugged in Jack's gut. He crossed over, folded her up in his arms and nuzzled the top of her head. She felt soft and warm and smelled like sunshine. If Angelica was okay when he called back, maybe they could stay an additional couple of days. Or three, or four.

"I missed you," he murmured against her hair.

She laughed. "You've been awake two minutes."

"One minute."

Pulling away, she spotted the phone in his hand. When her smile cooled, he felt a spike of guilt—which he shouldn't.

"I wasn't sure if we got reception out this far," he said.

"It's patchy. Any messages?"

"A few."

While her eyes still shone, her mouth tightened. "Anything important?"

"You don't want to know."

"Angelica?" Jack nodded. "You going to call her back?" She held up her hands. "Sorry. Stupid question. She might be planning a coup for this afternoon. You wouldn't want to miss that."

Jack caught her as she turned to leave. "Becca, this was always a tricky situation."

She kept her gaze on the wooden floor. "I didn't think it'd get *this* tricky."

Ah, hell.

He brought her close again and, lifting her chin, searched those sparkling green eyes. "Are you sorry we came?"

"Up until a second ago, for so many reasons, I wasn't. I wanted to take you away from everything that drives your need to win. I wanted you to live a simple life and appreciate it, even for a couple of days. I thought you might see how little people need, and how easy it would be for everyone to have that if we all cared enough. But now..."

"What we shared last night was amazing. But I still have to help Angelica. I just *have* to."

"Because someone has a gun to your head?"

Jack struggled and then admitted, "I can't explain."

"No need. It's pretty obvious."

He studied her wounded, defiant look and then put the phone down on the side table.

Her gaze snapped from the phone back to him. "You're not going to call her?"

"Angelica can wait."

But then his phone rang. Becca swept it up and held it out for him, daring him to refuse, hoping that he would. He wanted to ignore the call, but now it had rung a bigger part wanted to reconnect and plug into what was going on beyond the walls of this cabin. He couldn't walk away from this deal, not even for Becca.

He took the phone, connected. It wasn't Angelica.

"Hope I didn't catch you too early," David Baldwin said. "I left a message—"

Annoyed, Jack cut in. "What can I do for you?"

"I'm having a get-together this afternoon. I know you're probably busy."

Chichi pranced in with a stick between his small, pointy teeth. Jack turned toward the window view. "A bit, yeah."

"But if you could make it over, just for a few moments... it's important."

"David, I really don't think—"

"Don't give me your answer now." He gave a time for the event. "At the shop. Hope to see you there."

David Baldwin could hope all he liked.

Chichi was going to town, chewing his stick on the cot. Becca, however, had disappeared.

As Jack headed for the doorway, she marched by, carrying the ice chest. He strode out and took it from her. *For Pete's sake.*

"What exactly is the rush?" he asked.

"It's time to go."

"You said two days and two nights."

"I've changed my mind. Things have gotten off track. This won't work."

Jack put down the chest and turned off his phone. "Weren't we fixing bacon and eggs?" Amid the giggling and kissing last night, there'd been some mention of cooking breakfast before she'd fallen asleep.

"I'd rather just get back on the road. You know...get back to reality."

"I didn't mean to upset you."

She knotted her arms over her chest. "I'm not upset with you. I'm upset with *me*. For a second there, I'd actually talked myself into believing that I might have reached your human side. A *caring* side that didn't have stealing and then raping Lassiter Media as next on his to-do list. But you can't wait to get back into it."

Jack flinched. Well, that stung.

"One day," he said, "I promise, we'll sit down and I'll give you the lowdown on this Lassiter business from my perspective. Just...not today. I can't today." He filed his fingers back through her silky hair and waited for her to meet his gaze. "Now, can I make us a coffee?"

"That won't fix anything."

"It sure won't hurt."

When he grinned, she bit her lip, exhaled and finally nodded. As they headed back to the kitchen, she said, "I guess there's still a part of me who believes in a fairy godmother. She was just here, expecting a miracle."

"Could be that's what I like most about you," he said. "Your faith." He stopped and turned her in the circle of one arm.

"You mean my temper," she said.

"Your tenacity."

"My stubborn streak."

"I like this about you, too."

His lips met hers and lingered there. Closing his eyes, he drank in all that sassy, strong-headed goodness. When he drew away, her eyes narrowed even as those succulent lips twitched.

"Next you'll be suggesting we take our coffee back to bed."

"Well, just remember." He lowered his head to kiss her properly. "It was your idea."

When she brought it up again, Jack didn't try to talk her out of leaving the cabin. She didn't need for matters between the two of them to get any more complicated than they already were, and he obviously needed to get back to see what Angelica was up to.

He'd tried to phone Angelica a number of times. When he'd failed to reach her, he'd grown more and more preoccupied. He even admitted that he wondered if Angelica was purposely avoiding his calls now because she planned to do something he would stop if he could. When they finally got on the road after lunch, Becca couldn't shake the sense of guilt.

She had allowed her emotions to get the better of her where Jack was concerned. She'd taken him to the cabin not to give in to the attraction brewing between them, but to somehow help him gain perspective away from his cut-throat corporate world. She wanted to show him in a hands-on way he would remember that lots of people went without even the bare necessities. Had her scheme done any good at all, or had she only made matters worse?

Still, what Jack and she had shared at the cabin was more than physical. At least it had been for her. However much she abhorred Jack's business tactics and egocentric mind-set, whenever they had been together in an intimate sense, she hadn't been able to help falling just a little in love with him.

Chichi had sat on Becca's lap all the drive back to Santa Monica. When Jack pulled into the quiet beachside parking lot in a space right next to Hailey's café, the dog was quivering with excitement. Then Becca opened the car door; she couldn't stop Chichi from bolting up the ramp into the café's rear entrance.

Jack got out and hauled the ice chest off the backseat.

"Want to chow down while we're here?" Becca asked, joining him.

"Best to keep going."

He was eager to get back to L.A. He needed to call on Angelica, keep that Lassiter takeover ball rolling and on track. Becca had felt his preoccupation building for the whole drive back. Now, as they walked up the café's ramp together, he seemed disconnected.

As they made their way around the veranda, Hailey and Chichi appeared.

"How was the trip?" Hailey asked. "Hope Chichi behaved himself."

Jack set down the chest. As they took their usual seats and Hailey poured coffee, Becca let her friend know what had happened with Chichi the previous day at the lake... minus the bits about Jack and her being, well, otherwise occupied.

"I'm sorry," Becca said. "We should have kept a closer eye on him."

Hailey waved it off. "Way I see it, he probably just wanted to give you two some space."

When she flicked a knowing glance Jack's way, he held his expression, no hint of cheekiness or denial. But Becca's chest tightened. In his mind, he'd already moved on. What they had shared at the lake was in the past. He was back in corporate-raider mode and focused on bringing down his current target.

When neither Jack nor Becca commented, Hailey's expression grew concerned. "Oh, God," she murmured. "You don't know. There's no TV out at the cabin."

Jack's brow creased as he sat forward. "What happened?"

"It was on this morning," Hailey went on.

"You mean the interview from the reporter who ambushed us yesterday?" Becca asked.

"There were clips from that interview...." Hailey pressed her lips together. "It's the photos that got everyone talking."

Becca suddenly felt dizzy and she couldn't feel her face.

"What photos?" she groaned. She wasn't sure she wanted to know.

"You must have been followed," Hailey said. "They had shots of you both in that lake, taken with a telescopic lens, so they were kinda grainy. But it's pretty clear what you all were doing."

While Jack sat back like he'd been shot in the chest, the

knot of horror in Becca's stomach pulled apart and spread through every inch of her body. Everything around her, other than Jack's scowl, seemed to funnel back and fade to black.

Becca was always fighting the hard fight, standing up for morals and justice. Now she shut her eyes as that darkness enveloped her.

Despite keeping an eye out, Hailey said they must have been followed. Had they been followed back here, too?

She had to phone the office again and make certain Evans McCain understood. Things had gotten—confused, but she was still one hundred percent on his side.

"There's more," Hailey said, wincing.

Jack rubbed his brow. "Of course there is."

"Angelica Lassiter has called a press conference," Hailey went on, "scheduled for this afternoon."

Jack thumped the table and everyone, including Chichi, jumped. When he pushed to his feet, the action sent his chair skating and clattering into the one behind it.

Becca stood, too, hugged her friend and whispered in her ear, "I'll call you later."

Becca followed Jack around the veranda and down the ramp. Before he reached the driver's-side door of her Bambino, he stopped abruptly and spun around. She almost ran into him.

He held out his hand. "Keys."

Becca fumbled in her bag and slapped them in his palm. "You're going to see Angelica," she said.

"As soon as humanly possible."

Jack threw open the car door. As Becca skirted around and jumped in the passenger side, he turned the key in the ignition. The lights flashed up on the dash…but the engine didn't kick over. He growled and tried again.

Nothing.

He set his teeth, raised his fists, but held off somehow
from smashing down on the wheel. If Becca was upset,
Jack was livid. And then…

Things went from bad to a hundred times worse.

Twelve

"That's just great. That's *exactly* what I need."

Becca scowled across at him. "You're not the only one stuck in this car, you know."

"It's your car!"

As the tabloid show truck sailed into the parking lot and pulled behind them blocking their escape, Becca opened her mouth then simply sat back and crossed her arms tightly over her T-shirt while Jack brought up an app on his phone and sent a text for a cab.

He'd apologize for raising his voice later. Right now he needed to get them the hell out of this predicament. He didn't care who had tipped them off again or whether he and Becca had been followed the entire time. The director of the Lassiter Foundation had been seen repeatedly with the man who wanted to bring the whole lot down. He needed to get Becca out of this mess then he'd find Angelica before she purged in front of a microphone and said something they both might regret at that press conference.

When Angelica had wavered the other day, Jack thought he had been persuasive enough to get her back to where he needed her to be. Once again she had seemed set upon a path that would lead to a takeover of the company that was rightfully hers. But when she'd called this morning early and he hadn't been able to get in contact with her since, Jack had begun to worry. If Becca hadn't decided to call her cabin stay short, he'd have insisted.

As the camera crew and the reporter from the other day loped over, he threw open the door. "Get out of the car," he told Becca.

He met her around her side, grabbed her hand and headed for the road. She had to trot to keep up.

"Where are we going?"

"We're getting the hell out of Dodge."

As they reached the pavement, she yanked her hand from his. Her face was flushed but her bearing was almost regal.

"I'm not going," she said. "You've had Angelica dancing on your strings. Everyone knows she doesn't do anything without consulting you first. If Angelica's called a press conference without your permission or advice, it can only mean she's distancing herself from you. It might even mean that she's decided to step down from a takeover bid. I'm not going to tag along while you try to badger her into changing her mind."

The cab he'd ordered swerved into the gutter. Swinging open the door, he eyeballed Becca. "You coming?"

"I'll hold my head up and face the firing squad square on, thank you."

He had to admire her courage. "When you have a moment," he said, "I'll give you a lesson on how to avoid unnecessary trouble."

"You haven't done such a great job of it lately."

So it would seem. He should have flat-out refused

to give Becca an audience in the first place. Of course that would've meant missing out on getting to know her more—a once-in-a-lifetime experience. There'd never be another Becca.

"I'll call," he told her.

"Please don't."

"I can't change your mind?"

She only crossed her arms. Defiant to the end.

Jack hung his head, considered the repercussions and, leaving the cab door open, joined her again. "Then I'll stay, too."

Her eyes widened as her arms dropped to her sides. "I don't need you."

"Right now I think we need each other."

Stopping in position before them, the reporter shot out her first question.

"Mr. Reed," she began, "what do you have to say about the photos of yourself and Ms. Stevens circulating this morning?"

Jack surprised Becca. He didn't growl. Didn't try to divert the issue. He simply looped his arm around her waist, tugged her closer and announced, "Ms. Stevens and I are late for an engagement. So, if you'll excuse us…"

Then he crowded Becca toward the open cab door, leaving her no chance to argue. He scooted in the backseat after her. As he reached to close the door, the reporter persisted.

"Mr. Reed, wait…did you say engagement? You and Becca Stevens are engaged to be married? Does Angelica Lassiter know? Are you backing out of a takeover bid of Lassiter Media?"

The door slammed shut. The reporter's microphone hit the glass. Tires squealed as the cab pulled out.

"Where to?" the driver asked in an Eastern European accent.

"Beverly Hills."

Looking in the rearview mirror, the cabbie reached for a candy dispenser on the dash. He shook a mint into his mouth and sucked for a moment. "You are Jack Reed and the lady from the Lassiter charity, yes? I see pictures of you on TV."

Becca wanted to smack her forehead. Seemed everyone had seen those photos except them.

"No worries, Mr. Reed," the cabbie said with a lopsided grin. "I will lose those leeches. My mother-in-law, she worked for a big-time newspaper. She's still Mrs. Snoopidy Snoops." He sneered. "Always on my case, sticking in her nose where it might get cut off."

The cab swerved off the main drag down a side street.

"We get back on the highway a few miles down." The cabbie looked back at them over a shoulder. "Feel free to talk. What happens in cab, stays in cab."

After a few moments, Jack dared to look across at Becca. Her lips were tight, cheeks were pink. Her hands were balled up in fists at her sides.

"You tricked me," she growled.

"I did what I thought was right."

"You did what was right for *you*. I told you—" she pointed to Jack's brow "—you've got rocks in your head if you think I'm going with you to talk to Angelica. If you do, I'll tell her that she's being a fool. That she's destroying her family over the illusion of power. I'll ask her where the hell she put her priorities."

In this mood, Jack had no doubt that she would.

"I'll drop you off at your office," he said.

She slumped back and held her head. "They'll probably lynch me."

"Then I'll drop you home."

"That's not really addressing the problem, is it, Jack?"

He shut his eyes, his patience running thin now.

"I don't know what you expect me to do," he said. "If

you're waiting for a halo to magically appear above my head and a plea for forgiveness, don't hold your breath."

She stared at the ceiling, tears in her eyes. "I'm a fool. I was attracted to you and I let that ruin everything."

"Depends on how you look at it."

Her voice was thick, resigned. "There's only one way to look at it."

He didn't think so. "I want to see you again, Becca." And he didn't care who knew.

She froze, mouth half-open, eyes wide with shock. Then she shook herself and self-righteousness ruled again.

"You actually want to throw more fuel on this fire? Maybe you want to screw with my affections so much that I'll crumble and lead a munity of Lassiter management and employees against McCain?"

"That's crazy talk."

"Yeah, well, maybe I'm crazy."

"We're not going to get anywhere if—"

"That's it, Jack. We, you and I, are not going to get anywhere. Because this is over. O-V-E-R."

Angelica sent another text after Jack had dropped Becca home. She asked that he meet her at Lassiter Grill. He tried to ignore the ball of unease growing in the pit of his gut. The location was a sure sign. For her to suggest they meet there, she must have reconciled with her brother, Dylan, the one who'd been left controlling interest of the Lassiter Grill Group, including the restaurant here in L.A.

Jack would hear what she had to say. Then, if there was any doubt whatsoever about her caving in to the terms of J.D.'s will, he'd do his damnedest to talk her out of it.

When the cab dropped him off, Jack gave the driver a huge tip. As he walked into the restaurant, with its trademark rustic elegance, he spotted Angelica at a booth not far from the floor-to-ceiling stone fireplace. She sat staring into her coffee cup, looking like a jumper about to take that last step.

"Hello, Angelica," he said, sitting opposite her.

Angelica's head came up. Her expression was scathing. "What in the name of God were you thinking?"

Jack thatched his fingers on the table in front of him. "You're referring to Becca Stevens."

"The company, particularly the foundation, has been hit hard enough by this tug-of-war. Why in the name of everything sane would you go and sleep with that woman?"

"I didn't exactly plan it, Ange. Or not the way it turned out anyway."

She straightened in her seat. "I spoke with Logan. He was speechless."

And Jack was supposed to…what? Go to his room for time-out? "I am an adult. I don't need to ask permission."

"You sure as hell do when you're dragging my name down along with hers." She shook her head, incredulous. "I thought you said you weren't trying to get Becca on our side."

"I wasn't."

She blinked and frowned. "So, this was purely for sport?"

His teeth set so hard, his jaw ached. "I like Becca Stevens."

"Well, that's a shame because you just destroyed her."

It was bad, but not that bad. And Jack sure as hell didn't know why he was copping all the blame. "Becca's an adult, too. I didn't tie her down."

"She's no match for you." Angelica's anger turned into concern. "No one is."

Time to get back on topic. He took a breath and focused. "You wanted to see me."

"I want to… I mean, I'm pretty sure that I want to…"

"Walk away from your rightful inheritance?"

She raised her voice. "I want things back the way they were."

"We *can't* go back. We can only go forward. With commitment and justice on our side." He believed that to his bones.

Her head slowly tilted as she evaluated him through narrowed eyes. "You're saying the words, but somehow you don't sound as convinced."

That was news to him. But, granted… "It's been a long battle. When things are worth fighting for, it's never easy."

"Becca Stevens didn't get to you, did she? Here I am thinking you've used her, but I wonder—"

"If she had an effect on me?" Jack threw up his hands. "You know, in fact, *yes,* she did. She's a special lady with a big heart and too many other assets to count." He leaned forward. "But none of that changes what you and I are trying to achieve. *Will* achieve. Just think, Angelica. You won't have to live with the label of the snubbed daughter of J. D. Lassiter for much longer."

Her eyes glistened with moisture.

"You're not as strong as J.D.," Jack said. "You're stronger. And when you need a rest, like now, I'm here to stand guard on the battlements."

She blew out a shaky breath, then rested her elbow on the table and held her brow. "You don't know what it feels like to have to choose, Jack."

He might consider her fortunate. He was never given a choice.

When Logan had informed him of the part he was to play in this unfolding drama, Jack had wanted to refuse. But a friend was a friend; that didn't change once they died. And so he had agreed to comply with the special clause in J.D.'s will, which was meant solely for him and Angelica. Since that day he'd led her closer and closer toward a corporate showdown against Evan and anyone who stood behind him. The way Jack had looked at it, either outcome would be a victory.

Now…he only wished Becca Stevens didn't have to be part of the collateral damage.

Angelica called off the press conference, and Jack left her in a better state, although he didn't have a lot of faith in what the immediate future might bring. Angelica was an educated, capable woman. But he wondered how soon she would have crumpled and given in to the terms of the will if he hadn't been stirring her pot.

Jack ordered another cab, his intentions being to call in at the office—the first time ever wearing jeans, unlike Ms. Stevens. Not that he was in the mood to sit behind a desk. Truth be known, he felt like fishing…beside a quiet lake, simply to enjoy the atmosphere, the fresh air. The company.

As eventful as his time with Becca had been, he had an ice cube's chance in hell of rekindling those flames. Which got him thinking…just how long had it been since he'd been with a woman? The press played up his womanizing past. Jack's take? If a guy was single and able, damned if he'd want to sit at home singing to his cats. But he wasn't as ruthless in that department as the media made out. Of course it wasn't every day a man came across someone as intriguing as Becca.

She was in every way his match, including her annoying headstrong streak. And when they made love…she was wild and smart and incredibly generous. There were times when she exhausted him. She *always* inspired him.

And he sincerely doubted she'd ever want to see his hide again.

Jack was tossing around whether to tell the driver to ditch his earlier address and simply take him home when his cell phone beeped with a text. He prayed it wasn't

Angelica. Hoped against hope it might be Becca. It was neither.

David Baldwin. Again.

Still hope to see you this afternoon.
Best, Dave.

Jack felt bad for the man. He wished he could help the way David wanted him to. That was out of the question. But there was something more he could do. He had an afternoon to fill in anyway.

The cab dropped Jack off in front of the Baldwin Boats office and factory. The signage across the front of the main building was faded. The *o* in boats was gone completely. The yard was free of workers. He glanced at his watch. After quitting time for the factory.

As he neared the entrance, an odd, prickling feeling ran over his skin. He'd just take five minutes to tell Baldwin that not only was the deal still on the table, he would up the offer. Becca was right. How much money did one man need? And Dave had mentioned in one of the conversations that he had six kids. *Six.* What a scary thought. Four boys, two girls. What was it like growing up in a houseful of siblings? Noisy. Scary. Certainly never lonely.

When the receptionist spotted him strolling in through the automatic entry doors, she shot to her feet.

"Oh! Mr. Reed. Dave was expecting you. Well, he'd hoped…" She grinned like a kid who'd discovered every tree in the backyard had turned into a ball of cotton candy. "I'll go tell him you're here."

As she scurried off, Jack strolled around the reception area. Framed photographs hung on the walls, pictures of power catamarans, officials at boat launches. Quite a few of David, the earliest from perhaps twenty years ago. Before putting the contract together, he'd had a full back-

ground check compiled. David was only a little older than
Jack, although he looked at least, ten years older. Stress
could do that to a person. And while Jack lived with stress,
it wasn't the kind where he had to scramble to find the next
mortgage payment, or wonder when the utilities might be
turned off. He didn't have to worry every week whether
or not he could make the payroll. Jack knew that had been
Dave's dilemma pretty much since the recession had hit
and turned the economy on its head.

Dave ambled out from his office, a big smile plastered
on his face. When he held out his hand, Jack took a hold
and shook. There was a lot to be said about a man's hand-
shake and Dave Baldwin's was firm without being cocky.

"Jack, glad you could make it," Dave said, ushering
him down the corridor. He was a tall man. Almost as tall
as Jack.

"Seems I'm too late for that get together," Jack said.
Looked like everyone else had gone.

"Not too late at all."

They sat in tub chairs in Dave's office, a room that
overlooked the factory yard. Outside Jack saw a couple of
fixed cranes, several boat molds, numerous trailers, trol-
leys meant to shift upward of six tons. There was plenty
of value in those assets. From previous conversations, Jack
knew that Dave would never consider downsizing, which
would mean putting people on unemployment. Men of
Dave's ilk lived by two mottos: natural attrition only, and
the captain must go down with the ship.

"Can I get you a coffee, Jack?"

"Got a beer?"

Dave brought two back from a bar fridge tucked under
a counter covered with engineering plans. Jack cracked
open the beer and downed a couple of much appreciated
mouthfuls.

"Hmm. Cold," he said.

"I like it so cold that my lips turn numb."

Jack grinned. "Me, too."

"Cheryl and I have four boys, you know?"

"You mentioned."

"Oldest turning twenty-one next spring. Old enough to drink, to vote. It's scary how quickly time goes. I was twenty-one when I first got into this business. I worked my rear end off. When the owner decided to retire, he asked if I wanted to buy in. I learned everything from that man. He was like a father to me."

"That's a long time in one place. I understand why you think of your employees as family."

"Family..." Studying the floor near his feet, David nodded deeply. "It's the most powerful word in the dictionary, don't you think? Just the idea of family makes a person feel warm and included." He caught Jack's gaze. "And sometimes a little overwhelmed."

Dave was looking at him so curiously, as if his face was a mask he wanted peeled back to see what lay underneath. Jack, however, couldn't help thinking about the Lassiter family, how it had all come together only to be recently torn apart.

"You have two daughters, too," Jack said.

"They're the youngest. Twins. Only six. My wife worries that we're old parents. That we might not be around to see our youngest grandkids. I tell her that our memory and our love will live on. Those girls, the boys too, will always know where they came from and that they were loved."

Jack sipped his beer. Was that too much information? And yet after the week he'd had, sitting here, tipping back while Dave philosophized on the context of family seemed somehow acceptable. Even agreeable.

It was good to truly shirk off the Lassiter problem for a while. To forget how upset Becca had still been when he'd dropped her home. No matter how combustible the chemistry—no matter how much Becca had wanted what they'd shared—he couldn't believe she would ever want to lay eyes on him again. How could something so good end up so bad?

"You grew up an only child, right?" Dave was saying.

"My mother had health problems. My parents rated it a small miracle that I was conceived."

Jack always felt a kind of bond between Ellie Lassiter and his own mother because of that.

"Did you ever wonder what it would be like to have a sister or brother?"

Funny he should ask. "One of my first memories was asking my dad if he could stop on his way home from work and pick one up for me."

They both chuckled. Jack was enjoying the downtime, but he supposed it wouldn't do to get *too* friendly. He needed to wrap things up and get back on the road soon.

"Dave, I've been thinking about our deal. I'd like to throw a bit more into the hat."

Jack offered a figure—more than he'd even intended. When Dave simply sat there studying him with the hint of a smile on his lips, Jack shifted in his seat, cleared his throat. Perhaps he needed to clarify his position.

"I like you, Dave. You're a stand-up guy. But I'm not looking at this with the prospect of becoming business partners."

"You're not."

"No, I'm not."

"How about brothers?"

Jack's stomach knotted but he held his gaze. "I'm sorry. I can't become part of your family."

"You already are."

Jack breathed slowly out. Okay, this was getting awkward. He pushed to his feet. "I should head off."

Dave remained seated. "I'd rather you stay. We still have so much to talk about."

When Dave's oddly calm expression held, Jack confronted him. Something more than a business deal was going on here. "What's this all about?"

"I told you—"

"Family?"

"I only found out two months ago."

"Found out *what?*"

"Two months ago, my mother was in hospital. Complications with diabetes. She passed away."

Jack exhaled. What was he supposed to say to that? He lowered his voice. "I'm sorry. My own mother died ten years ago."

She'd been a loving, selfless person. Jack had shed tears at her funeral and wasn't ashamed to admit it. He was shell-shocked when his father had followed her only months later.

"Before she died," Dave went on, "she said she needed to pass something on. A story about me that also involves you, Jack."

"You're not making any sense."

"Your father never knew…"

For God's sake. "Spit it *out.*"

"Your father dated my mother when she originally lived in Cheyenne. They had a disagreement and broke up. It seemed his family didn't think she was good enough. Not long after that, he married your mother and my mom moved and married my dad." He sat back. "She didn't want her new husband to know that she was pregnant with John Reed's baby. That she was three months pregnant with me."

As Jack's ears began to ring, he simply stared and then coughed out a mirthless laugh. "You want me to believe…what? That I have a half brother…that you're my half brother and my father hid it from me my entire life?"

"He never knew."

Jack's ears and brow were burning. *What a crock.* There wasn't a single memory that so much as hinted that any of it was true. David Baldwin needed his head examined if he thought for one moment he would swallow this. Jack ought to walk away from the whole deal right now.

"For decades my mother followed your family's lives," Dave went on. "She particularly followed your accomplishments, Jack."

"Why are you doing this?"

"Because I want to make up for all those lost years. I thought you might want the same."

Jack wanted to tell him to get a grip on reality. But the emotion shining in Dave's eyes stopped him. It was affection. Compassion.

Brotherly love?

Jack collapsed back into the chair. After he drained that beer, he squeezed the empty in his hand and groaned out, "I'll need another drink."

Dave pushed to his feet, headed for the bar. "I'll make it Scotch."

Thirteen

Becca was gutted when Angelica Lassiter's press conference didn't take place. It didn't take her much to guess who had swooped in and got to J.D.'s haunted daughter before she could make any kind of announcement.

Catching up with a friend about the upcoming wedding, Felicity was in town again. When Fee arrived on her doorstep that evening, Becca was pretty much over the whole Lassiter mess. Over pretty much everything. For the first time in her life, she wanted to crawl in a hole and not bother coming back out.

As she opened the door, Fee simply stood there, looking disappointed and confused. Becca had kept her emotions under tight rein these past hours. Now despair rose in her throat, choking off air. Becca felt so miserable, she could only shrug and murmur, "Guess you heard."

The world must know by now…Jack Reed and Becca "Brainless" Stevens had blown off L.A. to get it on. And not in some motel room. Out in the great outdoors.

Shoot me now.

"I won't waste time asking if it's true," Fee said.

"I haven't seen the photos." Becca *never* wanted to see them. Never mind anyone else's opinions—what would her parents say?

In her favorite Raiders jersey and thick comfort socks, Becca led her friend through to the kitchen where Fee presented a bottle of red wine.

"Thought you might need a drink," she said. "I know I do."

"That'll go perfectly with the cheesecake."

Becca had already eaten half of it—the remaining half sat on the counter, next to a used plate.

Fee looked stupefied. "Tell me you didn't eat all that in one afternoon."

"It was a piece of cake." Becca gave her friend a withering grin. "That was a joke."

"Sorry," Fee said, "but you don't look like you've been yucking it up."

"Getting high on sugar is better than slitting my wrists."

"Don't talk like that. Nothing's ever that bad. Even this."

Becca thought of all the kids at risk of self-harm and suicide and flinched, ashamed. Of course, Fee was right. Nothing was worth taking your own life. That didn't mean that she didn't feel like hell.

Fee found two goblets while Becca cracked open the Merlot. She poured two generous servings and proposed a toast.

"To the world's weakest woman," Becca said and downed a mouthful.

Fee refrained. "Maybe alcohol isn't a good idea right now."

"Liquor has never been my problem." At the moment, nagging self-pity was.

"You are *anything* but weak."

"Except where Jack is concerned."

"Honey, forgive me for saying, but you're not alone there."

Good friends were always honest, and Fee was right on the money. She wasn't Jack's first conquest and she wouldn't be his last. One more notch on the bedpost.

"I knew Jack's reputation with women. He's a lady-killer. He wouldn't deny it. That's what my brain says. Then my heart got mixed up somewhere along the way and, suddenly, somehow, he looked like Prince Charming. It's crazy, but there's something about his voice—about his *everything*—that drags me in. I thought I could control it."

Fee narrowed her eyes. "You haven't fallen in love with him, have you?"

"Is falling in lust any better?" Becca set down her glass and covered her flushed face with her hands. "What am I going to do?"

Taking a hold of an arm, Fee hauled Becca over to the breakfast nook and sat her down.

"First you need to know that you have a lot of friends at Lassiter Media," she said, sitting down, too. "People who won't throw you under a bus, no matter what. But, yeah, this doesn't look good. I can't see Evan McCain being so understanding."

"Evan and I spoke. He wasn't pleased, to say the least. He knows I had all the right intentions. It was my execution that was off."

Whenever Becca thought about facing her coworkers' disappointed faces—their curious glances—she shuddered.

"I'd already arranged to have the rest of the week off." And she hadn't had a vacation break since starting at the foundation, so there were days up her sleeve. "Evan suggested I go back into the office Monday. I guess he'll have figured out what to do with me by then."

"And Jack Reed?" Fee asked.

Just the sound of his name sent her blood pounding. "I would be happy if I never had to see that sexy, bloodsucking smile ever again."

Fee arched a brow. "So, you're not in love with the man? You kind of skated around that question earlier."

Becca crossed to the counter and forked cheesecake into her mouth. It didn't hit the spot. Didn't ease the pain.

"I wish I'd never laid eyes on him," she said, avoiding the question again. "I wish I could go back and erase everything that's happened this past week."

"So, when he calls—and he *will* call—you're unavailable? It's just I know what you're going through. Being a slave to your own emotions, wishing you could feel differently but not being able to get past the longing. It's all consuming. An irritating, breathtaking reality that just won't go away."

Understanding, Becca smiled softly. "You went through that with Chance."

"Oh, yeah. In the end, my surrender set me free."

"You're saying that I should, what? Follow my heart where Jack is concerned?" Becca shivered even as added warmth swirled through her veins at the thought of being with him again. "He's nothing like Chance Lassiter."

"But you're not attracted to Chance. For all his apparent faults, you're attracted to Jack." Fee joined her friend by the counter. "Have you asked yourself why you're so angry right now?"

"I know why. I allowed this to happen."

"You mean you couldn't *stop* it from happening."

Fee didn't get it. There was such a thing as responsibility. "I know you must be feeling like all the world is filled with roses and love songs right now. I am so, so happy for you and Chance. But there is no way this side of forever that Jack and I will ever end up a happy couple. We have less than nothing in common. I despise what he stands for. His antics with Angelica have done so much damage to the foundation, and he couldn't care less."

Fee took a few seconds and then cocked her head. "As hard as it is, I think you ought to force yourself to look at those pictures of you and Jack in that lake."

The thought of thousands ogling those ultraprivate moments made Becca want to puke. Or was that the cheesecake?

"They must be plastered all over the internet by now."

"To my mind," Fee went on, "they show two people who look as if they belong with one another. Call me Cupid, but I don't think you and Jack are done just yet."

There were two reasons Jack tucked in his tail and went home to Cheyenne.

First, he needed time and space to absorb what he'd learned from David Baldwin. Dave believed that he and Jack were half brothers...that they shared a biological father. Dave had finished by saying that, if Jack agreed, he wanted to provide DNA material for testing.

Jack's first thought had been that it was some kind of scam meant to glean or extort money. His second thought was to wonder how his life might change if Dave's theory were true. He had no aunts or uncles. Since his parents had passed away, no extended family at all.

Although he'd never dwelled on it, Jack had always felt a sense of aloneness most during holidays. Everyone had somewhere to go Christmas day. He worked his private life so that he wasn't short on invitations. But even at his age, Christmas without family felt kind of hollow. A nonevent.

Waiting for the DNA results was harder than Jack had imagined. Anticipation was made worse by the second reason he'd left L.A. Jack hated how he and Becca had parted company. He had hurt her, embarrassed her, and he cared

too damn much to ever want to risk doing that again. That
meant staying the hell away.

And so he'd gone to bunk down in the place he'd once
called home.

The single-story ranch-style house was modest compared to some of the neighboring places. Certainly a far
cry from the luxury of either of his L.A. abodes. But when
he set his bags down inside his childhood bedroom and
looked around at the high school pennants on the wall and
his first CD player, Jack felt a sense of peace...grounded
in a way he could never be in California.

He simply chilled for the first couple of days. The
freezer was stocked and the fridge had enough beer to
last. By the third day, he got itchy feet. He revved up the
ten-year-old pickup his dad had left in the garage. Slap-
ping a Stetson atop his head, Jack drove north, headed for
the Big Blue.

Thirty miles on, the famous ranch came into view. Originally two hundred acres, the Big Blue now encompassed
30,000 acres, breeding Wyoming's most sought after Her-
eford cattle. J.D.'s nephew Chance resided in the original
ranch house. The main house where Chance's mother lived
was an 11,000-square-foot two-story structure made of
hand-cut logs and wood shingles, built when Ellie and J.D.
had adopted the boys. Many times Jack and J.D. had taken
brandy out on the flagstone deck, off from the great room,
to discuss sport and finance. That seemed so long ago now.

Jack sat outside the gates with the truck idling for a
full five minutes. He'd come to fill a curiosity and see the
Big Blue again, but he had no intention of paying a call.
He wouldn't be welcome, not like in the old days when he
had been viewed a friend of the family rather than foe—
Angelica being the current exception, of course.

Maybe he'd go visit Logan downtown. The ambitious
attorney and he might not be buddies, as such, but at least

Logan understood Jack's current situation with regard to Lassiter Media like no one else could.

Jack was ready to perform a U-turn when another, newer truck pulled into the wide driveway. When Jack recognized the driver, he wound down his window, as did she.

"How you doing, Marlene?"

"I'm real good, Jack. You coming inside?"

Marlene had turned sixty this year. She wore her brown hair in a short, no-nonsense style. Her hazel eyes were round and kind. After her husband had died twenty-four years ago, she'd moved in here from the original house to take care of J.D.'s children. Rumor said that she also cared for J.D. in a wifely fashion. More power to 'em.

"I was on my way into town," he let her know.

"Gonna grab a steak from the Grill?"

And risk seeing Dylan if he was in town? Not likely.

"I was going to stop by Logan Whittaker's office."

"Give him my regards." Marlene propped an elbow on the window ledge. "I sure don't like the position J.D.'s will has put you boys in."

Jack appreciated her concern but this was neither the time nor place to get into it. "It'll all work out," he assured her.

She leaned in closer and lowered her voice as if someone might overhear. "I know what this is about. At least, living with J.D. and his concerns, I'm pretty sure I know."

Jack took a moment and then smiled. He wondered if Marlene had worked it out, or whether J.D. had mentioned something before that final fatal night when he collapsed at Angelica and Evan's wedding rehearsal dinner. Either way, at this point in time, Jack was under obligation to keep quiet. If things unraveled the way he believed they would, the true nature of the part he had played in this tug-of-war would be revealed soon enough.

What would Becca say?

"J.D. was a good daddy," Marlene said. "He loved his princess more than anyone. More than anything. I'm glad she has a good friend to look after her now that he's gone."

That touched Jack in a way he hadn't anticipated. He was used to being viewed in a far less positive light. His mother had always said a kind word went a long way.

Sitting back, Marlene put her truck into gear. "Take care, Jack. Be sure and come back when this is all over."

For Jack, that couldn't be soon enough.

David Baldwin contacted Jack at the end of that week. The results were in and they confirmed his suspicion. When Jack heard, he flew back to L.A. and went directly to his brother's house.

He met the kids—Jack's very own nieces and nephews—and then enjoyed a big family meal of mashed potatoes and meat loaf in a room full of conversation and laughter and so much...well, *love*. By the end of the evening, he'd accepted that these people were indeed family. He planned to get to know them all a whole lot better.

Saying good-night on the front porch, Jack wanted his brother to know one important thing.

"I'm not upset with your mother for keeping her secret all those years. I get she was only trying to protect the people she cared about most."

"I'm sorry I never met your father." Dave eased into that familiar lopsided smile. "*Our* father. I wish we'd had the chance to know one another."

Those thoughtful eyes, his warm laugh... "Dad was a lot like you, you know."

Dave's eyebrow's lifted. "Really?"

Jack brought his brother close for a man hug. In some ways, this news was like receiving a gift from beyond the grave. The opposite of Angelica's situation.

When her father had died, she'd received what might equate to a kick in the pants. But the show wasn't over yet. Jack still hoped it would all work out for her, even if that meant it wouldn't work out for him. He'd like to believe that discovering that he had a brother—family—had changed his view on how he conducted business. In one important way, it had: he wouldn't be taking over and ransacking Dave's company. Other plans were in store there. Family was family.

He would not, however, reconsider his move on Lassiter Media. Evan McCain had cemented his stand and Jack Reed was standing by his. He had no choice.

Jumping in his car, Jack switched on his phone. Angelica had left a message asking him to call her as soon as possible. She answered on the first ring.

"How was Cheyenne?" she asked.

"Quiet."

He had let her know before leaving where he'd be. He could have been back in L.A. if she'd needed him here within a couple of hours.

"How's things with you?"

He heard her draw down a breath. "I had planned to speak to you in person about this…you've done so much to try to help. But there's really no need for you to waste time coming over."

He braced himself. "I'm listening."

"I've decided I'm going to step back."

Jack's chin went up. "Go on."

"I can't do it. I *won't* do it. My family means more to me than raging or crying over something I thought should be mine."

"Angelica—"

"No, Jack. Not this time. Let me finish. Dad was the smartest man I've ever known. I loved him. I respected him. It's time for me to make peace with his final wishes, with my family but, most of all, with myself. It's over. I'm backing away from the fight."

He waited before replying, "In the end, that's your decision."

"I'm glad you understand. And there's one more thing."

"Anything I can do to help."

"I want you to know that if you ever try to take over Lassiter Media anytime in the future, I'll do everything in my power to make certain that you fail. So will my brothers."

Jack rapped his fingertips on the steering wheel. "And Evan?"

"As long as Evan is the CEO of Lassiter Media, I will support him in that capacity."

A smile eased across Jack's face even as he kept his tone solemn. "Is there any way I can convince you to reconsider?"

"Nothing in this world you or anyone else can say will change my mind."

As soon as she disconnected, he put through a call to Logan. The attorney sounded apprehensive.

"I'm hoping this is good news," Logan said.

"The *best*."

Logan's voice dropped. "Are you saying what I think you're saying?"

"I just got off the phone from Angelica. She's made up her mind. She's throwing in the towel. Tossing it away for good."

"There's no way to talk her around?"

"None."

"You're certain?"

"To quote Angelica, it's over." Smiling, Jack shut his eyes and dropped his head back on the rest. *And thank God for that.*

* * *

As soon as Jack Reed appeared, his impressive physique filling the doorway of her office, Becca shot to her feet.

Today she had returned to work. It had been difficult facing her co-workers. Even harder would be her scheduled appointment to meet with Evan later in the day. She was prepared for the worst. If she were in his position, regardless of any good intentions, she would throw herself out the door.

Now that time had passed since that last incident outside of Hailey's café, she'd assumed that Jack had swept her from his mind. Trust him to show up here, at the Lassiter Media Building, and make a big performance. Did the man have no shame? Did he not care at all about her future? Her feelings?

As he shut her office door, Becca backed up a step. "How did you get in here?"

"Security downstairs was either asleep or didn't recognize my mug shot. I made my own way from this floor's reception area. I think your cohorts were all too stunned to stop or question me. Not that it would have done any good if they'd tried."

She snatched up her phone extension at the same time she told him in a firm clear voice, "Kindly leave."

If he wouldn't go, she would call security. The police. Hell, she'd bring in the National Guard if she had to. Word would have reached Evan. If her goose hadn't been cooked here before now...

"You need to hear what I have to say," Jack said, striding over to join her behind her desk. "You'll want to crack open a bottle of champagne when I'm through."

She was shaking inside and out. "I'll say it one more time. Leave, Jack. Leave now before this turns ugly."

Like the last time they'd seen each other. She loathed recalling how the reporter had smirked at their predicament that afternoon. Only now, with Jack standing so close, more pleasant memories began to rise to the surface, like how incredible and secure those strong arms had felt whenever he'd held her. Without meaning to, she breathed in his scent and suddenly she was reliving the heat she'd enjoyed whenever his mouth had claimed hers.

But all that was past. She had washed her hands of him. Nothing could make her want to go through that torment again. Not even that heart-thumping, devilish grin.

"I do wish you wouldn't smile at me like that," she said, turning away and punching that call through to security.

Reaching over, he took the receiver and dropped it back in its cradle.

She blinked at him. "Excuse me? You can't just waltz in here and tell people they need to listen to you. You don't own the place yet."

"Looks like I won't own it anytime in the future, either." His eyes shone down into hers as he edged nearer still. "Will I order up the ice bucket now?"

The floor tilted beneath Becca's feet. She had to unravel her arms and lean against the desk before her knees gave way. Was she reading this right?

"You mean...there's not going to be a takeover?" He'd stepped back from helping Angelica in her fight to take over Lassiter Media? No. Surely that was too easy. Too good to be true. Becca looked at him through narrowed eyes and took two full steps back.

"I don't believe you."

"You don't have to. I have no doubt it'll make this evening's news."

She waited, listening to her pulse beat in her ears. He wasn't laughing. Wasn't lying?

"You mean it?"

"Every word."

As reality sank in, happy tears welled in her eyes. Unimaginable pressure lifted off her shoulders. "When...?"

"Angelica and I spoke last night."

A laugh escaped from Becca's lips. She wrapped her arms around his neck and laughed some more. He felt so solid. So reliable and, at the end of it all, understanding. She wanted to kiss him until their lips were bruised.

Then she remembered Angelica. As much as Becca wanted this outcome for so many reasons, poor Angelica must be feeling gutted. Jack was her last hope of regaining control of this company.

She stepped back but held his right hand in both of hers. "How did Angelica take it? She must be upset."

"It was Angelica's call. Not mine."

"Oh?" Okay. That made a difference. "Did you try to talk her out of it?"

"Of course I tried. But this time there was no turning back. She'd made up her mind to put family first, corporate aspirations second."

Becca dropped his hand.

"You mean she's just giving up...walking away from the fight?" *And no thanks to you?*

When he nodded, Becca gathered herself. Those warm fuzzy feelings cooled. Other less favorable feelings were taking their place. Suddenly Jack didn't look so reliable.

"Well, I know why I'd want champagne, but you tried to talk her out of it." *And not for the first time.* "Why are you so happy?"

"It's really quite simple." Jack leaned back against the desk, crossed his ankles then his arms. "J.D. always meant for Angelica to run Lassiter Media, but he didn't want her to make the same mistakes he'd made."

"What are you talking about?"

"J.D. devoted all his time and energy to business, right?"

"Right."

"Corporate matters overshadowed every facet of his life. After the first heart attack, when Angelica stepped up to the plate, she became so engrossed in work, J.D. became worried that, when he went, his daughter would leave behind everything, including family, in the pursuit of corporate power."

Jack caught Becca's hand and drew her over to the couch.

"She did seem totally committed," Becca said, sitting down beside him.

"When J.D. made changes to his will in those final months, he also had a secret codicil drawn up. Logan Whittaker and I were the only ones who knew it existed. If and when Angelica accepted the will's terms and supported the family and Evan going forward, it would trigger the codicil. She would then be awarded controlling voting interest in Lassiter Media, which had been J.D.'s wish all along."

Had he said this was simple? "Only when she accepted the terms of the will…?"

"The way J.D. saw it, Angelica needed to understand and appreciate the importance of family first and foremost. He wanted her to run the company but, above all else, he wanted her to enjoy the rewards of a balanced life."

Becca slumped back. Poor Angelica. She thought she understood now what J.D. had been trying to accomplish, but what a test! Not only had it driven a wedge between Angelica and her brothers, she had gone to war with a man she had wanted to marry. If J.D. had wanted his daughter to embrace the benefits of family, to Becca's mind, he'd gone about it in a weird way.

"You were part of this scheme?" she asked.

"It was my job to push her as hard as I could in the other direction."

"Toward a hostile-takeover bid? That's…*twisted*."

"J.D.'s plan, not mine. He wanted her to struggle with it, if necessary. He wanted her to be sure."

"J.D. probably expected Angelica to be married before he died and the will went into effect. Did he consider the stress it would bring to Angelica's marriage to Evan?" She thought for a moment. "Or did he want to test the honesty of Evan's intentions somehow, too?"

"I only know he chose me to push the barrel."

"He obviously thought you were the man for the job." As unbelievable as it seemed, the plans and its resolution were sinking in. Jack hadn't been the bad guy in all this drama. He'd been a *good* guy willing to *look* like the bad guy. Which made him *extra* good.

He hadn't planned to steal from the rich to give to the poor exactly, but neither had he plotted to trick Angelica into a takeover and then sell off the pieces under her feet. For Jack, that was big. Heck, it was huge!

Becca's smile stretched from ear to ear. If Jack felt relieved, she felt euphoric!

Falling forward, she planted a closed-mouth kiss on his lips. "Sorry. I'm just so happy this nightmare has turned out so well. Angelica gets control of her company."

"Don't apologize." Tipping close, he brushed his lips over hers. "Best part is, when word gets out, any negative publicity the foundation has weathered will be reversed."

"But Evan…"

"He gets a big payout."

"I don't know how much compensation would be enough for losing this company *and* the woman he loved. Maybe still loves."

Jack tried to sound convincing. "Evan will bounce back."

"And you…do you know what you are?" She cupped his jaw and then grazed her thumb over the stubble of his chin. "You're a hero."

He drew back a little. "I was only following instructions."

"I wish I'd known."

"I wish I could have told you."

Her heart was throbbing, aching in her throat. God, his lips looked good. And now it didn't matter who took their picture. The truth was out and her Jack was back.

As her palm trailed down his shirt, she shifted closer still. His body heat steamed through his shirt, warming her all over, making her sigh.

"So, what are you doing now?"

His lips brushed hers as he answered, "I'm kidnapping you."

"A copycat strategy. I like it." She squeezed his thigh and thought to add, "Not that I'm in favor of the general nature of your business."

"The corporate-raiding stuff. Then you might like my other news. But I'm afraid it'll take most of the day to relay every detail, so you might want to inform your assistant that you'll be unavailable."

When he kissed her again, deeply this time, the fireflies humming around in her stomach began to burst into flame.

Coming up for air, she murmured, "Should we leave a ransom note?"

"Let's say, *gone fishing*."

Thirty minutes later, they were naked in his bed.

Fourteen

He and Becca walked out of that office and away from the Lassiter Media Building without a care in the world.

Or it sure had seemed that way at first.

Jack had hoped that Becca would take his news concerning Angelica well. He had wondered whether she might have struggled with believing him. He'd imagined her telling him to leave and not come back even after the facts had been verified. He'd been pleasantly surprised, to say the least, when she'd accepted the truth so readily. He had read her eyes, her body language, in those first moments when she'd been trying so hard to hate him.

In reality, she missed him, like an addict missed her drug. He knew because he felt the same way. All the pieces had fallen into place. This morning, he'd arranged for his bank to wire a sizable sum to the Lassiter Charity Foundation—specifically to help Brightside House and its endeavors. It was a good cause. And there was the added benefit of making Becca happy, because when she was happy, he was happy. Happier than he'd ever been.

He took her to his penthouse and let a valet park his car while he grabbed Becca's hand and rushed her to his private elevator. As soon as the metallic door whirred open and he had her inside, alone, he gathered her close, grazed his palms up and down the back of her red designer dress and forced himself to wait a moment more.

"You're more beautiful than I remembered."

She fanned her fingers over his chest, watching the action before looking up at him from beneath her lashes. "Aren't you going to kiss me?"

He gripped her tush and drove her hips against him. She laughed and then coiled her arms around his neck. With those killer heels, she was the right height to feel *just* how much he wanted to kiss her.

"If I start here and now," he growled against her lips, "we might be riding this elevator all day."

"So?" She tilted her head. "You own the building, don't you?"

Good point.

His mouth was one thumping heartbeat away from taking hers when the doors whirred open. He swept her up into his arms and strode to the center of the living room.

"Do you have a Merv here?" she asked.

"There's just the two of us."

The morning light flooding in through the wall-to-wall windows caught a flicker of unease in her eyes. "No cameras?"

He lifted her until the tips of their noses touched. "We have nothing to be ashamed of. Do you hear me?"

"I hear you. That's all behind us now."

So true. He did have some additional news to share, but it could wait.

He kissed her, lightly at first, a feathery brush of lips.

The contact sent rounds of pleasure ricocheting throughout his veins. Then he covered her mouth with his completely and leaned in as those sensations fired harder, longer. A thousand times deeper.

They had until morning. By then everyone would know that Evan was out, Angelica was in and Becca would need to attend to issues stemming from the switch. But what he would give to convince her to take a week or two leave. So they could spend every moment in bed.

With his mouth working over hers—while she was still in his arms—he crossed to the corridor that led to the master suite. He set her down at the foot of the bed and ran his hands up her back. With his brow resting on hers, he drew the zipper of her dress all the way down and then slipped it off her arms. Red linen rustled and fell around her feet.

He hadn't meant to get hung up at this point, but that lingerie was ten miles past sexy. He took a step back to get a better look. With a sultry grin, she cocked one hip and set her hands on her hips.

"You like?"

"You love to mix it up as far as office attire is concerned, don't you?" he asked, taking in the provocative picture from top to toe. "One day jeans, the next..." He wagged a finger. "What exactly do you call those things?"

"A garter slip. Satin and mesh." She performed a slow turn. "The color is raspberry."

He moved close again, letting his palms drift over the curvy satin all the way down to the strip of firm flesh left bare at the top of each thigh. A hand-span below that, the bands of her silk stockings began. He grazed his jaw lightly up one side of her cheek and then scooped her hair aside. Sliding the strap of her garter slip off a shoulder, he lowered his mouth to that smooth sweep of skin. She smelled fresh and...the only word that fit was *classy*. He ran the tip of his tongue along the ledge joining shoulder to neck then all the way up the side of her throat. He felt her shiver, a delicious, delicate quiver that only cranked the heat up all the more.

"Take off your shirt," she murmured. "Sit on the edge of the bed."

He nipped her earlobe. "You like to be the boss?"

"I'd like to take turns."

Jack had no objection to letting her go first.

He backed up toward the bed, at the same time releasing the buttons on his cuffs and shirt front. He took a seat while Becca made a tantalizing show of slipping down the second shoulder strap. After slipping off her shoes, she strolled forward and lifted her leg, setting her foot on the quilt next to his thigh. She flicked the stocking snap and leaned forward. Using her palms, she rolled the silk all the way down.

Jack was torn—should he look at that scrumptious toned leg or the closer, perhaps even more tempting view of her breasts wanting to spill out of their low-cut bra cups? Then there was the glimpse he'd caught of her panties when she'd switched legs to lower her other stocking.

He wound out of his shirt and tossed it on the floor. Then he reached for her hands but her fingers slipped through his as she moved back, a grin on her face.

Happy to play, he leaned back on his hands while she caught the hem of her slip and eased the satin up over her belly, ribs, breasts, until she stood holding the slip in one hand, wearing only panties.

The room's shutters were slanted, letting in strips of light that highlighted parts of her beautiful body. She moved forward with so much poise and confidence, Jack's anticipation turned a cartwheel and ramped up again. It had near killed him to keep away these past days. But the wait had been worth every minute.

He heeled off his shoes and got rid of his pants, briefs

and socks before she'd closed the distance and crawled up onto his lap. As she tasted his lips, she used her weight to ease him down onto his back. Straddling him, she kissed him deeply. Her arms curled around his head while her breasts brushed over his chest. When she tried to draw away, he gripped the top of her arms to bring her back. She only laughed and slid down the length of his body. Her lips trailed his throat, the center of his chest, over the ruts of his abs....

Then her tongue was looping a slow, purposeful circle around his navel, setting off a series of fireworks. His fingers filed through her hair as his hips rocked up.

She slid down more until the seam of her lips skimmed the tip of his erection. He felt her fingers wrap around the base of his shaft, squeeze and then drag up at the same time her amazing mouth went down.

He gripped the quilt and grit his teeth. This was scorching, intense. He could feel the beginnings of a climax burning, begging for release. He focused on the sublime rhythm she'd created, the tow of her hand working in perfect sync with the pump and pull of her mouth. Her other hand was spread over his chest, rhythmically kneading one side like a kitten preparing its bed.

As her mouth drew away, cooler air met warm wet flesh. It was a good thing she stopped when she did. He'd almost forgotten how much he wanted to satisfy her rather than the other way around. He caught her around the waist as she straightened. Then he cupped her breasts, grazing palms over distended nipples. He slid a hand down the front of her panties. She was swollen, wet. As ready as he was.

He urged her over onto her back and dropped a line of slow, moist kisses around each breast before angling lower. He hooked a finger into the side of her panties' crotch, pulled aside the satin and tenderly kissed her there. He heard her sigh before she arched into his caress. He tasted her again, relishing the scent and feel of her beneath his lips before he whipped off her last scrap of clothing and found a condom in a drawer.

When he was sheathed, he joined her again. She felt warm and soft and her eyes held nothing but trust. He positioned himself between her thighs while she ran her fingers through his hair.

He felt as if a furnace were burning inside of him. Her brow and the valley between her breasts were damp, too. He pushed inside of her, closing his eyes and tilting his face toward the ceiling as he buried himself to the hilt.

Her legs coiled around the back of his and she whispered to him how wonderful he felt, how she never wanted this to end. He built the friction as they moved together until he felt as if he was a part of her and she a part of him.

He was aware of her inner walls squeezing, of her fingers digging into his shoulders and her head rocking back. He watched the line crease between her brows, studied the smile lifting the corners of her parted lips. As he upped the tempo and force of each thrust, he felt her panting breath warm on his face. He lowered his mouth close to hers at the same time her legs clamped down hard.

Then he closed his eyes and held her tight as they both let go at once.

Fifteen

"You're not going to believe this," Becca said, gaping at a message on her smartphone.

Jack rolled over and stole another glorious morning kiss and then murmured against her lips, "You've decided you want to order in Danishes?"

"All my cravings have been well and truly satisfied." She tasted his lips again then amended, "For now."

They had stayed in Jack's penthouse the entire day *and* night. They'd ordered in dinner and had devoured barbecue ribs and butter pecan ice cream sitting out on the balcony, their feet propped up on the railing. Around ten, they'd fallen asleep on a soft-as-clouds leather lounge while they watched *Forrest Gump*. An hour ago they'd taken a long, sudsy shower together before Jack had dialed up the AC and pulled her under his duck-down duvet.

Becca hadn't checked back in with Sarah. Worse, she'd turned off her phone until now. She'd had an amazing time playing hooky with her bad boy, but it seemed lots had happened while she'd been away.

"Sarah says word is out about Angelica being reinstated as CEO. With you out of the picture, donations are already pouring back in." She sent Jack a sympathetic look. "No disrespect intended."

"None taken." He snuggled into her neck, tickling and arousing her as he nuzzled. "And so, all is right with the world."

Sighing, she beamed up at the ceiling while he nibbled her shoulder. "This has all turned out so well. I'm waiting for the bubble to burst."

He looked into her eyes. A soft, sexy smile tugged one corner of his mouth. "I guess sometimes there are happy endings."

"I guess there really are."

He kissed her again, long and slow and deep, before sitting up against the headboard alongside of her. "What are you doing Thanksgiving?"

"Are you asking me on a date?" she teased.

"I'm not sure. Is a family occasion classified as a date?"

"You don't have any family."

"As of yesterday, I officially do."

He passed on everything that had happened between himself and David Baldwin this past week. Jack Reed had a brother? Nieces and nephews?

"My God, Jack. That's *fantastic*. Why didn't you tell me sooner?"

"I wanted this other Lassiter stuff to be settled first." He lifted her hand and dropped a kiss on the underside of her wrist. "One victory at a time."

"You're not an only child anymore. How does it feel? Amazing, right?"

"The truth?"

"Of course."

"It feels almost too good." He leaned in to kiss her shoulder. "Like it feels almost too good to be holding you again."

She moved to run her fingers through his hair. "We should accept good things when they come our way."

"I'm beginning to understand that."

Their next kiss felt like the first of all their tomorrows. Which was thinking too fast, too soon. But she couldn't help wanting to take a hold of this fantasy and actually believe they could live it.

As the kiss broke, she curled into his arm and leaned her cheek against his chest.

"So, what's happening with your brother's business?" she asked.

"Take a guess."

"You're going to become partners."

"Uh-huh."

Her jaw dropped. "You're kidding."

"I offered to gift him the funds. He refused. Then he put it in a way I couldn't turn my back on. He said that through no fault of our own we were separated. Now it was within our power to be close, and stay close. Working together, becoming partners, would mean we'd be in touch most days, not just holidays. He doesn't want to simply maintain the connection. He wants to build on it. So do I."

"You're really going to be building a company up?" She laughed. "Call a medic!"

He tickled her until she begged him to stop.

"It's time we got something clear," he said, bundling her up in those big beautiful arms again. "I may make money out of applying a keen business eye to enterprises that can provide a larger profit operating as smaller entities."

"Say that again slowly."

"That does not, however, make me Scrooge."

"I know, I know. You give to charity. In fact, Sarah

mentioned in her text that Reed Incorporated had made
the biggest of the foundation's recent donations so far."
She dropped a kiss on his scratchy chin. "Thank you."

"You're very welcome. And I want you to know that this
latest, shall we call it *coming together of minds,* had no
influence on the size of that donation. Although, it would
be remiss of me not to mention that I am open to bribes."

"Like this?"

She shifted to straddle his lap all the while kissing her
way slowly and thoroughly around his neck and chest. He
groaned.

"*Exactly* like that. Keep it coming."

As his fingers trailed up and down her back, a thought
popped into Becca's head. She'd wondered about it last
night halfway through the movie, but it had drifted off
again until now. When she felt him growing harder against
her belly, she straightened. If she didn't ask this minute,
she might never get around to it.

"I'm not sure on one thing," she said, as his palms
trailed down her sides.

"What's that?"

"Your job was to keep pushing Angelica toward a takeover bid, right?"

"Right."

He leaned in to draw a nipple into his mouth. She quivered and closed her eyes. It was hard to think straight
when he did that.

"You've been actively acquiring shares and positioned
your company so it would be ready to move," she said. "I
would have thought very soon."

He was running his tongue around her other nipple now.
"These things take time."

"It's just…Jack, what would have happened if Angelica
hadn't backed down? What if she'd gone ahead with the
takeover and you both won?"

"Then she and I would have become partners."

"And you'd have managed all the Lassiter interests together." When he didn't answer, she looked down.

"Jack?"

"We would have worked together, yes."

She waited for him to add something more. Like, *But I would never turn around and do what I've done with every other company I've obtained through fair means or foul.* When nothing came, every hair on her head stood on end. Damn it! She *knew* this was too good to be true.

She shifted off of him and scrunched the duvet up under her arms.

"You were planning to sell off parts of Lassiter Media, weren't you?"

He scratched his head. "I can't say it didn't cross my mind that we could make a huge fortune without a whole lot of work."

"You mean by ripping apart someone else's work of a lifetime."

"There would have been discussions."

Oh, come on. "Angelica is no match for you."

"You've said that before but what about the way she stood up to me yesterday? Her father would have been proud."

Becca's throat was aching now. Suddenly she felt empty. Betrayed. Or was that merely foolish?

"You would have made it difficult, made it ugly, then you would have talked her into folding before the selling price was affected."

"You give me too much credit and Angelica not enough." He sat up straighter.

"What would have happened to the foundation?"

"We would have worked something out there."

"An offer I couldn't refuse?"

"I'm not a criminal, Becca. I'm only being honest with

you. It doesn't matter now because the game is played out and Angelica is where she was always meant to be."

"She'll never know how close she came to bringing it all down on her head."

"And that's the end of it." He reached for her. But his smile didn't look sexy now; she imagined it looked patronizing. Predatory.

She edged away and got to her feet, dragging the duvet along to cover herself. "There is no moving along until we get past this."

"Why worry about something that cannot, will not, happen? This, you and me, we're not about business."

"I know what I'm about. Ethics. Principles. Making the tough decisions so I can wake up in the morning and look at myself in the mirror. Guess what? That's gotten harder since I hooked up with you."

He opened his mouth, shut it again and then stood, too. "Shine a little light on something for me here. You never liked me, and you don't like me now because I'm a selfish, money-hungry, insensitive moron."

"You're not a moron."

"Thanks for clarifying that." He skirted the end of the bed until he stood an arm's length away. "Tell me, how could you lower yourself to sleep with me? And not just once. I must be losing my mind because I thought it was good. *No.* I thought it was *great.* The best."

That took her aback. She struggled for a response.

He moved closer, looming. "You know more about me than anyone. You might not trust me but, damn it, Becca, I trusted you. And for my trouble, you want to rake me over the coals."

She huffed. He would see it that way. "This isn't about you. Not anymore. It's about my feelings, my future, my decisions."

"Right, because my feelings don't count."

"You don't have feelings." She winced. That was going too far. "Or not like you should. If you did, you wouldn't be arguing with me now."

"You think J.D. was an angel?" he drawled. "Do you want to hear about the low deals he cut so that you could crow about all the great works your charity does? There has to be a *take* in order to have a *give*. Someone has to make the money to give it away, and no one makes money, real money, by sitting on a delicate behind letting other people make the choices that need to be made."

She spoke through her teeth, which had to be a damn sight better than speaking through tears. "Don't try to justify your behavior."

"I'm not. I won't. Not to anyone."

She marched toward the bathroom.

He called after her. "Where are you going?"

"Back to reality. *My* reality. Where people own up to their flaws and maybe try to do something about them."

He slapped his thighs. "Right. *Good.* I'm evil because I had good parents, was born with a brain and a drive to succeed."

"You were born with a will to *dominate*."

He shook his head as if he couldn't believe it. "I'm not wrong about most things," he said quietly. "But I was wrong about you."

"You thought you could convert me."

"I thought you could *care* about me." He stabbed a thumb at his chest. "*Me.* Not the money or connections or the name, Jack Reed."

Tears were so close, she could taste them. "Well, whaddya know?" The door swung shut as she finished. "You were wrong!"

Sixteen

"If I'm your sidekick, I hope this doesn't make me Friar Tuck."

Standing at the shooting line on the back lawn of his Beverly Hills house, Jack spun around and frowned. What was Sylvia doing here?

He lowered his bow as she crossed over to join him. She was right to carry her shoes. Those high-priced heels would ruin his lawn—not that he imagined for a minute that had been her motive for taking them off.

"Merv the Man let me through," Sylvia let him know.

"What's up?"

She eyed the distant target. Arrows were scattered all over the place. The bull's-eye, however, remained untouched.

"I was wondering when the boss might be coming back in," she said.

"You don't need help running the office. You have one of the most efficient business minds I know."

"Flattery doesn't work with me, Jackie boy."

"I'm doing other things."

"Like building boats with David Baldwin?"

Sylvia knew that story.

"That's the one good thing to come out of this month's firestorm."

Sylvia offered him a genuine smile. "No one's happier for you than I am."

He redirected his attention to the target. He and Sylvia did bottom-line analysis, not deep and meaningful conversation.

He sucked air in between his teeth. "I have other projects I'm working on."

"Any involve Becca Stevens?"

Eye still on the target, he growled. "No."

"You've been in contact with her, though."

"After I made myself clear, she made herself crystal clear."

In the briefest of summaries, he had also let Sylvia know that, due to the fallout surrounding the twist in J.D.'s will, his and Becca's "challenge" had come to an acrimonious end. He hadn't given up the finer details.

"I admitted to her that I would have followed through with the Lassiter Media takeover if Angelica hadn't changed her mind."

Of course, Sylvia didn't look the least bit surprised. "And since she ditched you, you haven't been able to think straight, right?"

"It's a matter of willpower."

He strode back to the line and fired a shot—which sailed over the top.

Damn!

Sylvia crossed over to join him. She took a long moment to study the target.

"Silly idea," she said, "but why don't you call her?"

Don't you know I want to?

"Sometimes in a relationship," he explained, "we say things we don't mean. Words can hurt. They can cut to the bone. But people can apologize, deeply, sincerely, and then get back to the good stuff. Becca and me...we went way beyond that."

Sylvia examined his face, particularly his mouth.

"Wait a minute," she said, and wriggled a finger. "Your bottom lip. Is that a pout? Are you *pouting,* Jack?"

Sylvia was like that. She never let herself, or anyone else on her radar, feel sorry for themselves. She could give a friend money, advice, she would work through the night if a job needed to be done. But no one could ask her for pity.

Jack crossed to the bench and sat down heavily. He swallowed against the lump lodged in his throat and then dealt out the bottom line.

"Becca told me exactly what she thinks of me. I could get over the argument, but she never will. She could never reconcile who she is, what she stands for, with being with a wrecking ball like me."

Sylvia sat down beside him.

"I could chase her," Jack said. "We'd fall into bed again. It'd be good for a while. Then she'd remember who I am, what I've done and the shame would creep back in. The guilt. She'd resent our being together. She'd resent me." He let his bow drop to the ground. "Not a recipe for happiness."

"Sorry," Sylvia said. "I was wrong. I thought you must really care for that woman. I thought she was the reason your schedule has been up the creek and we haven't seen your designer pants in the office for weeks."

"I'm the same Jack Reed," he said. But that was a lie.

"You're hiding."

"I am not *hiding.*"

"What are you so afraid of?"

"I'm *not* afraid."

"C'mon. Spit it out."

"No."

"Do it."

Fine! "I'm afraid I'll destroy her. That I'll let her down. I'll let her down and then…" He sighed. "Then I'll have made things even worse. I'm not good at long-term, Sylvia. I'm controlling. I have a controlling personality."

"I bet she'd like the chance to work things out."

His grin was entirely humorless. "I humbly disagree."

"She's taking a sabbatical from the foundation. Rumor is she's going to work in a mission overseas."

"What's the plan, Sylvia? I pack a bag, follow her and we save the world together?"

"I thought you might like to say goodbye at least."

"Why the hell would I want to do that?"

She gave a wry grin. "I've known you to be flippant, ruthless, but never cruel. Never stupid."

"I so don't need this." He pushed to his feet.

She got to hers. "I'm trying to help you."

"I don't need help."

"Everyone needs help sometime, for some reason. Some of us are even big enough to accept it. Don't be a dope. Go to Becca before she leaves, even if she slams the door in your face." She touched his arm, lightly at first and then more firmly. "Take the word of a lonely woman who always needs to be right. Talk to her. You'll regret it if you don't."

Standing on the beach, Becca watched Jack pull up, get out of his car and study Hailey's café before wandering down over the sand to join her.

When she'd answered his call earlier, her hand had shaken, she'd wanted to hang up so bad. But there'd been something different in his voice. Something…real. Had she imagined the self-effacing tone?

It didn't matter now. She'd agreed to meet him. But she had wanted to choose the place. To finish here in Santa Monica on a more adult, less hostile note would bring this episode full circle. And then hopefully she would be able to put aside this constant ache in her chest…in her heart.

She held her breath as he stopped in front of her. In that moment, she saw only his eyes, heard only the waves.

"Where's the Bambino?" he asked.

"I sold it."

"Get outta here. Really?"

"To Hailey's brother."

"Wow. Big step."

"Yeah." She slotted her hands in the front pockets of her denim pedal pushers and dragged a bare foot through the sand. "Moving on."

His smile faded and that different tone she'd heard on the phone was there again.

"Thanks for seeing me," he said.

"Guess you heard about the sabbatical."

He nodded as the wind combed his hair. "Where are you off to?"

"Haven't decided yet."

"The foundation will sure miss you."

Will you miss me, Jack?

She cut off that thought and focused on the ocean until she'd gathered herself again.

"I'm hosting a final auction night next week," she said, speaking to the waves. It hurt too much to look at him here like this. "Then I need time away."

She heard distant barking and turned toward the café. Chichi was scampering down the ramp and onto the sand. He sped right up to Jack, who dropped onto his haunches to play wrestle with him. Becca figured that Chichi would find a stick and the rest of this short time she and Jack had here together would be mediated by this brash third party. Not a bad thing.

But suddenly Chichi turned a tight circle and shot off again. Becca hadn't heard anything, but dogs had good ears; Hailey must have called him back.

"I want you to know," she said, "I'm not angry with you." Not anymore. "In fact, I want to apologize. Being so self-righteous isn't very pretty. I have no right to judge others when my behavior has been less than glowing. I was frustrated." And hurt mostly.

Looking up at her, his dark gaze turned stormy. "Then why are you leaving?"

"I need to work on myself. The best way to do that is to help others. Sort out what's important and what's not." He sat all the way down on the sand, facing the waves with his legs bent, forearms resting on his knees.

"I had a long conversation with a friend," he said. "She thinks we ought to give it a go."

Becca's legs went weak. She'd expected something but nothing as direct as this. After all those nasty things they'd said to each other?

"You and me?" she asked. "Like a *couple?*"

He reached out his hand. She took a hold and knelt beside him, still processing what he'd just said.

"I want us to be together," he went on. "I want to make it work."

She let that sink in. Obviously he didn't know what he was saying.

"What do you mean 'make it work'?"

"I mean negotiate. Compromise. Maybe move in together."

Whoa.

If he wasn't beating around the bush, neither would she.

"Do you want forever?"

A line formed between his brows but he didn't look away.

"That girl I told you about," he said. "I told you I'd proposed. In fact, we were going to be married the next day."

His eyes were reflective now, glassy, like he was living in the past and wasn't in a hurry to come back. Becca felt sick to her stomach. It was bad enough to have a loved one take her own life, but to be faced with that tragedy a day before they were supposed to begin life's most wonderful journey together... *Unimaginable*.

"You still love her," Becca said, wanting to cry for him all these years later.

"She was my best friend." He blinked slowly. "I wonder sometimes if she hadn't met me whether she'd still, you know...be around. The truth is I pushed her too hard. I thought I was helping. So, this is a tough one for me." He blinked a few times as a pulse beat in his jaw. "I want to push you to stay, but there's also that part of me that says—that *always* says—don't try to hold on. It's best to let go."

Becca held her stomach. She didn't think she'd felt so sorry for anyone in her life.

She got to her feet and forced out the words before they got stuck in her throat. "I honestly wish you nothing but happiness."

He looked more resigned than disappointed. "What's happiness? That's the sixty-four-thousand-dollar question."

"It's being at peace with yourself."

Before she walked away, she squeezed his shoulder and prayed that Jack found his.

Seventeen

One week later, Becca was ready to make an announcement.

This Lassiter Charity Foundation Auction Night had been wildly successful, with exceptional items up for grabs and an astounding amount of money having been raised. The high-neck black sheath she wore somehow suited her bittersweet mood. The foundation would not only survive, it would flourish under Angelica's reinstated reign at Lassiter Media. But this was also Becca's last public appearance as director of the Los Angeles-based charity she believed in so much.

A moment ago, Sarah had suggested it was time to offer the guests a final thank-you. Becca had been on her way to the lectern when she'd glimpsed someone standing alone in the back of the ballroom.

He was exceptionally tall with dark hair. His masculine physique was made all the more eye-catching by the tuxedo he wore. As he headed for an exit, she actually considered for a third of one second to simply let him go. However, in her professional capacity here this evening, that wouldn't be right.

Becca wove through the crowd. In her hurry, she bumped into one gentleman's paunch and then immediately knocked darling Mrs. Abernathy and her glass of punch. She apologized profusely to both and kept rushing toward the exit. She caught up the moment the man pushed open the door.

"Jack. *Jack!*"

He turned around. He was so handsome...when he smiled, the entire room seemed to light up.

"I've tried to contact you today," she said. "I spoke to your PA. Jack, I can't thank you enough for your generosity."

"She passed on your invitation. I'm glad the bow and arrowheads brought in a good price."

Good price? More like incredible. "I've never seen such a bidding war. I'm so glad they went to a museum, even if it's overseas."

"I'm glad, too."

They held each other's gazes while music wove through the room and crystal flutes tinkled.

"I'd better let you get back to your guests," he said at last, and turned toward the exit again.

"Wait." She had something she wanted to ask. "Have you heard from Angelica?"

"We spoke today. She's feeling right at home in the CEO's chair. Sage and Dylan are happy for her, too. I'm not sure what's happening with Evan McCain, other than there are rumors he's going to start up his own company with the money J.D. left him via that codicil. Guess he was very generously compensated but he still feels burned by the whole thing."

"It'd be nice if those two got back together. But I understand why she might think Evan somehow conspired with her dad to get controlling interest of the company. That's a lot of hurt to get over on both sides."

"Miracles happen."

When his broad shoulders rolled back and he glanced at the door, she threw in another question.

"How's your brother?"

"We touch base every other day. And I'll see the whole crowd on Turkey Day. And Christmas will be here before you know it. I'll have to do some research on buying gifts for people under sixteen."

"You'll have fun with it."

Sarah appeared at Becca's side.

"Sorry to interrupt. Becca, we need you to announce the total amount that was raised tonight. The mayor's about to leave."

Becca nodded. "I'll be right there."

"Duty calls," Jack said. "Good luck, Becca."

She took a deep breath and let it out on a wistful smile. "Same to you."

When the last of the guests left the ballroom, Sarah gave Becca a congratulatory hug.

"This has to be the most successful fund-raising night in history."

Becca laughed. "I wouldn't go that far."

"I just hate that you're leaving the charity. It's been such a buzz working with you. I've learned so much. But I understand. You have things you need to do. It must be hard leaving, though. Letting go."

"I'll find another job in charity when I get back."

"I mean leaving Jack Reed. You two have some amazing chemistry going on."

Becca hadn't spoken much to Sarah about her dealings with Jack. Of course her assistant had seen those shots taken at the lake…who hadn't? But the look on Sarah's face now—it was as if she believed in fairy dust or something. Real life wasn't like that.

The women said good-night. Sarah had shared a ride with a couple of the other girls from the office. Becca said she'd get a cab home.

Alone in the elevator, Becca hit the button for the ground floor. A moment later, she was crossing the quiet hotel foyer. The click of her heels on the marble tiles echoed through the large glitzy space.

But she didn't want to go home just yet. She wanted to do what she'd never given herself permission to do before: be idle and simply waste time window-shopping on one of the world's most famous streets, Rodeo Drive. It was strange to think that next week it would be a hard task to buy necessities that most people who lived in the States took for granted.

This street was lined with fairy-lit trees and filled with the boutiques of some of the most revered names in the fashion world. She studied the displays, clothes, jewelry, ridiculously priced handbags. And then she came across a window filled with exquisite gowns…beautifully crafted. Most of them were white.

One in particular caught her eye.

The gown was antique-white with a fitting, puff-sleeved satin bodice adorned with a sparkling sea of crystals. The skirt was extra full, flaring from low on the waist. The outer layer was gauzy with a satin band three-quarters down and a floral wreath in the same satin embroidered on the lower front half. It was a reflection of a bygone era when a member of the fairer sex had been encouraged to be fragile and endlessly romantic in the hope of finding her prince.

A dress like that, a dream like that, would need nothing more than the perfect ring. And, needless to say, the perfect groom.

Becca let the illusion wash over her a little more. She saw herself in that gown, her face beaming and eyes filled with love. Beside her stood a man, exceptionally tall, with dark hair, his masculine physique made all the more eye-catching by the tuxedo he wore. And then, the reflection spoke her name. As in…

It *actually* spoke.

Becca spun around. Embarrassment and panic set in so fast, her cheeks caught light. "I thought you'd gone."

Jack only smiled and commented on the window display. "That's some dress."

How must it have looked, her fawning over a whimsical wedding gown alone late at night?

"It's a good street to window-shop," she mumbled.

Jack followed when she set off at a brisk pace, putting the dress behind her.

"I thought it might be something you were thinking of for Felicity's wedding," he said, easily keeping up.

"Oh, she wouldn't have anything so…big."

"Would you?"

She kept her gaze dead ahead. "I might."

"It was very, well, sparkly. I don't think I've seen you wear a piece of jewelry other than a watch."

Slowing her pace, she slid over a defiant look. "I might be saving it all up for one revoltingly gaudy occasion."

"A dress like that would need a pretty impressive ring." He stopped and pulled a small box out of his pocket. "Maybe like this."

As he opened the clasped lid, Becca's jaw dropped. The most amazing piece of jewelry sat glittering up at her from its white satin bed.

"It's sapphires and a pearl." His finger circled the setting. "But you also like diamond and rubies, right?" He pulled out another box. When she stood rigid, overcome with shock, he prodded her. "Go on. Open it."

This couldn't be happening. It felt like everything was moving in a weird kind of slow motion. Someone reached to open the lid. Becca realized it was her. A beautiful white diamond shone up at her. It was mounted in a pool of blood red rubies. Both rings were just as she had imagined they would be way back when she was a girl.

Becca finally formed some words. "Jack...what is this?"

"I want to marry you."

She swallowed against the ache of so many emotions clogging her throat. "We said goodbye...God, I've lost count how many times."

"I worked it out. It's really quite simple. The fact is I love you. And if you love me, why wouldn't we try to work through this...through anything to stay together?" One dark eyebrow lifted as he leaned closer. "You do love me, don't you, Becca?"

Tears stung behind her eyes. No matter how much she tried to hide the truth, everyone else seemed to see it. What was the point in denying it now?

"Of course I love you," she told him. "So much it hurts."

His dark eyes glistened as he gave her a grateful smile. "Let's fix that."

His mouth took hers and, in that instant, sparks tingled and fell through her body. Nothing seemed impossible. She could surmount any problem. Achieve any dream.

When he broke the kiss, Becca felt light-headed, floating, as if her feet no longer touched the ground.

"Are you going to choose?" he asked with his lips still close to hers.

She couldn't argue with him. Not this time. She wanted to say, *I choose you. I choose love.* But he meant the rings. As she looked down to study them again, her vision grew misty with tears. They were both so beautiful. So...*her.*

"I don't think I *can* choose."

"Then you'll have both. As soon as you say yes." He put the boxes in his pocket and drew her close. "I love you, Becca. I want you to be my wife. I don't want to lose you. We *can't* lose each other."

"You really want to do this?" she asked.

"Yeah." He dropped a kiss on her brow and murmured, "I really, really do."

"I have a condition."

He grinned. "Sure."

"That we respect and honor each other for the rest of our lives."

"Just give me the chance."

"We'll both make the rules."

"I only have one."

"Tell me."

After he whispered in her ear, she laughed and wound her fingers into his jacket's lapels. "I think I can handle that." Then she cupped his jaw and fell into a tender gaze that held nothing but adoration for her. "I guess sometimes there really are happy endings."

"Oh, baby." Jack got ready to kiss her again. "Now I know there are."

* * * * *

REUNITED WITH THE
LASSITER BRIDE

BY
BARBARA DUNLOP

Barbara Dunlop writes romantic stories while curled up in a log cabin in Canada's far north, where bears outnumber people and it snows six months of the year. Fortunately she has a brawny husband and two teenage children to haul firewood and clear the driveway while she sips cocoa and muses about her upcoming chapters. Barbara loves to hear from readers. You can contact her through her website, www.barbaradunlop.com.

For my sisters, with love.

One

There were days when Evan McCain wished he'd never met the Lassiter family. Today was definitely one of them. Thanks to J. D. Lassiter, at thirty-four years old, Evan was starting his professional life all over again.

He pushed open the door to his empty storefront office building in Santa Monica. By rights, he should have sold the compact building two years ago after moving to Pasadena, but it was only a block from the beach and the investment value was solid. As things turned out, he was very glad he'd kept it.

He had no intention of touching any of the money left to him by J.D. The bequest in his former boss's will felt like a payoff for Evan's unwitting participation in J.D.'s complex scheme to test his daughter Angelica, Evan's ex-fiancée. She'd eventually passed the test, proving she could balance her work and her life, and replaced Evan at the helm of Lassiter Media. But she'd failed Evan in the process, ending both their romantic relationship and his employment at Lassiter Media.

He dropped his suitcase in the reception area, hit the overhead lights and moved to the counter to test the telephone. He got a dial tone and mentally checked off two steps in his implementation plan. He had electricity, and he was connected to the outside world. Those were the basics.

The blinds on the glass door rattled as someone opened it behind him.

"Oh, how the mighty have fallen." It was the voice of his long-time friend Deke Leamon.

Evan turned, blinking against the streaming sunlight, baffled to see Deke silhouetted in his doorway. "What on earth are you doing on the West Coast?"

Deke grinned, dropping a red duffel bag on the vinyl reception seat beside Evan's suitcase. He was dressed in faded jeans, a Mets T-shirt, and a pair of scruffy hikers. "We did it before. We can do it again."

Evan stepped forward to shake his former college roommate's hand. "Do what again? Seriously, why didn't you call? And how did you know I'd be here?"

"Educated guess," said Deke. "I figured there'd be too many memories in Pasadena. This seemed like the logical place. I assume you're going to live upstairs for a while?"

"Good guess," said Evan.

The upstairs apartment was small, but he'd make it work. He needed an immediate and total change of scenery. Luckily, despite its proximity to downtown L.A., Santa Monica had a personality all its own.

"Figured you might be feeling sorry for yourself," Deke continued. "So, I thought I'd wander over and give you a kick in the ass."

"I'm not feeling sorry for myself," said Evan.

Life was what it was, and no amount of complaining or wishing would change it to something else. It was a hard lesson, but he'd learned long ago that he could roll with the punches. On his seventeenth birthday to be exact, he'd realized just how resilient he could be.

"And you don't wander," he finished.

His friend was contemplative and deliberate in every action he undertook. Deke didn't do anything on a whim. Now, he dropped into one of the vinyl chairs and stretched out his legs, crossing them at the ankles.

"Okay, so I flew here on purpose." He glanced around the empty office space. "Thought I could probably lend a hand."

Evan leaned back against the reception countertop, bracing himself and raising a challenging brow. "Lend a hand doing what, exactly?"

"Whatever needs doin'." Deke glanced around the office. "So, what's the plan? What happens first?"

"The phones are up and running." Evan realized that he was still holding the cordless receiver, and he set it down.

"Good start. You got any leads? Got a website?"

Evan was both touched and amused by what he knew Deke was doing. "You don't need to be here."

"I want to be here. I left Colby in charge at Tiger Tech. Told him I'd be back in a month or so."

Colby Payne was a young, innovative genius who'd been Deke's second in command for two years.

"That's ridiculous." Evan wasn't about to let Deke make that kind of sacrifice. "I don't need your pity. Even if I wanted you here—which I don't—you've got a business to run."

Deke's massive technological prototyping facility in Chicago was filled with everything from computerized lathes to 3D printers. It helped budding innovators turn their ideas into commercial products. His unique brand of savvy and entrepreneurship had launched dozens of success ventures.

Deke shrugged. "I was getting bored. I haven't taken a vacation in two years."

"Go to Paris or Hawaii."

Deke grinned. "I'd go stir-crazy in Hawaii."

"You've seen the tourism photos, right? The surf, the sand, the girls in bikinis?"

"There are girls in bikinis right here in Santa Monica."

"I can take care of myself, Deke."

Sure, it was a blow, summarily losing his job with Lassiter Media when J.D.'s will codicil kicked in and gave control of the company to Evan's ex-fiancée Angelica. But he was already on the road to recovery.

"Don't you remember how much fun we had?" Deke asked. "You, me, Lex, holed up in that crappy apartment in Venice Beach, worrying about student debt while we tried to build a business?"

"It was fun when we were twenty-three."

"It'll be fun again."

"We failed," Evan noted.

Instead of getting rich, the three of them ended up going their separate ways. Deke went into technology, Evan into business management, while Lex Baldwin was rising fast in the ranks of Asanti International, a luxury hotel chain.

"Yeah, but we're way smarter now."

Evan couldn't stop a chopped laugh. "All evidence to the contrary?"

"Okay, I'm smarter now."

"I want to be completely on my own this time," said Evan.

He'd enjoyed working with J. D. Lassiter. The man was a genius. But he'd also turned out to be a manipulative old schemer. Family came first for J.D., always. And since Evan wasn't family, he'd ended up as collateral damage when J.D. had set out to test the loyalty of his daughter.

Not that Evan blamed anyone for supporting their own family. If he'd had a family, he'd have supported them through thick and thin. But he had no brothers or sisters. And his parents had died in a car accident the day he turned seventeen.

He'd planned to have children with Angelica. He wanted a big family, big enough that none of them would ever have to be alone. But that obviously wasn't going to happen now.

"I've got your back," Deke told him, his tone low and sincere as he scrutinized Evan's expression.

"I don't need anybody to have my back."

"Everybody needs somebody."

"I thought I had Angie." As soon as the words were out, Evan regretted them.

"But you didn't."

"I know."

Angie had seemed like the woman of Evan's dreams. But she'd bolted at the first sign of trouble. She'd turned her back on him and everybody else, isolating herself, refusing to trust him or her family.

"Better you found out before the wedding."

"Sure," Evan agreed, because it was the easiest thing to do.

Secretly, he couldn't help but wonder what might have happened if J.D. had passed away after the wedding. As his wife, would Angie have tried any harder to trust him?

"She's out of your life, Evan."

"I know that."

"You don't look like a man who knows that."

"I've got my head on straight. It's over. I get that. I'm here in Santa Monica because it's over."

Maybe Evan would find someone else someday. Not that he could imagine when, how or who. If Angie wasn't the real thing, he couldn't fathom who was.

"I'm going to hold you to that," said Deke, coming to his feet, rubbing his hands together. "Okay, first up, we get your business back on its feet. At the very least, your accomplishments at Lassiter Media will impress future clients."

"They will be impressed," Evan agreed. They'd be impressed with what he'd accomplished there. Some might even be impressed that he'd walked away.

* * *

Angelica Lassiter needed a fresh start. If there was a Reset button for life, she'd press it right now.

She'd fought with her family over her father's will for five long months, only to discover J.D. had a master plan all along to test her ability to balance work with life. Although he'd first seemed to hand it to Evan, in the end, her father had given her exactly what she longed for: control of Lassiter Media. But she wasn't proud of the way she'd fought for it. And she wasn't proud of the way she'd treated Evan.

It was bad enough that she'd pushed her ex-fiancé away while she fought for her heritage. But she'd accused him of lying to her, of betraying her and conspiring to steal her inheritance. She'd been wrong on all counts, but there was no way to take it back.

"Ms. Lassiter?" Her administrative assistant appeared in the doorway of the empty boardroom.

"Yes, Becky." Angelica turned from where she was gazing across the heart of downtown L.A.

"The decorators are here."

Angelica squared her shoulders and gave her assistant a determined nod. "Thanks, Becky. Please show them in."

Angelica knew her decision to renovate the top floor of the Lassiter building and relocate the CEO's office was going to cause a lot of talk within the company. But she also knew it was her only option.

Maybe if the power transition had gone smoothly she could have moved directly into her father's office. After all, she'd been at the helm in all but title prior to her father's death. But with the original will leaving control to Evan, the transition had been anything but smooth. And now she needed to put her own stamp on Lassiter Media. She'd decided to convert the top floor boardroom into her own office and turn her father's office into a boardroom.

"Angelica." Suzanne Smith entered the room first, followed by her partner Boswell Cruz. "It's so good to see you again."

Suzanne's expression and tone were professional, but she couldn't quite hide the curiosity lurking in her eyes. The Lassiter family's troubles had been all over the media these past months. Angelica couldn't really blame Suzanne for wondering what would happen next.

"Thanks for coming on such short notice," said Angelica, moving forward to shake both of their hands. "Hello, Boswell."

"Nice to see you again, Angelica," he returned.

"Tell me how we can help you," said Suzanne. Her expression invited confidence.

"I'd like to build new office. For me. Right here."

Suzanne waited for a moment, but Angelica didn't offer anything more.

"Okay," said Suzanne, gazing around at the polished beech wood paneling and the picture windows on two sides of the room. "I have always loved this space."

"It'll give me some extra light in the morning," said Angelica, repeating the rationale she'd decided to use for the move.

"Light is good."

"And J.D.'s old office is closer to the floor's reception area, so it'll make a more convenient boardroom." It was another perfectly plausible excuse that had nothing to do with Angelica's real reasons for making the switch.

Boswell had a tablet in his hand and was already making notes.

"Anything in particular you want to keep from J.D.'s office?" asked Suzanne. "Furniture pieces? Art?"

"Nothing," said Angelica.

The twitch of Suzanne's mouth betrayed her surprise at the answer.

"Maybe keep the historic Big Blue mural," Angelica

added, rethinking the sweeping decision. "It can hang in the new boardroom."

The painting of the Lassiter ranch in Wyoming had hung in J.D.'s office for over a decade. Moving it would cause talk and speculation, possibly even more speculation than Angelica's moving her office to the opposite end of the thirtieth floor.

She wasn't turning her back on her roots. And, despite what the tabloids had surmised, she had forgiven her father. Or at least she would forgive her father, eventually, though maybe not all at once. Emotionally, she had to sort some things through first.

"That's it?" asked Suzanne. Her tone was neutral, but it didn't quite mask her surprise. Some of J.D.'s pieces were very valuable antiques.

"We can put the rest in storage."

"Certainly. Did you have any initial thoughts on your office?"

"Lots of natural light," said Angelica. "I like the fresh feel of the atrium, so plants for sure. Not ultra-modern, no chrome or anything. And I don't want bright white. But definitely lighter tones, neutrals, earth tones perhaps." She paused. "Am I making any sense?"

"This is all good," Suzanne assured her. "It gives us a nice starting point. Now, you've got plenty of room in here. You'll want a desk area, a meeting table, and a lounge area. Would you like us to include a wet bar? A private washroom?"

"Only if you can do it discreetly. I want it to look like a business office, not a playboy's downtown loft."

Suzanne's alarm showed on her face. "Oh, no. It won't look anything like that."

"It would be nice to be able to offer refreshments."

"Done," said Suzanne. "And we'll make it discreet, I promise."

The door opened and Becky appeared again. "Ms. Lassiter? Sorry to interrupt. But your three o'clock is here."

"We'll get out of your way," said Suzanne. "Would the end of the week be soon enough for some mock-ups?"

"End of the week is fine," said Angelica.

She'd rather have the mock-ups in the next ten minutes, but patience was one of the characteristics she was practicing at the moment. Patience, composure and a work-life balance.

Before his sudden death, her father had complained that she worked too hard, that she needed balance in her life. When he'd taken away her position at Lassiter through his will, she'd been forced to reevaluate her balance.

She'd made progress, and she'd promised herself to give it a fair shot. She was even thinking about taking up a hobby, and maybe a sport. Yoga, perhaps. People who did yoga seemed very serene.

"We'll be in touch," said Suzanne as she and Boswell left the boardroom.

The door closed behind them, and Angelica took a moment to focus on her composure. Her next meeting was with her close friend Kayla Prince. Kayla was engaged to Lassiter Media account executive Matt Hollis, so she'd been along for the ride on the family discord over the past five months.

Angelica knew that many of the Lassiter Media executives worried she'd put the company at risk by working with corporate raider Jack Reed and attempting to contest the will. And her recent single-minded focus on regaining control of the company meant she hadn't seen much of Kayla or any of her other friends. She could only imagine what Kayla might have heard from Matt at the height of the conflict.

So, when the door opened again, she was ready for anything. But Kayla surprised her, rushing through the door and quickly pulling her into a warm hug.

"I'm so glad it's over," said Kayla. She drew back to peer

at Angelica. "You okay now? Congratulations. You deserved this all along. You're going to be a fantastic CEO."

Angelica's brain stumbled for a moment, and then a warm rush of relief nearly buckled her knees. She hugged Kayla back. "I've missed you so much," she confessed.

"Whose fault is that?" Kayla asked on a laugh.

"Mine. It's all my fault. Everything is all my fault."

Kayla drew back again, this time briskly rubbing Angelica's upper arms. "Stop. That's enough. I don't want to hear you say that again."

Angelica was about to protest, but then she spotted Tiffany Baines in the doorway. "Tiff?"

Tiffany opened her arms, and Angelica rushed to greet her other close friend.

"Angie," Tiffany sighed. "It's so great to see you at the office."

Angelica took a step back, sobering. "I've got a lot of work to do here." She glanced at Kayla as well. "There are a lot of fences to mend and a whole lot of decisions to make."

"You'll do great," Tiffany stated with conviction. "There's nobody better than you to run Lassiter Media. The stupid will put you in an impossible position."

"I could have handled it better," said Angelica.

"How were you to know it was a test? What if it hadn't been a test? What if your father had truly lost his mind and left the family company to Evan? You were right to fight it."

"I think you're the only person in the world who feels that way," Angelica said to Tiffany.

"I doubt it. But it doesn't matter. What matters now is that you're going to be an amazing success." A mischievous grin grew on Tiffany's face, and she shifted her attention to Kayla. "Go ahead. Tell her."

"Tell me what?" Angelica took in Kayla's matching, wide grin. "What's going on?"

"We've set a date," said Kayla.

"For the wedding?"

Kayla nodded.

"That's fantastic news. When? Where? How big?"

Kayla laughed. "End of September. I know it's quick. But they had a cancellation at the Emerald Wave. We'll be oceanfront in Malibu, just like my mother always dreamed we'd be. We can have the ceremony right on the cliff. I know it'll be spectacular."

"It sounds perfect," said Angelica, ignoring the tiny spear of jealousy that tried to pierce her chest.

It was too late for her own fairy-tale wedding. That was simply the reality of it all. And she was genuinely delighted for her friend.

"Now that we've finally made plans, I can't wait to marry Matt."

"Of course you can't."

"I want you to be my maid of honor."

The jealousy was immediately obliterated by a wave of warmth. Angelica was surprised and touched. "I'd love to be your maid of honor. After everything—" she stopped, gathering her emotions. "You are so sweet to ask."

"Sweet, nothing. You're my best friend. You always have been, and you always will be."

"And I'm going to be a bridesmaid," sang Tiffany. "We're going to have a blast."

"We are," Angelica agreed, putting conviction into her tone. "This is exactly what I need right now."

She *would* forgive her father. And she truly did want to honor his wishes. What could be more conducive to work-life balance than being maid of honor at a wedding?

Kayla's expression tightened ever so slightly. "There is one small complication."

"What's that?"

"Matt is going to ask Evan to be the best man."

Angelica's equilibrium faltered.

Evan as the best man, while she was the maid of honor? She and Evan together, dressed to the nines, at a dream wedding with lace, flowers and champagne, but not getting married? For a second, she didn't think she could do it. She didn't see how she could survive an event like that.

"Angelica?" Kayla prompted, worry in her tone.

"It's fine," said Angelica, her voice only slightly high-pitched. "It'll be fine." She gave a little laugh through her fear. "Hey, unless he leaves L.A., we're going to run into each other eventually. I can handle it. No problem." She gained determination. "I'm going to be the best maid of honor ever."

Angelica's sanctuary was the rose garden at her family's mansion in Beverly Hills. She'd had the gazebo built five years ago to take advantage of the quiet, fragrant setting. At the end of a busy day, filled with dozens of meetings and the blare of the television screens that followed the five Lassiter networks, she could settle into one of the padded Adirondack chairs and sip a glass of wine.

It was peaceful out here. She could read through the latest ratings, check reviews on the programming from Lassiter Broadcast System, take note of the successes and failures of the competition, and wrap her head around strategic direc-tions for each of the Lassiter Media networks. It might only be September, but contingency plans for the inevitable Janu-ary scheduling adjustments were well underway.

She heard footfalls on the brick pathway from the main house and assumed it would be a member of the kitchen staff checking to see if she wanted dinner. She really wasn't hun-gry, and she didn't want to give up the peace of the garden just yet. She'd ask them to hold it for her.

"Hello, Angelica," came a distinct, male voice that sent a buzz of reaction twisting down her spine. She tightened the grip on her wine glass, whirling her head to see if she was imagining him.

She wasn't. Evan was standing in the middle of her rose garden, his steel-gray shirt open at the collar, and a pair of faded blue jeans clinging to his hips. His unshaven jaw was set, his hazel eyes dark and guarded.

"Evan?" she responded, memories of the times they spent out here coming to life in her mind. They'd made love more than once in this gazebo, the cool, evening breeze kissing their sweaty skin, the scent of roses wafting over them, the taste of red wine on his lips.

She swiftly set down her wineglass.

He took a couple of steps forward, coming to a halt at the short staircase that led up to the gazebo. "I hope you're ready to put on your maid-of-honor hat."

She sat up straighter, taking in his expression. "Why? Does Kayla need something? Is something wrong?"

"Yes, something's wrong." He paused. "I'd never show up here unless something was very wrong."

The disdainful words cut her to the core. He didn't want to be at the mansion, didn't want anything more to do with her. She understood that. She'd prefer to stay away from him as well, but not for the same reasons.

They'd been forced into each other's company on several occasions since the breakup. Through it all, she'd had her anger to shield her. But now, all that was left was embarrassment and guilt.

"You heard Matt and Kayla were delayed in Scotland?" he asked.

She told herself to brazen it out. Evan couldn't read her mind.

"Yes," she said. "Matt called in to the office yesterday. He's taking a few extra days of vacation."

Matt and Kayla had flown to Edinburgh to take advantage of a last-minute opportunity to secure a significant art exhibit for Kayla's gallery. As Angelica understood it, after they'd arrived, they'd been told a senior member of the church council had to personally approve some of the pieces leaving the country. They'd been forced to travel to his retreat in the north of the country to meet with him.

"I've been trying to call them all day," Evan continued. "But with the time difference and the spotty cell reception in the countryside, I couldn't get through. And then I thought to myself, what are they going to do from Scotland anyway except worry? We'll have to fix it for them from here."

"Fix what?" She sat up straighter. "What's wrong, Evan?"

He put his foot on the first stair and braced his hand on a support post, but seemed unwilling to enter the gazebo. "There was a fire at the Emerald Wave."

"Oh, no. Was it bad?"

"Bad enough. It gutted half the kitchen. Luckily, nobody was hurt."

Angelica was grateful to hear everyone was safe, but her mind immediately went to Kayla. "We're only three weeks from the wedding."

"No kidding."

"We need to find them a new venue."

"Are you going to continue stating the obvious?"

She felt her nerves snap to attention. "Are you going to continue being a jerk?"

"Oh, Angie." His tone was soft, and his use of her nickname sent a new shiver of awareness through her body. "I haven't even begun being a jerk."

She reached for her glass of merlot, needing something to fortify her. "What do you want from me, Evan?"

He came up the three steps, filling the doorway to the gazebo with his six-foot-two height. "I need your help. I went to see Conrad Norville today."

"I don't understand." What did movie mogul Conrad Norville have to do with repairing a kitchen?

"To ask if we could use his Malibu mansion for the wedding."

The explanation set her back for a moment. But she had to admit, it was a good idea.

Conrad Norville owned a monster of a mansion on the Malibu oceanfront. The seventy-something man was renowned for being gruff and eccentric, but his house was acknowledged as an architectural masterpiece.

"It's the only place anywhere near Malibu that has a hope of fitting all the guests," said Evan.

"What did he say?"

"He told me, and I'm quoting here, 'No way in hell am I getting mixed up with that Lassiter circus. I've got a reputation to protect.'"

Angelica felt her defenses go up on behalf of her family. "*He's* got a reputation to protect?"

"No," said Evan, his tone admonishing. "He's got a house we want to borrow."

"But—"

"Don't get all high and mighty—"

"I'm *not* high and mighty."

"Well, whatever you are, this is no time for you to get into a fight with the man."

"He already turned you down," Angelica pointed out. How could it possibly matter if she fought with Norville or not?

"I'm willing to take another run at it," said Evan. "For Matt and Kayla's sake."

The statement made her curious. "You think you can change his mind?"

"I was thinking *you* could help me change his mind."

"How could I do that? I've barely met him in passing. And it sure doesn't sound as though he likes my family."

"I thought we could alleviate his fears, present a united front. Show him there are no hard feelings between us, that the rumors about the power struggle were overblown."

The rumors weren't overblown. When her father's will left

control of Lassiter Media to Evan, it had resulted in all-out battle between the two of them. Even now, when they both knew it had been a test of her loyalty, their spirits were battered and bruised, their relationship shattered beyond repair.

But Kayla's happiness was at stake. Or, more specifically, Kayla's mother's happiness was at stake. Angelica was willing to bet that Kayla would marry Matt anywhere. In fact, they'd probably prefer to be married in Cheyenne, where they'd made their home. But Kayla's mother had been looking forward to this day since Kayla was born. And Kayla would do anything for her family.

"So, you're asking me to lie?" Angelica stated in a flat, uncompromising tone.

"I'm asking you to lie," Evan agreed.

"For Kayla and Matt." That might be one of the few reasons she'd consider it.

"I'd do a lot more than lie for Matt," said Evan.

She took in the determination on his handsome face. Experience had taught her that he was a formidable opponent who let absolutely nothing stand in his way.

"I shudder to think how far you'd go to get what you want."

His expression tightened. "Yeah? Well, we both know how far you'll go, don't we?"

It was a cutting blow.

"I thought I was protecting my family," she defended.

When she'd learned of the terms of the will, she couldn't come up with any explanation except that her father had lost his mind, or that Evan had brazenly manipulated J.D. into leaving him control of Lassiter Media.

"You figured you were right and everyone else was wrong?" he asked.

"It seemed so at the time."

His steps toward her appeared automatic. "You slept in

my arms, told me you loved me, and then accused me of de-
frauding you out of nearly a billion dollars."

All the pieces had added up in her mind back then, and
they had been damning for Evan. "Seducing me would have
been an essential part of your overall plan to steal Lassiter
Media."

"Shows you how little you know about me."

"I guess it does."

Even though she was agreeing, the answer seemed to
anger him.

"You *should* have known me. You should have trusted
me. My nefarious plan was all inside your suspicious little
head. I never made it, never mind executed it."

"I had no way of knowing that at the time."

"You could have trusted me. That's what wives do with
their husbands."

"We never got married."

"Your decision, not mine."

They stared at each other for a long moment.

"What do you want me to do?" she finally asked. Then
she realized her question was ambiguous. "About Conrad."

An ironic half smile played on Evan's lips. "Don't worry.
I know you'd never ask what I wanted you to do about us."

He backed off a couple of paces. "Come with me to see
Conrad. Tomorrow night. Pretend we're pals, that everything is terrific between us, and he doesn't have to worry
about any public fights."

The request brought a pain to Angelica's stomach. Nothing was remotely terrific between her and Evan. He was
angry and she was sad. Because now that their dispute over
Lassiter Media was over, she missed so many things about
their former life.

"Sure," she agreed, forcing her misery into a small corner
of her soul. "I'll do whatever it takes to help Kayla."

"I'll pick you up at seven. Wear something feminine."

She glanced down at her slim, navy skirt and the collared, white blouse. "Feminine?"

"You know, ruffles or flowers, and some pretty shoes. Maybe curl your hair."

"Curl my hair?"

"You don't want to look like my rival. He's an old-fashioned guy, Angie. He remembers a different time, a different kind of woman."

"When? The 1950s?"

"That sounds about right."

"You want me to simper and giggle and bat my eyelashes to get a wedding venue for Kayla and Matt."

"In a word, yes."

She'd do it. She'd definitely do it for her best friend. But she wasn't going to like it, and she wasn't going into it without a protest. "Shall I cling to your arm as well?"

"Cling to anything you want. Just sell it to him." With that pronouncement, Evan turned on his heel, left the gazebo and disappeared along the pathway.

Two

Evan stood in the high-ceilinged foyer of the Lassiter mansion, gazing in amazement as a transformed Angie descended the grand staircase. She looked beautiful, feminine and deceptively sweet. Her chestnut hair was half up, half down, wisps dangling at her temples and curling enticingly along her shoulders in a silk curtain. The color was lighter than he remembered it, and he instantly realized he liked it this way.

"You're wearing pink," he couldn't stop himself from observing.

"Now who's stating the obvious?" As she covered the last couple of stairs, Evan noticed her simple, white pumps that matched a tiny purse tucked under her arm.

"I've never seen you in pink." The dress was snug in the bodice, with cap sleeves and flat lace across the chest. It had a full silk skirt and a discreet ruffle along the hem. She wore simple diamond stud earrings and a tiny diamond pendant on a delicate gold chain. She truly could have stepped out of the 1950s.

"I hate pink," she noted as she came to a halt on the ground floor. Then she donned a brilliant if slightly strained smiled and pirouetted in front of him. "But do you think this outfit will get Kayla the dream Malibu wedding her mother wants for her?"

Evan wasn't sure the outfit would get them a wedding. But it was definitely getting him turned on. He'd seen Angie in no-nonsense suits, opulent evening gowns and the occasional classic black cocktail dress. But he'd never seen her looking so alluring and demure, and so incredibly kissable.

"If it doesn't," Evan found himself responding, "nothing will."

"Good." Her expression relaxed, and her smile looked more natural. "Then let's get this over with, shall we?"

He held out his arm to escort her, but she didn't take it. She walked pointedly past him, drawing open the front door and marching onto the porch.

"He needs to believe we're still friends," Evan cautioned as he trotted down the staircase after her.

His dark blue Miata convertible was parked halfway around the circular driveway. He'd picked Angie up in this spot countless times, taking her to dinners, to parties, occasionally away for the weekend. And for a few heartbeats, it felt exactly like old times. He had to stop himself from taking her hand or putting an arm around her shoulders. Touching her seemed like such a natural thing to do.

"I can act," she responded breezily.

He slipped past her to open the passenger door. "I'm sure you can."

She slid into the low seat, pulling her dainty shoes in behind her. "Conrad knows we're coming?"

"He knows. I imagine we'll get an earful about some of the stories in the tabloids."

"I can cope with upset people."

"Can you keep your cool when they come after your family?"

"Of course, I can."

"Angie?" Evan cautioned.

She stared straight ahead. "Don't call me that."

"You want me to call you Ms. Lassiter?"

"My name is Angelica."

He waited for a moment, until curiosity got the better of her and she raised her eyes to look his way.

"Not to me it isn't," he told her firmly. Then he pushed the door shut and rounded the hood of the car.

He knew he shouldn't goad her, and he probably shouldn't use her nickname either. But they'd been lovers once, best friends, engaged. They'd been mere hours away from getting married. They'd laughed. They'd fought. And she'd cried naked in his arms. He wasn't about to pretend it had all never happened.

They both stayed silent as he pulled onto Sunset, pointing the sports car toward the Pacific Coast Highway.

"You can do it for one night," she told him as he navigated traffic beneath the bright streetlights.

"Do what for one night?" He wondered if she was aware of the many interesting ways that statement could be taken.

She'd probably slap his face if she knew what he was picturing right now.

His mouth flexed in a half smile at his own thoughts. If this really were the 1950s, she would slap his face, but he'd kiss her anyway, pinning her hard against the nearest wall. Then she'd quickly capitulate and kiss him back, because she was only protesting out of a duty to be a good girl, not because she was unwilling.

"Call me Angie," she answered, startling him out of the daydream.

"I can call you Angie for one night?"

"While we're at Conrad Norville's pretending to be friends. But that's it."

"I don't think you can control what I call you," he countered casually.

She fussed with the hem of her skirt, and there was something defiant in her tone. "I can control what I call you."

"Call me anything you like."

"What about incompetent and irresponsible?"

"Excuse me?" He swung a glance her way for a second before returning his attention to the winding highway. "You're planning to insult me in front of Norville?"

"Not Norville. I had a phone call this morning. Somebody looking for a reference on your work with Lassiter Media."

"Who?" Evan immediately asked.

"Lyle Dunstand from Eden International."

Anger clenched his stomach, and his tone went iron-hard. "You'd actually undermine my business out of spite?"

She was silent for a moment. "Relax, Evan. I told them you'd done a fantastic job under trying circumstances. I gave you complete credit for last year's expansion into Britain and Australia, and I said your instincts for people were second to none."

His anger dissipated as quickly as it had formed.

"My point is," she continued. "I'm treating you with respect and professionalism. You could at least do the same for me."

"I didn't give anyone your contact information," he assured her. "I was hoping they'd avoid checking with Lassiter."

"I can't see that happening. You were with us for several years." She angled her body to face him. "So, you're opening up the consulting agency again."

"I have to earn a living."

"My father left you a lot of money."

Evan coughed out a cold laugh. "Like I'm going to touch Lassiter money."

She seemed to consider his words. "Are you angry with him?"

"Hell, yes, I'm angry with him. He used me. He messed with my life like I was some pawn in his private game."

"He assumed we'd be married by the time he died."

Evan twisted his head to look at her again. "And that makes it better? He sets me up as CEO in order to test your loyalty to him, and then he cuts me loose to do what? Play second fiddle to my own wife at Lassiter?"

She seemed to consider his statement. "Are you saying you'd have a problem working for me? If we were married, I mean?"

"Yes."

"But you'd have been okay with me working for you?"

He gave a shrug. "It might not be logical or fair. But, yeah, I could live with that."

"Now who's living in the 1950s?"

He didn't disagree. "It's a moot point. Neither of those things is ever going to happen."

"Because we'll never be married."

"Stating the obvious again, Angie."

"Angelica."

"You said I could have one night." He wheeled the car into a left turn, and down the private road that led to Conrad Norville's estate.

They met Conrad in the great room of his oceanfront residence. Even though Angelica had spent years living in the Lassiter mansion, she was taken aback by the size and opulence of the home. The great room was accessed through a massive foyer and a marble pillared hallway decorated in ivory and gold. The room was huge, rectangular, with a thirty-foot ceiling. Its beachside wall was completely made of glass. In the center of the glass wall, several panels were drawn aside, turning the patio into an extension of the house.

The patio itself was beautifully set up for entertaining, with different tiers that held tables, comfortable lounge furniture groupings, and gas fire pits surrounded by padded chairs. The lowest tier jutted out over a cliff, offering a spectacular view of the rocks and waves, while a side area held a swimming pool, complete with a pool house and a massive wet bar.

As Conrad shook her hand in welcome, he gave Angelica's outfit a critical once over. He didn't make any comment, and she couldn't tell what he thought.

"Your family's been in the news lately," he stated, giving a signal to a waiting butler who immediately moved forward with a silver tray of drinks.

"Things have stabilized now," said Angelica, standing next to the open doorways, appreciating the fresh ocean breeze. "I think we're all ready to move forward on a positive path."

"You never want to become the story." Conrad took a crystal glass from the waiter's tray. It contained a small quantity of amber liquid.

"Being in the media wasn't something any of us enjoyed," Angelica agreed.

The butler offered her a drink, and she took it, guessing it was probably single malt, since Conrad owned a distillery in Scotland and often sang its praises. She hated single malt, but she'd drink it if she had to.

"Is your daddy a crazy man?" Conrad asked, studying her expression while he waited for her answer.

Though they'd tried to guard the details of J.D.'s will, with Conrad's industry and social contacts, he'd likely have learned more than most people outside the family.

Before she could answer, Evan stepped in. "J. D. Lassiter loved his family very much. It's one of the things I admired most about him."

"My stepkids are leeches," said Conrad, switching his piercing attention to Evan. "No good, blood-sucking losers."

Angelica glanced at Evan, but he didn't seem to know how to respond to that either.

"I'm sorry to hear that," she offered into the awkward silence. "Do they live here in Malibu?"

Conrad gave a gruff laugh. "Can't afford their own houses. At least not the kind of houses they think they deserve." He upended his glass, swallowing the entire shot.

Angelica took an experimental sip. It was single malt all right—bold, peaty scotch that nearly peeled the skin from her mouth.

Evan finished his in one swallow.

"They're both in Monaco right now," said Conrad, signaling the butler to bring another round. "Some fancy car race through the city. Nothing but girls and all-night parties, I'm guessing."

"Kayla Prince runs an art gallery," Evan offered. As he spoke, he shifted a little closer to Angelica.

She assumed he was trying to perpetuate the ruse that they were still good friends.

"One of those snooty, high-brow places?" Conrad asked. "Always trying to get me to spend millions on some nouveau crap. Can't even tell what's in those pictures. A monkey might have done it for all I can tell."

"I once bought a water color painted by an elephant," said Angelica.

Her instinct was to defend Kayla, but she didn't want to risk an argument with Conrad. She decided it was better to distract him with a new thread of conversation.

Evan gave her a puzzled look, but Conrad jumped right in on the topic.

"Could you tell what it was?"

"Blue and pink lines. The elephant's name was Sunny. Cost me five hundred dollars."

That got a grin from Conrad. "The elephant's probably more talented than that artist, and he charges millions. One of the kids bid at an art auction last month, and I nearly had to mortgage my house."

She found herself glancing around while she tried to imagine how much you'd have to bid at an auction to warrant a mortgage on this particular house.

The butler returned, and while Conrad was distracted, Evan smoothly switched glasses with Angelica, discreetly downing her drink. She couldn't help finding the action chivalrous. She attempted to refuse a second drink, but Conrad insisted, so she accepted, declaring the scotch delicious.

"You probably want to see the patio," Conrad said to Angelica, sounding like he didn't particularly want to show it to her.

"I would love to see the patio."

He gestured. "Well, come on outside. Evan here says you're going to convince me the scandal is over, and it's safe to be associated with the Lassiters."

"The scandal is over," she assured him as they stepped outside.

Soft, recessed lights came on in the perimeter gardens, whether triggered by motion sensor or an alert staff member, Angelica couldn't tell.

"And you're at the helm now?" Conrad asked her.

"I am."

Conrad looked to Evan.

"She's at the helm," Evan agreed. "And she'll do a fantastic job."

Though she knew he was only playing a part, Evan's words warmed her.

Conrad got a cagey expression on his face. "Angelica, while I'm deciding whether or not to lend you my mansion, what would you say if I told you Norville Productions had a series we think would be perfect for Lassiter Broadcast System?"

"I'd tell you at LBS we have always created our own programming."

"And if I reminded you that I have something you seem to want?"

She paused. "I couldn't offer you quid pro quo, but I can tell you I'll get your idea in front of an acquiring executive, and we'll take a look at it."

"But no promises?"

"We'll give it full and fair consideration." She was sincere in that. Just because they'd never commissioned a third-party program for LBS didn't mean they never would.

"And your brothers?" Conrad took a healthy swallow of his new drink. "Are they aware that the scandal is over?"

"They are. They're each involved in the corporation in different ways."

"But not on the media side?"

"Not on a day-to-day basis," said Angelica. "But the family it united." It was a bit of a stretch. There were certainly some fences left to mend, but Angelica was confident her brothers wouldn't say anything publicly that would disparage her father or the family.

"And Jack Reed?" Conrad asked, giving yet another nod to the butler.

Angelica hadn't even touched her second drink. Luckily, while Conrad momentarily turned away, Evan once again deftly switched glasses with her, drinking it himself.

"Jack is completely out of the picture," she said. "There was some confusion about his role at first, but he was also acting on my father's wishes."

Conrad arched a bushy brow. "Your father *wanted* his company to be taken over and split apart?"

The butler returned, and they all exchanged their empty glasses for fresh drinks.

"My father," Angelica admitted with frank honesty, "set it up to test how I would react if that became a possibility."

Conrad cracked a grin. "A wily old coot, was he?"

"I would say so."

Evan joined in. "Everyone passed the test with flying colors. The family pulled together, and Lassiter Media is going to thrive."

"They didn't pull together right away," Conrad noted.

Evan gave a shrug and took a hearty swallow of what was now his fifth glass of scotch. "Nobody does the right thing right away."

Conrad gave a wheezing laugh at that.

"First we look at the angles," Evan continued. "Then we decide what we want. Then we decide what's best. But the last decision is the only one that counts."

Angelica forced herself to take a sip of her drink. She wished the glass contained a liquor she enjoyed. She needed something to counteract her burgeoning appreciation of Evan. He sounded quite sincere in his defense of her behavior.

"And what about you two?" Conrad asked, glancing from one to the other.

"We're friends now," Evan offered simply.

"No, you're not," Conrad countered with conviction, his bushy brows coming together, creasing his forehead.

Angelica stilled, worried they were caught.

"In a relationship like yours," he continued, "you either love each other or you hate each other. There's nothing in between."

"You can't believe what you read in the tabloids," said Evan.

"It's not what I read. It's what I see. Picture after picture tells me you two had it bad." His wrinkled hand gestured back and forth between the two of them. "I'm no fool. You're makin' nice now, but it'll go off the rails in the blink of an eye. The story will hit the tabloids, and this wedding and my mansion will be smack dab in the middle of a scandal."

"You're right," said Evan, and Angelica shot him a look of amazement. But then his hand closed around hers with a reassuring squeeze. "Truth is, we've been thinking about getting back together."

He raised her hand to his lips and gently kissed her knuckles. A familiar buzz of awareness traveled along her arm to her heart, and she had to struggle to mask her reaction.

"You have not," said Conrad. "Nobody keeps a secret like that in this town."

"We do," said Evan, sounding completely convincing. "Look at her, Conrad. I'd have to be a blind fool to give her up."

Conrad's gaze took in every facet of Angelica's appearance. She told herself to hold still and try to look like some kind of 1950s dream girl, the kind you forgave, took back and married, even when she messed up your life.

Conrad finished his drink, and Evan followed suit.

"You've got me there," said Conrad.

"I think you've had enough to drink, sweetheart." Evan lifted the glass from her hand and drank it himself.

Angelica focused on looking calm, serene and in love.

"I'll be damned," said Conrad, his expression relaxing for the first time since they'd arrived.

"I'm no fool," said Evan.

"I guess you're not. So, you're telling me I don't need to worry about wading into a scandal?"

"I'm assuring you this won't blow up in your face."

"What was that date again?"

"Last weekend of the month."

"*This* month?"

"I realize it's short notice. I told you about the fire at the Emerald?"

"We'd need extra staff and security," said Conrad.

"We'll take care of all the details," Evan assured him.

Angelica held her breath.

Conrad nodded his head. "I'll leave the details to you."

"Thank you so much," Angelica reflexively gushed,

reaching out to shake Conrad's hand with both of hers. "Kayla will be so excited."

"Yeah, yeah." Conrad gruffly brushed away the thanks and seemed to mentally withdraw.

"We've imposed on you long enough," said Evan polishing off the last drink. "Thank you for this, sir. Is there a staff member we can contact?"

"Albert will bring you a business card."

The butler, who had remained nearby, came forward to give the card to Evan.

"Goodnight, Conrad." Evan tucked the card into his suit pocket and shook Conrad's hand.

Conrad gave Angelica a parting smile. "I guess I'll be seeing you again soon."

"You will," Angelica agreed. "I'll look forward to it."

Evan put his hand at the small of her back and guided her back through the great room toward the hallway. As soon as the front door was closed behind them, he leaned down to whisper. "You were amazing."

"Are you okay?"

"How do you mean?"

"You drank six single malts."

"Oh, that. Getting him a little drunk seemed like a good strategy, and I couldn't very well throw you to the wolves." Evan blew out a breath as they approached the car. "But I am a little woozy. I think you'd better drive."

"No kidding."

He walked her to the driver's side door, extracting the keys. "Do you know how to drive a stick?"

"I can manage."

"She's peppy," he warned.

Angelica's back was to the car door, and she couldn't help smiling at the warning. "I'll be fine."

Then he went silent, and she suddenly realized just how close to her he was standing. The warmth of his body swirled out to meet her skin. She picked up his familiar scent on the breeze. He smelled good, so good, and she felt herself sway involuntarily toward him. Her hormonal reaction to Evan hadn't changed one bit.

That was bad.

"I mean it," he said in a gravelly voice. "You did great in there."

"So did you," she told him sincerely.

He inched ever so slightly closer. "We make a good team—you and me."

"You're drunk, Evan."

"Maybe a little."

"Your judgment is impaired."

"My judgment is perfect. You're incredible, Angie. And I wanted you just as badly sober as I do now."

Before she realized what was happening, his lips were on hers. Magic exploded inside her brain, colors flashing, music playing, the taste of Evan overwhelming her senses. The kiss went on for long minutes before he finally pulled back.

She was breathless, and not nearly as horrified as she ought to have been. She had to get it together here.

"That did *not* demonstrate good judgment, Evan," she told him tartly, holding out her hand for the car keys.

He just grinned and dropped the keys into her palm. "Sure it did."

The Lassiter Media building's twenty-seventh floor patio, with its adjacent café, was normally open to all the company executives. But today, it was closed for Angelica's private meeting with her brothers and cousin. Together, the four controlled the broader Lassiter conglomerate group.

At her request, they'd agreed to coordinate trips to L.A. Chance and Sage were in from Wyoming, where Chance ran the family's Big Blue ranch and Sage took care of his own business interests. Dylan managed the Lassiter Grill Group.

They were at a dining table beside the fountain as Dylan popped the cork on a bottle of Chateau Montegro, a signature wine of Lassiter Grill. Chance was telling Sage about the adventures of a couple of the ranch cowboys.

Feeling like she needed to clear the air, Angelica broke into the lighthearted story. "Before we go any further, can you please let me apologize?"

They all looked at her, falling silent.

"This isn't a celebration," she reminded Dylan.

She forced herself to look at each of them in turn, Chance with his strong face and ranch-weathered complexion, Dylan with his ready smile and compassionate eyes, Sage with his closed expression and tight rein on his feelings.

"Please let me get this out. I am so profoundly and incredibly sorry for putting you all through this."

Dylan was quick to speak up. "It isn't your fault."

"But it is." She wasn't going to back away from this.

"You got the short end of the stick," said Chance. "The will took us all by surprise. I can't honestly say what I would have done if I'd been shafted like that."

"You'd have walked away," Angelica told her cousin with conviction. She glanced at her brothers as well. "All of you. If J.D. had left you out of his will, you'd have accepted it and walked away."

Sage spoke up. "That's because we wouldn't have been surprised. His relationship with us was a lot more strained than his relationship with you."

"You mean he spoiled me." She was determined to be completely honest here.

"He loved you," said Dylan. "He loved you and you expected, you *knew*, you always knew above everything else that he'd take care of you. And he didn't. Or it looked like he didn't."

"Ultimately, it was his choice," said Angelica. "It was his money, his companies. He was free to leave them to whomever he pleased." She swallowed a catch in her throat. "I should have accepted his decision right away."

Sage reached out and put a hand on her shoulder. "Don't beat yourself up, little sister."

The unexpected endearment made her tear up. Sage wasn't one to demonstrate emotion. "I'm so sorry," she managed.

"Okay," said Dylan, raising the bottle of Chateau Montegro. "You're sorry. It's done. We accept your apology."

Both Sage and Chance nodded with conviction.

"We're family," said Chance. "It's up to us to stick together now."

The obvious love in their expressions made the weight slowly lift from Angelica's shoulders. Her tears dried, and she managed a weak smile.

Dylan began pouring the wine.

"I don't know why he even left me the twenty-five percent of Lassiter Media," Sage said to Angelica. "I'm busy running Spence Enterprises. I'll sign the shares over to you anytime you want."

She shook her head. "No, you won't. I'm through second-guessing our father. You're a significant shareholder in Lassiter Media, and you're staying that way. If I had to guess, I'd say he wanted to make sure you felt like part of this family. Besides, I want to be able to come to you for advice."

Sage grinned. "You don't need any of my advice on Lassiter Media. Evan's the one who—" He abruptly stopped himself, looking apologetic.

"You're allowed to say his name," said Angelica.

"Have you spoken to him? I mean, since the day you took over?" asked Dylan, handing her a glass of the red wine.

"I have," she confirmed. "We talked yesterday."

All three men looked surprised by the news. They waited for her to elaborate.

"We're standing up for Kayla and Matt," she explained. "They're getting married at the end of the month."

There was a further beat of silence all around. All three men looked decidedly worried.

"It's fine," she assured them.

"How can it be fine?" asked Dylan.

She waved away their concern. "We're friends—" She stopped herself, realizing that lying to her family was ridiculous. "Okay, we're not friends. We've hurt each other in too many ways to ever even contemplate forgiveness. But we can pretend to be friends—we *have* to pretend to be friends—for Kayla and Matt's sake."

"You want us to talk to him?" asked Sage.

Angelica fought a bubble of laughter. "And say what?"

"If he steps out of line," growled Chance.

"Stop it," she ordered. "You guys like Evan. You've always liked Evan." She straightened the silverware in front of her, telling herself it was vital to keep the honesty flowing. "There were times when you liked him better than you liked me."

"Never," said Dylan.

"It's fine," she assured them again. "It's going to be just fine." Her voice went softer. "But, thank you. Thank you for caring, and thank you for supporting me."

Dylan raised his glass, and they all followed suit. "This is long overdue. To J.D."

"To J.D.," they echoed.

"To Dad," Angelica whispered, her heart beginning to heal as she took a first sip.

Three

"Why are you even still here?" Evan asked Deke as they slowed to a walk on the beach pathway north of the Santa Monica Pier.

"I'm helping," Deke answered through labored breaths. He angled his way through the colorful afternoon crowd of tourists, buskers and rollerbladers, going toward the slushy kiosk. They'd ended their jog a couple of blocks from Evan's building.

"You're not helping at all." Evan followed along without complaint because he was incredibly thirsty.

"I got a hot lead this morning."

"*I* got a hot lead this morning. You just answered my phone."

"I provided excellent service. Two large lemon mangos," Deke said to the kiosk clerk.

"How do you know I want lemon mango?"

"You want something else?"

"I don't care." As long as it was cold and wet, Evan would be happy.

Deke handed a twenty to the clerk. "Then why are you griping?"

"I want a little control over my life."

"You want a little control over Angelica Lassiter."

"Say what?" How had Angie gotten into the conversation?

"You're sexually frustrated, and you're taking it out on me."
The clerk smirked as he handed Deke his change.

"I'm not sexually frustrated," Evan said in a loud voice,
as much for the clerk's benefit as anything else. His lack of
a sex life was purely by choice.

"You want Angelica. You can't have her. So you're pissy."

"Hey, I kissed her. Just last night. And she kissed me back."

The clerk had turned away to operate the slushy machine,
which was chugging out the lemon mango, so Evan couldn't
tell if he'd heard the brag.

"The hell you say," said Deke.

"I say."

"Where'd you kiss her?"

"Conrad Norville's."

"Is that above or below the waist?"

"Ha, ha."

"So, what does that mean?" Deke asked, going serious again.

Evan shrugged, already regretting having shared the information. "I don't know," he admitted.

It meant nothing. He was a fool to have mentioned it. He'd
all but forced that kiss on Angie. Her return kiss had been
reflexive, an obvious result of shock and surprise. It might
have been fantastic, but she hadn't meant it. Afterward, she'd
been nothing but annoyed.

The clerk slid the slushy drinks across the counter, and
they each took one.

"When are you seeing her again?" asked Deke as they
turned away.

"In an hour. The Emerald Wave faxed Matt and Kayla's
plans for the wedding so we could pick up the ball. We'll
need to contact the florist, the bakery, the musicians. And
we need to check out a new caterer."

"Does Matt know about the fire?"

"He does now. I finally got a text from him this morning. But it looks like they'll be a couple more days getting back." Evan plopped down on a bench facing the ocean and took a long, satisfying drink.

Deke sat down next to him. "You're not meeting her at Lassiter Media, are you?"

"Good grief, no," said Evan. The Lassiter Media building was the last place on earth he wanted to be.

"You want company?"

Evan's first reaction was to grin. "You think I need protection from Angie?"

"More like she needs protection from you."

"It's all under control."

Evan had everything in perspective. He just needed to keep his emotional reaction to Angie separate from his intellectual understanding of the situation. And he could do that.

Her lack of trust in him had destroyed any chance they had as a couple. But that didn't mean she wasn't attractive. She was just as gorgeous and sexy as she'd ever been. And the fact that he could picture her naked in such vivid and astonishing detail was to be completely expected.

But he could handle it. He had no choice but to handle it.

"You just told me you kissed her," said Deke.

"It was nothing."

"Kissing your ex-fiancée is not nothing."

"It was a slipup. She was standing there. I was standing there..." Evan struggled to keep his mind from going back to that incredible moment.

"And if she's 'standing there' again today?"

"She won't be."

Deke gave a choked laugh.

"You know what I mean." Evan took another drink.

The sun was hot on his sweat-damp head, burning along the back of his neck. The shrieks of children on the sand swirled around him, while the moist, salt air sat heavily in his lungs.

"I'm coming with you," Deke announced. "And afterward we're hitting a club or two and dancing with some new, hot women."

Evan was about to refuse. But he realized Deke was right. He had to nip this in the bud. Angie was his past, not his future. Once they were done with Matt and Kayla's wedding, they were going their separate ways. Letting himself fantasize about her would only delay his recovery.

"Fine," he agreed. "Suit yourself."

"Thanks for helping out with this," Angelica said to Tiffany as she drove her ice-blue sports car into the parking lot of the Terrace Bistro where she and Evan had agreed to meet.

"Why are you thanking me?" Tiffany asked. "It's my job. Kayla needs me. Besides, there's no way I'm letting you face Evan alone."

"I faced him alone last night," Angelica pointed out.

Not that she was looking forward to doing it again. Their kiss last night had completely rattled her. It should have felt awkward. It should have felt strange. She should have recoiled from the feel of his hands and the taste of his lips.

But it had felt familiar. It had felt like coming home.

"You okay, Angie?" Tiffany reached out to touch her arm.

"I'm perfectly fine." Angelica shut off the ignition and set the car's emergency brake. Then a wave of anxiety hit her, and she latched her hands on to the steering wheel, gripping hard for a second.

"Angie?"

"I'm over him." She released her grip on the steering wheel. "And he's definitely over me. Let's go."

"He kissed you, didn't he?" Tiffany had already heard the entire story.

"That was an... I don't know what that was. But it wasn't

a regular kiss. He was making some kind of debating point or maybe a power play, or he was mocking me."

"Well, I'm here for you if he tries anything over dinner."

"Thank you," Angelica told her sincerely. "He won't. And I don't care one way or the other. He's just another guy to me."

"If you say so." Tiffany sounded doubtful.

"I say so," Angelica responded with conviction. She pocketed her keys and opened the car door.

The two women made their way across the parking lot to the non-descript, little café. Inside, Angelica spotted Evan at a corner table. The second his gaze met hers, her stomach fluttered with anticipation, and all her hopes of pretending he was just another guy flew out the window. This was Evan. He was never going to be just another guy.

A moment later, she realized he wasn't alone.

"Who's *that*?" Tiffany whispered from behind her.

"Deke?" Angelica asked the question out loud, quickening her steps. She had only met Evan's college friend Deke a few times, but she'd always liked him. He was slightly shorter than Evan and had dark hair. He was very handsome, and one of the smartest people Angelica had ever met.

He came to his feet, giving her a broad smile. "Angelica." He pulled her into a brief hug that felt entirely natural.

"What are you doing in L.A.?" she asked.

He shrugged. "I got a little restless." His gaze went past her to abruptly stop on Tiffany.

Angelica quickly introduced them. "This is Tiffany. She's Kayla's other bridesmaid."

Deke held out his hand to greet Tiffany, and Angelica quickly stepped out of the way. She realized too late that the action put her in position to sit next to Evan on the bench seat of the booth. Doing anything to switch back would look ridiculously awkward. Besides, Deke was already motioning Tiffany in next to him.

Resigned, Angelica sat down.

"I see you brought reinforcements," Evan noted in an undertone.

"As did you." She settled her purse on the bench seat as a barrier between them.

"Deke's staying with me for a few days."

"In Pasadena?"

"I sold the house in Pasadena."

The words took her by surprise, and she automatically glanced at him. "You did? When? Why?"

"Last week."

"But, you loved that house."

"At the moment, I need the money more than I need a big house."

"But you have—"

"I am not using his money, Angie."

"You'd take a loss on principle?"

"I didn't take a loss. But, yes, *I'd* take a loss on principle."

"What's that supposed to mean," she hissed under her breath as Tiffany and Deke got settled.

Evan handed her a printout on Emerald Wave stationery. "It means, unlike certain other people, I stick to my principles even when it's inconvenient."

"I stuck to *my* principles." Which were, at least in part, to ensure the health and security of Lassiter Media.

"Principles like respecting your father?" he drawled.

"Evan," Tiffany put in smoothly from across the table. "You should shut up now."

Deke gave a muted chuckle.

A waiter appeared at the table. "Good evening."

Angelica gratefully switched her attention to the man.

"Our most popular themes are Mediterranean, southwest and continental." The man handed around some sheets of paper. "I'll give you a few minutes to discuss it, and then I'd be happy to talk about wine pairings for your choices."

Angelica shot Tiffany a confused glance. They had to agree on a theme? What kind of a restaurant was this? Why couldn't they just order from the menu?

"Thank you," said Evan. "We'll let you know what we decide."

"Have you been here before?" Angelica asked him as the waiter stepped away.

"Never." He arranged three sheets of paper in front of him. "But our options were limited at this late date."

"It's a Wednesday." How busy could Malibu restaurants be? It was only five-thirty in the evening.

He gave her a confused look. "I mean our catering options for the wedding."

She blinked. Then she glanced down at the papers in front of them. They listed price points per guest and per platter.

"These are catering menus," she observed.

"Can't get one past you."

"I thought we were here for dinner. I thought you were bringing the Emerald Wave information for us to discuss."

"I am. I did. But we're also sampling the caterer's menu."

Tiffany jumped in. "That sounds like fun."

"I'm game," said Deke. "Not to brag, but I excel at eating."

Tiffany smiled as she gave Deke a sidelong glance.

"You could have told me," Angelica, embarrassed by her own confusion, said to Evan.

"I thought I did tell you when we talked on the phone. Maybe you just didn't listen. Mediterranean, southwest or continental."

Angelica didn't exactly believe him, but she let it go, scanning the catering menus.

"Continental has my vote," said Tiffany.

"I'd be happier if we knew what Kayla wanted."

"I finally got a voice mail from Matt in response to my text," said Evan. "He says thanks. He trusts our judgment. And they'll appreciate anything we can do before they get back. The connection was pretty bad, because I think he said something about the moat being flooded."

"The *moat*?"

"The only logical explanation I could come up with is that the retreat is at a castle somewhere. I know there's a pretty big storm off the North Sea. The upshot is they won't be able to get home for a few more days. We're on our own."

"I agree with Tiffany," said Deke.

Evan glanced up. "Of course you agree with Tiffany. You're flirting with Tiffany." He looked pointedly at her. "Watch out for this guy."

She grinned.

"Southwest is a bit overdone lately," Angelica noted. And the décor at Conrad's mansion definitely lent itself to something a little highbrow.

"Matt's not a huge fan of Mediterranean," Evan put in. "Does that settle it?"

"Sure," said Angelica. "Let's go with continental."

"So, old world wines?"

"Bite your tongue," said Angelica. "California wines, for sure."

Evan smiled without looking at her. He knew full well the Lassiter family had many close friends in the wine business in Napa Valley.

"Are you *trying* to pick a fight with her?" Deke asked him.

Evan seemed to be doing his best to look offended. "I can't make a joke?"

Tiffany put up her hand to signal the waiter. "This seems like a great time to get the wine tasting underway."

"I like the way you think," Deke muttered.

After some consultation with the waiter, they chose several wines to taste along with a selection of appetizers, entrees and desserts from the continental menu.

Despite the rather humble surroundings of the restaurant, the food turned out to be delicious.

Angelica bit into a warm brie and smoked trout appetizer, enfolded in phyllo pastry and garnished with a light herb paste.

"Oh," she groaned, setting the remainder of the morsel down on her plate to savor the mouthful. "This is the best one yet."

"Try the shrimp," said Tiffany. "Oh, man. I'm getting stuffed, but I just can't stop."

"I need some real food," said Evan.

"Get them to bring you the duck or the lamb," Angelica suggested. "But I think I'm going to have to trust you on how those taste. I couldn't possibly eat anymore."

"You'd actually trust me on something?" asked Evan, a lilt to his tone.

She turned to rebuke him for the sarcasm, but then she caught the sparkle in his eyes. She realized she had to stop being so touchy. He'd always had a dry sense of humor. She used to enjoy it.

"So long as you don't try to steal what's rightfully mine," she countered.

In answer, he snagged the remaining bite of brie and smoked trout from her plate, popping it in his mouth.

"Hey!" she protested.

"Guess you shouldn't have trusted me after all. Wow, this is good. Definitely add that to the list."

"You stole my trout."

"You left it unguarded."

"You said I could trust you." She knew she should be annoyed, but she was only barely able to keep from laughing.

"I believe you were the one who offered to trust me."

"Clearly, I was wrong about that."

"Clearly."

She sniffed. "Well, you owe me some trout."

"I'll trade you for some duckling."

"Are you ordering the duckling?" asked Deke. "Then I'll try the veal."

Angelica glanced at the menu. "You mean the duck flambé? With orange brandy?"

"That's the one," said Evan.

"You got yourself a trade." She was about to shake on it, then quickly realized it was a mistake, and redirected her hand to her wineglass, lifting it and taking a sip of the rich merlot.

Evan smirked. He reached below the table between them, squeezing her other hand. She nearly inhaled her wine.

He leaned close, muttering in an undertone as Deke commented to Tiffany about the stuffed mushrooms. "It's okay to touch me, Angie."

At that moment, Evan's fingertips brushed the hem of her skirt, contacting her bare thigh. They both instantly stilled. Arousal radiated along her leg, electrifying her skin, contracting her muscles.

"Orgasmic," Tiffany declared.

Angelica whimpered under her breath.

Evan's warm hand curled open, his palm spreading across her thigh, sliding ever so slightly beneath her skirt.

"Please," she managed to whisper.

"Something wrong?" Tiffany asked her, looking concerned.

"Nothing," she managed, distracting herself with another swallow of the wine. She shifted, but Evan's hand moved with her.

Deke signaled the waiter, asking the man for the duck and the veal.

Evan leaned toward her, his voice a ragged whisper in her ear. "Tell me to stop."

She tried. She opened her mouth, but the words didn't come out.

His hand slipped higher, and her grip tightened on the wine glass.

"Angie?" Tiffany's voice penetrated the haze inside her brain.

"Hmmm?" she managed.

"I said do you have a preference for desserts?"

"Uh. No."

"Torte? Éclairs? Maybe cheesecake?"

"Sure. Yeah."

Evan's fingertips swirled lightly against her skin. The sensation took her back months in time. For some reason, she remembered a particular morning when they'd lounged in bed at his house in Pasadena. It had been pouring rain, and he'd made hot chocolate, lacing it with coffee liqueur.

"Maybe the pecan tarts?" asked Tiffany.

"Okay," Angelica managed.

Tiffany peered at her strangely. "You look flushed. Are you having an allergic reaction?" Her glance darted from dish to dish. "Were there almonds in something?"

"No, no." Angelica put in quickly. "I'm good. I'm fine." She put her hand down on top of Evan's. She'd intended to push him away, but somehow it didn't happen. Instead she pressed down on his hand, pushing it harder against her thigh.

"The chocolate truffles," said Evan. "Get them to bring some of the chocolate truffles."

Tiffany smiled. "I *love* chocolate. It's so richly decadent."

Evan's touch was richly decadent, and indulgent, and Angelica had to stop him.

"Are you dating anyone?" Deke asked Tiffany.

"Seriously?" asked Evan. "You're hitting on her during dinner?"

"I'm asking her out," said Deke. "There's a big difference."

"I can tell the difference," Tiffany offered breezily. "And he's hitting on me."

Deke pulled back in his seat in mock offense, his hand on his heart. "You wound me deeply."

As Tiffany answered back, Evan leaned in close to Angelica's ear again. "In case you're wondering, I'm also hitting on you."

His words gave her the strength to tug his hand away. He gave in easily, but she was left quivering.

Evan knew it was his turn to make sure Angelica got home safely. By the time they made it through the all the wines, she was in no condition to drive, and Tiffany was probably over the limit as well. He paid the bill and slid his keys across the table to Deke. Then he held out his hands for Angelica's keys.

"I'm fine to—" She stopped herself. "You're right. I'm not driving anywhere. But I can call a driver."

"Don't be ridiculous. It'll take them until midnight just to get here."

"They're on call for a reason."

"And I'm already here. I trusted you to drive my car, and it's a whole lot more expensive than yours."

"Can you drive an automatic?" she asked, humor lurking in her slightly glassy eyes.

"I'll manage." He flicked his gaze to Tiffany. "We'll have to put you in a cab."

The sports car was a two-seater.

"I'll take her home," Deke offered.

"Oh, no you don't," said Evan.

"You'll love Evan's convertible," Deke said to Tiffany.

She looked at Evan. "I'm more worried about you with Angie than I am about Deke with me."

"Seriously?" Evan asked, honestly offended. "How well do you know me?"

Tiffany studied his expression for a critical moment. "I don't want you fighting with her."

"I'll be a perfect gentleman," said Evan.

Truth was, fighting with Angie was the very last thing on his mind. Seducing her, now that was the real danger.

But he could absolutely control himself. His hand might still be warm where he'd caressed her thigh, and he might remember the unique, arousing texture of her skin, but he was keeping it in context. He *had* to keep it all in context.

"You'll be okay with him?" Tiffany asked Angie.

"I have to get my car home somehow."

"You're not drunk?"

"I'm not drunk. I'm merely over the legal limit from doing my duty as a bridesmaid."

"Fair enough," said Tiffany. "I on the other hand did my duty with the dessert." She popped the last chocolate truffle into her mouth.

"How *do* you stay so slim?" asked Deke.

"Give the compliments a rest," she responded with a laugh. "They're not going to work."

Watching the exchange, Evan couldn't help feeling envious of Deke. He suddenly wished he and Angie had just met tonight, that they had no baggage between them. If that were the case, he'd also be putting on a full-court press.

"You ready?" he asked her, resisting the urge to smooth stray wisps of hair away from her forehead.

She reached for the purse between them. "I really didn't think this through."

"I'll get you home safe," he told her.

She gave him a nod of agreement and slid from the booth. The two couples separated at the bottom of the café steps. Evan settled Angie into the passenger seat before starting her car and pulling onto the highway.

As he drove, he struggled to push away the memory of her warm skin. But instead, he found himself wondering what she'd thought. When he'd caressed her thigh, she hadn't immediately pushed him away.

Maybe she was too shocked by his behavior to react. Or maybe she'd been sitting there fuming mad. He knew nothing good could come of bringing it up again. But that didn't mean he could stop it from ticking through his mind.

He made it fifteen silent minutes down the Pacific Coast Highway before he cracked. He wheeled into a dark parking lot overlooking the surf and the moonlit night.

"What?" Angie was clearly confused by the unexpected stop, glancing around outside.

He angled his body to face her. "Should I apologize here?"

Her jaw went lax in obvious shock, and her eyes went round in the dashboard glow. "You'd actually do that?" she asked in an awed whisper.

It took him a moment to realize what she was thinking. She thought he was talking about how he'd gone along with J.D.'s will. For some reason, she'd guessed he meant the big apology, the one where he told her he'd been wrong all those months, that she was justified in not trusting him, and that the problems between them were his fault, not hers.

That was never going to happen.

"For what I did in the restaurant," he clarified.

"The...oh. Okay." She schooled her features and glanced away from him.

"I didn't do it to upset you." Half his brain was telling him to shut up already, while the other half seemed hell-bent on ploughing forward. "It was an accident. Well, at first. But then...you didn't seem to mind."

"I minded a whole lot."

"You didn't stop me."

She looked at him again. "You took me by surprise."

"I took me by surprise too," he admitted.

They both fell silent, and the air seemed to thicken inside the dim car. His gaze moved to her full lips, and her taste from last night invaded his senses. He wanted to kiss her again, wanted it very badly.

"Evan, don't."

"Don't what?" He hadn't made a single move here.

"I can see what you're thinking."

"You can read my mind, Angie? Really?"

"You're remembering what it was like between us." She swallowed. "You remember it being good."

"It *was* good."

"Sex is always good."

Her words were like a bucket of cold water. "*Always*?"

"Evan, don't."

"You've had a lot of sex lately, have you?"

She smoothed the hem of her skirt. "That's none of your business."

"With who?"

"Stop."

Hard anger invaded his stomach, turning his voice to a growl. "Who, Angie? Who've you been sleeping with? Was it Jack Reed?"

"Jack's with Becca now."

"Doesn't mean he wasn't ever with you."

"I am *not* having this conversation." She abruptly swung open the door.

He leaned across the car, reaching for her, but she slipped out too quickly, slamming the car door firmly behind her. He was out his side in a shot, pacing his way to her.

"Tell me the truth," he demanded. It wasn't the first time he'd wondered about Jack Reed. And it wasn't the first time he'd wanted to take the man apart.

She glared defiantly up at him, her back against the car. "Why? Why would you even care?"

"That's a yes."

"It's *not* a yes," she retorted.

"How long?" he asked, his tone deceptively soft. "How long after you left my bed were you in his?"

"I never slept with Jack."

"I don't believe you."

"Believe whatever you want, Evan. But I have never lied to you, and I'm not about to start now. I haven't slept with anyone since we broke up." She gave a slightly hysterical laugh. "When would I have time for a relationship? And you, of all people, *you*, Evan—" she jabbed a finger against his chest "—should know I don't just jump into any man's bed."

He trapped her hand, holding it against his thudding heart. "Nobody?"

Her eyes were black as the night around them. "Nobody. And I'm insulted that you asked."

"You're a beautiful woman, Angie." He wasn't entirely sure if it was an explanation for his suspicions or an observation in the moment. Every time he saw her, he was blown away by her beauty. "Men must hit on you all the time."

"I understand how to say the word no, Evan."

"Yeah?" He felt himself swaying forward.

"Yeah," she told him with conviction.

"Then tell me no."

To be fair, he didn't actually give her time to answer. His lips were on hers again before she could even draw a breath. In the back of his mind, he realized he had to stop doing this. He had no right to kiss her, no right to touch her, no right in the world to ask about her sex life. But right and wrong seemed to fly out the window when she was near.

Before he knew it, she was in his arms, their kiss deepening. Somehow, she had imprinted on him. The memory of making love to her was burned into his spinal column. He knew to wrap one arm around her waist, bury his fingers in her hair, caress the back of her neck, tease her tongue with the tip of his own. Her little moan was familiar to his ears, while the scent of her hair took him back in time.

The next move was his hand at her waist, slipping under her blouse, rising up to cup the lace of her bra.

"We can't," she cried, pushing her hands against his chest and turning her head away.

He ordered himself to let go, but it took his body a moment to react.

"We can't let that happen." She pressed herself back against the car.

He eased off, putting some space between them, his breath ragged. "I didn't plan it."

There was an edge of hysteria to her voice. "You think I did?"

"No. No. Of course not. I'm only saying—" After all they'd been through, he shouldn't want to make her feel better about the slipup, but for some reason he did. "I'm only saying the physical attraction is still there. It doesn't have to mean anything."

"It doesn't mean anything." She paused. "Okay, it means we have to be careful."

"We do," he agreed. They seemed all but combustible when they got close to each other.

He also realized that the kiss had answered his original question. There was no need to apologize. He tried to rein in his ego, but he failed.

He voiced his suspicions. "You liked it. That's why you didn't stop me. You liked my hand on your thigh."

"I did not," she snapped.

"You said you wouldn't lie."

"I told you, it shocked me."

"But you liked it," he challenged.

She looked him straight in the eyes. "Like I said, we have to be careful."

She might not have confirmed it. But she hadn't denied it.

He couldn't help the self-satisfied grin that spread across his face.

Four

"Angelica?" Her brother Dylan's voice came over the speakerphone on the meeting room table. "Is there something you want to tell us?"

Angelica had temporarily set herself up in a comfortable meeting room on the twenty-eighth floor of the Lassiter Media building, leaving the top floor boardroom and J.D.'s office free for the renovators.

"Tell you what? And who is us?" she asked as she continued to page through a financial report.

"The *us* is me and Sage. The *what* is the article in the *Weekly Break* newspaper about you and Evan getting back together."

Angelica snatched up the telephone receiver, glancing worriedly at the open meeting room door. "*What*?"

"That's what I'm asking you," Dylan responded mildly.

"I don't know where they'd get that." Her mind flipped frantically back to last night when she'd kissed Evan at the parking lot on the highway. Could a reporter have possibly gotten a shot of them in that moment? "Is there a picture?"

"Is there a picture?" Dylan parroted. "Are you telling me there might possibly be a picture?"

"There can't be a picture," she lied. "Unless it's an old

one. You know, maybe with a current newspaper Photo-shopped into it."

"It's not a ransom demand."

"I realize that." She didn't know what else to say.

"Angie?" Dylan's tone was searching. "What's going on?"

"*Nothing* is going on."

She caught a flash of movement in the corner of her eye and glanced up to see Evan in the doorway, a copy of the *Weekly Break* in his hand.

"I have to go," she said to Dylan.

"Angie."

"I have a meeting." Her eyes locked with Evan's. "It's nothing. They've made up a story is all."

"Are you sure, because we'd all be very happy—"

"Goodbye, Dylan." She quickly hung up the phone.

"You heard?" asked Evan, walking into the meeting room.

"You shouldn't be here."

She came to her feet, crossing the room to close the door.

"You might not want to close that," he observed.

"Speculation is probably better than having them overhear our conversation. What happened? What does it say?" She reflexively put a hand to her forehead. "Oh, man, how is Conrad going to react to this?"

Evan tossed the paper onto the top of the meeting table. "I think Conrad's the source."

She glanced down to see a damning headline on the front page. There was a picture of them, but thank goodness it was from last year.

"They didn't catch us last night?" she asked, spinning the paper right-side up in her direction.

"Now, *that's* the kind of thing you don't want people to overhear."

She frowned at him. "You know what I mean."

"There's no new photo," he confirmed. "But an unnamed source quoted me as saying I'd be a blind fool to give you up."

Angelica closed her eyes for a long moment. "Conrad."

"Unless it was the butler."

She opened her eyes to look at Evan. "Butlers get fired for a lot less than that."

"My money's definitely on Conrad."

"But why would he do that? He said he wanted the Lassiters to stay *out* of the tabloids."

"Maybe he's calling our bluff."

"No." But she hesitated. "You think?" She glanced down at the article. "What would be his motivation?"

"I don't pretend to have the first clue about what makes that man tick."

"What are we supposed to do now?" They couldn't let this stand. But they couldn't let Conrad know the truth either. Kayla's wedding was at stake.

"We may have to ride it out."

Angelica did not like the sound of that. She dropped back into her chair, voice going low, trepidation rising. "What do you mean, ride it out?"

"I mean…" He pulled out a chair across from her and sat down. "We don't deny anything to anybody until after the ceremony."

"And let the world think we're getting back together?"

Evan shrugged.

She shook her head. "Uh-uh. No way."

"I'm not saying it's a good answer."

"We can't do that."

"The alternative is to tell Conrad we lied."

She continued shaking her head. "We can't do that either."

"Then tell me the third option."

She frantically searched her brain. But there was no third option. She brought the side of her fist down on the paper. "How did we not see this coming?"

"We never guessed he'd go to the tabloids."

"We shouldn't have assumed he'd keep it a secret." She could have kicked herself for being so stupid.

"Well, I was drunk," Evan drawled.

"This isn't funny," she snapped in return.

"I don't think it's funny, Angie. But nobody's going to die from it either. It's two-and-a-half weeks. And then we're done. We fake a breakup and walk away."

"I am not going to lie to my brothers." It would be bad enough having strangers think they were a couple.

"I understand."

"I mean, after all we've been through. We just got back on an even keel. I can't possibly do that to them, Evan."

He seemed to ponder for a moment. "I do understand. Trouble is, Sage can't lie to Colleen and Dylan can't lie to Jenna."

"Of course they can't," she agreed.

"And you want Chance to have to lie to Felicia?"

Angelica set her jaw.

"Exactly how big do you think we can make the conspiracy before somebody accidentally trips up?"

She felt her throat close up. No matter which way she turned, somebody got hurt. "I can't do this."

His tone turned gentle. "You don't have to lie, Angie."

"How do I not have to lie? How can I possibly not have to lie?"

"Answer me this. If I was to come to you on bended knee, telling you I was sorry, that it was all my fault, that I thought we should give it another try, would you dismiss the idea out of hand, or would you at least think about it?"

It was a ridiculous scenario. "You are never, *ever* going to do that."

"I'm not," he agreed. "But if you were to come to me on bended knee, telling me you were sorry, that it was all your fault, and that you thought we should give it another try, I'm pretty sure I'd at least think about it."

"That's your loophole?"

"So, when you say to someone—*if you were* to say to someone—that we both knew we had a lot of issues to work through, that the chances were slim, but we had discussed getting back together, it wouldn't be a lie."

"Technically, no," she allowed.

"Precisely no."

Her chest had gone heavy with pain. "And that's what you want us to do? You want us to let the entire world think we're giving it another shot?"

"Think about the benefits, all of the benefits. There's Conrad, of course, and the wedding venue. But also Kayla and Matt's emotional comfort. They won't have to tippy-toe around us. Everybody at the wedding will be more comfortable. You and I won't feel like we're under a microscope."

That was exactly how she'd expected to feel at the wedding.

"It's traditional for the best man and maid of honor to dance together," Evan continued. "Can you imagine what the guests would be thinking? 'Is she frowning? Is he grimacing? What are they saying to each other? Are they fighting?'"

"You've given this a lot of thought." She hated to admit that she had as well. She was trying desperately not to dread the reception, but she was losing the battle.

"I like to think I'm a realist, Angie."

"You promised to call me Angelica."

He gave a small smile. "I don't remember promising. But now that we're thinking about getting back together, you'll have to put up with it for a couple more weeks."

She glanced back down at the headline. "You really think we should do this?"

"It'll be over before you know it."

* * *

"What, exactly do you think you're doing?" Deke asked as he strode into Evan's office in Santa Monica.

"Manual labor," Evan answered, holding one of the metal brackets for a shelving unit against the wall, his cordless drill groaning as he anchored the screws.

The door banged shut behind Deke, the blinds rattling with what was becoming a familiar sound. "I read the tabloid story."

"I had nothing to do with it." Evan reached for another screw on the counter beside him.

"You're quoted in it."

"Don't believe everything you read."

"So, you're not getting back together with Angie?"

Evan thought through his words. "We're talking. We're thinking. We're spending a little time together."

There was a moment of silence. "Are you using recreational drugs?"

Evan snorted a non-reply.

"Seriously, Evan. Have you completely lost your mind?"

"No."

"Then, *what the hell?*"

Evan immediately realized that deceiving Deke was never going to work. The only way he could pull this off was if Deke was in on the ruse. His friend knew him too well, and Deke would be around him too much this month to get away with lying.

He gave in. "Fine. Okay. It was a ruse to get Conrad to let us use his mansion."

It seemed to take Deke a moment to process the statement. "You told Conrad you were getting back together with Angie."

"It was the only way."

"It was a stupid way."

Evan smiled to himself, lining up the final screw. He

drilled it firmly through the bracket and into the wall. "Well, it's too late to turn back now."

Deke crossed his arms over his chest. "I was your first phone call. Remember? I know the state you were in the day you and Angie split up."

Evan's hand tightened on the drill grip. "I remember."

"It was a bad day, buddy."

"No kidding," Evan repeated.

It wasn't a day he talked about. He refused to dwell on it. He simply pointed his life forward and took it one step at a time. He turned back to the counter and set down the drill.

Deke took a step forward. "You can't go through that again."

Evan retrieved a box cutter from his tool kit and set to work on the cardboard box that held the wooden shelves. "We're faking it, Deke. Pretending to like each other. We won't break up again, because we're not getting back together."

Deke followed Evan's lead, locating another cutter and slicing through the tape at the opposite end of the long box. "You still like her. Hell, I think you still love her."

Evan's heart gave a little lurch inside his chest. "It's impossible to love someone who doesn't trust you."

"Maybe." Deke sounded skeptical as he peeled back the box flaps.

"There's no maybe about it. I don't love her." Evan pulled away the packing tape and opened the box. The cherrywood planks were wrapped in bubble plastic.

"It's not an on-off switch."

"It's a do-don't switch," Evan responded with conviction. "And I don't."

"I saw the way you looked at her last night."

"That was lust."

"So, you admit you're still attracted to her?"

Evan knew there was no point in denying it to Deke or

to himself. "I may not be in love with her, but I remember what she looks like naked."

Deke cracked a smile at the answer. "I hear you. I'm still trying to find out what Tiffany looks like naked."

Evan lifted the first shelf from the box. "Good luck with that."

"She's hot. And she's funny. And she's killer smart."

"Angie's going to warn her about you."

"What's to warn? I'm a perfectly nice, perfectly rich, perfectly decent-looking guy."

Evan placed the shelf on the top bracket. "With a perfect track record of short, meaningless relationships."

"See, that's why I worry about you. You claim it's lust, but you buy into the whole hearts-and-flowers thing. You, my friend, have a perfect track record of long, meaningful relationships."

"I did it *once*," Evan pointed out.

"With Angie."

"Your point?"

"I don't believe you're over her."

"I am." It wasn't like Evan had a choice.

"You're going to get hurt."

"I can take care of myself." Evan might still be attracted to Angie, but he was a realist. He was going into this thing with his eyes wide open.

Deke handed him the next shelf. "Just so you know, when it all goes bad and you feel like you have to call in the cavalry—"

"Yeah, yeah. Don't call you."

"What? No. *Do* call me. At least I'm experienced now. We'll head over to Italy and rent a chateau on the Mediterranean. Jeez, Evan. Just because you're stupid, doesn't mean I don't have your back."

Evan couldn't help but chuckle. "Thanks, man. But it won't be necessary."

"We'll see."

The office door swung open, and both men turned toward the sound.

"Lex?" Evan spoke first, astonished that their former roommate was standing in his doorway. "I thought you were in London."

"I heard you were starting over." Lex glanced around the disorganized office. "You do know you can hire carpenters and decorators to do this kind of thing."

"You can?" Evan dusted his hands on his blue jeans as he rounded the end of the reception counter.

"There's this thing called Handyman Listing on the internet...."

Evan grinned as he reached out to shake Lex's hand, clasping his shoulder at the same time. He hadn't seen his friend in over a year. "I'm keeping myself busy. What on earth are you doing in L.A.?"

"Asanti's holding some corporate meetings in New York." Lex nodded to Deke and reached over to shake. "Hey, man. Good to see you again."

The answer was ridiculous. It was clear to Evan Lex was hiding something.

He pressed. "So, you were just on the continent and thought you'd stop by?"

"Something like that."

Evan turned to Deke. "You called him."

"Of course I called him. You weren't going to call him."

"Because there was nothing to tell him."

"You lost your job," said Deke. "You lost your girl. And you're all but destitute."

Evan knew this had gone far enough. "I'm hardly destitute."

Both men raised their eyebrows.

"Seriously," said Evan. "You two want to compare the zeros in our bank accounts?"

Lex laughed.

But Evan wasn't finished. "Deke might have a share in all those technology patents, but I know how to invest." He looked at Lex. "And all you have is a salary." Admittedly, it was probably a very good salary.

"And stock options," said Lex.

"Yeah?" Deke asked with obvious interest.

Lex nodded. "In fact, I'm seriously thinking about cashing them in and buying the Sagittarius."

"Say what?" asked Deke.

"The Sagittarius Resort?" Evan pointed in the general direction of the Pacific Ocean. "*That* Sagittarius?"

Lex nodded.

The five-star complex had close to a thousand rooms and sat on a stunning stretch of beach north of Malibu. It was one of the crown jewels of the California tourism industry.

"I figure it could be the start of a new chain," said Lex.

"You can afford it?" asked Deke.

"I'd need a partner. Maybe two partners." He sent a meaningful glance in Evan's direction.

"Oh, no, no." Evan took a step backward, glancing at Deke, knowing a setup when he saw one. "I don't know how you two lost your collective minds, but you are not riding in here to rescue me. I'm fine. I am completely fine, professionally, financially and romantically."

"What makes you think this is about you?" asked Lex.

"Of course it's about me." Evan was equal parts touched and horrified that his friends would suggest such an outlandish scheme.

"This is the first I'm hearing about the Sagittarius," said Deke.

Evan didn't know whether to believe him or not.

"I'd have to be a silent partner," Deke continued, looking for all the world like he was taking the idea seriously. "I don't have time for any day-to-day responsibilities. Then again, I wouldn't need to draw a salary either."

"No problem," Lex responded. "I can run a hotel with my eyes closed. Evan will be in charge of international expansion. You just pony up with a check."

Deke was nodding thoughtfully.

"Stop this," Evan demanded, glancing from one man to the other. "You two have completely over-estimated the magnitude of my problems."

"It's not all about you, Evan," said Deke.

"Ha," Evan barked.

"What is *with* him?" Lex asked Deke.

"He isn't over Angie yet."

"I am absolutely over—"

"Well, *get* over Angie," said Lex. "And think logically here. Tell me that the three of us going into business together would not be an absolute blast? I don't want to work for someone else for the rest of my life. You and me, all three of us, we're smarter now, more experienced, and we have some serious capital at our disposal. I know the tourism industry. You know international business. Deke, well, maybe he can build us a robotic cleaning system or something. But he can come to the annual shareholders' meetings. We'll have them in Hawaii, find you a hot girl, get you over your heartbreak."

"I'm not heartbroken." But Lex's words had him wondering if this might not be such a bad idea.

How amazing would it be to go into business with his two old friends? Lex and Deke were both brilliant. They were innovative and hard-working. Together, the three of them would have a real shot at building something successful.

He could throw all of his energy into the venture, totally focusing on business for the foreseeable future.

"Just how far have you thought this through?" he asked Lex.

"I just spent fourteen hours on airplanes. So, fourteen hours, plus a three-hour layover."

"Is the Sagittarius even for sale?"

"It will be," said Lex. "The family who owns it is having some…challenges. That's what kicked off my plan. Rita Loring just discovered her husband is sleeping with his assistant, putting the pre-nup in her favor. I know she'll sell her share. The woman couldn't care less about the hotel, and she'll get a kick out of ruining Lewis Loring. Her daughter will support her. If I offer, both women will sell their shares of the business and go on a shopping spree. And Lewis will be left with a choice between staying on as a minor shareholder and cashing out. Since the place has lost money the past three years in a row, I'm betting he'll cash out."

"How do you know all this?" Deke asked.

"I talk to people," said Lex. "I buy them drinks. Sometimes I sleep with them."

"You slept with Rita Loring?" Evan voiced the first thought that popped into his mind.

Lex's expression twisted into a grimace. "I slept with her daughter."

Deke coughed out a laugh. "I'm in."

"The daughter's not ticked off?" asked Evan.

"The daughter's already moved on. She's got bigger fish than me to reel in. It'll take me a week or two to put the deal together. But we've got to move fast."

Both men stared at Evan.

"I have to decide right now?" He glanced at the half-built shelves, thinking his evening plans had taken a huge left turn.

"Yes, you have to decide right now," Lex mocked. "What's to decide?"

It was a fair question. Of all of them, Evan was the guy in the best position to make a big change in his life. He had to make a change. The status quo had ceased being an option over a week ago.

His mind shifted to Angie. He told himself, really *truly*

told himself, that it was over. There was absolutely no going back. Forward was his only choice.

"Okay," he said, forming a plan in his mind as he spoke. "I've got some liquid investments and the cash from the Pasadena house. And J.D. left me several million dollars in his will. I was going to donate it to charity or maybe burn it in protest. But I suppose it's honorable to contribute it to the cause."

"You're in?" Lex asked with a grin.

"I'm in," Evan stated with conviction.

"We need a very old bottle of scotch," said Deke, fishing his car keys out of his pocket, "to toast our new venture."

Angelica had dressed in an ultrafeminine outfit once again in an effort to impress Conrad. But she needn't have bothered. He wasn't at home, and it was Albert, the butler, who showed her and Evan inside. They were meeting with the catering manager and the florist to tour the house and settle some questions about the setup and décor for the wedding.

Kayla and Matt had made it as far as Edinburgh on their way back home. They'd sent several texts while in the airport changing planes. They were thrilled with the wedding plans and reported that everything seemed set for the art exhibit. By now, they'd be over the Atlantic on their way to New York. Once they made it to California, the wedding planning was going to get a whole lot simpler for Angelica and Evan.

Albert, who seemed exceedingly good at his job, had offered her a glass of chardonnay this time instead of the single malt. Evan had chosen a beer.

The group worked their way through an impressive kitchen and dining area, agreeing that the bride should come down the grand staircase, and discussing how the great room should be set up for the ceremony. The guests could then mingle on the terrace and even on the beach at low tide, while staff replaced the folding chairs used for the ceremony and set up the tables for a sit-down dinner.

The caterer seemed impressed with the kitchen, and had requested extra prep tables in the breakfast room. The florist took pictures and measurements, and went over photos of the arrangements Kayla had already chosen, ensuring they would still work with the new décor. Soon they had what they needed.

While Albert showed the florist and caterer out, Angelica wandered across the terrace, trying to imagine Kayla's smile and her mother's delight at the amazing surroundings. She made her way to the lowest level of the terrace then gave in to temptation, taking the narrow staircase down to the beach level.

The tide was out, leaving a wide strip of damp sand exposed beyond the rocky shore. She kicked off her shoes to pick her way to the shore.

The sky was clear, and the half-moon illuminated an orange buoy about thirty yards out. She captured her hair in her hand, holding it against a gust of wind. Her aqua silk wraparound dress rustled against her legs. As she moved toward the water, she heard the sound of Evan's footfalls behind her.

"Reminds me of the opening scene in *Jaws*," she observed.

"Going skinny-dipping?"

"Not on your life."

"Chicken," he mocked softly.

"Uh-huh," she agreed, taking a sip of the crisp wine. "Do you think they'll be happy?"

"Matt and Kayla?"

"Yes. Not with each other. That's a given. I mean with the arrangements we're making. I know we've done our best, but it's hard to second-guess people." It was shaping up to be a wedding that Angelica would love. But what bride wanted someone else to do the planning for her?

"It was their decision to go to Scotland," said Evan. He was standing beside but slightly behind her as she gazed out at the dark water.

"They didn't expect the storm."

"Or the need for the extra approval."

"At least they got the exhibit." Kayla had come across as very excited in her texts to Angelica.

"It's all coming together for them." There was a wistful note in Evan's voice.

Angelica could relate to that emotion. When they'd first introduced Matt and Kayla to each other, she and Evan had been the stable couple, happy, in love and newly engaged. Back then, it had been Matt and Kayla helping with preparation for Angelica and Evan's wedding. A lump formed in her throat at the memories.

"You okay?" Evan asked.

"Fine," she lied, gathering her emotions. "How about you?"

"It's all good."

She forced herself to carry on with small talk. "Are you getting settled in Santa Monica?"

"I am."

"How's the business?" She knew leaving Lassiter Media had to have been a professional setback for him, and she truly wished him well.

"Deke and I might start working together. Lex, too."

She turned to him. "I thought you were going out on your own."

"I was planning on it. But we're looking at a possible deal that involves all three of us."

"What is it?"

"I'm not in a position to say."

Of course he wasn't. And even if he was, it was certainly none of her business. "I'm sorry. I didn't mean to pry."

"Everything going okay for you?" he asked.

"I'm moving my office. I didn't…" She stumbled a bit, re-alizing she was about to share the truth with him. "I mean, I couldn't…well, bring myself to take over Dad's office. So I'm converting the top floor boardroom into an office for me."

Evan was quiet for a moment. "That seems like a good idea, differentiating yourself for your father."

"That's my plan."

The sound of the waves filled in the silence between them.

"So, did Conrad really bring you an idea for a television series?" Evan asked.

"He's been in contact. He hasn't sent us anything yet, but it looks like he's serious."

"I thought he was just testing you."

"I did too. But he actually gave me an idea for a new di-rection for LBS."

"I'm glad you have some new ideas."

"I've always had ideas," she said defensively.

"I wasn't criticizing you, Angie."

She hated it when he used that nickname. Okay, she liked it when he used that nickname. But she hated that she liked it. It was endearing and intimate, strumming her memories. How many times had he said it while they'd made love?

I love you, Angie, he'd whisper in her ear. No matter how often he said the words, her breath would catch, and her heart would sing, and her world would settle into a perfect dome of contentment. Even now, she was fighting an urge to lean back against him.

"Angie?"

She shook herself and headed toward the waves, letting the cold water shock her to reality. She waded to her ankles, her knees, her thighs.

"Whoa," Evan caught her arm.

She shook him off.

"I thought we'd decided against skinny-dipping."

"I don't need your help." She didn't need it here or anywhere else.

"I honestly wasn't criticizing you. I have nothing but respect for your abilities at Lassiter Media."

"Is that why you fought so hard to keep me out?"

"Is that how you remember it?"

"I remember." She paused, gathering her thoughts as the waves pushed against her legs, washing the sand from beneath her feet. "I remember being abandoned by everyone I ever loved."

"Yeah?" There was a funny note to his voice. "How did that make you feel?"

The question struck her as absurd. "How do you think it made me feel? Terrible. I felt terrible."

There was a lengthy silence, and then his tone was hollow. "Do you know how many people in this world loved me?"

For some reason, each of his words felt like a punch to her stomach.

"You," he continued. "You were the only one, Angie. So, yeah, I know exactly how that makes a person feel."

Her chest contracted with pain. She turned, and a wave splashed up, dampening her dress.

"Evan…" She didn't know what to say. She knew his parents had died when he was a teenager, knew he had no brothers or sisters. Her family might be scattered and unorthodox, but it was definitely a family in every sense of the word.

"You were supposed to be my other half." He spoke softly into the night. "You were supposed to have my babies and turn this solitary existence into a big, rambunctious, loving family."

Her chest turned into one big ache, and tears threatened behind her eyes. Then a big wave pushed against her side. She staggered, then fell, gasping as the cold water engulfed her, the wave swirling over her head.

In a split second, his hand was on her arm, yanking her upright.

"What the hell?"

"I tripped," she sputtered.

He scooped the wineglass full of seawater from her hand. "Let's get out of here."

She trotted miserably toward the shore, his hand firmly on her upper arm, tugging her along. Her heart ached with regret. She'd made some terrible mistakes these past months. She'd been angry, disappointed and despondent.

But in all that time, with all those disputes and maneuvers, she'd never felt as heartsick as she did in this moment.

Angelica arrived at the Lassiter mansion still soaking wet. Albert had given her a fluffy, white robe to cover her ruined dress, and she'd combed out her hair and washed off the worst of her smudged makeup in Conrad's powder room. But she still looked like a drowned rat.

The last thing she needed was to find her two brothers waiting for her in the front foyer. She'd known they were both in town with their wives, but they'd fallen out of the habit of staying at the mansion.

"Explain this to us so that we understand," Dylan began, as they came to their feet.

"I fell in the ocean." She shut the door behind her. She was too tired for this, so she slipped past them into the study, helping herself to a brandy snifter and uncapping a bottle of cognac.

They both followed on her heels.

"We're talking about you and Evan," said Sage.

"That's a l—" She stopped herself mid-word.

She'd been about to confess that it was all a lie. But she knew that Evan was right. If she told her brothers the truth, she'd have to ask them to lie to their loved ones. She couldn't do that. But she also couldn't risk an accidental leak before Kayla's wedding.

"It's a long shot," she said instead, her back to them as she poured a measure of the cognac into the blown crystal glass.

"What the hell happened?" Dylan demanded. "One minute you can't even contemplate forgiveness, the next the newspaper has you reuniting."

"It's complicated," she said, turning to face them. "You'll have to leave it at that for now."

"I don't think so," said Dylan, advancing on her.

"We talked," said Angelica, looking her brother square in the eyes. "We reminisced." She inwardly winced as she recalled tonight's hurtful conversation. "We agreed that we'd both made some mistakes. And we've decided to spend a little time together."

There. Everything she'd just said was true. She took a sip of the cognac.

Sage moved to stand beside Dylan. "What aren't you telling us?"

"What I'm not telling you, is how this all ends. Because I don't know how it all ends."

They both peered at her with obvious suspicion.

"We were very much in love," she told them. "What we went through was painful and emotional. We're both battered and bruised, and we don't know where that leaves us."

Her brothers' gazes softened in sympathy.

She realized they were buying it.

She also realized that the reason they were buying it was because she was buying it. Because it was true. It was all so frighteningly true that she wanted to weep.

"Oh, Angie," Dylan sighed, drawing her into his arms.

She held her drink out to one side and accepted his hug.

"I wish I could explain better than that," she whispered.

"We understand that you can't," said Sage, giving her a rub on the arm. "We can wait."

She drew back, wishing she could be completely open with them. "Thank you. Thank you for being patient with me."

"You're freezing," said Dylan, tightening his hug and rubbing his hands up and down her back.

"I am. And I'm exhausted. I think I'm going to take a bath and go straight to bed."

"That's a good idea," said Sage. "Do you want me to get Colleen to come over?"

Angelica managed a smile. "I don't need a nurse. What I really need is a good night's sleep."

"Okay," Sage agreed.

Dylan plunked a kiss on her head. "Call us if you need anything."

She hiccupped out a laugh. "I'm not used to you guys being this way."

"I suppose not," Dylan agreed. "But I like it better when we're not fighting."

"So do I," said Angelica, battling a surge of guilt. She stepped away from Dylan, feeling as though she was accepting their affection under false pretenses. "Now, you two get out of here so I can warm up."

They both wished her good-night and headed down the hall to the front foyer and out the door.

Angelica sipped at the brandy as she made her way up the main staircase to her bedroom. She was chilled to her bones, aching and shivering uncontrollably as she stripped off her wet dress and clinging underwear, tossing them into the sink to rinse off the saltwater, wondering if there was anything she could do to save the patterned silk. Then she turned the taps in the oversized tub, and hot bathwater churned from the big faucet to fill it.

Leaving the dress to soak, she dumped some scented oil into the bathwater, lit a few candles, and then finally sank into the deep water. She laid her head back and let the warmth seep into her skin.

Evan's image immediately bloomed in her mind. His anger and disappointment hurt as much now as it had in those moments on the beach. She'd known all along that he wanted a big family. She'd wanted one, too. She'd also known he was alone in the world. But she'd never imagined him being lonely.

She felt a ridiculous urge to reach out to him, comfort him, help him somehow. But she knew there was nothing she could do. She'd made her choice five long months ago when she'd decided to mistrust him, to team up with Jack Reed and fight Evan for Lassiter Media. She reminded herself for what seemed like the hundredth time that there was absolutely nothing she could do to fix things now.

Five

As he and Deke made their way across the ten-story atrium lobby of the Sagittarius Resort, Evan considered the possibility that Deke could be right about the danger of spending time with Angie. Last night, when he'd pulled her dripping and vulnerable from the surf, protectiveness had welled up inside him. He'd wanted to hoist her into his arms and carry her off. He'd been forced to slam a lid on the urge before he could figure out where he'd carry her and what he'd do when he got there.

"Maybe we should spend a couple of days here incognito," Deke suggested. "Get rooms, check out the facilities, see how things are run."

Lex was looking into the company's financial records, while Evan and Deke were taking a more hands-on approach to investigating their potential purchase. So far, they'd toured the beach, the pool, the beachfront café and the gourmet restaurant on the top floor. Now, they were on their way to the eighteen-hole golf course.

Before Evan could decide on the usefulness of taking things undercover, Deke redirected his attention. "Look. There's the sports bar."

They altered their path, swerving to take in a couple thousand square feet of steel-gray leather, brick work and big screen TVs. The floor was worn wood, the bar top immaculate, and the pool tables in the back looked beautifully kept.

"What we should do," Evan suggested, "is hold Matt's bachelor party here. A round of golf, a game on the big screen, brews, burgers and a few pool matches. Then we can all book rooms and stay over. We'll poll everyone in the morning and see how they liked their stay."

Deke grinned. "Kill two birds with one stone? I like it. Maybe we can get Kayla and the bridesmaids to check out the spa."

Evan's brain wrapped itself around the thought of Angie in a spa, or anywhere else for that matter.

"I'm not interested in a hot stone massage," Deke continued. "Never mind a facial or some waxing."

Even shook off the image of Angie. "Ouch."

"Yeah. Ouch. I say we sacrifice the women."

"That kind of thinking is why you'll never have more than one-night stands."

"Who wants more than one-night stands?"

Evan's phone chimed in his pocket.

"Most guys over the age of twenty-one," he noted as he answered the familiar number. "Hey, Matt. You're on the ground?"

"Taxiing to the terminal at LAX," came Matt's reply.

"Welcome home."

"Thanks. It's been an adventure. You around tonight?"

While Evan talked, he and Deke exited the sports bar and began to make their way to the golf course. "Sure. Absolutely. Deke and I are just checking out a place for your bachelor party."

"Deke's in town?" asked Matt.

"He is."

"Can he stay for the wedding?"

"Hang on." Evan moved the phone away from his mouth. "Matt wants to know if you can come to the wedding."

"I already told Tiffany I'd be her date."

The information took Evan by surprise. "You did?"

"She asked. And I still haven't seen her naked."

"You watch yourself," Evan warned.

But Deke just laughed.

"He's coming with Tiffany," Evan told Matt.

"That's great." There was a muffled sound at Matt's end of the line. "Kayla wants to know when you and Angelica got back together."

Evan made a guess of what had happened. "She read the *Morning Break?*"

"She found it online while we were at JFK."

"We aren't back together," Evan corrected. "Yet."

"Well, get a move on, will you?"

"Sure. No problem. How do you feel about the Sagittarius Resort golf course and sports bar?"

"What for?"

"Your bachelor party."

"Sounds expensive. Who's paying?"

"Deke's paying."

Deke gave an unconcerned shrug.

"Then I leave it in your capable hands, best man." There were some pings in the background, followed by a voice over the airplane loudspeaker. "We're at the gate. I'll call you from the apartment. I think Kayla just set up the final tux and dress fittings at the his-and-hers wedding place for tonight."

"Text me the details."

"Will do. And, hey man, thanks for all your help this week."

"Happy to do it." Evan signed off.

Deke pushed open a glass door that led to a patio and the pro shop.

"I'm not crazy about this thing with Tiffany and the wedding," Evan felt compelled to state as they walked.

"Why not? She doesn't have a boyfriend, and I already know Matt and Kayla. It seemed like a pretty logical solution."

"But you're not dating her. You're only trying to sleep with her."

"Of course I'm trying to sleep with her. Have you looked at her?"

"She's Angie's friend, Deke."

"And you're Angie's ex. So you shouldn't even care. Besides, I haven't exactly kept my goal a secret. She knows perfectly well that I've got the hots for her."

"I hope you used those exact words."

Deke chuckled. "I did. She told me not to hold my breath."

They came to the edge of the patio, where clusters of dining tables overlooked the golf course. Evan braced his hands on the rail, letting the topic slide. Deke was right. Tiffany knew the score, and Evan knew Deke wouldn't push it if she said no.

As expected, the golf course was magnificent. Wide, emerald fairways followed the natural contours of the land. Palm trees swayed in the wind, while the overall layout sloped down to the cliff's edge, offering stunning views of the blue ocean.

"They host three professional tournaments a year," said Deke. "Plus top-flight amateur events. And their list of VIP members is impressive. I say we buy the place for the Rolodex alone."

Evan's phone chimed again.

Deke nodded toward the sound. "It's hard to believe you're currently unemployed."

"It's hard to believe your phone is staying so quiet."

Deke patted his shirt pocket. "I forwarded all the business

calls directly to Colby. You know, I'm beginning to think I don't actually have a personal life."

"You're a workaholic," Evan reminded him.

"True enough."

Evan didn't recognize the number, so he assumed it was a business call. "Hello?"

"Mr. McCain?"

"Yes."

"This is Geoff Wilson, *Los Angeles Star Daily*."

Uh oh.

"I'm doing a story on Lassiter Media, and I was wondering if you had any comment on the recent revelation that your engagement to Angelica Lassiter is back on?"

Evan knew he couldn't alienate the press without losing Conrad's support, so he didn't hang up. Instead, he chose his words carefully, hoping to drop enough breadcrumbs to keep the reporter happy. "My relationship with Ms. Lassiter is a private matter."

"She's pictured in the *Weekly Break* without an engagement ring."

"I haven't seen that *Weekly Break*."

"Does it surprise you that she's not wearing her engagement ring?"

"It does not." Evan covered the receiver with his hand, whispering to Deke. "Get Angelica on your phone." He needed to warn her about potential calls from reporters. And they needed to make sure they kept their stories straight.

Deke's brows went up, but he extracted his cell phone and dialed.

"So, you're saying there's no engagement?" asked Geoff Wilson.

"I'm saying it's a private matter."

"Where's the ring?"

Evan decided stalling was still the best way to go. "Ms. Lassiter and I would appreciate privacy while we—"

"Are the two of you back together or not?"

"Ms. Lassiter and I would appreciate privacy while we discuss our reconciliation."

"You do know this is L.A., right?"

Evan couldn't help but crack a smile. "The Lassiter family has been through a difficult time."

"How will you feel about playing second fiddle to your wife at Lassiter Media?"

"That's not an issue, since I'm no longer working at Lassiter Media."

Deke had turned away, and was talking in a low voice on his phone.

"Did she fire you?" the reporter asked.

Evan wished he could end the call, but he wanted to keep the press satisfied, and the last thing he needed was to ramp up the story any further. "I resigned from Lassiter Media. I'm now pursuing some independent business opportunities."

"Will you go back to Lassiter Media after you marry Angelica?"

"Lassiter Media is in very capable hands. Angelica Lassiter will make an excellent CEO. And I'm certain her father would be proud."

"Proud of the way she fought his will?"

Evan felt like he was navigating a mine field. "It was a complicated situation. But we're all focused on the future. And I'm afraid I have another pressing appointment right now. Do you have a final question?"

"Did you give her back her ring?"

Evan hesitated for a moment. "Can I go off the record?"

Geoff Wilson paused. Evan knew the man would hate to get a juicy scoop off the record, but he'd hate it more to miss a juicy scoop altogether.

"Sure," he finally answered. "Off the record."

"Not yet. But I am planning to give it back."

"When? Where?"

Evan chuckled. "If we decide we want our pictures in the paper, you'll be the first person we call. Goodbye, Mr. Wilson."

"But—"

Evan disconnected the call.

"Off the record?" asked Deke. "Are you kidding me?"

Evan took Deke's phone and pressed the microphone against his leg to block his voice. "I know it's a long shot that he'll respect it. But I had to give him something. And it would be worse if he printed his suspicions that we're not really getting back together."

Evan raised the phone to his ear. "Angie?"

"What's going on?" She sounded breathless.

"Are you okay?"

"Fine."

"Are you running from someone?"

"I'm on an exercise bike."

Evan struggled not to picture her in tight exercise pants and a cropped T-shirt. "I just had a call from a reporter. A guy from the *Los Angeles Star Daily.*"

Her tone turned guarded. "What did he want?"

"To grill me about our relationship. You're going to the fitting tonight?"

"The bridesmaid dresses? Yes. Grill you how?"

"The usual. Are we back together? How do I feel about it? Am I working at Lassiter Media again? I'll pick you up, and we can go together tonight."

"I can get there myself."

"If the press is calling me, they're likely following you. We have to make this look good."

"Evan, I am not going to spend the next two weeks—"

"Yes, you are. You're going to spend the next two weeks pretending you like me."

"Evan."

"We're too far down the road to back off now. I'll pick you up at seven."

"I won't be home."

"Where will you be?"

She went silent, and he could feel her stubbornness right through the line.

"Fine," she huffed. "I'll be home."

"I'll see you at seven."

Kayla had a flare for the feminine and the beautiful, and everything about her custom-made wedding reflected her good taste. Her bridal gown was both traditional and spectacular. Made of pure, white satin, the wraparound bodice hugged her slim torso. A band of delicate jewels accentuated her bust, while the full skirt, with its cascading jeweled vine pattern, started at her hips and flowed to the floor where it flared out in a three-foot train.

"It's absolutely stunning," Angelica breathed, blown away by the picture Kayla made in the dressing area of the wedding store.

"You look like a fairy princess," said Tiffany, moving around for a look at the back.

"I was thinking hair up," said Kayla, demonstrating.

"Definitely," Angelica agreed. "Do you have a diamond necklace?"

"And dangling, diamond earrings," said Tiffany.

Angelica moved closer to check out the pattern of the jewels on the dress. "I've got the perfect thing," she told Kayla. "It's a four-row diamond choker." Then she wondered if she was being too presumptuous. "If you'd like something borrowed, I mean."

"I don't remember it," said Tiffany.

"I don't wear it very often. My brothers gave it to me for my nineteenth birthday. It's a little too dressy for most occasions."

"I'd love to borrow it," said Kayla. Then she took a step back, turning away from the mirror. "Now let me get a look at the two of you."

Angelica focused on the mirror, gazing at herself in an ice-pink, full-length bridesmaid gown. The tight, strapless, satin bodice glistened with silver sequins. It laced up the back, starting at the base of her spine and ending several inches below her shoulder blades in a sexy, low, V cut. An organza skirt, scattered with sequins, floated like a cloud around her ankles.

Given the time constraints, they were buying off the rack. But the store had a huge variety of styles to choose from.

"You both look perfect," said Kayla.

Tiffany twirled around. "I feel like dancing already."

"Matt says you're bringing Deke as your date," Kayla said.

"That's right. He's a fun guy and a really good dancer."

Tiffany stopped twirling, and the three women stood side by side in front of the mirror.

"You've been dancing with Deke?" Angelica asked, curious.

"Just that one night after dinner. Neither of us was tired. Nothing else happened."

"I assume you'd tell me if it did."

"Maybe." Tiffany grinned.

"I think it all works," said Kayla.

Angelica pulled her attention back to the mirror. She agreed with Kayla. The dresses looked exquisitely beautiful—a little girlie for her normal tastes, but definitely beautiful.

"Well, that was quick," said Tiffany.

"I'm nothing if not efficient," said Kayla.

Both of the other two women groaned at the joke. Kayla could shop until she dropped.

"So, is the thing with Deke serious?" Kayla asked Tiffany.

Angelica found herself wondering the same thing. She knew Tiffany was attracted to him, and the reverse was obviously also true. But she'd thought it was more of a flirtation than anything else. She had been surprised when Tiffany invited him to the wedding.

"He's hot," said Tiffany.

"That doesn't answer the question," Angelica noted.

"It's not serious," said Tiffany, but her glance moved away as she said it. "Can't a girl have a good time?"

"Of course you can," said Kayla, an apology in her tone. "We don't judge. You should have as many good times as you want."

"Okay, I didn't have *that* good a time."

"My point is that you can," said Kayla.

"I agree," Angelica said with conviction. "All flings don't have to be romantic."

A fleeting expression of guilt crossed Tiffany's face.

Before Angelica could consider what it meant, Kayla turned. "Can somebody unbutton me?"

As Angelica started unfastening the long row of tiny buttons, she couldn't help wonder if Tiffany was masking deeper feelings for Deke. Could she be worried about Angelica's reaction? Angelica didn't mind if the two of them dated. Just like she didn't mind that Kayla and Matt were a loving couple.

Her and Evan's friends had gotten together, while she and Evan had split apart. That was life. It was ironic that she and Evan had been the ones to introduce both couples, but it didn't change the fact that she wished them every happiness.

"You guys stay dressed up," said Kayla as she made her way into the changing room. "We can't let Matt see my dress, but I want to put you beside the groomsmen and see how you look."

"It's okay if you like him," Angelica told Tiffany as the curtain shut behind Kayla. "Don't hold back because of me."

"Who says I'm holding back?" Tiffany was silent for a moment, then said, "I saw that you drove here with Evan?"

It was Angelica's turn to feel a pang of guilt. She knew Tiffany had seen the *Weekly Break* article, but they hadn't had a chance to talk about it yet. She felt sick at the thought of lying again.

She swallowed, girding herself to tell the fake story. She couldn't look Tiffany in the eyes. "We're, uh, trying to spend a little time together. You know…to maybe see what happens."

"Angie."

"Yes." Angelica couldn't seem to bring her voice above a whisper.

"Deke told me."

"Deke told you what?"

"About the two of you tricking Conrad."

Angelica was speechless.

"I understand why you're doing it," Tiffany continued, "but I have to say, I'm not sure it's such a good idea."

"How did Deke figure it out?"

"Evan told him."

"But…" Anger formed in the pit of Angelica's stomach. She went hot, then cold, her tone a hiss. "We swore. We swore we weren't going to tell anyone. Not even my brothers."

"I won't tell anyone."

"I trust *you*. It's Evan who betrayed me. I can't believe he did that. I *lied* to my own brothers."

"You're mad at him. That's a good thing for your psyche. Hold on to it."

Kayla pulled back the change room curtain with a clatter. "What are you guys doing for shoes?"

"We should match them," said Tiffany, easily changing topics and looking down at her feet.

Angelica forcibly pushed aside her frustration and anger. She didn't want her problems to impact on Kayla's happiness.

"You think white?" she asked, in the calmest voice she could muster. She glanced down at the western boots she'd put on with her jeans this morning. "Or silver? Silver's probably better. Open toed or closed."

"Should we shop?" asked Kayla.

"I'm up for it," Angelica agreed.

"Heck yeah," said Tiffany. "You're the bride. We'll do whatever you want."

Kayla grinned. "This is fun. What else can I get in the next two weeks?"

"Anything you want," said Angelica. "Just name it."

"I want a spa day."

"I'm definitely in on that," said Tiffany.

"Apparently the guys are doing golf and a kegger."

An entire day at the spa sounded like a very big time commitment to Angelica. But she reminded herself she was striving for work-life balance. She'd figure out a way to swing it. It would take a few extra late nights, but she'd make up the time.

"Let's do it," Angelica said with conviction.

"It's a date," said Kayla. "Now, let's go see how the guys look." She ushered Angelica and Tiffany toward the doorway.

Leaving the dress shop, they passed through a storefront full of flowers, stemware and satin accessories, then passed under an archway to the tux fitting area.

Though there were several men in the room, Angelica's gaze immediately zeroed in on Evan. There was no word for him but magnificent. Standing in front of a triple mirror, he wore a classic black tuxedo, with a black vest and a white shirt. His tie was silver, with a subtle stripe of ice pink. The other groomsman, Silas, was wearing an identical outfit, while Matt had differentiated his outfit with a silver vest and a plain, black tie.

"Go stand beside them." Kayla sounded excited. "Matt, get out of the way."

"Are you turning into bridezilla?" Matt joked, stepping aside.

"Tiffany says I have two weeks to get everything all my own way."

Evan's gaze came to rest on Angelica, sweeping from her head to her toes and back again. It left a trail of heat in its wake.

Tiffany gave Angelica a subtle nudge, reminding her she was supposed to go stand next to Evan. She took a deep breath and forced her feet to move.

His gaze stayed on her as she approached. The warmth in his eyes was unmistakable. But she reminded herself she was angry with him. He'd told Deke their secret, after swearing he wouldn't.

"Nice dress," he offered in an intimate tone.

"Nice tux," she returned a little more crisply.

"Shall we?" He gestured to the big mirror.

Girding herself, she turned.

Her breath immediately caught in her throat. She knew it was the clothing, but they looked like the perfect couple. For a long moment, she was certain, someplace deep down in her soul, that they belonged together.

She frantically shook off the feeling.

"I'll be taller." She came up on her toes, trying to do something, anything, to erase the perfect picture. "I'll have higher shoes."

"I'll still have you beat," he pointed out. He was right. Her height was far from being a match for his.

"It works," Kayla called out from behind them. "You guys look terrific together. Everybody strike a dance pose."

Angelica dropped her heels back down to the floor, and shifted sideways. The last thing she wanted to do was hug Evan. But he slipped an arm around her waist, using the momentum to turn her around, and pull her snug against his shoulder.

"Act natural," he whispered against her ear. "Remember, they think we're back together."

She found her voice. "Deke doesn't." A welcome wall of anger went up around her feelings. "You told Deke."

"Smile," said Evan.

"I lied to my brothers, and you went and told Deke."

"Can we not talk about this right now?" He took her hand in his and struck a dance pose.

"He told Tiffany. So now she knows."

Evan snuggled her to his body, and a rush of desire flooded her skin. "Later."

"Why did you tell Deke?"

"Because it was more dangerous to keep him in the dark."

"You want me to trust you, yet—"

"I wanted you to trust me five months ago. You didn't."

"And it turns out I was right."

"Angie? Is everything okay?" Kayla's tone was searching.

Angelica quickly planted a smile on her face. "It's perfect. I love the dress. Evan is just arguing with me about shoes."

"What's to argue?" Kayla asked. "We haven't even bought them yet."

"He's afraid the heels will be too high," said Angelica. "And he'll look short."

"He can always come shopping with us," Kayla offered.

"Great idea," said Angelica. "Let's take Evan shoe-shopping."

"I'm afraid I'm busy," said Evan, while Matt and Silas laughed at him.

"We can reschedule, so that you can come along," Kayla offered sweetly.

"No need," said Evan. "Whatever the bride wants will be perfectly fine with me."

"That's the spirit," said Matt.

"What the bride wants is for everyone to be happy," said Kayla. "So, no more arguing."

"Yes, ma'am," said Evan. "I'll do everything in my power to keep Angie's temper in check."

"Excuse me?" Angelica retorted. "You're suggesting *I'm* the problem?"

"There is no problem, sweetheart," said Evan. Then he dropped a kiss on her mouth.

Through the roar of her body's reaction, she heard Kayla say, "It's so great to see you two back together again."

Angelica knew she had to put some distance between her and Evan. A minivan had followed them home from the dress fitting last night. It didn't take a rocket scientist to figure out it had been a reporter.

Since the Lassiter mansion was partially visible from the gates, Evan had made a show of walking her to the front door. He'd suggested coming inside to make it look good, but she'd flatly refused, prompting him to give her a lingering good-night kiss. She'd almost kissed him back. She'd come within a split second of giving in when he finally broke away.

Afterward, she'd lain awake half the night in frustration. When she finally fell asleep in the early morning hours, she dreamed of making love to him. She knew she had to get away.

It took her half the day to come up with a viable excuse to get out of L.A. But then Noah Moore, the vice president of LBS family programming at the Lassiter Media offices in Cheyenne handed it to her on a silver platter.

While Evan had been in charge of Lassiter Media, he'd bought up the licensing of several stations in Britain and Australia. Then this morning, Angelica had reviewed the drama series proposal from Conrad Norville. It was an undeniably exciting show idea, targeted to LBS.

She was impressed with Conrad's work, and made a quick

decision to commission a first season. Once she got past the mental roadblock of only using original programming developed in-house on LBS, she realized Lassiter could make an American version of the top-rated shows from the new British and Australian affiliates.

But Noah Moore hated the idea. Which meant Angelica needed to bring him on side. And it made sense for her do that in person. Normally, she'd have asked him to fly to L.A. But right now, she was jumping at the excuse to get out of the city for a couple of days.

At Van Nuys Airport, she went out onto the tarmac and mounted the steps to the Lassiter Media corporate jet. The plane comfortably sat twelve, but it would only be Angelica today, since she didn't see any need to drag her assistant along.

She'd meet with the managers who worked from the Lassiter offices in Cheyenne, convince Noah Moore of the merit of her plans, then spend some time at Big Blue. There was no place better than Big Blue with its rustic beauty for her to rest and regroup. There wouldn't be a single tabloid reporter for hundreds of miles.

The jet pilot greeted her at the door. "Welcome aboard, Ms. Lassiter."

She gave the fiftyish man a smile. "Hello, Captain Sheridan."

"Looks like a smooth flight tonight." He stepped back so that she could easily enter the aircraft. "They're calling for a bit of turbulence over the Rockies, but I think we can avoid it if we take a higher altitude."

"That's great to hear, Cap—" As she turned into the body of the aircraft, she stumbled to a halt. "What are *you* doing here?"

"Is something wrong?" asked Captain Sheridan from behind her.

"Going to Cheyenne," Evan answered with a lazy grin.

He was sitting in the second row, wearing blue jeans and a tan T-shirt, an ankle propped up on the opposite knee. A half-full bottle of beer sat on the table in front of him.

"Who invited *you*?"

"Chance," said Evan.

"Ms. Lassiter?" the captain asked.

She turned back. "Evan is not coming with us."

"I don't understand. Mr. Lassiter advised us that we would have—"

"Hey, Angie." Tiffany came into view behind the captain.

"Tiff?" Angelica reached out to steady herself on the back of a white leather seat. "Is something wrong?"

Tiffany grinned. "Everything's great."

"Four passengers tonight," the captain finished.

Deke appeared behind Tiffany. "Good evening, Captain." He shook the man's hand. "I've never seen Big Blue," he told Angelica. "I can't wait."

"Stop," Angelica shouted.

Everyone went silent.

"What's going on here?"

Evan rolled to his feet, moving close to her, lowering his voice. "We're going to Cheyenne."

"No, *we're* not. *I'm* going to Cheyenne."

"And the rest of us will keep you company."

"Is this a joke?"

"No, it's a con. Remember?" He tipped his head toward the back of the plane. "Let's talk in private."

Angelica quickly skimmed through her options. She could stamp her foot and kick them off the aircraft. She could leave herself, refusing to go on the trip. Or she could give in and let Evan get his way.

None of the options appealed to her.

"We're ready to go, Sheridan," Evan told the captain.

Angelica opened her mouth to protest. Evan wasn't the

CEO any longer. This was her airplane. The captain was her employee.

"Very good, sir," Captain Sheridan replied.

Tiffany had flown on the jet in the past, and she helped herself to a mini bottle of wine from the cooler.

"You thirsty?" she asked Deke.

Evan snagged his beer and began backing away toward the rear of the plane.

"Come on," he told Angelica. "I need to talk to you."

"I'll take a beer," said Deke. "Are those cashews?"

"I can't believe you're pulling this stunt," said Angelica. He was ruining her entire plan. The only reason she was flying to Cheyenne was to get away from him.

He took another backward step. "I can't believe you're running away."

She gave up and followed him. "I'm not running away. Because you're coming with me. And you're the thing I'm running from. So, why are you here?"

"Piece of advice, Angie. Don't ever try to make your living as a con artist. The question on everyone's mind is, are they reconciling or not? How's it going to look to someone like Conrad if you take off without me?"

"Like I have a job."

"It looks better if we're together."

"I don't want to be together."

There was an edge to his tone as he gestured to the seat in the last row. "Tough break. This isn't all about you."

"I never said it was."

The jet engines whined as the pilot poured on power, and she quickly took her seat.

"It's about Matt and Kayla," said Evan as he belted into the seat across the narrow aisle.

"I'm aware of that," she answered tartly.

The jet began to taxi.

"And we're all doing things we'd rather not."

Something in his tone send a jolt through her brain. It was suddenly crystal-clear that he didn't want to be with her either. The situation was as inconvenient and frustrating for him as it was for her. Difference was, he was taking it in stride, while she was complaining like a little girl.

What was wrong with her? Hadn't she learned anything from her father's will? It truly wasn't all about her. She had to pitch in and serve the collective good instead of being so focused on herself.

"I'm sorry," she said to Evan.

His jaw dropped open just as the jet rushed to full power, pushing them back in their seats as it accelerated along the runway.

"Excuse me?" Evan asked above the noise.

"You're right, and I'm wrong. Everybody's inconvenienced by this. You, me, Tiffany, Deke. But it's about Kayla and Matt, and I need to shut up and get on with it. The house at Big Blue is huge. I'll try to stay out of your way."

The jet lifted off the runway, climbing into the setting sun.

He studied her in silence for a long moment. "You surprise me."

She wanted to move on. "Why did you bring Tiffany and Deke?"

"I thought you'd be more comfortable with chaperones."

She nodded. "I am. It was nice of them to come."

"Deke's never seen Big Blue. He's curious."

Angelica found herself smiling, and some of the tension eased from her stomach at the thought of spending some time on the family ranch. "It's a fantastic place."

"It is," Evan agreed, his posture relaxing. "So, something going on in the Cheyenne office?"

"I need to talk to Noah Moore. He disagrees with a direction I want to take for LBS."

"That's what happens when smart people work together. You get different ideas."

"You still think I'm smart?" The question was out before she thought through the wisdom of asking.

"You're brilliant, Angie. That's never been the problem."

"I'd ask what the problem was, but I'm pretty sure I know the answer."

"You're fanatical, controlling and way too myopic."

"I didn't ask."

"That one was for free."

She leaned her head back on the soft headrest, staying silent as the flight leveled out. She drew a deep breath. "I am working on those flaws."

His voice was low and slightly cautious beside her. "Okay, now you're just freaking me out."

"I know I'm not perfect, Evan."

He didn't respond for a moment. "At the risk of bursting this Zen-Angie bubble thing you've got going, I have something to ask you. And it's probably going to make you mad."

Angelica didn't particularly like the sound of that. But she promised herself to try to take it in stride. "Ask away."

"I think you should wear your engagement ring for a while."

She turned to gape at him.

"It'll convince everyone we're serious."

Her mind galloped to catch up to his words. "You still *have* my engagement ring?"

"Of course I still have your engagement ring."

"I don't understand. Why would you keep it?"

"What would I do with it?"

"Return it. Get your money back."

He shook his head. "It's custom-made. And it's been in dozens of photographs. In the middle of the press frenzy, did you really want the Angelica Lassiter engagement ring to show up for sale on-line?"

"I never thought of that," she admitted.

"Yeah, well, you were a bit distracted."

"Thank you," she found herself saying. "Even when you hated me, you were thoughtful."

"I never hated you, Angie. I admit, I was mad as hell."

"So was I."

A beat went by. Then he reached into his pocket and produced a small, black leather box.

Everything inside Angelica stilled. Her chest went tight with intense anxiety. She gazed down at the familiar solitaire. She'd always loved the way the stylized band winked with tiny white and blue diamonds. It was traditional, with a twist. That was how she'd always thought of her relationship with Evan. It had all the elements of a typical romance, but then there was the added spice of their energetic lives. At one time, it was enhanced by their mutual love of Lassiter Media with all its facets and foibles. But that was gone.

"Angie?" he prompted.

She moved her gaze from the ring to him. "It would be difficult," she told him honestly.

"I know. But the press is outright asking why you're not wearing it. And I'm more convinced than ever that Conrad is calling our bluff."

"You think he knows we're faking?"

"I think he suspects. And it's occurred to me that he might use it as an excuse to mess up the wedding."

Angelica knew this wasn't about her, and she knew she had to be tough. But when she reached for the box, her fingers trembled.

"Go get me a really big glass of wine," she told Evan, determinedly taking the box from his hand. "And I'll put it on."

He seemed to hesitate for a moment. "Sure. Okay. No problem." He unclipped his belt and rose from his seat.

Angelica stared at the beautiful ring, imagined the cool, smooth platinum settling on her finger, the weight of the big diamond, the wink of the band whenever her hand moved across her peripheral vision.

"You okay?" came Tiffany's soft voice.

"Not really." Angelica looked up. "Did you know he was going to do this?"

Tiffany shook her head. "Though it makes sense."

"Never occurred to me in a million years," Angelica admitted. "I guess I thought Conrad would keep it to himself. Then I thought we'd tell a few friends, and everybody would give us space while we pretended to think about getting back together. But now… How am I going to do this?"

"You don't have to wear it."

"Yeah, I do."

Kayla's happiness was at stake. Evan was keeping up his end of the deal. Angelica had to step up as well.

She determinedly tugged the ring out of the display slot. Then, without giving herself time to think, she shoved it onto her finger.

"It doesn't burn or anything," she joked to Tiffany.

"That's encouraging," came Evan's voice as he returned with a glass of red wine.

"Hand it over," said Angelica, waving him forward. "And keep 'em coming."

Six

Evan had always loved the Big Blue ranch. It was symbolic of J.D. and the entire Lassiter family. It could be harsh and unpredictable, but it was self-sufficient and endlessly resilient. It stood like a sentinel, protecting those who sought its refuge.

It was good that Angie had come here. Despite their differences, he knew this was hard for her. He had to admit he was baffled by her attitude on the airplane. He couldn't quite get past the shock that she'd agreed to wear her engagement ring. And, unsettlingly, he couldn't quite shake the idea that she might have truly changed these past months.

"Angie," Marlene greeted her niece with open arms as the four trooped into the great room.

Though Marlene was Angie's aunt, she had been more of a mother figure, since Angie's own mother had passed away when she was just a baby. The older woman enfolded Angie in a warm embrace.

When Marlene pulled back, her attention turned to Evan. "It's *so* wonderful to have you back," she beamed, moving to give him a hug as well.

"Wonderful to see you, Marlene."

Marlene then glanced curiously at Tiffany and Deke.

Angie stepped in. "You remember my friend Tiffany? And this is Evan's friend Deke. Tiffany is also going to be a bridesmaid at Kayla's wedding."

"Welcome to Big Blue," Marlene offered warmly, leading the way into the great room.

She chatted with them there for a few minutes but soon apologized for being tired and retired to her own wing in the huge house.

Angie offered everyone a snack then dispensed guestroom assignments, putting Deke and Tiffany on the second floor near her own bedroom, while relegating Evan to one of the first-floor bedrooms behind the kitchen. He supposed he should be grateful she hadn't put him in the bunkhouse.

He wasn't tired, so when the others went upstairs he made his way outside to the huge, flagstone patio. The ranch stretched out around him for miles, a patchwork of groves and lush paddocks. It was peaceful now; the equipment was all shut down for the night and the animals were quiet. The big sky arched above him, scattered with bright stars and a crescent moon.

He sat down on one of the padded deck chairs facing away from the house, drinking in the fresh air and absorbing the ambiance.

"Not much like L.A.," said Deke, as he approached from the house. "Or Chicago for that matter."

"I like it," said Evan. "Oh, maybe not full-time like Chance does. But it's a great place to come to get your head on straight."

"Your head's not on straight?"

"Getting more crooked by the minute," Evan admitted.

"I tried to talk you out of this," Deke reminded him, swinging into the chair beside him.

"You try to talk me out of a lot of things."

"Sometimes I'm right."

"You're always right. I just don't often care."

Deke chuckled. "If things work out well with the Sagittarius, maybe we should buy a dude ranch next. That way, you can work on your head on a regular basis."

"It's usually not a problem. So, why aren't you upstairs finding an excuse to bother Tiffany?"

"She's with Angelica right now. But the night is young."

"You really think you have a shot?"

Deke shrugged. "I think she can see right through my usual charm."

"Has that ever happened before?"

"Not in recent memory. But I'm up for the challenge. So, how come you're not warning me off her anymore?"

"Because I know she's got your number."

Deke tapped his fingertips against the wooden arm of the chair. "Sad, but true. So, what's up for tomorrow? Are we going to ride horses, wrangle cows? Maybe drive a tractor?"

"Do you know how to ride a horse?"

"I do not."

"Angie's going into the office in Cheyenne."

"Are you going to follow her?"

"I wish I could. She said she was in a disagreement with one of the executives. Noah Moore. I'd like to know what it's about. Noah can be opinionated, but he knows his job. He's got a lot to offer the company."

"You don't work there anymore."

"I know that."

"Any chance I can talk you out of all this?"

Evan shot him an arched look. "I haven't decided to do anything yet."

"Sure you have. The woman's got your ring back on her finger."

"It's a ruse."

"Keep telling yourself that." Deke brought his hands down on the chair arms and propelled himself to a standing position. "I'm going to check things out upstairs."

"Good luck," Evan offered automatically.

"Right back at you, buddy." Deke clapped him on the shoulder before he walked away.

Evan settled back into the deep chair, letting his focus go soft on the stars that glowed on the horizon. Deke knew he was still attracted to Angie. No bombshell there. He'd be attracted to her until the day he died. But that didn't mean there was anything more to the engagement ring than a convenient distraction for Conrad and the press.

A ring in and of itself didn't mean a damn thing. It was the emotion behind it that counted. It was love, honesty and respect between two people that made an engagement ring, a wedding dress, even a couple's wedding vows have meaning. Without those things, the ring was just a piece of stone.

"I didn't see you there." Angie's voice interrupted his thought. "I'm sorry, I'll just—"

"Don't be silly. It's your house. I can move to somewhere—"

"You don't have to leave on my account."

"I'll stay if you'll stay," he offered. "It's not a bad idea, you know. For us to practice talking to each other."

"You think we need practice?"

"I think we're a little stilted right now."

"Fair enough." She sat down in the chair vacated by Deke.

He took note of her glass of wine. "Anaesthetizing yourself against the ring?" He was a little surprised she still had it on.

She covered the diamond with her thumb. "I should have offered you something. Are you thirsty?"

"I'm fine. You don't have to treat me like a guest." Then he realized the way that might sound. "Not to say I'm family. I meant that I know I'm an interloper. You can feel free to ignore me."

She took a contemplative sip of the wine. "You know, that's not the dumbest thing you've ever said."

"Thank you." He paused. "Just out of curiosity, what was the dumbest thing I ever said?"

She thought about that for a moment. "It was at the Point Seven sailing regatta the day we met. On the dock next to J.D.'s yacht, Purshing's Pride. You said: 'Hello, Angelica. I'm Evan McCain. I work for your father.'"

"You remember the moment we met?"

"You don't?"

"You were wearing navy slacks and a white cotton blouse. It had dark blue buttons, and I could just barely see your lacy bra underneath."

"You were checking out my bra?"

"I was checking out your breasts."

The light was dim on the patio, but he was pretty sure he'd made her blush.

"A gentleman would be ashamed of himself," she stated.

"A gentleman might not have said it out loud, but he'd be doing exactly the same thing."

"You're lucky my father never knew."

"Your father planned it all along."

"He did," she agreed. "He might be shrewd, but he's not subtle." She went quiet. "Why do you think he did it?"

"Which part?"

"Us. You and me."

"You and me is a lot of real estate, Angie."

She nodded then took another sip. "We've never talked about it, you know. His will, the grand scheme, what it did to us."

"We've shouted about it," said Evan.

"I guess we have." Her thumb was stroking over her engagement ring. She had beautiful hands, beautiful arms, beautiful shoulders.

He watched the diamond wink in the starlight, his emotions moving to the surface even as he tried to ground himself in reality. "I'm not sure there's anything more to say."

She lifted her gaze to his. "It would be nice if there was. It would be nice if there was a conversation that would get us from A to B in a way we'd understand and accept, so that we could move forward."

He gave in to temptation and took her left hand, holding it up so that he could gaze at the ring. "I'm only looking as far as the next two weeks."

"Understandable." She rose.

He stood with her. "Can you see past that?"

"I have to see past that. The January replacements are already underway."

"Always business with you."

Her voice was a whisper, but the hurt was clear. "That's not fair."

"Isn't it?" He drank in her beauty.

"I'm doing everything I can to help Kayla."

He couldn't stop himself. He had to touch her. He ran his index finger along the curve of her chin.

His voice was guttural. "While I'm doing everything I can to save myself."

She didn't bolt, and he stroked his spread fingers into her hair. Then he leaned down to mesh his lips to hers, letting the power of his longing obliterate all good sense.

Angelica knew that the last thing in the world she should be doing right now was kissing Evan. But she didn't stop. She couldn't stop.

His lips were tender, firm, hot against her own. He knew just when to apply pressure and when to back off. His tongue flicked out, setting off a spiral of sensation through her body, drawing a moan from deep in her chest. She stepped in, pressing full length against him, blindly setting her wineglass on a side table.

His free arm went around her waist and he pulled her close, kissing her deeply. Then he moved to the corners of her mouth, across her cheek, down her neck, easing open the collar of her shirt.

"We can't do this," she murmured, more to herself than to him.

"We won't," he breathed. "We never do."

His words didn't make sense. "We don't?"

He popped a button on her shirt. "I always wake up far too soon."

"Oh. Okay." She'd dreamed about him too. She didn't always wake up too soon, but she wasn't about to admit that he'd satisfied her many times in her sleep.

He popped another button. His lips were warm, the autumn breeze cool on her skin.

She ran her fingers through his short hair, inhaled his familiar scent, closed her eyes and let herself revel in the cocoon of Evan. Her free hand went to his shoulder, sliding over his bicep, and she was reminded of his strength. She kissed his chest through his T-shirt, fighting an urge to tear it off. She wanted to taste his skin.

Before she knew it, her shirt was open. He slipped his hands beneath, moving them to her bare back. She felt her nipples tighten against her bra, and she pressed her breasts to his warm, broad chest.

His voice was strained. "This feels so damn right."

"I know." Her hands had moved to the waist of his jeans. She was pulling his T-shirt free, reaching beneath it to stroke his bare skin.

He swore under his breath. Then his hand fisted around the hem of her blouse. He took a step backward, tugging her along. She stepped forward. Then she took another step, knowing where they were going. They'd been there before, made love there before, in a secluded alcove at the edge of the patio, screened by a rose-covered trellis.

She dared to look into his eyes. They were dark and intense, smoldering coffee. She knew she should tell him no.

One of them had to put a stop to this, and Evan looked like he was past the point of reason.

But her vocal cords weren't working. His intense gaze trapped her own, and she felt her pulse rate jump. Her skin was flushed with arousal, itching against her tailored blouse and straight skirt.

The light dimmed around them. As he backed up against the log wall, the momentum propelled her forward, and she braced her hands on his shoulders, coming flush against his body. He instantly kissed her. His lips were hotter than before, more intense, his tongue probing deeper.

This was such a terribly bad idea.

But his hands were on the clasp of her bra. And then it was free, and he pushed the shirt and bra from her shoulders. His hand closed over her breast, and she moaned against his lips. He stroked her nipple with his thumb, making her knees go weak.

"I've missed you," he rasped, even as his hand stroked over her rear, coming to the hem of her skirt before reversing to slide upward.

"Evan," she managed.

She didn't know what else to say. She could stop him with a word, but she'd missed him so much. She'd missed his kiss, his touch, his voice and his scent.

His fingertips grazed her panties, and passion surged within her. She couldn't wait another second.

"Now," she whimpered. "Oh, please, now."

He'd heard the words before, and he jerked to action. He stripped off her panties, still kissing her deeply. He loosened his jeans. Then he lifted her, turning to brace her against the wall.

He was inside her in seconds, and she nearly wept with relief. The sensation was so familiar, so satisfying and so intensely arousing. He moved, and she pressed her face to the crook of his neck. Her hands clasped his back, fisting into the fabric of his T-shirt.

His breathing was heavy. He'd broken out in a sweat. He knew just when to slow down and just when to speed up. His fingertips teased, while his lips left moist circles on her neck and shoulders.

All she could do was hang on tight, while her world tilted over the horizon, and color and sound hazed her brain.

"Evan," she cried, and his hand closed over her mouth. She cried out again, but the sound was muffled.

"Angie," he whispered in her ear. "Angie, Angie, Angie."

Her body contracted, and her arms convulsed. Evan groaned, holding her tight, kissing her hard, his body shuddering and then going still.

After long minutes, she blinked her eyes open to see the stars, the black outline of the barn, the glow of the deck lights filtering through the rose bush. It was the intensely familiar sight of Big Blue. Reality was all around her, and she was practically naked in Evan's arms.

"Uh oh," she muttered.

"I know we shouldn't have done that."

She drew back to look at him, her body still joined with his. "Can you think of a single dignified move I can make here?"

"I can't," he admitted.

"This is mortifying."

"Yeah. Okay. Well, maybe in a minute I'll work my way up to mortified. Right now I'm still feeling pretty satisfied."

She bopped him in the shoulder. "Well, stop."

"I'll try."

"Evan, we just had sex."

"No kidding."

"We *can't* do that."

"Turns out, we can."

"Will you please be serious?"

"I am being serious. I'll be appalled in a minute. But right now, well…" He glanced at her bare breasts. "I want to memorize the moment."

"You have to forget all about this moment." She was going to find a way to do exactly that.

"Okay," he agreed.

"I mean it, Evan. We have to forget this ever happened."

"I will."

But then he kissed her, and she automatically kissed him back. It was tender and sweet, and it felt like goodbye.

"I'm sorry, Angie," he whispered as he eased them apart.

He set her gently on the ground, smoothing her skirt and adjusting his jeans. Then he stepped away to pick up her blouse and bra.

In the few seconds it took him, she struggled to regroup. It had been a slipup, for sure. But now that they'd done it, now that the urge was out of her system, perhaps things would get easier.

"You're going to the office in the morning?" he asked handing her the clothes.

"Yes." She shrugged into the lacy white bra, trying to forget that he was watching.

"You want some help?"

She felt a flash of annoyance. "I don't need your help."

"I got to know Noah pretty well over the past few months."

Having her shirt back on gave her confidence. "I can handle Noah."

"I'm not saying you can't. They're going to see your ring."

She reflexively glanced at her left hand, fighting a surge of emotion that came along with the sight of the diamond.

"They'll think I'm back in the game," Evan continued. "It wouldn't be so strange for me to show up with you."

"I'll tell them you're not working for Lassiter Media. We're not pretending that," she warned. "Not even temporarily."

"I agree."

"That's a first."

He took a step closer. "Hey, I agreed we shouldn't make love."

"Fat lot of good that did me."

He flexed a grin. "What is it you and Noah disagree on?"

"None of your business."

"I'm trying to help."

"Don't."

"Seriously, Angie. Is there some kind of trouble?"

"No trouble, Evan. None at all." Well, except for the fact that she'd just had sex with her ex-fiancé. That was definitely trouble.

She refastened the last button then met his eyes. She didn't have the faintest idea what to say in this situation. Simple seemed best.

"Goodnight, Evan."

"Goodnight, Angie."

She moved past him.

"Sleep well," he called from behind.

She didn't acknowledge his words. Instead, she retrieved her wineglass on the way across the patio and headed for the staircase to her bedroom. She *would* sleep well, she told herself. For a few hours at least, she was going to forget about everything complicated in her life.

Tomorrow would come soon enough. Tomorrow, she'd compound her lies by wearing Evan's ring in public.

Evan left Deke and Tiffany to a morning horseback ride under the capable care of a Big Blue ranch hand, while he headed into town. Angie's decision to fly to the Cheyenne office had been unexpected and abrupt. Evan wasn't a fool. If something wasn't seriously wrong, she would have waited until after the wedding.

He still had plenty of people he could trust at Lassiter

Media. He was going to sleuth around, see what he could find out. There were a lot of nuances and complexities to the expansion he'd managed while he was CEO. He hadn't explained them to anyone, because he was ticked off when he left. But he didn't want Angie walking into a hornet's nest.

He parked the borrowed ranch pickup truck in the historic district, pocketing the keys in his blue jeans as he headed for the reception area of the red brick, six-story Lassiter Media building. In contrast to the exterior, the inside of Lassiter Media looked like it belonged in L.A., with chrome and glass, plenty of light and television screens showing the fare of the various Lassiter Media networks.

"Evan." The receptionist greeted him with a wide smile.

Clarissa was in her mid-thirties, friendly and down to earth, and she had a knack for keeping the entire building organized. If Evan had stayed, he'd have made her his personal assistant in the Cheyenne office.

"Morning, Clarissa," he offered as he approached the high counter.

"Are you looking for Angelica?" Clarissa gave him a wink. "I saw the rock was back on her finger."

"It is," Evan acknowledged. "But, no. I'm sure she has everything under control in the boardroom. I was wondering if Max was around."

Clarissa picked up her phone and punched a few buttons. "He should be in his office. But if he's not, I can page him. Will you be in town long?"

"Just a few days." It was a guess on his part.

"Max?" she said into the receiver. "Evan's here to see you." She paused and a smile grew on her face. "Yes, that Evan. You didn't see Angelica? The wedding's back on."

Evan kept a smile pasted on his face, knowing there'd be no stopping the gossip mill now. Next thing, there'd be speculation on a new wedding date.

"I know," said Clarissa, nodding at whatever Max had said. "You want to go on up?" she asked Evan.

"I was thinking we'd step out for a coffee."

"Can you come down?" she asked Max. "He wants to do coffee." She paused again. "Okay." Then she hung up the phone.

"He's coming right down. We've missed you, boss."

"I've missed you too."

"Any chance you'll come back?"

Evan shook his head. "That's not in the cards. I'm working with a couple of old friends on some deals in L.A."

"But you'll visit Cheyenne. You'll come to town when Angelica does."

"I hope so."

"When's the wedding? It'll be at Big Blue, right? I'm dusting off my dress and rewrapping the gift."

Evan wished he could tell her to return the gift. He hoped she hadn't spent much on it.

The elevator door whooshed open, and Max Truger appeared. Barely into his thirties, he was director of integrated content at LBS, but he generally had his finger on the pulse of Noah's priorities in family programming.

"Welcome back," Max said, reaching out to shake Evan's hand.

"I'm not back. Not at Lassiter, anyway. Have time for coffee?"

"You bet." Max turned to Clarissa. "Can you bump my ten o'clock?"

"Sure thing."

"I don't want to mess up your day," said Evan.

"It's an internal meeting. No problem." Max turned for the door. "The Shorthorn Grill?"

"Sounds good." Evan would enjoy the walk.

They exited through the wide front door, onto a sidewalk lined with well-preserved, historic buildings. The mid-morning traffic was light, but several pickup trucks sped by, along with a shiny, vintage red Cadillac that belonged to a famous local rancher.

"So, what's going on?" asked Max, watching Evan with an astute expression. The two had worked closely together, and Max knew more than most about Evan's relationship with Angie.

"I wanted to ask you the same question. Something up with Noah?"

"In what way?"

"He's meeting with Angie?"

"You're jealous of Noah? The man's pushing sixty."

"Of course not. What's the matter with you?"

Max shrugged as he walked. "You're the guy asking questions."

"I got the impression something was off between them. A business something. Good grief, man. Jealous of Noah?"

This time Max grinned. "Well, we're all getting used to having her at the helm. It's funny. You moved into the big chair with barely a ripple whereas Angelica seems to be floundering."

"Floundering how? She understands every facet of the organization."

"I agree."

"She was all but running it before J.D. died She's smart. She's prepared. You all know she has J.D.'s blessing."

Max was quiet for a moment as they crossed an intersection. "Maybe it's the way she got here."

"You mean the way she tried to fight the will and teamed up with Jack Reed."

"I suppose. Or maybe we just geared up to follow you, and then bam, the world changed around us, and now we're all scrambling."

"She's going to do a great job," said Evan.

"I know she will. I have faith in her. But leadership's a tricky thing."

"How do you mean?"

They rounded a corner, making their way past one of the colorful eight-foot-tall cowboy-boot sculptures that dotted the city.

"When she seems to be going off in a risky direction, I'm not sure some of the older guys want to follow." Max held up his palms. "Don't get me wrong. I'm the integrated media guy. I'm all for going off in new directions."

"What do you mean, risky?" This was certainly news to Evan. Angie was stubborn, sure. But Lassiter Media was her life. He couldn't imagine she'd take risks with it.

"I'm talking about commissioning programming from non-Lassiter producers."

"You mean Conrad Norville?"

"According to Noah, it started with Conrad Norville, but now she's talking about making American versions of the top-rated affiliate programs."

Evan gave a laugh of comprehension. "She's eroding the powerbase of the existing Lassiter producers."

"And funding their competition. Like I said, I'm all for taking new directions. Heck, I think we should do a web-only series next summer. There's nobody internal who can produce that, so I'd be looking outside. But she's stepped into a minefield. Noah's not the only one who'll fight her."

"Who's on her side?"

"You mean, besides the British and Australian affiliates who'll get the licensing fees?"

"Yes. I mean, who's on her side in America."

"Me. And I assume, you? And, why haven't you guys talked about this?"

"I don't work at Lassiter anymore."

"But you're marrying the woman. Warn her. And why are you coming to me to—?" Max stopped in the middle of the sidewalk and turned to face Evan. "How is it that you don't know about this?"

Evan considered lying. Then he considered telling the truth. Neither was a realistic option. "It's complicated."

"Yeah. You said that. Complicated how?"

"You know what the family's been through."

Max thought for a moment. "But you're engaged again."

"She took back my ring."

"Have you set a date?"

"No."

Max watched Evan closely. "Is it better if I don't ask questions?"

"Yes."

Max gave a sharp nod. "I'm on her side, Evan. But I'm a director, and they're vice presidents."

"So, she's stepped into a hornet's nest?"

"Worse than that. She's busy breeding the hornets."

Seven

Angelica's day had been mentally exhausting. It was going to be harder than she'd expected to get the vice presidents on board. She could order them to commission non-Lassiter content, but that approach would be doomed to failure. It was hard enough to develop a successful television series, without having senior executives going reluctantly or half-heartedly into the effort.

It was dark when she parked her car in front of the house at Big Blue. She'd managed to put Evan out of her mind for most of the day. But now that she was home, memories of him were back, full blown in her mind.

She gripped the steering wheel for a long minute, willing away the sound of his voice, the tingle of his touch, the scent of his skin. They'd given into temptation last night, and she regretted it.

Though, in the light of day, she had realized the slipup was probably natural. Their relationship had ended so abruptly that there were bound to be lingering sexual urges. But that was all it had been. And it left her feeling hollow.

She eased the car door open and stepped out, looking toward the front porch. After a few seconds, she let her gaze wander to the pathway that led around back of the house.

There was nothing saying she had to go inside right away. She had no desire to face Evan, and she knew Marlene was bound to spot the engagement ring. It was pure, blind luck that she hadn't seen it last night.

Angelica truly wasn't ready for her aunt's excitement.

She firmly shut the car door then made her way along the pathway to the backyard. There, she made her way down the sloping lawn to the cottage that served as a pool house.

The large pool had been designed to blend in with the natural surroundings. Grass led up to its shallow edge, giving it the feel of a lake. She'd loved it here as a child, and she had happy memories of catapulting from the overhead tree swing. But tonight, all she wanted was to stretch out her muscles, burn off a little energy and postpone seeing anyone else for a little while longer.

It was a simple matter to find one of her bathing suits in the cottage. She changed, took a striped towel out to the deck, then waded into the cool, salt water. Goosebumps came up on her skin as she submerged. But once she started stroking her way across the deep end, she quickly warmed up.

She breathed deeply. Oxygen pumped its way through her limbs as she focused on putting power in her kicks and lengthening her strokes. She let her thoughts drift back in time and, eventually, both Evan and Lassiter Media vanished from her mind.

"We heard you drive up and wondered where you'd gone." Evan's voice interrupted her peace as she executed a turn.

Startled, she lost concentration and scraped her ankle.

"Marlene has dinner almost ready."

"I'll be up in a bit." Angelica determinedly pushed off the wall, leaving him behind.

He didn't take the hint and was still standing in the same spot silhouetted against the house when she returned.

"How did it go today?"

"Fine," she answered shortly. Then she turned to do another lap.

Again, he didn't go anywhere. "Something upsetting you?"

"No." She went under, holding her breath as long as possible, nearly making it back to the center of the pool before she came up for air.

At the end of her next lap, Evan was sitting on a deck chair.

"I'll meet you inside," she told him.

"I don't mind waiting."

"I might be a while."

He smiled in the dim light.

"What do you want, Evan?"

"To know how things went at Lassiter Media today." He glanced at his watch. "It's nearly seven."

"Your point?"

"It's late."

"There were a lot of people for me to see in Cheyenne."

"Socially?" he asked.

"Professionally."

"You do remember your father's will."

Angelica clamped her jaw, turning abruptly to start another lap. How dare Evan criticize her for working late. She'd worked until six tonight, merely an hour past regular quitting time. Big deal. Work-life balance was allowed to include work as well as life.

He was there when she returned.

"Swimming is life, not work," she told him.

"Did you have lunch?"

"What?"

"You heard me. Did you have lunch, or did you have meetings straight through?"

"We sent out." Somebody had brought in a platter of sandwiches during a noon-ish meeting.

"Did you eat?"

"Of course I ate."

She clearly remembered putting a turkey sandwich on her plate. She'd definitely had a drink of iced tea. But she'd been talking quite a lot at that point, and she couldn't say for certain how many bites she'd taken of the sandwich.

She did ten more laps without looking at him, but he still didn't leave.

Finally, she was forced to admit she was tired. Her arms and legs were beginning to feel like jelly. She waded out to the lawn, retrieving the fluffy towel she'd left on a lounger.

Evan approached. "You need anything out of the cabin?"

"I'll get it."

"Sure. Whatever."

She tucked the towel around herself sarong style and paced her way barefoot to the cabin. Evan walked alongside.

"How did it go today?" he asked again.

"I told you it was fine."

"You and Noah seeing eye to eye?"

"*You* and Noah ever see eye to eye?" she asked.

Everyone at Lassiter Media knew that Noah took a contrary position in most discussions. He seemed to like arguing.

"Occasionally," said Evan.

"I really don't want to talk about it." She entered the small cabin and retrieved her purse and clothes.

They walked along the concrete path to the house, but he continued to glance at her every few steps.

She stopped and turned to look at him. "Evan."

His gaze zeroed in on hers, and she lost her train of thought. Lassiter Media, Evan, their fights, making love, everything morphed together in a kaleidoscope in her head.

"Yes?" he prompted.

The silence stretched.

"I don't know," she finally admitted. "This is weird. It's all so incredibly confusing."

"I know. I really do. Tell me how it went today."

His tone was kind and there was concern in his eyes. And he was probably the one person in the world who did understand everything.

She gave in. "Not well. Not well at all. I hate to pull the gender card and say 'I can't get no respect because I'm a woman.' But I can't help but think he wouldn't react this way if I was J.D."

"Noah?"

"Yes," she admitted. "Noah."

"You're probably right about Noah's attitude," Evan agreed. "And maybe some of the other VPs, too. J.D. had the advantage of being experienced, venerated and male. But you have strengths he didn't, and you should learn to use them."

"What strengths?" she found herself asking. "What do I have that he didn't?"

"Vitality, fearlessness and youth."

"I suppose I'll eventually outlive Noah."

Evan grinned. "It is a good idea, though."

"What's a good idea?"

"Licensing hit series from the affiliates and remaking them in America."

Her suspicions instantly rose. "How did you know about that?"

"I asked around."

"You spied on me?"

"Of course I spied on you. If you don't want me to spy on you, then answer my questions when I ask."

"Evan, you can't spy on me."

"Actually, I'm pretty good at it."

"Angie?" Marlene's came down the patio stairs and took in Angelica's appearance. "Oh, good heavens, girl. Come inside. You're going to catch cold. I've got jambalaya and orange peel cookies."

Angelica felt her stomach rumble to life.

"I'm starving," Evan stated in a loud voice.

Marlene made her way down the stairs. "Let's get you into some dry clothes, young lady."

"Yes, ma'am," Angelica agreed. She had no intention of fighting with Evan in front of her aunt.

"Your fingers are turning bl—" Marlene gasped and lifted Angelica's left hand to gape at the ring. "Oh, my goodness." She looked to Evan, beaming with obvious happiness. "Oh, my goodness."

Angelica forced a smile, but her stomach went hollow around her lies. She couldn't imagine how she was ever going to extricate herself from all this.

Evan's heart went out to Angie, and he couldn't shake the feeling that he ought to apologize. Marlene had finally bid them good-night, but she'd left Angie looking positively shell-shocked amidst a cacophony of bride magazines, fabric swatches and invitation samples.

Through dinner, Marlene had ridden a crest of unbridled excitement at the idea of planning a new wedding. Though Angie protested that they hadn't even set a date, her aunt strongly recommended summer, outside, at Big Blue. And with that, she'd been off.

In the silence left in Marlene's wake, Angie zeroed in on Evan. "I can't believe you spied on me."

The accusation took him by surprise. "*That's* what you want to talk about?"

"I want to know where you get off interfering in Lassiter Media."

"What happened at Lassiter?" asked Tiffany. She and Deke were lounging at opposite ends of a big brown leather sofa.

"Forget Lassiter," said Deke. "It looks like The Wedding Show exploded all over Angelica."

She glared at him. "Not funny."

Tiffany covered a grin.

"Stop," said Angie.

"I'm sorry," said Tiffany. "I know it's not funny. But I can't help thinking there's a reality TV show in this somewhere."

"Reluctant brides?" asked Angie, looking like she might be considering it for a Lassiter channel.

But she quickly returned her accusatory glare to Evan.

He held up his hands in surrender. "Believe me, if I knew how to slow Marlene down, I'd do it."

"I'm not worried about Marlene." She paused. "Okay, I am worried about Marlene. But I'm more worried about Lassiter Media at the moment."

"I can help you with that," said Evan.

"I don't need your help."

"I'm the guy who set up the acquisitions in Britain and Australia. I know all the players."

"My problem isn't with Britain and Australia. It's with Noah, and the last thing I need is some man riding to my rescue. That'll only compound the problem." She came to her feet.

"So, what's your next move?" Evan asked.

"Are you kidding me?" She looked at Deke. "Is he kidding me? What part of *none of your business* don't you understand?"

Instead of answering, Deke took Tiffany's hand. "We should go to bed. These two need to talk."

Tiffany snapped her hand back. "Nice try."

"I didn't mean it that way." But his smirk said otherwise.

"Yeah, you did. But you're right. Angie, you guys need to talk. I wasn't in favor of this ruse, but now that it's gotten away from you, you better come up with an exit strategy."

"Maybe we can stay engaged for a while after Matt and Kayla's wedding," Evan offered.

"And draw this out?" Angie blinked at him in obvious dismay.

"That's our cue," said Deke, rising and drawing Tiffany to her feet.

"It would give people time to get used to our breakup," said Evan.

As Deke and Tiffany headed for the grand staircase, Evan moved to an armchair closer to Angie.

She was twisting the engagement ring around on her finger. "I can't believe we got ourselves in this deep."

"It seemed like a good idea at the time," he said. "And it worked. We got Conrad's mansion for Matt and Kayla."

"That's true. I am glad about that. But talk about unexpected consequences." She flopped back in the big chair.

"No good deed goes unpunished?"

"Something like that. And now I can't shake this nagging fear that we'll tell one or two more lies and accidentally end up married."

Evan chuckled at the joke, but something inside him warmed to the idea. Oh, he knew it was impossible, but as he gaze flicked to the wedding gowns pictured in the magazines left open on the coffee table, he acknowledged there was something compelling about Angie as a real bride, his bride.

"I've been thinking about the affiliates' top shows," Evan said, changing the topic. "*The Griffin Project* and *Cold Lane Park* would both be good choices for remakes."

"Traditional cop shows?" she asked, frowning.

"Tried and true. They're incredibly popular."

She seemed to forget to tell him to back off. "I was thinking something more cutting-edge, maybe super heroes or criminal procedural."

"*Alley Walker*?" he asked. "It's doing okay in Australia, but viewership has leveled off."

"We could use a younger hero, introduce a love interest. It's got that nice, edgy, paranormal aspect to it. And the leather outfit could reel in the teenage girls."

"If you had exactly the right actor," he mused.

"Eighteen to twenty-five demographic," said Angie. "That's where we need to focus."

Evan didn't disagree, but it was a tough audience to gauge. "What do you think of Max Truger?"

The question obviously took her by surprise. "In what way?"

"Is he doing a good job?"

"I guess." She sat forward and began stacking the bridal magazines.

"I was thinking he was young, and if that's where you want to focus, he might make a good VP."

Angie glanced up. "Are you telling me how to reorganize Lassiter Media?"

"I'm saying I buy into your vision of reaching a younger demographic."

She smacked the stack of magazines with energy and purpose. "And now you feel compelled to instruct me on how to do that?"

"Why are you so touchy? You're reacting emotionally to a perfectly logical suggestion."

"Because I'm a woman?"

Evan clamped his jaw and counted to five. "I'm not Noah."

"You sure sound like Noah."

"Well, I hope you don't sound like this when you're talking to him."

She rose up, her eyes darkening to burnt chocolate, and he immediately regretted the outburst. He didn't think she was a hysterical woman. He knew her to be cool, controlled and intelligent.

He stood with her. "I'm sorry. We've both had a long day. I know you're good at your job."

To his surprise, her features smoothed out, eyes cooling to their normal bronze. At first he was relieved. But then he realized it meant she'd withdrawn. He couldn't help but miss the emotion.

"You're right," she told him in a crisp tone. "This isn't a good time to discuss anything. Not that there'll ever be a good time for you and me to discuss anything about Lassiter Media. I've done all I can here in Cheyenne. We'll fly back to L.A. in the morning and get this wedding over with. After that, I can turn all of my attention to Lassiter."

He didn't like the single-minded determination in her eyes. "That's not what your father wanted, Angie."

"Are you *trying* to pick another fight?"

"I thought you were getting that now. He was truly worried about you. You should take another day, stay in Cheyenne and do something fun. Ride a horse or walk in the woods. Don't even go into the office."

She gave her hair a little toss. "I have too much work to do in L.A."

"That there is exactly why he was so worried. There will always be more work that needs doing. It's not a goal line, Angie. It's a treadmill. And you have to be really careful about letting the speed go up."

"There was and *is* absolutely nothing for my father or anyone else to worry about. I love my job, and I have it all under control."

She started to move, but he reached out to her, his hand landing on her elbow.

"This isn't about you controlling Lassiter Media. It's about Lassiter Media controlling you."

"Let go of me, Evan."

He searched her remote expression. "I need you to think about that."

"You lost the right to need anything from me a long time ago." She shook him off and turned on her heel.

As he watched her walk away, he couldn't help thinking he still needed a lot of things from her. Lovemaking was only the first on the list.

Thunder woke Angelica from a fitful sleep. Rain clattered on the roof above her, spraying in through the open window. She pulled back her covers and got up, crossing the room. As she wrestled the window closed, cold rain dampened her tank top and the soft pair of shorts she wore as pajamas.

Lightning flashed above the hills, illuminating both the sky and the ranch yard. She knew her cousin Chance and all the hands would be up and outside working, checking on the animals, securing anything that might blow away. The power could easily go out, but the ranch had emergency generators. When the weather turned nasty, the ranchers were in better shape than most people in town.

She shook rain droplets from her fingers, catching a glimpse of Evan's ring. She'd meant to take it off before bed, but somehow she'd forgotten. She touched it now as the lightning flashed off the diamond and thunder shook the big house.

She was angry with Evan for trying to interfere in Lassiter Media. Worse, his suggestions showed a complete lack of trust in her judgment. Didn't he remember that she'd all but run the company while her father was still alive?

During her conversation with Noah today, she'd realized the senior executives didn't have faith in her abilities. They were fine when they assumed J.D. was behind the scenes, vetting her decisions and actions. But now that she was on her own, they were questioning her.

A soft knock sounded on her door.

"Angie?" It was Tiffany's voice.

"Come on in," Angelica called.

The door cracked open. "Did the storm wake you too?"

"It did."

Tiffany moved through the doorway, her worried expression highlighted as another streak of lightning flashed through the sky.

"Are we in danger?" she asked.

"We're fine." Angelica flicked on a small lamp. "It's a powerful storm. But we get those every once in a while. Biggest problem is that it scares the cattle and blows everything all over the yard. But Chance and the hands will take care of that."

"That's a lot of rain." Tiffany sat down on the end of the bed, curling her bare feet beneath her. Like Angelica, she'd substituted casual clothes for pajamas, wearing a pair of black yoga pants and a cropped T-shirt.

"Something's sure to flood. Probably the ponds in the lower field. Hopefully, it won't be too hard on Marlene's vegetable garden." Angelica returned to the bed, popping her pillow against the white wooden headboard to lean back.

"How'd it go with Evan after we left?"

"Predictable," said Angelica. "He thinks he's right, and I think he's wrong."

"Did you talk about your fake engagement?"

Angelica shook her head. "Mostly about Lassiter Media and what he thinks I should do there. He just can't help poking his nose into it. I don't need his advice. He needs to back off and let me work."

"I think he's trying to help."

"Whose side are you on?"

"Yours, absolutely. I'm just wondering why else he'd do it."

"It's a compulsion. Do you know how many times I wanted to call him up over the past six months and tell him he was crazy?" Angelica couldn't seem to stop herself from smiling at the memory. "I still had spies, you know. My dad might have taken me out of the CEO chair, but many people were loyal. They told me what Evan was doing with the British network purchase, then the Australian one. He spent a whole lot of corporate money in a very short time."

Lighting flashed and thunder boomed all around the house as the storm increased in intensity. Footsteps sounded on the stairs and on the floor below, and muffled voices sounded in the foyer. It would be all hands on deck outside.

It was coming up on 3:00 a.m. In another hour or so, Marlene would get up and start cooking in the kitchen; she'd be ready with food for anyone who needed sustenance. Angelica would go down to help. In addition to their efforts in the main house, the cook shack would already be humming with activity. Cowboys needed plenty of coffee, eggs, sausage and biscuits to keep them going in this.

"Was he wrong?" Tiffany asked.

"Hmmm?"

"Was Evan wrong to buy the networks?"

"I thought so then. And I'm still worried. But right or wrong, it is what it is. We now own those affiliates, and we need to do the best we can within that reality."

"Do you think he had a long-term vision?"

"What I think is that he's an empire builder. Even Lassiter Media wasn't big enough for him. He had to try to increase the size."

"I think he likes you."

The unexpected comment threw Angelica. "What?"

"I was watching him watch you tonight. I think he's still attracted to you."

"Physically maybe." Physically, Angelica still had it bad for Evan.

"Did he kiss you again?"

Angelica debated how much to tell Tiffany.

"Angie?"

"He kissed me again." She tippy-toed up to the truth.

"When? Where?"

"On the patio. Last night."

"Did you like it?"

Angelica hung her head and gave a sigh of defeat. "I always like it."

"How many times has it happened now?"

"Twice. Well, three times. Four if you count the one at the fitting."

Tiffany leaned in. "Big kisses? Small kisses? Give me some context here."

Angelica looked up. She realized she didn't want to lie or hold back. "Big kisses. Lots of them. So many that I lost count."

Tiffany's brows shot up.

"Especially last night. A dozen, a hundred, I don't know."

Tiffany's voice rose. "A *hundred?*"

"Shhh."

"I don't think they can hear me over the thunder. *A hundred?*"

"We had sex." It felt good to blurt it out.

Tiffany blinked. "You don't mean last night."

"I do."

Tiffany opened her mouth, then she closed it again. Thunder rumbled ominously.

"I know. I know." Angelica waved away the inevitable criticism. "It was a colossally stupid thing to do."

"I'm stunned."

"So was I."

"You…like…I mean…how…?"

"I'm weak," Angelica confessed. "He's a good-looking, sexy guy. And it's been a very long time since anyone held me close. And it was so easy, so familiar, so…unbelievably good." She fisted her hands around her quilt and squeezed in frustration.

"Uh oh."

"You have a gift for understatement."

"So, now what?"

"Now, nothing. We agreed to forget it ever happened."

"And how's that working for you?"

"Not well," Angelica admitted. "I didn't fall in love with him because he was a jerk. He's a good guy. We might not have been able to survive everything that came at us. But they were extraordinary circumstances. And, truth is, I don't know that he did all that much wrong."

Tiffany stretched out on her stomach on the far side of the bed, propping her elbows on the mattress and her chin on her hands. "You ever think about trying this reconciliation for real?"

"No. *No.* Not at all. Too much has happened, Tiff. When push came to shove, I—" Angelica swallowed, suddenly afraid she might cry. "I let him down." She drew a shaky breath. "He won't forgive me. He can't forgive me."

"Maybe you should—"

"No!" Angelica gave an adamant shake of her head. "I missed my chance with Evan. I've got Lassiter Media to think about now. It's going to take all of my focus. I'm not going to delude myself into dreaming about anything else."

"I suppose." Tiffany's agreement seemed reluctant.

There was a banging on the door.

"Angelica?" This time, it was Deke.

"Come in," she called.

Deke swung the door wide. "I just talked to Evan. He said to tell you they're sandbagging Williams Creek."

Angelica rolled off the bed and came to her feet. "Are they worried about the road?"

Deke nodded.

"It hasn't flooded there in years." While she talked, she pulled open a drawer and threw a sweatshirt on.

"It's risen two feet at Norman Crossing."

"What do we do?" asked Tiffany from behind her.

Angelica tossed her a warm shirt. "We can go help sand-bag. Last time this happened, the only way we could get to town for over a week was by off-road, four-wheel drive."

Evan couldn't help but be impressed by the way the Chey-enne ranchers pulled together in a time of crisis. There were at least fifty people out in the pouring rain, and they'd been working at it for hours. Men, women and teenagers lined the creek bank, filling bags from the back of a pickup then moving them in human chains to the low section of the road where it paralleled the creek.

Evan was working with Deke and Chance at the lead-ing edge of the barrier, stacking the largest sandbags in a base layer, while Angie worked in a small group farther upstream, finishing off the top layer. Even from here, she looked exhausted. Her raincoat was plastered to her body. The hood had long since fallen down, and her hair was dark and stringy, making her face look pale.

He longed to go to her, pull her into her arms and escort her someplace warm and dry. But he knew she wouldn't stop working. Many of the women had already taken breaks, in-cluding Tiffany, who'd all but fallen over before one of the ranchers had dragged her off to sit on the hillside and drink a cup of coffee. But Angie hadn't slowed down. She'd been plugging away, sandbag after sandbag.

Refocusing, he went back to work, building the founda-tional layer, making sure it was solid.

When he looked up again, Angie was farther upstream. She seemed to be on her own, doing a final check of the barrier's integrity. The others were making their way back.

Evan was reminded that the woman he'd first met at a so-cial event, then came to know in the boardroom and escorted to L.A.'s hotspots, had also spent a good deal of her life on a working ranch. She was used to physical work, and would step in and help out wherever she was needed. He stopped feeling sorry for her, and started being impressed.

Chance suddenly grasped Evan's arm, squeezing it tight. "Do you hear that?" he called out, drawing Deke's attention as well.

Evan listened. His heart sank. A low, ominous rumble was coming from upstream.

"Get back! Quick!" Chance shouted to everyone, urging people to run. "Across the road! Up the bank! Everybody *move*, now!"

Deke echoed the call, as did Evan, rushing along the creek, ordering everyone back from the bank. The sound was growing louder, and Evan could see a roiling flood of water and debris barreling down on them.

"Angie!" he cried out.

She was the farthest away, cut off from safety by the curve of the creek and a grove of trees. She was running toward him, and he broke into a faster sprint along the rocky bank.

"Go," she cried out to him, motioning for him to get to safety. "I'm coming."

But she wasn't fast enough. He could see the water rushing up behind her.

"Run," he cried out to her, pumping up his own speed.

Then she tripped. She went down on the rocks, and his heart stopped in his chest. While she lay motionless, everything inside him screamed in agony.

"Angie!"

Eight

Evan had thirty feet to go to get to her, then twenty, then ten.

She sat up and rose unsteadily to her feet.

He finally reached her, wrapped an arm firmly around her waist, all but carrying her as they headed for the road and the safety of the bank beyond. Fifty sets of eyes were riveted to their progress.

"My shoulder," she gasped.

"Hang on." There wasn't a second to lose.

Chance started toward them, but then he looked past Evan, and his face turned ashen. Evan knew exactly what the other man was seeing—soupy, gray water laced with rocks, tree trunks and branches about to overtake them. It wasn't humanly possible to outrun it.

Quickly changing tactics, he hauled Angie to the nearest tree. He grabbed her thighs and hoisted her up as high as he could reach.

"Grab on," he called. "Grab anything."

"I got it," she shouted back, using one hand to pull her butt onto a wide branch and scrambling for a foothold.

He was out of time.

The freezing, debris-ridden water engulfed him. He instinctively took a deep breath, closed his eyes and wrapped his arms around the tree trunk, holding on for dear life.

The trunk protected his face and body from direct hits, but branches battered him on all sides, scratching his arms, bruising his legs, bouncing off his shoulders and hips.

His lungs were about to burst, when the water receded. He sucked in air.

"Evan!" Angie's cry seemed high above him.

But then the water closed in again.

This time, he couldn't fight the cold. It was numbing his fingers, making it impossible to hang on. Deep down in the base of his brain, he realized he was running out of time. Angie was safe, he told himself. At least Angie was safe.

The water receded again, and he drew another breath.

"Climb," Angie called to him. "Climb, Evan!"

The water was at his neck. He opened his eyes, and his brain registered the chaos around him, foaming water clogged with debris. The sandbag wall had disappeared, as had part of the road. But the sandbagging crew was high on the bank, out of harm's way.

"Come on, Evan," Angie shouted. "Get up here."

He gritted his teeth and reached one arm up. He managed to grasp a branch. It bit into his freezing hand, and it was all he could do to hang on. But he reached up with his other hand, getting it slightly higher. His feet scrambled along the trunk. Then one of them connected with a foothold. He pushed with all his might, grabbing a higher branch, then another and another.

His body finally cleared the water, and he heaved himself onto a broad branch next to Angie.

"Thank God," she breathed. Her face was wet and pale, her right hand clinging to the tree, her left arm dangling by her side.

"Damn," he ground out.

"You okay?" she asked.

"Forget me." He eased his way toward her. "Your shoulder's dislocated."

"You nearly died."

"I'm fine. Dammit." He knew she had to be in agonizing pain.

She swallowed. Then her teeth started to chatter, and her eyes went glassy.

"I think I can help you." He reached forward.

"Don't touch me," she begged.

"You have to trust me."

"They'll come and get me. Chance will have called the medics by now."

He continued inching himself toward her. People on the bank were calling out to them, and the water continued to roar beneath them. They rain pounded down, but Evan's focus was completely on Angie.

"I'm going to wrap my arm around your waist."

"Evan, don't."

He did it anyway. "Relax, Angie. If your muscles are relaxed, you're going to feel better."

"I can wait."

"I know it hurts like hell."

"I'm fine."

He put his other hand gently on the forearm of her injured side. "Relax," he whispered in her ear. "Please sweetheart, just relax and trust me."

"Okay," she whispered. Then she gave a shaky nod.

"I'm going to move your arm slowly and gently. I won't do anything sudden." He kept talking as he worked, hoping to distract her. "You're right. They are coming for us. Help is going to be here soon, and you'll be home and dry in no time." He bent her elbow, pivoting her forearm. "I bet Marlene will make hot chocolate, with whipped cream, and cookies. She'll have been baking all day." He eased her shoulder out straight. "I hope she made monster cookies. Oatmeal and pecans, they really stick to your ribs." He moved her arm higher pivoting the shoulder.

She gasped a breath, but then the shoulder popped back into place.

She gave a small exclamation of pain.

"That's it," he quickly told her. "It's back in."

Angie relaxed against him, gasping in deep breaths.

"How does it feel?"

"Quite a lot better."

He gave in to impulse and kissed the top of her head. "Good."

"You just saved my life."

"You climbed the tree with a dislocated shoulder. I just gave you a shove."

She was quiet for a moment.

"Evan?" Chance called, his voice loud and worried. He was as close to them as he could get without wading into the overflowing creek. "You guys okay?"

"We're good," Evan called back. "But Angie's going to need a doctor."

"What's wrong?"

"She hurt her shoulder. Nobody's bleeding. We're just cold."

"You're bleeding," said Angie.

Evan glanced down at his body. His sleeves and pants were torn, and several deep scratches oozed blood.

"It's not bad," he told her.

"I thought you were dead."

He gave a choppy laugh. "For a second there, it didn't look so good. But I'm fine. Clearly, I'm tough."

"You're tough," she agreed.

He glanced at the landscape around them. "This is a mess."

"I've never seen it this bad. I guess I won't be going back to L.A. today. You need a doctor."

"Not anymore. So, how did you learn to fix a dislocated shoulder."

He hesitated to tell her. "YouTube video."

"Is that a joke?"

"It's not."

"Weren't you worried you'd do it wrong?"

"A little," he admitted. "But I dislocated my shoulder when I was a teenager. So I know how it feels. I was more worried about you being in such terrible pain."

She seemed to think about it for a moment. "Well, I guess that's nice."

"How's it doing?"

She flexed it a little. "Much better. Maybe you should watch a brain surgery video next, since you learn things so quickly."

He liked that she was joking. "That way, if my business management gig doesn't work out, I'll have a fallback?"

"What's your business management gig?"

Evan shifted to a more comfortable position in their perch. "Can I trust you to keep it confidential?"

"Yes, you can."

"You won't go running to the tabloids like Conrad did?"

"I never talk to the tabloids. Though, maybe we should tell them about this." She cupped a hand around her mouth. "Hey, Chance!"

"What do you need?" her cousin called back.

"Get a picture of us, will you?"

Even from this distance, Evan could see Chance's grin. "We've already got about a hundred."

"A picture of all this should keep Conrad satisfied," Angie said to Evan. "Try to look ecstatic about saving my life."

"I am ecstatic about saving your life."

"That's the spirit."

"I *am*."

"Tell me about your business management gig."

"Okay. But it really is confidential."

"I understand."

"Lex, Deke and I are looking into buying the Sagittarius." The surprise was clear in her tone. "The resort?"

"That's the one."

"You're going to *run a hotel?*"

"We are."

"But…I mean, Lex I can see, but Deke? And *you?*"

"Your confidence is overwhelming."

"You know what I mean. You don't have any experience running hotels."

He frowned at her. "Seriously, Angie? 'You don't know what you're doing' is the thing you want to say to the guy who just saved your life?"

"You know what I mean. You didn't jump up and buy Lassiter Media. You spent years learning the ropes before you were in charge."

Evan supposed that was true enough. "And now I'll learn about hotels. Maybe there's a YouTube video available."

"So, you're using J.D.'s money?"

"I am. I haven't decided exactly how. I'm thinking about setting up a trust, using the money as a shareholder loan, and then donating the proceeds to a worthy cause."

"Why not just put it in as equity?"

"Because it feels like a bribe, like your father paid me to mess with your head. I hate that, Angie. I never, *ever* would have agreed to a scheme like that."

Sirens sounded in the distance, and flashing lights appeared down the road.

"Looks like the cavalry is here," said Angie.

"I hope they brought a boat."

Angelica felt like she'd been transported back in time to her teenage years. It was nearly ten o'clock now, dark and raining outside, and further cleanup efforts were going to have to wait until morning. In the great room at Big Blue, Marlene was handing around steaming mugs of hot chocolate. Chance was regaling them with stories of action, hard work and heroism, not the least of which was Evan's rescue of Angelica.

Happily nobody else had been injured in the flood, but several of the area ranches had been damaged. People were coming together to move livestock, drain fields, fix buildings, and make donations to their neighbors. The main road had been wiped out in a couple of places. Construction crews would arrive in the morning so that work could begin as soon as the rain stopped.

After taking an X-ray that confirmed Angelica's shoulder was correctly in place, the doctor had given her some pain pills and told her to take it easy for a week or so. She felt pleasantly tired and fuzzy as she moved her gaze past Chance to Evan. He had literally saved her life today, risking his own to do it. How did she thank him for that?

"How's the cocoa?" asked Tiffany, curling into a spot next to Angelica on the leather sofa.

A fire crackled in the big, stone fireplace and the aroma of fresh-made monster cookies wafted in from the kitchen. Rain splatted against the windows,

"Marvelous," Angelica answered, taking a sip.

"Was it like this while you were growing up?" Tiffany asked, glancing around at the homey atmosphere.

"Just like this," said Angelica. "I really miss it sometimes."

Tiffany cradled her own mug of cocoa. "We're definitely not in L.A."

"I like them both," said Angelica.

Though, at the moment, she preferred Cheyenne. She'd love to hole up here for a few more days and think about nothing at all.

"How are things between you and Evan?"

"Okay. Fine. He saved my life, so I guess I might have to forgive him for spying on me."

"You might," Tiffany agreed.

Angelica's memory went back to the moment he'd shoved her into the tree. "Do you think—?"

"What?"

"Well, I mean, do you think he'd have done that for anybody? He really could have died. He almost did."

While he held her dripping wet in his arms, Angelica had admitted to herself how much she missed him. Soon, once the wedding was over, he'd go off into the world and be somebody else's hero. The thought made her intensely sad.

"You know him better than I do," Tiffany answered softly.

"He would. He'd have risked his life to save anybody. He's that kind of a guy."

Tiffany put a hand on Angelica's good shoulder. Her voice was gentle. "Is this getting complicated?"

"It is."

"Are you going to get hurt?"

"Probably."

"Okay, but one small point to make here. You're a little high on painkillers right now. This might not seem as complex in the morning."

Angelica couldn't help but smile. "I hadn't thought of that."

"Plus, the man saved your life. You're probably experiencing some gratitude hormones."

"Is there such a thing?"

"I bet firefighters and police officers get laid all the time. Or, at least get offers. Though I imagine they're professionally obligated to say no."

Angelica could well believe they got offers. In the aftermath of the flood, she'd have hopped into bed with Evan in a heartbeat.

His gaze suddenly caught and held hers from across the

room, well out of hearing distance. His smile was slow and tender, and a wave of emotion clogged her chest. Again, she went back in time, to when they were engaged, happy and in love. Those moments had been incredibly precious, yet she'd taken them for granted.

Evan said something to Chance, then crossed the over to her.

"Want me to leave?" asked Tiffany.

Angelica grasped her hand. "Stay."

"You got it. Hi, Evan."

"How are you doing, Tiffany?"

"Tired," she replied. "I haven't worked that hard in years. Well, maybe never."

Evan gave her an answering smile. "I don't imagine sand-bagging comes up very often in corporate real estate."

"I once had to call a plumber to fix a kitchen faucet, but that's as close as I've come to flood control."

Evan turned his attention to Angelica. "How about you?"

"I'm high on pain killers."

"So now would be a good time to ask you a favor?"

A flutter of nerves passed through her stomach. "That depends."

"Don't look so scared. It's nothing too painful."

"But I won't like it."

"Probably not. Let me help you with Noah."

She didn't even consider it. "No."

"You're going to see him again before you leave Cheyenne?"

"I plan to."

Evan perched on an armchair at the corner of the sofa. "I genuinely want you to succeed, Angie."

"I am going to succeed." In case nobody had noticed, she was the CEO. She could, in fact, make unilateral decisions if she wanted.

"I can help."

Tiffany stepped in. "I don't think Angie should be arguing right now. She should be resting."

"You're right," said Angelica, taking the opportunity to exit the conversation. "I should go to bed."

She didn't want to fight with Evan. But she didn't want to give in to him either. Though she hated to admit it, at the moment, a little help with Noah seemed like a good idea. And that was clearly a dangerous line of thinking.

She polished off her hot chocolate and rose to her feet.

Saying goodnight to everyone, she made her way to her bedroom. Her shoulder was tender, but she managed to get out of her shirt and bra and into a clean tank top. It was a bit of a chore to wash up and comb her hair, but she managed.

Once she was ready for bed, she sat down to reassemble her cell phone. She'd opened it up and pulled out the battery and SIM card in an attempt to dry everything out. She pressed the On button and was happy to see the screen light up. Satisfied, she set the alarm and crawled into bed.

Her quilt was warm, her pillow soft, and a lighter rain now drummed above her. The pain pills had done their job, and her shoulder was no longer throbbing. She floated quickly into sleep.

What seemed like only moments later, her phone rang.

Angelica dragged her eyes open, squinting at the screen to find it was barely after eleven at night. The number was Kayla's, so she picked it up.

"Hello?"

"Angie? It's Kayla. You okay?"

"A little groggy. But good, yeah." Angelica let her head drop back on the pillow.

"We saw the flood footage on LNN. Is Big Blue okay? Any damage?"

"Very little here. We're just soggy. It rained and rained. In fact, it's still raining."

"We've booked a flight to Cheyenne in the morning.

We're coming home to help. The Dysons got hit pretty bad, and I heard the hospital is going to need a new generator."

"The community is pulling together."

"I know. And we want to be there."

Angelica understood the sentiment. She was going to have to return to L.A. soon, but she'd stay as long as she could, and Lassiter Media would make a hefty donation to the reconstruction effort.

"I'm sorry to call so late," Kayla continued. "But I wanted to let you know right away, and to tell you personally." She seemed to hesitate. "With all this going on. Well, Matt and I were talking, and…it doesn't seem like the right time to have a splashy, Malibu Beach wedding."

Angelica sat up, wincing as the movement stretched her shoulder. *"What?"*

"We're thinking of postponing. We need to be in Cheyenne, and we can't be there and still be planning the wedding here. I know how hard you've worked." Kayla's tone was apologetic.

Angelica scrambled to recover. "It's not about me. It's your wedding. You should do what feels right."

Kayla let out a relieved sigh. "I just couldn't do it. I couldn't sip champagne in a three-thousand-dollar dress while our friends and neighbors back home were struggling to restore power and water."

"I understand," said Angelica. She truly did.

"Matt is calling Conrad Norville, and the caterers, and the florist, and the musicians. But can you let Evan know?"

Angelica swallowed. "Sure."

"Thanks. And thank you so much for understanding. Will you still be in Cheyenne tomorrow?"

"I will," said Angelica. "For a couple more days, anyway."

"That's great. I'll call you when we get there."

"Good. Great. I'll talk to you tomorrow."

"Bye," said Kayla.

Angelica set down her phone and swung her legs from under the covers. She was guessing Kayla expected her to simply roll over and tell Evan about the cancellation. Since she thought they were back together again, it made sense Kayla would expect them to be sleeping together.

She sighed and rose to her feet. The house was silent. Not surprising, since everyone would have an early morning and a busy day tomorrow. She didn't know Deke's plans, but she'd overheard Evan last night offering to help.

No wedding, she said to herself as she padded to her bedroom door. *No wedding*, she repeated, opening the door and slipping through, heading down the great staircase. Okay, so no wedding.

She made her way through the kitchen, back to the guest room where Evan was staying. She knew her way blindfolded, but light from the yard filtered through the big windows, making it easy to see her way. Pale light was visible under Evan's door, meaning he was likely still awake.

She knocked lightly.

"Yes?" he called from within.

She cracked open the door. "It's me."

A small bedside lamp was on. "Angie? What's wrong? Are you in pain?"

"I'm fine," she assured him, opening the door wider and going inside.

"You sure?" He closed a book and set it on the night table.

She shut the door behind her and nodded as she crossed the room. The floor was cold under her bare feet, so she perched on the end of his bed, pulling her soles from the floor.

"What's going on?" he asked.

"Kayla called."

He waited.

"They saw footage of the flood. They're coming back to Cheyenne."

"I'm not surprised."

"And they're canceling the wedding."

Evan drew back against the headboard. "Canceling it how?"

"They don't want a posh party in Malibu while there are people in trouble in Cheyenne."

"I guess I can understand that."

Their gazes met and locked. Then his dropped to her left hand, and the engagement ring.

"So," he ventured, "I guess our secret plan—"

"Was a very big waste—"

"Of time."

"I was going to say effort."

"That too." He raked a hand over his short hair.

"Not to mention all the lies." She reached for the ring, pulling it from her finger.

But he sat forward, his hand closing over hers, stopping the action. "Don't."

She looked up in confusion.

"Breaking it off now is going to seem very abrupt."

"So what? It's not like there's going to be a better time."

"People have enough to worry about already."

"The two of us pretending to stay together is not going to help the flood reconstruction."

"That's true," he agreed. But he didn't remove his hand. "What about Lassiter Media?"

She felt her guard go up. "What about it?"

"You've already got trouble with Noah. You're trying to build credibility and trust. How's it going to look if you get reengaged for a few days and then change your mind?"

"Who says it's me changing my mind? Maybe it was you who broke it off."

"That'll make them ask why."

"Evan, for goodness' sake."

"If I break it off, you run the risk of people thinking I had a reason."

"How is that fair?"

"Gossip's never fair. And you're more of a celebrity than me. Who do you think will be the target?"

She had to admit, he had a point. Not that she was agreeing with the idea. She rubbed her hands up and down her chilled arms. "We can't just stay engaged."

He shrugged. "We can for a while."

"How long is a while? Or maybe we should just get married." Her voice went higher as she spoke. "That would really throw them off. If we actually went through with the wedding, who would ever suspect the engagement was a sham?"

"There's no need to be sarcastic."

"Yes, there is. We have an honest-to-God problem here."

"And we have an honest-to-God, if temporary, solution. I'm not saying forever, Angie. We can shut it down anytime we want. But not tonight. Not tomorrow. Let's let a few of these other things work themselves out first. It'll be easier that way."

"You think this is easy?"

It sure wasn't easy for her, spending time with Evan, talking to him, laughing with him, experiencing his little touches in front of Marlene and others to keep up the charade. Every minute of every day, she remembered more and more about their life together. She remembered why she'd fallen in love with him, and how badly it had hurt to lose him.

She shivered at the memory.

"Cold?" he asked.

She didn't answer, but she was. Her shorts and tank top didn't give much warmth.

He pulled back the covers. "Hop in."

"Are you *crazy?*"

"You're injured. You're doped up. And you're freezing. I think I can manage to be a gentleman for a few minutes."

She hesitated, but the promise of warmth was too much to ignore. She scooted up to sit next to him, and he flipped the covers over her legs. They weren't touching, but the warmth of his skin swirled out to her.

"Better?" he asked.

She nodded.

"We don't say anything for a few days."

"I don't like it."

"I know you don't. I don't blame you."

"What about you?" she asked. "This can't be any fun for you either."

He angled his body to look at her. "I really don't mind. It's not like I have a girlfriend to worry about. And I like your family."

"But you have to hang around with me. You have to pretend…"

"That I like you? I've always liked you, Angie. You might be kind of quirky and misguided."

"*Excuse* me?"

"And you nearly got me killed today."

"Okay, that part's true."

"But, all in all, you're not that objectionable."

She whacked him in the thigh, realizing too late she'd used her sore arm. She groaned in pain.

He was instantly concerned. "You okay?"

"No. I'm an idiot. Ouch."

"It's the drugs. You're a bit addled right now."

"Is that why I'm agreeing to stay engaged to you?"

"No, that's the smart part of your brain talking."

The throbbing was subsiding in her shoulder. "What's in it for you?"

"I'm still hoping to help with Noah."

"I'm not going to let you. Besides, that would technically be for me. And why do you want to do it anyway?"

He gently wrapped an arm around her shoulders. "I was

in love with you once, Angie. Very, very much in love with you. And feelings like that don't just evaporate into thin air."

She knew what he meant. She felt it too. She tried to frame it in words. "Ghost feelings."

"That's right. You're haunting me."

"You're haunting me too," she admitted.

He squeezed her ever so gently. "Maybe that's why we made love."

A flush warmed her body. It was the first time either of them had mentioned it.

"I guess," she said.

His tone went low. "For a few minutes there, it was as if we'd never been apart."

She was afraid to answer, because she agreed.

The air thickened between them.

He reached over to smooth back her hair. Then he brushed the pad of his index finger along her cheek. He looked deeply and intensely into her eyes. "No one would ever know."

Arousal throbbed in the depths of her body, heating to life. She understood what he meant. If they did it again, no one would ever know. And what could it change? They'd already given in once. It hadn't made things better, but then it hadn't made things a whole lot worse either. She was as confused and conflicted before making love to him as she had been after.

He kissed her oh so tenderly on the lips. "Tell me if I hurt you. Tell me if I hurt you, and I'll stop."

Nine

With an arm around her waist, Evan eased Angie down into his bed. Her tank top shimmied up, exposing her flat stomach, her smooth skin. She was everything he'd ever remembered and loved.

"You're so beautiful," he breathed.

"And you're so strong." Her palms skimmed his bare shoulders, moving along his biceps.

He was wearing boxers, but nothing else.

She frowned as she took in his torso. "You really got hurt out there."

"Just scrapes and bruises. They'll heal."

"They look painful. I'm afraid to touch you."

"Please don't be afraid of that." He settled his palm against her bare stomach. "Because I'm dying to touch you."

He brought his lips to hers again, hoping to reassure her. The last thing he wanted was for her to have second thoughts. It had been months since she'd been in his bed. And now that she was here, he realized how desperately he wanted her this way.

She accepted his kiss. Then she kissed him back. Her arms wound around him, her small, soft hands coming up against his back.

Conscious of her shoulder, he hugged her around the waist, bringing them together, her softness against his tension. He deepened the kiss, and her tongue answered his, sending sweeps of passion through his body, pushing every other thought from his mind.

Angie. This was Angie in his bed again, finally.

He let his hand slide up and skim the side of her breast, which was bare beneath the tiny tank top. Then he moved on to her shorts, running his fingers over her hip, the curve of her rear, the smoothness of her bare thigh. She curled her body against him. The sensation was so familiar his throat went raw.

"I've missed you," he moaned.

Her hand framed his chin, and she kissed him deeply. "This is so confusing."

"It's going to be okay. I promise."

On some level, he realized his words made no sense. But he wanted it to be true. He desperately hoped he'd never have to hurt her again.

She slipped off her tank top, a little awkwardly around her sore shoulder. But she'd revealed her beautiful breasts, and that was all he cared about. He settled her skin against his, absorbing her warmth and softness.

She kissed her way along his bruised chest. "Am I hurting you?"

"You're healing me."

There was a smile in her voice as her lips brushed his skin. "I don't think sex has any medicinal properties."

"Let's test that theory."

Impatient to have her naked, he stripped off her little shorts and tossed them aside. Then he kicked out of his boxers. In seconds, they were full length, skin to skin. He rolled slowly onto his back, bringing her with him.

"Tell me if anything hurts," he said.

"Nothing hurts." She gave him a lingering kiss. "I can't feel a thing."

"That's disappointing." He slipped his hand between her thighs. "Can you feel that?"

She gave a low moan.

He caressed her more intimately. "That?"

"Oh, Evan."

His breathing grew ragged as his arousal ramped up. "That?" he managed.

She hugged him more tightly, and buried her face in the crook of his neck. "Don't stop. Don't— Oh, my."

Unable to wait a second longer, he guided himself inside. The moist warmth of her body closed around him, sending lasers of arousal sweeping through his brain.

He tried desperately to take it slow, but it wasn't going to work.

It was impossible to talk. He guided her onto her back.

"It's good," she assured him as she sank back into the mattress. "So good."

She arched her hips against him, and he braced himself on his forearms. He gazed at her beautiful, flushed face, as his body went on autopilot. Her eyes were closed, lashes thick against her creamy skin. Her hair was mussed and sexy. Her cheeks were pink, lips full, red and slightly parted. He could get aroused simply by looking at her.

A moan escaped from her lips, and her legs wrapped around him. She arched her hips further, ankles locking in the small of his back. He'd wanted to be gentle, promised himself he'd be careful, but his instincts had been hijacked by need, and his body pumped faster and faster.

"Evan!" she finally cried out, head tipping back into the pillow.

He felt her shudder and convulse. He was instantly over the edge, ecstasy pairing with oblivion in huge waves that rocked his body to the core.

It took a long time to recover, before he could move, before he had the presence of mind to turn them over so that he didn't give in and crush her to the bed.

He lay back and dragged a quilt overtop of them. Her long hair tickled his neck as she rested her head on his chest. Her soft curves settled perfectly around the planes and angles of his body. Nothing hurt anymore, not in the slightest; he felt as though he was drifting on a plane of heaven.

He stroked her messy hair. "You're amazing." He wanted to say more. He wanted to marvel at how good they were together. Making love with Angie was like nothing else in the world. But that conversation would take them somewhere they couldn't afford to go. For now, it was enough that she was here in his arms.

Her fingertips traced a pattern on his chest. "I can't believe it was all for nothing."

"What's that?" He wondered if she meant the sandbags.

"Me, you, Conrad, the tabloids, my brothers, *Marlene*."

"Oh, that. Yeah, well, who could have predicted the flood of the century?"

"If we hadn't made up the story, hadn't lied to a single person, everything would have turned out exactly the same."

He disagreed. "If we hadn't lied, I never would have followed you to Cheyenne, and you might have been swept away by the flood."

"So our lies saved my life?"

"I'm going with that one."

She seemed to ponder for a moment. "If we hadn't lied, I wouldn't have talked to Conrad, and I wouldn't have come up with the idea of remaking the affiliate's hit shows. Then Noah and I wouldn't have disagreed, and I never would have been in Cheyenne yesterday."

"But it's a good idea," Evan countered. "If you don't do it, Lassiter Media could start losing market share. If you'd never come up with it, the company might have spiraled downward, eventually going bankrupt and taking the entire Lassiter empire with it."

He felt laughter rumble through her chest. It was another sensation that was achingly familiar.

"We've just saved the Lassiter empire by lying to my family and the entire world?"

"We never lied to Deke and Tiffany. But yeah."

Sleep was creeping into her voice. "You really do need to get yourself a white charger, Evan McCain."

"Your horse Delling is a dapple gray. That's pretty close."

Her voice got softer. "Too bad you didn't marry me. He'd have been half yours."

As she relaxed into sleep, the words bounced around inside Evan's brain. *Too bad you didn't marry me.*

If he could go back in time, he honestly might have dragged her to the altar.

Angelica crept back up to her bedroom at 6:00 a.m. Evan had roused her from a sound sleep to give her the choice—staying with him a while longer or going back to her own room before the family got up. For a split second, she'd been tempted to stay. But she knew it was a ridiculous impulse. They weren't a couple any longer.

She silently twisted her bedroom door handle, pushing the door inward on smooth hinges. Then she startled, sucking in a breath when she saw Tiffany sitting on her bed.

"You've been downstairs?" Tiffany asked, a suspicious expression in her eyes.

"Kayla called." Angelica silently closed the door behind her, leaning back against it. "I had to talk to Evan. They've canceled the wedding."

Tiffany rolled to her feet. "And how long did that take?"

Angelica thought about lying, but this was Tiffany. "About six hours."

Tiffany's expression softened. "You want to talk?"

"I don't know." Angelica honestly didn't. She crossed the room to her dresser, sliding open a drawer, realizing the logical thing to do was get dressed and go on with the day.

"If you did want to talk," Tiffany continued, moving toward her, "what would you want to say?"

Angelica gripped the half-open drawer, giving up on holding her emotions at bay. "That Evan is the best lover in the entire universe."

There was a split second pause. "Okay. Well. That's… uh…hmmm."

Angelica turned. "I couldn't agree with you more."

"What are you going to do?"

Excellent question. "First, I'm getting dressed." Angelica retrieved a pair of blue jeans and a hunter-green shirt from her drawer.

She stared at the clothing that she only used on visits to Big Blue. It suddenly felt like her past, and she tossed it onto the bed, not sure if she should wear it.

"No," she decided. "First, I'm going to brush my teeth."

"Okay. But what about the big question?"

"There is no big question. He didn't ask, and I didn't ask. Nothing's changed, Tiff. We just couldn't quite keep our hands off each other a couple of times."

Tiffany was silent for a moment. "I meant with Kayla and Matt. But please do continue talking about your sex life."

Angelica rolled her eyes, then pivoted and headed into the bathroom.

"They're coming to Cheyenne to help out," she called back. "They don't want to host a splashy wedding party while people are recovering."

"That makes sense," said Tiffany. "When you think about it, what else would people like Kayla and Matt do?"

"I know." Angelica nodded as she squeezed toothpaste onto her brush.

"Wait a minute." Tiffany appeared in the doorway. "That means you and Evan don't need to fake it any longer."

"That's what I told him last night."

"Yet somehow, you ended up sleeping with him instead? You want to walk me through that logic, Angie?"

Angelica held her toothbrush under the faucet. "He doesn't want it to be too sudden. For my family, mostly, especially for Marlene. He thinks we should let them down more gently. Plus, he thinks making up and breaking up in such rapid succession will make me look like a flake to the Lassiter Media brass." She shut off the tap. "I'm not sure he's wrong. I think I've already got trouble on that front."

Tiffany had moved to lean in the bathroom doorway, talking while Angelica brushed. "You're the Lassiter Media brass, Angie. You can tell them to stuff it."

Angelica knew it wasn't that easy. "My father handpicked those men. They're the backbone of the company."

"You're the head of the company. They have to follow you now."

Angelica spat and rinsed her brush. "I'm confident we'll get there. But they have to respect me, not fear me. The faster I can make that happen, the easier my job gets. It's true that looking like I have an erratic love life isn't going to garner me any respect."

"So, what's the long-term play here? Are you going to have to marry Evan so you don't look like a flake in front of the vice presidents?"

Angelica couldn't help laughing. "That's exactly what I said to Evan."

"What did he say?"

"He told me I was being sarcastic. I was. It wasn't helpful, but I was kind of rattled at the time."

"And then?"

"And then he told me I wasn't too objectionable, and he

could tolerate hanging around with me for a while longer, for the good of the cause."

A smirk grew on Tiffany's face. "Smooth talker. I can see why you jumped into bed with him."

"No, that happened when he said he'd once been very much in love with me, and feelings like that didn't evaporate into thin air."

Tiffany sobered. "Oh. Well, yeah. I can definitely see that working."

Angelica wandered back into the bedroom, plunking herself down on the bed next to her jeans. "I should know what to do here. I shouldn't feel so confused."

Tiffany sat down with her. "Do you want him back? Do you want to try again?"

"Setting aside for the moment that I not only burned that bridge, I blew it sky-high and buried the ashes, I'm not as sure as I once was that I don't want him back."

Tiffany blinked for a moment. "Let's pretend I actually followed that train of logic. You're saying you might want him back?"

"I'm saying I no longer know that I don't."

"You've been talking to too many reporters."

"I don't know. I'm confused." Angelica snagged a pillow and pressed it into her stomach.

Tiffany sat next to her and put a hand on her shoulder.

Angelica's phone rang. The display indicated it was her assistant in L.A.

She squared her shoulders. "Hi, Becky. What's up?" It was very early on the West Coast.

"I just got a message from someone at the Cheyenne office."

"Is something wrong? Did the flood get worse overnight?"

There hadn't been any reports of damage yesterday in

the historic section of town. But it had continued raining all night long.

"Nothing like that," Becky put in quickly. "It's Noah. Apparently he's on an early flight to L.A. this morning."

Angelica came to her feet. "What for?"

"I don't know. But it was a very sudden trip. I can't put my finger on it, but something feels off."

"I'm on my way back. Thanks, Becky." She ended the call.

"What's up?" asked Tiffany.

"You better pack. I'm taking the jet home to find out."

"What happened?"

"One of the hostile vice presidents, Noah, is on his way to L.A. It could be nothing. It might be nothing. But I know he's tight with Ken and Louie, and I need to get to them first."

Angelica crossed to the dresser. She put back the blue jeans and T-shirt and moved to the closet instead. There, she selected a white blouse and a pair of black slacks to go with a tailored black blazer.

She felt more like herself again. She knew she'd feel even better once she got back to the L.A. office.

Noah beat Angelica to L.A., and when she arrived at the office, he was already meeting with Ken Black and Louie Huntley, vice presidents of drama and comedy series respectively. She was annoyed by Noah's move, but there was nothing specific to call him on. Vice presidents met with each other all the time, with or without the CEO.

In the newly decorated boardroom, the landscape of Big Blue hanging proudly on the wall, the men were deep in a discussion. As she walked in and made herself known, Noah was just saying that LBS should continue to create all of its own content. What's more, he announced that her father would have wanted it that way.

"Angelica," said Ken in obvious surprise. "You're back,"

"I'm back," said agreed.

"You're all right?" asked Louie.

"I'm fine," said Angelica. She turned to Noah. "You were saying?"

"Welcome back," said Noah, his tone tight.

There was an awkward silence.

"It's a cornerstone of the network." Ken voiced his agreement with Noah, saying to Angelica, "It's how we distinguish ourselves from the competition. Lassiter Media *is* Lassiter programming. It's not up to you or anyone else to change that."

Becky quietly took a seat at the far end of the table.

"You have to admit, the industry is changing," said Angelica. "Take a look at some of the innovative things happening on cable, even online."

Louie stepped in. "Lassiter will *never* stoop to the trash being played online"

A subtle but satisfied smile played on Noah's lips.

"Who said anything about trash?" she asked them all. "What I'm proposing is new versions of top-rated series, most of them family-friendly. And they were created by our new affiliates, now part of the Lassiter Media family."

"They weren't created by Lassiter Media," said Louie. "Can't you see how you compromise the brand by diluting the creative?"

"They're terrific shows. They're popular shows."

"Since when is mass appeal our primary driver?" asked Ken.

It was on the tip of Angelica's tongue to ask since when vice presidents felt so free to disregard the wishes of the CEO. But she kept silent. She needed to co-opt these men, not alienate them.

"The bottom line still counts," said Angelica.

"So does integrity," said Noah.

"I'm asking you to pull together a team. Pick a series.

Do some storyboards. Let's at least see where it goes." She hadn't made it a direct order, but it was close.

The three men glanced at each other. Then Noah looked at the Big Blue landscape. It was clear he wished he could invoke J.D.

Angelica waited.

"Fine," said Noah. "It's a waste of manpower, but we'll put something together."

"Thank you." Angelica gave a sharp nod, and the men rose and left the boardroom.

Becky shuffled some papers at her end of the table. She'd been J.D.'s executive assistant for the past several years. She'd sat silently through the entire exchange.

Now Angelica turned to her. "What do you think?"

Becky seemed flustered by the question. "I don't know anything about programming decisions."

"You knew my father. You watched him interact with Noah, Ken and Louie, and a whole bunch of other managers."

"You're nicer than he was," said Becky. Then she seemed to catch herself. "That is…I mean…"

"It's okay. If I didn't want your unvarnished opinion, I wouldn't have asked for it."

Becky hesitated a moment longer. "They never would have spoken to Mr. Lassiter like that. They would have said yes, sir, no, sir, how high, sir. And that would have been that."

Angelica couldn't help but smile. "My father brought that out in people."

"He was a very smart man."

"He was. Just out of curiosity, which style do you think works better?"

Again Becky waited a moment before answering. "Maybe somewhere in the middle. Someone has to be at the helm, but other people have good ideas too."

Angelica found herself intrigued by Becky's insight. The woman had long been an observer of senior management.

meetings, and had been privy to J.D.'s thoughts and opin-
ons on a regular basis.

"What do you think of Max Truger?" Angelica asked.

Again, there was a small hesitation. "I like him. He seems
well respected. He's always struck me as smart in meetings.
And he's polite to the staff. But then he's younger than a lot
of the senior management. I think attitudes have changed
over the years. There's not as much hierarchy as there was
twenty or thirty years ago."

"I agree with you," said Angelica. "Anybody else that
strikes you as progressive?"

"Lana Flynn over in marketing. She's only a manager,
but she's bright. And Reece Ogden-Neeves in movies. He's
not that young, but he's open-minded."

Angelica liked Reece as well. Though he kept mostly to
himself, she'd always thought he was one of the company's
strongest assets.

After a pause, Becky said, "I'm not sure why you're asking me this."

"Because you've had a ringside seat to the inner work-
ings for years now. But mostly because I think you're progressive and bright."

Becky smiled at the compliment.

"I'm trying to make something work here," Angelica said.
"I'm trying to figure out when to push and when to be patient."

Becky nodded her understanding. "I think you should
trust your instincts. I mean, if you're still asking for my
opinion."

"Feel free to give your opinion anytime you like," said
Angelica. "You trust your instincts too. You've been doing
this a long time, and you seem to have a good head on your
shoulders."

"Thank you."

"Can you get me a meeting with Reece?"

Becky grinned again. "You're the CEO, Ms. Lassiter He'll drop everything and come right up."

"I suppose that's true," Angelica agreed. "Let's give it a try and see what happens."

Becky reached to pick up the phone on the boardroom table and connected to Reece's office. It took the man less than three minutes to show up.

"Can you excuse us please, Becky?" Angelica asked as Reece entered the room.

"Of course, Ms. Lassiter."

As Becky left, Reece sat down across the table.

"Is there a problem?" he asked, lips pursed.

"I wanted your opinion on something," said Angelica.

"Of course." He gave a sharp, unsmiling nod. "Whatever you need."

"I'm looking into the possibility of remaking some of the popular series out of the new British and Australian affiliates."

"I heard."

"You did?"

"I also hear you've hit some resistance."

"I have. Are you a resistor?"

Reece gave a slight smile. "I don't know enough about the projects to have an opinion one way or the other."

"In general, do you think we're compromising Lassiter Media's principles by commissioning content from outside that's not original?"

"In general, no. In specific, it depends on whether the content will be embraced by our viewers."

"And how do we determine that?"

"Up front? We can't. We have to try it, and see if it flies."

"Simple as that?"

"Simple as that."

She considered him for a moment. "We might lose a lot of money."

"We might make a lot of money."

"We might lose viewers."

"Or gain them." Reece sat back in his chair. "What are you really asking me?"

The astute question took Angelica by surprise. "If I decide to commission remakes, what can I do that would make you comfortable with the decision?"

"If you're comfortable, then I'm comfortable."

"Are you a yes-man, Reece?"

"In public, yes. In private, I'll give you my opinion, as fully and freely as you want. I'll point out all the potholes in the road. If you tell me to go around them, I will. If you tell me to drive over them, I will. If we crash, we crash. But we'll go down giving it our best shot."

She liked the answer. She liked it a lot. "How's the spring lineup coming?"

He opened a leather folder in front of him. "I brought the draft schedule with me. I thought that's what the meeting was about."

Angelic accepted the report, moving on to their day-to-day business. But she couldn't help thinking that if Reece was working in series instead of movies, her life would be a whole lot easier.

Since they'd returned from Cheyenne, Evan had tried to call Angie several times. She hadn't answered, and she hadn't returned a single message.

He knew he should give up. But some kind of perversity had him tracking her down in person tonight.

He tried to tell himself it was to keep up appearances, but he knew it was because he missed her. It was bad enough before Cheyenne. But since she'd slept in his arms, he hadn't been able to get her out of his head for a moment.

As of five o'clock today, he was the proud, one-third

owner of the Sagittarius Resort. He was pumped and excited, and he wanted to share it with her.

He'd gone ahead with the idea of setting up a trust for J.D.'s money. The trust was receiving a guaranteed return from the investment in Sagittarius, as well as having a profit position in the company. Inspired by the Cheyenne flood, he'd chosen disaster relief as the focus of the fund. There were plenty of ordinary families deserving assistance after any number of floods and storms.

Now, the elevator doors slid open on the twenty-eighth floor of the Lassiter Media building. He'd called Angie's office earlier with no success. Then he'd swung by the mansion, hoping she'd be home by nine o'clock. She wasn't, and her housekeeper confirmed that she didn't have a social engagement tonight. The Lassiter Media offices looked like his best hope.

The door to her temporary office was wide open, and she glanced up at the sound of his footsteps.

"What are *you* doing here?" she asked, looking past him. "And how did you get in the building?"

"I have some news. And the security guards all know me. The world thinks we're engaged again, remember?"

"I remember." She sat back in her leather chair.

He moved around the table. "What are you working on so late?"

"Storyboards."

"Reviewing them?"

"Fixing them."

"You're fixing somebody's storyboards?" It was a surprisingly low-level task. "You're the *CEO*, Angie."

"I'm aware of that."

"Why? What?" It was nine o'clock at night, for pity's sake.

"It's one of the series out of Australia."

He peered over her shoulder. "Not to backseat drive on

you, but don't you have staff who can do this? Maybe even during regular working hours?"

"How is that not backseat driving?"

"You should have gone home a long time ago."

"It's fine."

"Angie," he warned.

"Don't start in on the work-life balance lecture."

"Then tell me what's going on."

"It's Noah. And Ken and Louie for that matter." She seemed to hesitate. "I'm not so sure my approach is working."

Evan glanced at the panels on her computer screen, but they were out of context and didn't make sense. "What approach?"

"I basically ordered them to pick a series and work on a remake."

"Okay." He didn't really see a problem with that. If the VPs were going to be snarky, they deserved what they got.

"Their hearts just aren't in it."

"Their ideas aren't working?" Evan's suspicions were immediately aroused.

"Not at all. I'm playing with this one. I'm thinking if I can show them what I mean, give them an example using one of the series, things will smooth out on all three."

Evan glanced at this watch. "So you're working half the night because your VPs can't get their jobs done."

"I'd like to have something for the morning."

"Not a good plan, Angie."

"Truly none of your business, Evan." She rose from her chair. "You want some coffee?"

"Not this late."

She moved to a side counter and grabbed the coffee pot.

"Have you had dinner?" he asked her, wrinkling his nose at the stale smell of the coffee.

"I had a late lunch in the café." She sniffed at the coffee pot. "Right now, I wish it was still open."

"You want to go out for something?"

She shook her head. "I have to get this done."

He could see arguing would get him nowhere, so he changed the subject. "I've tried to call you a few times since we got back."

She poured the remains of the coffee pot into her cup. "I've been busy working."

"Every night?"

"Most nights, yes."

"You know, this is exactly what J.D. worried about."

She made an abrupt turn to face him. "Bully for J.D. and his perfectly balanced life. But he had *me* for support. He had *you* for support. And he had the loyalty of his entire staff. I'm operating under just a few more challenges than my father." Then her shoulders drooped. "Can we not talk about this? I don't have the energy to fight. Tell me why you came. You said you had news."

Evan wanted to keep hammering home his point. He wanted to grab her and shake some sense into her. Then he wanted to kiss her and make love to her. After that, he feared he might actually want to marry her. But the look on her face told him to keep that all to himself.

"We bought the Sagittarius," he told her instead.

She looked impressed. "You actually did it?"

"We'll make the announcement on Monday."

Her body relaxed a bit more, and she gave him a smile. "That's great news, Evan. I'm truly happy for you."

"I'm happy, too. I can't wait to start working with Deke and Lex." The fit between the three men felt perfect. He was more excited about his professional life than he'd been in months, maybe years.

But he was worried about Angie right now. Even when she smiled, her face was pinched. He wondered if her shoulder was still bothering her. Without conscious thought, he moved closer.

"Do you need to find some more help?" he asked. "Because, you're right, you know. Your father had both of us to share the load. Who've you got?"

She broadened her smile. "This is just a hiccup, Evan. It's all going to work itself out."

"I can—"

"No, you can't." Her tone was firm.

His cellphone rang in his pocket. He wanted to continue arguing with her, but she looked so fragile that he honestly couldn't bring himself to cause her any more distress.

He went for the phone instead.

"It's Matt," he told her as he took the call.

"Hey, Matt."

"Hi, Evan. How are things in L.A.?"

"All's well. How about Cheyenne?"

"We're working hard. Everybody's working hard. There's a lot to do here."

"I bet there is."

"The donation from Lassiter Media has been extremely well received."

"You should tell Angie, not me."

"Yeah, I keep forgetting. You might be back in the family, but you're not back in the firm."

"That's right," Evan agreed, watching Angie as he spoke, battling a desire to draw her into his arms and hold her comfortingly close.

"Kayla and I have come up with a new idea for the wedding," said Matt.

"Oh, yeah?"

"We'd like to have it here in Cheyenne. On the weekend."

"This weekend?"

"Yeah, yeah. I know what you're thinking. We must seem pretty impulsive to you. But I promise, you don't have to lift a finger this time."

"It's not that—"

"We'll have a simple ceremony."

"What about Kayla's mother?"

Matt's tone hardened. "She can come to us. Flights go both ways, you know. We're going to have a small wedding in the church, followed by a big bash at the town hall. The entire ranching community is invited. It'll be a break from all the cleanup."

Evan had to admit, it sounded like a very good idea. "I'll absolutely be there. And I'm sure the town will appreciate it."

The curiosity was clear on Angie's face.

"I think they will," said Matt. "So far, everyone's on board. A whole bunch of people are stepping up to help. Kayla's going to call Angie."

"She's right here," said Evan.

Though it didn't really matter anymore, he couldn't help thinking that the two of them being together helped validate their ruse.

"Ask her if she can make it."

Evan covered the phone. "Can you make it to Kayla and Matt's wedding in Cheyenne this weekend?"

Her jaw dropped.

"She'll be there," Evan told Matt.

"That's great," said Matt.

Angie's mouth moved, but no sounds came out.

"We can't wait," said Evan. "See you in a couple of days."

"Thanks, man."

"No problem." Evan ended the call.

"Cheyenne?" Angie asked, apparently regaining the power of speech.

"They've invited the entire ranching community to the reception. I think it's there way of supporting their neighbors."

"It's a lovely thought," said Angie. But her voice was flat as she dropped down into a chair. "I wish I had more time."

"Oh, no you don't. This is important. You'll spend whatever time it takes to make Kayla happy."

Angie gestured to her computer. "And who will take care of all this?"

"Your employees."

"My employees are rebelling."

"Well, that's a whole other problem. But your best friend is getting married, and you are going to be there with bells on."

Ten

Kayla had swapped her satin, jeweled wedding gown for a simpler dress. It was strapless, with a tight bodice covered in flat, ivory lace. The ankle-length skirt was made of raw silk and wispy chiffon, with a ghost pattern of pale lavender flowers. It was set off by a pair of soft, cream leather ankle boots, while a lavender ribbon had been woven into Kayla's light brown braid that dangled down the center of her back. The effect was simple and beautiful.

Angelica and Tiffany wore matching strapless, purple dresses. They had short, layered skirts. Taupe cowboy boots completed the look.

Barbecues smoldered on the deck of the big hall. Guests had feasted on steaks and grilled salmon prepared by the chefs of the local Lassiter Grill. Dessert would be the gorgeous multi-tiered lemon raspberry cake, baked and decorated by Lassiter Grill's head pastry chef.

After the ceremony and celebratory dinner were both over, Angelica's mind bounced between Cheyenne and L.A. She was delighted for Kayla and Matt but worried about the argument she'd had with Ken this morning.

A local band played on the small stage, and the guests had all gathered around the edges of the worn, hardwood floor.

The first waltz played to an end, and strains of another slow country tune came up. It was Angelica and Evan's signal to join the bride and groom on the dance floor.

Dressed in a steel-gray suit and a pair of cowboy boots, Evan took her hand, walking her to the center of the floor, where he took her in his arms. Her feet automatically picked up the rhythm, and she followed his lead, fighting the urge to settle against his chest, close her eyes and forget about the rest of the world.

"Your head's not here," he said to her.

"My head's right here," she countered. "So are my arms, my legs and my feet."

"You're thinking about Lassiter Media."

"You can read my mind now?"

"I can read your expression. And you keep looking at Noah and frowning."

"I've been smiling all day." At least she had been whenever she wasn't alone. "And I've been looking at Kayla. Isn't she beautiful?"

"You need to set it aside."

"Set aside the fact that the bride is beautiful? You think I'm jealous?"

Evan gave her a spin then reeled her back.

"Forget about work," he told her. "This is a wedding. You're supposed to be having fun."

"I am having fun."

"You're worrying at about a million miles an hour."

She pasted a bright smile on her face. "I'm having a blast."

Just then, she caught sight of Noah. He, Ken and Louie had come to the wedding, along with many of the other Lassiter managers and staff, since Matt had worked with them for many years. The three men were clustered in a corner, talking intensely to one another. While she watched, a woman joined the conversation. It was Noah's secretary, and she handed him a cell phone. Noah broke away, his glance catching Angelica's for a brief second.

Evan tugged her tight against his chest. "Stop it," he rasped in her ear. Then he turned her so she couldn't see.

"They're up to something," she told him.

Evan drew back. "Let it go. Your job can't be twenty-four seven."

"The networks run twenty-four seven."

"That makes it even more important for you to be able to get away. My hotel is open, but I'm not checking texts."

"You're not in a duel with your managers."

The song changed, but they kept right on dancing.

"Is the duel still going on?" asked Evan.

"It is. And that's what I'm worried about." She'd given Ken the updated storyboards, and he'd told her he'd play with them some more. She'd been waiting two days now for an update.

"What happened?"

"I think Ken's messing up my storyboards."

"So, ask him."

"I did. He's ducking the questions."

"Take charge, Angie. But do it on Monday. For now, dance with me."

"I can't—" She stopped herself mid-protest. There was no point in arguing any further with Evan. They'd just go round and round.

She forced herself to relax into his chest. She concentrated on the dance steps, on the feel of his strong arms, the scent of his skin, the sound of his heartbeat. The music filled her ears, and a rush of desire tightened her chest. If only she could escape with Evan, go somewhere for the night, or even an hour, and let their passion obliterate all the worries in her world.

"That's better." His voice rumbled against her ear. "You, me, Cheyenne. For some reason, it always feels right."

She knew she should argue that. His words were far too

loaded and intimate. But he was right. There was something in the untamed atmosphere, or maybe it was the glorious, star-filled nights. But it pushed them together.

"I want you, Angie."

Her throat closed over, and she couldn't speak.

He drew her hand in close and placed a soft kiss on the inside of her wrist. Sensation bloomed along her arm, warming the core of her body.

The song ended, and the master of ceremonies announced the cake cutting. His hearty voice jangled through the speakers, shocking Angelica back to her senses. What was wrong with her?

She pulled away from Evan and hurried off the dance floor. She'd been about to say yes. She'd been about to agree to yet another night in his arms, in his bed. How could she be so foolish?

She made it into the coat room, where it was dim and quiet. There, she grasped a shelf on the wall, steadying herself and taking deep, calming breaths.

"I'd like to see the lowest rated," said a male voice.

Angelica blinked, realizing the man speaking was around the corner from her, out of sight.

"Was that last year?" It was Noah who was talking. "So, season three?"

Angelica started toward him.

"A copy of the script would be perfect. Yes, please."

She came around the corner, and Noah spotted her. He immediately snapped his jaw shut.

"I'll call you back." He ended the call.

"Who was that?" she asked.

"Australia."

"Who in Australia?"

"Her name is Cathy, low-level assistant, nobody you'd know."

"What are you doing, Noah?"

He started to move for the exit. "Just getting some background information for the remake."

"You're working on a remake from Britain."

"Ken's remake."

Her suspicions were growing. "You've seen the storyboards?"

"The updated ones, yes."

"My updates?"

"Plus Ken's. You had some good ideas, Angie. I'll give you that."

"You'll *give* me that? Why, thank you, Noah. Nice of you to believe I have something to contribute to Lassiter Media."

"What's going on here?" Evan interrupted from behind her.

"Of course you have something to contribute," said Noah, his tone smoothing out. "You have plenty to contribute. Isn't that what I just said?"

For a second, she wondered if she could have possibly misinterpreted his meaning.

"We all loved your changes. We've elaborated on them."

"Why are you working on Ken's project?"

"Enough," said Evan. "Noah, this isn't the time or place."

"Butt out," Angelica said to Evan.

"Leave," Evan said to Noah.

Looking nervous, Noah glanced at Angelica. Then his attention shot back to Evan. A flash of trepidation appeared in his eyes, and he suddenly rushed past them for the door.

Angelica turned on Evan, struggling not to shout. "You can't undermine me like that."

His voice was flat. "They're cutting the cake."

"I don't give a damn about the cake."

He stepped forward, nearly pressing up against her. "Do you hear yourself? Do you?"

"He was talking to the affiliate in Australia, asking about

low-rated shows. I think they might actually be out to get me. I couldn't ignore it."

"Yes, you could. You can. You'll deal with this in the office on Monday."

"Is that an order?"

He clamped his jaw tight. "It's a friendly suggestion."

"You lost the right to make friendly suggestions."

"Did your father's machinations mean nothing to you? Did he put me, your brothers, the company, and everyone else through the ringer for six months and have you not learn a *single lesson?*"

"Shut up, Evan."

"No, I won't shut up. I can't shut up. You want to hear an order, Angie? If I was going to give you an order, here's what it would be. Fire Noah. Fire Ken. Fire Louie. Promote Max. Promote anyone you think you can trust. Then back off, Angie. Back off and let them do their jobs. You cannot do it all alone. You'll botch it, and you'll ruin your life."

Angelica's pulse pounded in anger. She'd been around Lassiter Media a whole lot longer than Evan. *She* was the one her father trusted. *She* was the one in charge. She all but growled at him. "Are you actually telling me how to run my company?"

"No," Evan answered softly. Then he lifted her left hand, rubbing his thumb across the diamond in her ring. "I'm telling you how to be my wife."

The world stopped dead in its tracks.

"A long time ago," he continued, "I met a beautiful, cheerful, wonderful woman. I fell in love with her, and I wanted to spend the rest of my life keeping her happy. But you've taken her, Angie. You've stolen her from me and I can't seem to get her back."

He let go of her hand, and his voice flattened out. "If she ever shows up again, give me a call." Then he turned and walked away.

Angelica started to shake. She gripped a shelf again, feeling woozy. She hadn't gone anywhere. She was still here. If Evan loved her, if he'd truly loved her, he'd know that she was all one package. He wasn't allowed to pull her apart, discarding anything that was less than perfect. That wasn't how love worked.

Evan spent three days regretting his outburst. Back in L.A., it played through his head over and over again. He'd pushed too hard. He'd pushed too fast. She might someday be ready to put her life on an even keel, but she wasn't there yet. He should have given her more time.

"Premier Tech Corporation conferences," Lex announced triumphantly as he walked into Evan's office at Sagittarius. "Five-year commitment, five days each month as they rotate through their regions, five hundred guests per conference."

"This came out of Deke's contact?" asked Evan, shifting his mind to business.

"On the strength of the commitment, we're sending you to trade shows in Munich, London and Paris." Lex slapped a stack of conference brochures down on Evan's desk. "Corporate business is the most lucrative of all. You leave Friday. Pick five staff to take along."

"I don't get a say in my own schedule?" Evan lifted an itinerary from the top of the stack.

"You're overseas expansion. Besides, it's London and Paris, not Siberia. Who doesn't love going to London and Paris?"

"I suppose," said Evan.

It was a great opportunity. And he knew he was foolish to keep waiting on Angie. She was stuck in her world, and he was quickly moving into his own. It couldn't be clearer that she didn't want his advice, that she didn't want him.

He leafed through a conference brochure from the stack. "I suppose I should start building a marketing team."

Lex sat down. "You can hire new, or you can see if we have any likely candidates already on staff."

"I like Gabrielle down in client relations. She's originally from Paris. She's fluent in French and Italian."

"She's also smokin' hot."

Evan frowned. "Now that's a quick route to a sexual harassment lawsuit."

Not that he was interested in any woman at the moment. If it wasn't Angie, well, he was going to have to take some time to think about how that worked.

"What I meant was, she might have some hot friends back home."

"I'll keep that in mind," said Evan.

"So Angie broke it off with you?"

Evan was through pretending. "We haven't spoken since the wedding."

"Isn't that pretty much the same thing?"

"I guess." Except that they'd never actually gotten back together in the first place. "It was doomed from the start."

"You okay?" asked Lex.

"I'll be fine. It's not like I haven't had six months to get used to the idea."

Lex considered him for a moment. "I get the feeling you never did. And having her back, well…you two seemed good together, Evan."

"We were, until we weren't anymore."

"Can the good times come back?"

"I thought maybe. For a while at least, I'd hoped so." The image of her sleeping in his arms at Big Blue surfaced in his mind. "For a little while there, I really thought we had another chance."

"Maybe you'll get over her in Paris."

"Maybe."

Lex came to his feet. "Take Gabrielle along. Hopefully her friends can help out."

Evan managed a smile. But a fling in France wasn't in the cards. He couldn't imagine making love to anyone but Angie.

Mid-morning, Angelica stared across the boardroom table at Noah and Ken. She'd wanted to be right. She'd desperately wanted to be right and for Evan to be wrong. The last thing her self-esteem needed was for her ex-fiancé to be better than she was at running her family's company.

"These are terrible," she said to the two men, covering the screen of her tablet computer on the revised storyboards.

Noah jumped in. "We think they're very much in keeping with the overall—"

"No," said Angelica. "They're terrible. And, what's more, you both know it." Her anger was rapidly replacing her disappointment. "You want this project to fail. You don't agree with the direction I'm taking, and you want to prove your point by compromising the project."

This time, Ken tried. "We took what you said and—"

"No," Angelica repeated. "You deliberately undermined me. And you compromised the good of Lassiter Media to support your own agenda. You don't get to do that."

She rose to her feet. Then she hit a speed dial button on her cell phone. Her assistant immediately answered.

"Becky? Please send security in here right away."

The color drained from Noah's and Ken's faces.

"Are you all right?" Becky asked.

"I'm fine."

There was a briefest of pauses. "They'll be right in."

Angelica set down her phone. "Someone from the finance department will be in touch with a severance package. It will include your pension plans. For now, security will escort you to your offices so you can pick up your personal belongings."

The boardroom door opened, and two Lassiter security guards entered the room.

"These two gentlemen are leaving Lassiter Media's employ immediately," Angelica said to the security guards. "Please give them a chance to pick up any personal items. They'll need to leave their company cell phones and their keys. And have the IT department shut down their accounts. I'll make arrangements with the Cheyenne office."

Noah came to his feet, and the two security guards instantly moved toward him.

"You can't fire us," he shouted.

Ken rose as well, but he seemed more stunned than angry.

"I just did," said Angelica, gathering her things.

"We have the support of the creative team!" Noah shouted.

"And I'm the CEO." She headed for the door.

"You'll *regret this*." Noah's voice followed her out.

Becky was there to meet her. "Are you okay?" She took the tablet from Angelica's hands.

"I'm fine. Really fine." A weight felt like it had been literally lifted from Angelica's shoulders.

"Can I get you anything?" asked Becky, her glance going furtively over her shoulder to where security was escorting Noah and Ken the opposite direction down the hallway.

"I'm heading down to twenty-one. Can you free up my next two hours?"

"Absolutely."

"Thank you." Angelica pushed the button for the elevator.

She made her way to the twenty-first floor, to Reece Ogden-Neeves's office.

"Angelica?" He looked surprised, but quickly asked the man and woman in his office to excuse them.

"I'm sorry to barge in," she began as he closed the door behind them.

"Not at all." He motioned to a chair at the meeting table next to his picture window.

Angelica couldn't help but note that L.A. was moving along as normal. Traffic was brisk. The flags were blowing.

And clouds were moving in from the ocean. It was going to be another beautiful afternoon.

She sat down, and Reece took the chair opposite.

"I've just fired Noah and Ken," she told him without preamble.

The surprise was clear on Reece's face.

"Louie is next."

"I see."

"I've decided to create two senior vice president positions, one for core operations and one for new ventures and expansion. My initial thought was you for core operations and Max Truger for expansion."

"So, you're not firing me?"

Angelica cracked a smile. "No, I'm not firing you."

"I wasn't sure there for a moment."

"Did I bury the lead?"

He grinned. "You did. And Max Truger?"

"What do you think?"

"I think he's great. He's smart, innovative and fearless."

"Is fearless bad or good?"

"Depends on your tolerance for risk."

"High," she answered.

Today it was very high. She was taking risks at Lassiter Media, starting now. But she was about to take an even bigger, personal risk right afterward.

"Then Max is your guy."

"I need people I can trust," she told Reece. "People who see the future the way I see it, and in whom I can put a lot of faith and decision-making power. This isn't a one-woman operation."

"It's not," Reece agreed.

"Are you up for the challenge?"

"I am."

Angelica rose, and Reece stood with her.

"I'm going to fire Louie now," she said. "After that, you want to come to Cheyenne and help me promote Max?"

Reece reached out to shake her hand, his smile going wide. "I'd like nothing better."

"The car will be out front in half an hour. It'll be a whirl-wind trip. I have something I need to do in L.A. tonight."

Evan was in no rush to get home. His flight left for Frank-furt at nine in the morning, and he didn't feel like facing an empty apartment tonight. Instead, he levered himself into a high leather seat in the Sagittarius sports bar. The chair was comfortable. The brickwork detail and low lighting gave a pleasing ambiance. And a major league game was just get-ting underway on the big screen.

He ordered a beer from the bartender. Barry was the man's name, and Evan had spoken with him a few times over the past week. But tonight, Evan didn't want to chat. He wanted to think. He wanted to sort through his emo-tions fully and finally, and leave it all behind when he got on the plane.

Maybe he would have a fling in Paris. Why not? Celi-bacy wasn't a realistic long-term strategy. He might as well get started now. Get that first encounter under his belt, and maybe it would become easier with time.

"This seat taken?" The soft voice sent a shot of reaction up his spine.

He turned slowly to see Angie standing beside him. She looked gorgeous and uncertain. Her hair was half up, half down, softly curled. She was wearing a pale pink dress with spaghetti straps and a layered skirt.

"Can I get you a drink?" asked the bartender.

"Brandonville Chablis," Evan quickly answered for her, hoping she'd feel obligated to stay for a while.

She climbed up onto the seat. "I was on my way home from work."

"Dressed like that?"

"I changed before I left the office." She set a small purse down on the bar. "I...uh...well. I wanted to give you something."

She reached out her hand, opening her fist.

He looked down and saw the circle of his engagement ring sitting in her palm. His heart froze, sending a sharp pain through the middle of his chest.

He'd known it would hurt. But he hadn't expected to feel like he was drowning. For a split second, he wondered if he'd ever breathe again.

"Charade's over?" he managed.

"Charade's over."

When he didn't take the ring, she set it on the bar in front of them. He couldn't bring himself to look at it.

"I fired Noah today," she told him conversationally.

The bartender set down the glass of Chablis. He glanced at Evan, looking like he might join in the conversation. But Evan's expression obviously warned him off, and he moved briskly away.

"Probably a good call," Evan told her.

"Then I fired Ken."

That got Evan's attention.

"Well," she continued. "I actually fired them both at the same time."

"What happened?"

She toyed with the stem of her wineglass. "You were right, and I was wrong."

He gave his head a little shake. "Excuse me?"

She looked at him. "Are you going to make me say it again? Because it's embarrassing. It seems you can run Lassiter Media better than me."

He struggled to wrap his head around her words. "What *happened*?"

"They were sabotaging me."

He paused. "Somehow, that doesn't come as a complete shock."

"I mean, it's one thing to disagree with your boss. And it's one thing to press your point. But to try to make something fail? To waste the company's resources? No. That wasn't going to happen. I fired Louie too." She lifted the glass to her lips.

"He was in on it?" Evan asked.

"Thick as thieves. I've never done anything like that before." She took another drink. "I need this."

Evan resisted an urge to take her hand. "I'm proud of you, Angie."

"Thank you. I'm a little proud of myself."

"You should be." His glance went to the diamond ring on the polished bar top.

"I promoted Reece."

"Reece is a good man."

Evan realized that Angie had finally come to her senses. The woman he loved was back, but she was breaking up with him all over again. The pain in his chest radiated out.

"We went to Cheyenne together."

"You and Reece?"

She nodded, and Evan felt a stab of jealousy.

He reached out and picked up the ring. That was it, then. It was over. He dropped the ring into his shirt pocket. He was going to have to stay away from Reece Ogden-Neeves for a while. Otherwise, he might end up with an assault charge on his record.

"I wanted Reece to be there when I promoted Max Truger. I'm really going to count on the two of them."

"You promoted Max?" Evan couldn't help but be pleased about that.

Angie turned and looked him in the eyes; hers were soft and fathomlessly dark. "You were right, and I was wrong. I need help at the top. I need it from people I can trust. And then I need to back off and let them do their jobs, so I can have a life."

He loved her. He loved her so much it hurt.

His throat was raw. "But you're giving me back the ring?"

"The engagement was fake, Evan."

He knew that. But it didn't change how he felt.

"I don't want a fake engagement." Her gaze fixed on his shirt pocket. "If I'm going to wear that ring again, it has to be real."

It took a moment for her words to penetrate. When they did, he couldn't believe it. "Are you saying...?"

She nodded.

He came to his feet, his body all but vibrating with joy. But this couldn't happen here. It couldn't happen in a sports bar.

He drew her from her chair, then out of the bar, down the wide hallway. It took him a moment to figure out where to go. But then he used his access key to let them into the dim, closed spa. He pushed the door shut, locking it behind them.

"Marry me," he told her, wrapping her in his arms. "Marry me, marry me, marry me."

"Yes," she answered simply, her dark eyes shimmering.

He kissed her then, deeply, thoroughly, passionately.

"I love you, Angie."

"I love you, Evan. I never thought I'd get to say that again."

He scooped her into his arms. "Say it as much as you like. Say it every day." He started to walk.

"Where are we going?"

"I don't know." He made his way down a narrow hallway. "I've never been in here. But I'm betting there's something back here that resembles a bed."

"We're going to make love in the spa?"

"It's closed and locked, and I own the place. So, yes, we're going to make love in the spa." They came into a lounge area with a softly lit fountain. He spotted a wide, low sofa.

"Here we go." He set her down on the sofa and gazed at the picture she made. "I love you in pink. You should always wear pink. Now, take it off."

She grinned up at him. "I just fired three men for not being deferential."

"Oh, I'll be deferential. I'll be *very* deferential. Just as soon as you're naked."

She held out her hand, wiggling her fingers. "Can I have my ring first?"

He dropped down on one knee, pulling the ring from his pocket. Then he smoothly pushed it onto her left hand. "This is *never* coming off."

"This is," she lightly joked. She slipped her fingers from his hand, drew back and pulled the dress over her head, tossing it to one side.

Epilogue

Spring had arrived at Big Blue. Flowers were blooming, birds chirping, and the bright sunshine heated the lush hills. Evan had warned Angie they were taking a chance with the garden wedding, but now he was glad they'd risked it. The sky was a perfect, vast blue. White folding chairs were set up on the lawn, azaleas, peonies and tulips making the landscape colorful.

Angie had walked alone down the aisle toward Evan and the preacher, who were standing under the natural wood canopy. Her brothers and Chance had all offered to escort her, but she'd said J.D. was with her, his presence in everything about Big Blue.

Evan had never seen her looking more beautiful. She'd chosen a simple white dress, knee length, made of delicate chiffon. Crisscrossing to a low, V back, the spaghetti straps left her shoulders bare. She'd woven wildflowers in her upswept hair and carried a tiny, cornflower bouquet.

It was nothing like he'd originally imagined their wedding, but it was perfect. And when he'd kissed his bride, he knew they were ready to stand together through anything life might throw at them.

Much later, he stood with Chance at the edge of a garden overlooking the natural swimming pool. The stars were a sparkling canopy above the ranch, while tiny, white lights decorated a temporary dance floor. Angie was dancing with her brother Dylan, while his wife Jenna watched, holding their baby son.

Deke was dancing with a dazzling Tiffany. Evan was in on the secret that his friend was proposing to her tomorrow night.

"Have you picked out a spot yet?" asked Chance, smiling, his gaze resting on his wife Felicia as she stopped to talk to Jenna. Felicia was several months pregnant with what they had just discovered were twins.

"Angie says we should build in the meadow beside Rustle Creek." Evan couldn't help but smile at the memory of their conversation. "I say a hundred feet up the hillside in case there's ever another flood."

Chance chuckled. "Don't blame you for that."

Although the ranchers had completely recovered from the fall flooding, nobody wanted to go through anything like that again.

"I can deed you the property," said Chance. "As much of it as you'd like."

Evan shook his head. "Not necessary. I don't think Angie wants to break the place up into pieces."

"She's keeping the mansion in L.A.?"

"She's not interested in letting go of any of the family possessions. We'll be here part-time, but we'll still need roots in L.A."

"It's a big house for two people." Chance gave Evan a sidelong glance.

"We hope it won't just be the two of us for long." Evan and Angie had tossed out her birth control pills last month. They were both content to let the babies come along whenever it happened.

Chance's gaze went back to Felicia and Jenna. "It looks like the Lassiter clan will be growing in leaps and bounds."

"I'm more than willing to do my part."

"I've set the bar pretty high," said Chance.

Evan laughed at the reference to the twins. He gazed around at the crowds of happy people, including Marlene dancing with the senior partner from Logan's law firm. The two had been inseparable since Christmas. Sage and his wife Colleen had announced they were also expecting a baby.

"I can't help but think J.D. would be happy with all this," he told Chance.

"I can guarantee he would," said Chance. "He'd have loved all the grandchildren, and especially the strong bonds between the family members."

Evan nodded his understanding and agreement.

The band ended the lively song then slowed things down to a waltz. Angie glanced around, and Evan knew it was his cue to join her.

"Catch you later," he told Chance, his feet taking him toward his bride.

"Later," Chance answered from behind him.

Angelica caught sight of Evan and flashed him a brilliant smile. His heart warmed, and the world around him seemed to disappear. He quickened his pace, scooping her into his arms, drawing her tight as they settled into the slow rhythm of the music.

"Hello, Mrs. McCain," he intoned next to her ear.

"Hello, Mr. McCain." She molded against him, letting him support her slight weight.

"Are you getting tired?"

"A little bit. But it's been a fantastic day, don't you think? Everyone seems really happy."

"As long as you're happy," he said. "That's all that counts."

"I am happy, Evan. I'm incredibly happy."

"I told Chance we wanted to build in the meadow."

She drew her head back. "Is he okay with that?"

"He's fine with it. I think he's looking forward to all the little Lassiter grandchildren that'll soon be running around Big Blue. He's bragging about his significant contribution to the effort."

"Felicia's the one doing all the work."

"He's still taking credit."

Angie went silent for a few minutes, swaying to the music.

"We can say goodnight anytime you want," he told her.

Chance had a horse-drawn carriage waiting to take them in true Big Blue style to a little cottage in the hills for their wedding night.

"A few more minutes," said Angie.

"Sure."

She drew a deep sigh. "It feels like the Lassiters are starting a whole new chapter."

"They are," Evan agreed. "And I am thrilled and proud to be part of it."

"Something fantastic is starting." She gazed up at him, her eyes shimmering in the tiny lights. "But something fantastic is ending too. I just need a little longer to savor the goodbye."

He wrapped her tight in his arms again, with the huge sky above them, the ranch around them, and the joy and goodwill of their family permeating the Wyoming night. "Take all the time you need, sweetheart. Take all the time you need."

* * * * *

MILLS & BOON®
By Request

RELIVE THE ROMANCE WITH THE BEST OF THE BEST

A sneak peek at next month's titles...

In stores from 12th January 2017:

* **The Tycoon and I** – Jennifer Faye, Kandy Shepherd & Barbara Wallace

In stores from 26th January 2017:

* **The Beaumont Brothers** – Sarah M. Anderson

* **Taming a Fortune** – Judy Duarte, Nancy Robards Thompson & Allison Leigh

* **The Package Deal** – Marion Lennox, Brenda Harlen & Jennifer Greene

0117/05

MILLS & BOON®

Why shop at millsandboon.co.uk?

Each year, thousands of romance readers find their perfect read at millsandboon.co.uk. That's because we're passionate about bringing you the very best romantic fiction. Here are some of the advantages of shopping at www.millsandboon.co.uk:

✱ **Get new books first**—you'll be able to buy your favourite books one month before they hit the shops

✱ **Get exclusive discounts**—you'll also be able to buy our specially created monthly collections, with up to 50% off the RRP

✱ **Find your favourite authors**—latest news, interviews and new releases for all your favourite authors and series on our website, plus ideas for what to try next

✱ **Join in**—once you've bought your favourite books, don't forget to register with us to rate, review and join in the discussions

Visit **www.millsandboon.co.uk**
for all this and more today!

puni ower ... ...ma agree.
d her hands ... d down her